# Judith LENNOX

## Summer *at* Seastone

REVIEW

First published in Great Britain in 2023 by
HEADLINE REVIEW
An imprint of HEADLINE PUBLISHING GROUP

First published in paperback in 2023 by
HEADLINE REVIEW

1

Cataloguing in Publication Data is available from the British Library

ISBN 978 1 4722 9827 0

Typeset in Joanna MT Std by Palimpsest Book Production Ltd, Falkirk, Stirlingshire

Printed and bound in Great Britain by Clays Ltd, Elcograf S.p.A.

HEADLINE PUBLISHING GROUP
An Hachette UK Company
Carmelite House
50 Victoria Embankment
London EC4Y 0DZ

www.headline.co.uk
www.hachette.co.uk

To Viv

# Acknowledgements

*Summer at Seastone* was inspired by the time in my life when I was bringing up three small sons and trying to establish a career as a novelist. Viv, Rosie and I were close friends, like Emma, Bea and Marissa in the novel. We were constantly in and out of each other's houses, we helped look after each other's children, we talked a lot and laughed a lot and offered comfort when it was needed. Very sadly, Rosie died of a short illness at the beginning of 2020, just before the pandemic kicked off. I miss her very much. It is to Viv that I dedicate this book.

Thank you, Jeanette Gilchrist and Vivien Cavallo, for your generosity in sharing your memories of working for British Caledonian.

Grateful thanks also to Adèle Geras and Rachel Meller – I have fond memories of our chilly, restorative walks in the depths of lockdown.

Heartfelt appreciation is due to my agent, Margaret Hanbury, to my editor, Clare Foss at Headline in the UK, and to Bettina Feldweg and Isabelle Toppe at Piper in Germany.

Thank you, Iain, as always, for your love, support and steadfastness.

# Prologue

They are loading up the ferry. Gulls shriek and dive while a fine, tall young man with a dark birthmark on the side of his face directs the column of vehicles onto the car deck with neat gestures of the hand.

She imagined blue skies for this Channel crossing, sunlight dancing on waves. But the sky is grey and rain is spitting and she can't yet see the sea. It's pointless, this errand of hers, she thinks as the vehicles crawl forward. No, worse – it's mad, and it's a mistake. It's arrogant of her to believe she has a hope of repairing this rift.

She could still change her mind. She doesn't have to board the ferry. She flips on the windscreen wipers to clear away the rain, which is falling more heavily now, and bites her lip, weighing things up. She might make it worse. She could nip out of the queue, turn round and drive back out of Portsmouth. Sometimes, she tells herself, the best service a friend can give is to stand back and pick up the pieces. Sometimes you have to face the fact that the only thing you can do is to offer comfort and solace.

The car in front of her, a red Fiesta, stalls, and she brakes. She threads her fingers together, thinking, hardly conscious of the impatient hoots from behind her.

The three of them: Bea, Emma and Marissa. She thinks of all they've shared. She remembers how her friends have celebrated her joys and successes and consoled her in her grief. She owes them so much.

She scrabbles for a tissue in her handbag to rub away the steam from the windows. Sometimes, she thinks, a friend has to do whatever she can to help. Even if she makes a fool of herself, even if she risks putting her foot in it. This is one of those times. She has to try; she has to embark on this journey: it's as simple as that.

At last the red Fiesta's engine starts up and the queue begins to move again. For a moment she pauses, irresolute, drumming her fingers against the steering wheel. Then she puts her car into gear and drives forward onto the ferry.

# PART ONE

# A FRESH START

# Chapter One

## 1970–1972

He said, 'They're hungry today, don't you think? They look like they could do with a sandwich.' The boy standing on the far side of the pond was addressing Bea. He had black curly hair and an Irish accent, and his school blazer was grey to her brown. Her mother had told her not to walk home through the park in case of strange men, but Bea liked feeding the ducks and didn't think this boy qualified as a strange man.

'I keep the crusts from my packed lunch.' She held out a piece of bread to him. 'Would you like to give them some?'

'That would be grand, yes, if you're sure.'

'I'm afraid they don't get enough food, living here.'

'I daresay other kind souls like yourself feed them.'

When he came to stand beside her, she saw that he was a lot taller than her. But then everyone was taller than her. Bea was seventeen and just about scraped five foot two in heels. She had inherited her dark hair and eyes from her French grandmother, and her petite vivacity from her mother, Vivien.

The boy threw a crust to a drab duck on the outside of the clacking circle. 'Good shot,' she said.

'It's one of my talents.'

'Have you others?'

'I can change a car tyre in twenty minutes.'

'Goodness.' When Bea's father's Wolseley had a puncture and he had to attend to it, it seemed to take him ages and much tutting.

'I work in the garage after school and weekends,' said the boy. 'I'm on my way there now. You wouldn't happen to have the time on you, would you? The winder's gone on my watch.'

'It's half past four. I'm Beatrice,' she said, offering him her hand. 'Beatrice Meade. Bea, actually.'

'Ciaran O'Neill.'

'Ciaran. That's a nice name.'

'Ciaran with a C. That's the proper way of spelling it.'

'I like your accent.' A blush flooded her cheeks. 'The way I speak is so boring, so . . . so out of date!' Someone had once told her she spoke like Celia Johnson. Bea had tried to rid herself of her cut-glass vowels ever since, to her mother's disapproval.

Ciaran laughed. 'I don't think so.'

'Which school do you go to?'

He gave her the name of the red-brick grammar she walked past each morning. He said, 'You go to a posh private school, don't you?'

'How did you guess?'

He put his head to one side. 'Your blazer. The handshake. It'll be white sliced when I come here tomorrow.' He said goodbye and walked away.

On her way home, Bea thought about Ciaran O'Neill. She hoped she would see him again.

*

6

The next day the weather was warmer. From time to time, during lessons and at break, she wondered whether he had meant it. Boys said things like that – *see you, bye then* – and the next time you encountered them they looked through you.

After the school day came to an end, she went to the park. She saw with a lift of her heart that he was standing by the pond. He had loosened his tie and slung his blazer over one shoulder.

'Hello there, Bea!' he called out. 'Did you have a good day?'

She made a face, but quickly turned it into a smile. Her mother scolded her for making faces. *You're a pretty girl, Bea, so why do you make yourself look like a goblin? No boy wants a girl who scowls and grimaces.*

'We had to do a French translation and I got into a hopeless muddle with the subjunctive,' she said.

'Don't the French themselves get into a muddle with the subjunctive?'

She laughed. 'How about you?'

'Chemistry practical test. It went all right, I think. Here.' He took the end of a packet of Sunblest out of his pocket and offered it to her.

'Do you want to be a scientist, Ciaran?'

'Eventually, yes. I want to go to university to read chemistry.' He lobbed a chunk of bread into the pond and the ducks dashed, quacking. 'I'll have to get good grades, though. If I make it, I'll be the first in my family to go to university. What about you?'

'I expect I'll do a secretarial course.'

None of the girls from Bea's school went to university. They did a secretarial course or a cordon bleu cookery course or they nannied for a suitable family or they went to a finishing school. Her mother said they couldn't afford a finishing school, so Bea must do a secretarial course.

Ciaran said, 'Is that what you want to do?'

No one had ever asked her this before. For as long as she could remember, her future had been mapped out for her. That the man she eventually married would be moneyed and from a good family was a necessity. If he were to have a title as well, her mother's wildest dreams would be fulfilled. Bea's pretty face and charm were the key to her glittering future. She was expected to meet this suitable boy at a cocktail party or on a weekend away. Failing that, she must complete the secretarial course and marry her boss, perhaps.

More and more her heart rebelled against a prospect that seemed out of date. When once she had expressed doubts, her mother had snapped at her. 'You'll run your house and you'll support your husband and entertain his friends and bring up your children. What more do you want?'

So much more, Bea thought, though she didn't dare say it. Though she enjoyed the parties her mother let her go to because she loved company and dancing, she knew that in this summer of 1970, in other parts of London not so very distant from her parents' mansion flat in Maida Vale, far more exciting parties were going on. She pictured smoky dives where loud rock music played and psychedelic lights cast sliding coloured discs along the floor. The girls would be wearing clothes from Biba or Bus Stop and the men would be the sort her father disgustedly termed hippies before muttering about bringing back National Service. The air would be sweet with the smell of joss sticks and marijuana.

She said, 'I don't know. I like being with people.'

'Maybe you could be a nurse,' he said. 'My sister Emer's training to be a nurse. She loves it.'

'Maybe I should.' The idea appealed to her. Was it possible?

'You'll be great, Bea, whatever you do.' Ciaran spoke as if it was not unreasonable for a girl like her to have ambitions.

On Friday, Ciaran bought her an ice cream from the van that stood by the park gates. He insisted on paying. Bea had noticed that his blazer was worn at the elbows and there was a patch on the knee of his trousers. She said she would buy the ices next time. When he protested, she said, 'You have to let me. What about women's lib?'

'Fair enough. Sorry.'

They stood beneath the trees, eating their cornets. Green light filtered through the branches and flickered across his eyes, which were the deep blue of cornflowers. Go-to-bed eyes, her mother would have labelled them.

Today he was wearing a watch. 'Did you mend it?' she asked.

'Fergal did. Fergal's my brother; he can fix anything. I have to go, Bea. I want to get a full-time job at the garage over the summer, so I mustn't be late. Gives a bad impression.'

'Will I see you tomorrow?' Immediately she regretted asking. Boys liked to do the running. Men tired quickly of demanding women. You should let a man chase you.

But instead of replying, he bent his head and brushed his lips against her cheek. 'I've been wanting to do that ever since I first saw you at the pond,' he said.

She moved a little so that he could kiss her mouth. His kiss tasted of vanilla. The city, the park reduced to the soft, dry touch of his lips on hers and the slight pressure of his hands on her hips. There was nothing else.

\*

Though she had kissed boys before, playing sardines in a cold country house or escaping for a few stolen minutes from the watchful mothers at a party, none of those kisses were like Ciaran's, which lit a fire inside her. Over the next few weeks, more kisses followed, each more blissful than the last, and soon they abandoned the duck pond for a patch of lawn screened by shrubs.

She fell for him so easily, so readily, it was as if she had been waiting for him, for his smile, for his voice with its soft Irish lilt and for his sweetness and generosity. Gloriously disorientated, she found herself headlong in love with him.

Ciaran lived in Notting Hill with his father and his elder brother. Both Mr O'Neill and Fergal were employed on building sites, though in the summer, Fergal worked on the motorways because the pay was better. Ciaran's father was in Ireland just now, staying at the family farm in County Cork, so only Fergal and Ciaran were living in the flat. 'It's Fergal who wants me to go to university, not Dad,' Ciaran told her. 'Dad thinks it's a waste of time. Fergal says one of us has to do well, and I'm the brainy one. He had to twist Dad's arm to let me stay on. Fergal left school when he was fifteen to work with Dad. If he hadn't taken my side, I'd have done the same. I'm lucky. I won't be hauling a hod of bricks round a freezing building site in the middle of winter.'

Bea knew that her mother would disapprove of an Irish boy like Ciaran, so she didn't say anything about him at home. She didn't tell her friends about him either. She wasn't sure why she held back. It wasn't that she didn't trust them, and it wasn't that she was ashamed, or afraid that they might think the worse of her for falling in love with the son of a labourer. Maybe it was because he was so special, special to her, that she didn't want to share him.

Her friends fell in love with all sorts of men. Some had steady boyfriends, though none of them admitted to having gone all the way. They gleaned their information about sex from magazines like *Honey* and *Petticoat* and were all terrified of getting pregnant. They didn't dare go on the Pill because they were afraid their doctors would scold them or tell their mothers. When they spoke of the possibility of pregnancy outside marriage, it was in a theoretical and alarming way. Someone knew a girl who had had to get married. Someone else had heard of a girl who had got rid of her unplanned pregnancy herself, using a knitting needle.

Bea and Ciaran talked about everything: about music and books and TV programmes and politics. He was a great reader of newspapers and lent her copies of *Private Eye* and *Melody Maker*. She felt her mind filling up with all sorts of new things. She told him how, when she was younger, she had longed for a brother or sister. Ciaran, who had four elder sisters back in Ireland as well as Fergal, said he had an excess of family and she could borrow a sister or two if she liked. His sisters were always poking their noses into his affairs. His mother had died when he was nine years old, and since then, Aislinn, Nora, Clodagh and Emer had taken it upon themselves to mother him. All four sisters wrote to him each week and expected a letter in return.

Ciaran was a dark smudge beneath a tree. Rain sheeted across the London streets, blurring the entrance to the park. They kissed as the rain pelted their heads.

'Awful weather,' Bea said. 'What are we going to do?'

'Fergal's away, up in Birmingham, working on the roads. We could go to the flat if you don't mind.'

'Why should I mind?'

11

He gave a half-smile. 'It's not grand, Bea, that's all.'

On the Underground train from Maida Vale to Ladbroke Grove, they stood face to face and kissed. Walking from the station to Notting Hill, they stopped to kiss some more. Rain drummed on the pavement and gathered in potholes in the road. She wanted to see where he lived because everything about him fascinated her and everything about him was attractive to her. They passed rows of small shops, a laundrette, a church where rivulets of water ran between weed-smothered gravestones. In an adventure playground, children roared round flimsy wooden climbing frames and rope swings, oblivious to the weather. Raindrops slid down the windows of a café, blurring the West Indian men and women sitting inside. Rain darkened the graffiti white-washed on a wall: *Power to the People*. From the open door of a tall, thin house the beat of Jimi Hendrix's 'Purple Haze' seemed to pulse in rhythm with the downpour. Two young men in patched jeans and torn singlets lounged in the doorway, smoking. The tall one with the Afro called out, 'Hey, Ciaran, who's the bird?' It was only a couple of miles from Maida Vale to Notting Hill, but it might have been another country. Families like her own were a remnant from a dying era, Bea thought. They lingered now only in small pockets of London.

The O'Neills' flat was in a side street. There was a betting shop and a long queue outside a fish and chip shop. Ciaran unlocked a green door. Inside, narrow stairs covered with cracked beige linoleum led up to a small landing. Bea could smell Dettol. A baby was crying; a couple were arguing.

Inside the flat, he found her a towel to dry her hair. While he hung their raincoats in front of a one-bar electric heater, Bea looked round. The room was sparsely furnished: a sofa, and a table with three chairs. There were some battered paperbacks on the table, along with a transistor radio and an ashtray.

'That's my dad's room,' Ciaran said, indicating a door. 'And that's Fergal's. I usually sleep on the couch, but I use Fergal's room while he's away.'

The smallness of the flat startled Bea. She wondered whether there was another room somewhere that she hadn't noticed.

Ciaran took the towel from her. She sat at his feet while he dried her hair. Now and then, as he ran the towel down a long, dark lock, his hand brushed against her cheek. She could smell the rain on his skin. She knew that soon they would go into Fergal's room and lie down on the bed.

There was a moment when they might have held back, when he said, 'Will it be all right? I haven't any johnnies, I thought we'd be at the park.' She said it would be fine, because by then she wanted him too much to stop. The rattle of the rain on the window receded, obliterated by a pleasure that soared and flew.

Later, buttoning up her dress in the bathroom, Bea inspected her reflection in the mirror and was surprised to see that she looked no different. After all, in losing her virginity, she had grown up, she had become a woman.

The summer term finished. Ciaran worked more hours at the garage and Bea took a little cleaning job, helping an elderly neighbour, Mrs Phillips.

It was the happiest summer she could remember and she would have liked it to go on for ever. After they made love, she liked to pad around the O'Neills' flat wearing Ciaran's shirt, making mugs of tea and slices of toast and pretending to herself that the two of them lived there together. Ciaran would put on one of his brother's records; Fergal had a great collection. Ciaran had a fine voice and liked to sing along to Bob Dylan or the Clancy Brothers. While they drank the tea, they made plans. Once they had left school the following year, once they were both eighteen, Ciaran would go to university and Bea would train to be a nurse. It wouldn't matter where they lived and it wouldn't matter that they hadn't any money, because they loved each other.

'We quarrelled this morning, Fergal and I.'

They were in bed in the flat and Ciaran's arm was round her. Bea's head rested on his chest and she felt the steady beat of his heart.

'What about?'

'About you. Though Fergal didn't know that, thank God. He's an idea something's going on, though. He's not daft. There we were, eating our cornflakes, and suddenly he's saying I've my head in the clouds all the time and was I seeing one of our neighbours' daughters.'

She craned round to look up at him. 'What did you say?'

'I told him he was an eejit even for thinking it. Fergal can be a right pain in the neck once he's got his teeth into something. He said he'd kill me if he found out I'd been fooling around with some girl instead of getting on with my school work.'

Hearing a hammering on the front door, they both froze. 'Jesus,' Ciaran muttered. 'Who the hell is that?' He slid out of bed. 'Stay there.'

He pulled on his jeans and went out of the room, closing the door behind him. Bea began quickly and silently to dress. What if it was Fergal, come home early from work, having forgotten his key? He would be angry if he found her there. He might tell Ciaran they mustn't see each other again. She heard a click as Ciaran opened the front door, then the murmur of conversation. Straining to catch the words, she fumbled as she clasped her bra.

Ciaran came back into the room and turned off the record player. 'It was my neighbour, complaining about the music.' He let out a breath. 'I forgot he's working nights this week.'

'Oh my God, I was so terrified . . .' As she zipped up her skirt, Bea gave a high-pitched laugh.

'I thought it was Fergal. Or my dad, come back from Ireland. Christ, that would have been a scene.' Ciaran pulled on his shirt.

She saw that his good mood had vanished. 'It's all right, love.'

But the warmth had gone from his eyes. 'Bea, what are we doing? I can't see where this is going, can you? We've been lying to our families for months. Doesn't that bother you?'

'If my parents weren't so snobbish and unfair, I wouldn't have to lie.' Her words echoed back at her, self-justifying yet weighted with guilt.

He sat on the edge of the bed. 'What are we going to do when the weather gets colder? My dad'll be back in London in a few days' time. We won't be able to come here then.'

Ciaran had skived off school that afternoon to be with her. Bea's school term would begin the following week. Outside, the leaves of the London planes were tinged with yellow. The summer had worn itself out.

'We'll find a way.'

He swung round to her, blue eyes wide. 'Will we? What if one day you just don't turn up? What then? Would I go round to your flat? Would I knock on the door and ask your ma where you were? I don't think so, do you?'

Bea stroked the nape of his neck. 'Don't, love, please.'

'Maybe we should give it a rest for a while.'

'Is that what you want?' She was close to tears.

He groaned. 'Of course not. How could I?'

They lay down on the bed, face to face, his hand resting on the hollow of her waist. 'I don't want you to get hurt, Bea,' he murmured. 'I don't want to be the man who hurts you.'

'You could never hurt me. I love you.'

'People hurt the people they love all the time. They don't mean to, but they do. Didn't you know that?'

They were late leaving the flat. Ciaran walked with her to the Underground station. They kissed, then Bea ran down the escalator and jumped onto a train just before the carriage doors closed. Jolted as they lurched from stop to stop, she felt upset and nauseous. *Maybe we should give it a rest for a while.* She had felt him retreating from her, mentally preparing himself for separation.

As she walked home from Maida Vale station, the sky was grey and oppressive. Laurels, their sheen diminished by black grime, pushed between iron railings. She wished she was a year older. If they had both been eighteen, they could have married without their parents' permission. They had met each other too soon, she thought, and the crushing panic she had felt earlier returned.

At home, Vivien was opening kitchen cupboards, staring at the rows of tins and packets. She looked up as Bea came into the room. 'Did you get the ham?'

'Sorry, I forgot.'

'Oh, for heaven's sake, darling!'

'Sorry, Mummy.'

Her mother's expression altered, irritation giving way to suspicion. 'Where were you? You're awfully late. I thought you said you were going to the Prices'?'

'No . . . well, I . . .' She fumbled for an excuse.

'I called Mrs Price and she told me Sarah was at the hairdresser.'

Bea thought of the O'Neills' flat and Ciaran. *We've been lying to our families for months.* Just then, it seemed a huge effort to think up another lie.

'I was late leaving Mrs Phillips' flat,' she said. 'Then I went for a walk.'

Vivien was still frowning. 'Perhaps I should have a word with her. She shouldn't take up so much of your time. I need you here, even though you're such a scatterbrain.'

'It's all right, Mummy, I'll make sure I get away earlier tomorrow. Shall I make you a cup of tea?'

'No, a gin and tonic.'

Bea opened the sideboard door. Her hand shook as she took out the gin bottle. Rising, she smoothed out the creases in her skirt. Her heart was pounding, and she was hot and sweating. In all the rush of leaving Ciaran's flat, she had forgotten to check her hair and make-up. Her hand went to her breast. A few weeks ago, Ciaran had given her a silver chain. She wore it only when she was meeting him. Had she remembered to remove it? It was the sort of thing her mother would notice. With relief, she felt its slight weight in her pocket and recalled taking it off as she entered the building. When she glanced in the mirror above the sideboard, she saw that her fringe plunged messily to one side and there was a smear of mascara

17

under her eye. She measured out the gin, tidied her hair with her fingers and dabbed at her eye to dislodge the smear. She must be more careful.

She went back into the kitchen. Her mother had opened a tin of beans and was taking eggs out of the fridge. The feeling that they had that afternoon narrowly avoided disaster persisted, and as she shook ice cubes from the tray, Bea mentally ran through her last conversation with Ciaran. She knew how much he hated lying to Fergal. When he spoke of his brother, it was always with affection.

Ciaran had a lot to lose. Though her mother often complained of being short of money, there was a difference between the Meades' version of hard-up and the O'Neills'. She had the horrible feeling that she and Ciaran existed in a shimmering, dancing bubble that might burst as soon as it was exposed to a cold gust of wind. Her fantasies of the two of them living in their own place were just that: fantasies. It would be years before they could afford so much as a bedsit.

Her mother cracked an egg, shining and gelatinous, into a cup. A wave of heat and nausea swept through Bea. She closed her eyes and pressed an ice cube against her forehead, but the tide of sickness was unstoppable, and her mother turned to her as she gave a little moan before rushing off to the bathroom.

She felt lousy all weekend and went to bed early each night. Her father brought her treats – a magazine, some peppermints, a cup of tea. Sick three evenings in a row, Bea thought she had a stomach bug. Her mother was more bracing, but then her mother believed that giving in to physical frailty was a weakness. The expression in Vivien's eyes worried Bea.

A wind had got up, whipping the leaves from the

sycamores and gathering them up in leathery brown heaps on the terrace. On Sunday mornings, Bea and her father were in the habit of walking to the newsagent to buy the paper. This Sunday, as Jack was getting ready to go out, Vivien told him he should go on his own. Bea thought it was because she hadn't been feeling well, but when the door closed behind him and she made to go to her room, her mother's sharp voice stopped her.

'Don't you dare run off.' Vivien slid a cigarette from a packet of John Player's. 'What's going on?'

'What do you mean?'

Frowning, Vivien tapped the cigarette against the packet. 'Have you been doing something you shouldn't? And don't you dare lie to me.'

Bea didn't feel anything at first, not even fear. Numbness was quickly followed by a blank despair. Her mother had somehow found out about her and Ciaran. She couldn't see how, though.

The click of a gold cigarette lighter. 'Well? Do I have to spell it out?'

'I don't know . . .' She honestly didn't, at that point.

'Have you been with a boy?' The lighter failed to catch, so Vivien flicked it again. She looked up. 'If you don't tell me the truth, I'll speak to your father. He can have the pleasure of finding out what his darling's been up to. Do you want me to do that, Beatrice?'

Bea shook her head. 'No,' she whispered.

'Are you pregnant?'

*Pregnant.* The suggestion was so preposterous she almost smiled. 'No, of course not!'

'I mean,' said Vivien acidly, 'is it *feasible* that you're pregnant? Have you been to bed with a boy?'

19

Bea thought of the flat and Fergal's bed. Herself, bare-legged as she made tea, wearing Ciaran's shirt. The Dubliners on the gramophone and the smell of the street, fish and chips and car fumes, through the open window.

She stared at her mother. 'But we were careful . . .'

'Oh my God, you stupid, *stupid* girl . . .'

They *had* been careful – except, she remembered with horror, that first time, when they hadn't. Her stomach lurched and she wanted to rush off to the bathroom again, but she didn't dare.

Her mother put her hand to her mouth and closed her eyes. The gesture was more frightening to Bea than anger. And then the glimpse of vulnerability was gone, and questions were hurled at her.

*Who was it? Was it the Price boy? No? Who, then?*

'I assume he has a name,' Vivien added contemptuously.

At first she tried not to tell her mother anything, but it dawned on her that her disbelief that she might be expecting a baby was fired by the fact that such a thing was too terrible to be possible. She knew so little about pregnancy, about babies. She kept thinking about her father, how he mustn't know, how she couldn't bear him to come home while this conversation was going on.

'Ciaran,' she said eventually. 'He's called Ciaran O'Neill.' Though she tried to say his name proudly, it sounded like a whimper. 'We met in the park.'

Her mother's eyes sparked with fury. 'You went to bed with some boy you met in the park?'

'It wasn't like that!'

They both heard the vestibule door open. Vivien muttered crisply, 'I shall take you to the doctor tomorrow morning and get this mess sorted out. Go to your room, Beatrice.

20

You're not to say anything to your father. I shall tell him you're still unwell. I'm afraid this will break his heart.'

A succession of ordeals followed, each more dreadful than the last. First the appointment with the family doctor. After he had finished examining her, Dr Wilton said as she dressed, 'Well, you've been a silly little girl, haven't you?' Then he spoke to her mother. Beatrice was around eleven or twelve weeks pregnant. He would do a test to make sure, but he had little doubt.

Even worse was that evening, when her mother told her father about the baby. Bea knew that she would remember the look in his eyes, of shock and hurt and disappointment, for the rest of her life. That he heaped all the blame on Ciaran only made it worse.

Her parents wouldn't let her see Ciaran or speak to him. Apart from the visit to the doctor, her mother wouldn't allow her to leave the flat and had told her school that she was unwell, so even though she wrote letters to Ciaran, telling him about the baby and explaining what had happened, she couldn't post them. She didn't know whether it was her pregnancy making her feel tired all the time, or if her fatigue came from her sense of being trapped in a nightmare.

Lying on her bed one evening in a stupor of misery, she drifted off to sleep. When she woke, thick-headed and dis-orientated from sleeping at the wrong time of day, she heard her parents' voices from the sitting room. Her mother was wearing a crimson cocktail dress and sitting on the chintz sofa in front of the French windows. There was a bottle and two tumblers on the occasional table, and her father was mixing drinks.

He looked round and smiled. 'Hello, love.'

Her mother said, 'Your father has spoken to the O'Neills.'

For the first time in days, Bea felt a flicker of optimism. 'To Ciaran, you mean? You spoke to Ciaran? What did he say?'

'I went to their flat. What a godforsaken hole.' Jack put the stopper back on the Cinzano bottle. In the washed-out evening light, he looked pale and weary. 'I didn't see the boy, poppet. Only the father.'

'I don't understand. Why didn't you talk to Ciaran?'

'Listen, love—'

'He's gone away,' Vivien interrupted.

'Gone away?' Bea stared at her mother. 'Where to?'

'He's gone back to Ireland. Your father wrote to Mr O'Neill about the situation a couple of days ago, to arrange a meeting. The boy must have cut and run when he found out about the baby.'

'You're lying. Ciaran would never do that. I don't believe you.' Bea heard her voice rise.

'I'm afraid it's true, poppet.' Jack, his back to Bea, was adding vermouth and a dash of bitters to the drinks. 'He's gone back to Ireland. Mr O'Neill told me.'

Bea gripped the back of the sofa for support. 'No, that can't be right. You've made a mistake.'

Vivien shrugged. 'Darling, there's no mistake. Men do that sort of thing all the time.'

Jack patted the arm of the sofa. 'Sit down, love.'

Bea did so. Her gaze fixed on her father. Ice cubes and a curl of orange peel; he handed the glass to her mother.

'I came across a few chaps like O'Neill in the army. They're rum fellows, never learn to handle responsibility. Something tough comes up, something that needs a bit of grit, and they do everything they can to wriggle out of it.'

'You need to face up to the truth,' said Vivien. 'The boy hightailed it back to Ireland as soon as his father told him about the baby.'

'He wouldn't do that. I'll write to him.'

'You will not.' Her mother's voice was sharp.

'Vivien, that's enough.' Her father's tone softened as he turned to Bea. 'Hey, love, don't cry. Here.' He gave her his handkerchief. 'Listen, poppet, we're not going to let him hurt you. Don't upset yourself. We'll make it better, I promise.'

'You can't . . . How can you possibly . . .' She was sobbing now. 'I *love* him!'

'You *think* you do,' said Vivien crisply.

'*Vivien*. Your trouble, Bea, is you have a soft heart.'

She pictured her heart red and raw, like a scarlet ball of wool unravelling, fraying, as her father went on speaking.

'He wasn't worth it, love. You'll soon forget him, you'll see. You're best shot of him. It'll be all right, I promise. Mummy and I, we'll look after you, we've worked out what to do for the best. You're going to wipe the slate clean, honey. A few months to get through, that's all, and then you'll be able to make a fresh start.'

In the car, driving to Gloucestershire, her father went over once more the plan he and her mother had made. Bea would stay with her aunt Muriel in her home in the Cotswolds until the baby was due. There was a nursing home nearby, in Stow-on-the-Wold, where the child would be delivered. Afterwards, the baby would be given up for adoption and Bea would be able to return to London and pick up her life as though nothing had happened, her father said. Her parents had told her school that Bea had decided that academic work was not for her and that she had gone to France for six months, where she would stay with her relatives and concentrate on improving her French.

Every day during that long, lonely winter, she took Aunt Muriel's three dogs – a Dalmatian and two cocker spaniels – for a walk. She picked a route that led her through a village so that she could post her letters to Ciaran. She kissed the letters before she put them in the postbox.

He never wrote back. Not once. Daily her emotions went through the same exhausting cycle: hope as she waited for the post to come, followed by despair when no letter arrived. By the time the baby was due, she had come to the conclusion that at least part of what her father had told her was true: that Ciaran had gone back to Ireland. His father and brother couldn't have been forwarding her letters to him.

*People hurt the people they love all the time*, he had said.

Her labour pains began one April morning. Aunt Muriel drove her to the nursing home. Bea's son was born in the early hours of the following morning. They were tidying her up when she heard someone say, 'Are we to let her see him?'

'Give him to me.' It came out a weak flutter, but the nurse put the baby in her arms. His tiny, perfect features were creased and reddened by his passage through the birth canal. One eye was open, the other a dark blue slit. The open eye swivelled round and fixed on her face, unwavering. Her love for him was unqualified and without measure.

'Hello, Patrick,' she whispered.

The night after they took her baby away, she had the dream for the first time. She was on an Underground train. There were other people in the carriage – her parents, a friend, a stranger. The doors opened and she got out onto the platform. No one else left the train, which set off, melting into the dark circle of a tunnel and leaving her alone. She went down some steps and into first one passageway, and then another. In all the gloomy, shadowed labyrinth she didn't see another soul. She was looking for her baby, but she couldn't find him. She was to blame; she had somehow forgotten him, had left him behind and couldn't remember where. Loneliness pressed around her like a heavy coat. When she dragged herself out of the nightmare, she was crying.

The next day, her father drove her home. Sitting in the car, her arms felt empty, weightless. The Maida Vale flat was unchanged, as though she had left it only yesterday, and yet it seemed at the same time unfamiliar, to have nothing to do with her.

Bea cried a lot and stayed in her room. It was her mother who insisted she eat her meals and take exercise each day. Her father didn't seem to know what to say to her. They didn't talk about anything much, but Vivien tucked Bea's arm through hers and steered her round the garden, and then, when she was getting better, the park.

When she was well enough, Bea took a train to Notting Hill. There was, she discovered, another family living in the O'Neills' flat. None of the neighbours knew where Ciaran and his father and brother had gone. The streets seemed shabbier now, less colourful.

The day after Patrick's first birthday, she travelled to France, to stay with her relatives in Provence. She and Chantal, her cousin, worked in the village bakery throughout the spring and summer. The sun shone and the air smelled of lavender and herbs. She didn't tell anyone about Ciaran or the baby, because her mother had told her not to.

She was nineteen when, in the autumn of 1972, she returned to London. She moved into a shared flat in Earls Court with a couple of friends and found a job as a photographer's assistant, working for a man called Vic, an East Ender who always had a fag in his mouth and who did interiors for magazines like *House & Garden* and *Country Life*. Part of Bea's job was to search out the right vase and flowers or the perfect junk-shop find to set off a room. One morning, Vic took his cigarette out of his mouth long enough to say, 'You're a clever girl, Bea. Don't have to explain nuffink to you any more, do I? You've got an eye for it.' She glowed with pride.

She went on the Pill, had plenty of boyfriends, and crammed her evenings and weekends with parties and dinners out. But last thing at night, wherever she was and whoever she was sharing her bed with, she prayed that Patrick was happy and healthy and well cared for. And then she told him how much she loved him and wished him goodnight.

# Chapter Two

## 1975–1976

He was a passenger on the Tuesday-evening flight from Genoa. Emma Romilly, an air stewardess on the plane, noticed him because when he opened his small bag of peanuts, they sprayed over the floor of the cabin. She felt sympathetic: it was the sort of thing she herself might do. He had the type of fine brown hair that always appeared dishevelled and the sort of looks she liked: tall and spare, with neatly chiselled features. She was twenty-three. He seemed to be much the same age, maybe a few years older.

As they both scrambled to pick up the peanuts, their heads knocked together.

'Oh God, sorry,' he said, backing off. 'Sorry, I'm so sorry. Are you all right?'

'I'm fine. What about you? I have a hard head.'

The knock had dislodged his wire-framed glasses. When he took them off and looked, blinking, directly at her, she saw that his eyes were the dark blue-grey of sea-washed slate.

'Let me sort this out,' she said. 'You sit down, sir.'

There were autumn storms, and they were flying over the

27

Alps. Emma gathered up the scattered peanuts; shortly after she finished clearing up, the seat-belt sign went on. The plane bounced and lurched. She went round the cabin checking that all the passengers were belted in, then the air hostesses sat down on their small fold-down seats. Emma sat next to her friend Kirsty. She shared a house with Kirsty and Sue, another stewardess. Kirsty had been with British Caledonian longer than Emma; it had been she who had suggested Emma apply for a job at the company. Emma suspected she had got the job because one of the men who had interviewed her was rumoured to have a thing for redheads. It certainly couldn't have been because of her flawless appearance or faultless efficiency. She noticed that her tights were laddered from crawling around on the floor and tugged down her skirt. The senior stewardess, Cecilia, was a stickler when it came to uniform, forever noticing chips in Emma's nail polish or loose red curls springing out of her bun.

Emma looked along the plane, searching for the man with the slate-grey eyes. She could see only the top of his head. He had seemed familiar to her, as if she had met him somewhere before, but when she had looked up his name on the passenger list (Dr Max Hooper), she hadn't recognised it.

After the plane landed at Gatwick and the seat-belt signs were extinguished, the passengers rose to queue in the aisle. Emma and Cecilia stood by the exit door, saying goodbye to them. Before he left the plane, Dr Hooper turned to her. 'So sorry about, you know, our collision.' He tapped his forehead.

She laughed. 'The concussion's not too bad. Do watch your step as you go down.' The metal treads were shiny with rain. Lights bounced and reflected on the tarmac.

In the arrivals hall, she came across him again, extracting a crumpled mackintosh from a briefcase. 'I'm no good in turbulence,' he said as they walked through the concourse. 'I always think I'm going to die. You looked so calm. I don't know how you do it.' He had slung the raincoat over his arm. Now and then it threatened to slither to the floor, but he seemed oblivious to its precariousness.

'It's part of the job.'

'Do you enjoy your work?'

'I love it.' This was true. She hadn't so much as sat in an aeroplane before she had started working for British Caledonian. The Romillys didn't go on foreign holidays. Over the last six months she had flown everywhere – Le Touquet, Lisbon and now Genoa.

She asked him whether he had far to go. 'No distance at all,' he said. 'I live in a farmhouse about six miles from Horley. I share it with some friends. Do you know the area?'

'I live in Horley. A farmhouse sounds nice.'

'It is. Seventeenth century, a good solid building. I moved here six months ago to join an architectural practice in Reigate. I've just about stopped feeling that I'm the new boy.'

'It's never easy, starting in a new place.'

Though she said this to reassure him, she did not believe it. She loved the adventure of a new house, a new job, a new country. As they parted, an impulse made her say, 'My name's Emma Romilly. One of the girls in my house has a birthday on Saturday and we're throwing a party. Come along if you'd like to meet some people. And do bring your friends.'

She had invited him to the party because she and Kirsty and Sue were always on the lookout for suitable men to even up the numbers. But that was not the only reason. Her attraction to him was instant and powerful. Like a crack on the head, it dazed her a little.

\*

Marc Bolan was singing 'Get It On' and the party was in full swing when, on Saturday evening, Emma let herself into the semi-detached house in Horley. She waved at Sue across the crowded front room and wished her a happy birthday, then went upstairs to her bedroom, stepping over the couples sitting on the treads. In her room, she changed out of her tartan uniform into a plum-coloured crêpe midi dress. She fluffed out her curly hair and touched up her lipstick and mascara. A quick spray of deodorant and Aqua Manda scent and she was ready.

In the sitting room, they had pushed back the furniture and couples were dancing. Her heart beat faster as she caught sight of Max Hooper, standing in the far corner talking to two other men. His back was to her and she noticed how well his denim-blue shirt sat across his shoulders. As she picked her way through the partygoers, she caught snatches of the men's conversation. *A semi in Reigate . . . Modernism hardly adapts to the British climate . . . Andy, I can't believe how stuck in the past you are . . .*

She touched his elbow. 'Hello, Max.'

He turned and smiled. 'Emma, how good to see you.'

'Sorry I'm late. Problems with the plane at Frankfurt. I'm so pleased you could come.'

Max introduced her to his friends. Phil was the broad-shouldered, fair-haired man crushed up against a bookcase; Andy was thin, dark and wiry.

'I brought a bottle,' Max said, brandishing it. 'Decent stuff. We kept it to share with you. I'm trying to make up for my debacle with the peanuts.'

He poured her a glass. The wine was cool and flinty. They talked about wine, then cooking. They had to shout over the music and chatter. After a while, Phil asked her to dance.

Once the song had finished, he drifted off to find more drinks. Emma touched Max's shoulder. The first lazy, loping chords of 'This Guy's in Love With You' poured from the cassette player as he took her in his arms. She felt the warmth of his hand as it rested on the small of her back, the movement of muscle and solidity of bone, and the slight roughness of the denim fabric beneath her fingertips. Kirsty was dancing with Phil. Emma watched as she leaned in closer and rested her head against his shoulder. She would have liked to do that with Max, but something stopped her. She wasn't sure where she stood with him. He was friendly, but nothing more.

She had assumed that what she had felt on the plane for Max Hooper would have faded by the time she next saw him; that it was a passing attraction, of no importance. But it was not so, and this took her by surprise. Since she had left university, she had bounced through life, doing this job and that before settling for working for British Caledonian, and sharing a house with one friend or another. She had had plenty of boyfriends, but no one special. She wanted to have fun and to have adventures and she preferred not to be serious. This, this sudden yearning and desire, wasn't part of the plan at all.

Before they left the party, the men from the farmhouse invited Emma, Kirsty and Sue to dinner the following weekend. Sue had a date with her pilot boyfriend so couldn't come, but she lent Emma her car.

A storm had got up and brown waves rose from the puddles as Emma negotiated the Mini along narrow country roads. Sue had warned her that the windscreen wipers didn't work very well, so she drove slowly while Kirsty, in the passenger seat, read the map. The countryside was black and solid and the fingerposts hard to decipher in the downpour, and they drove round in circles for some time before coming across a painted sign directing them along a rutted, muddy track.

Afraid that the car would get stuck, Emma parked on a patch of firm ground a short distance from the house. Rain pelted at them as they trudged through the mire to the front door. Phil welcomed them to the farmhouse and hung up their coats. Their boots were plastered with mud, so they took them off. Emma had forgotten to bring shoes to change into and padded after him in her stockinged feet.

He led them into a large kitchen towards the back of the building. Half a dozen people turned to look at them. A woman with platinum-blonde corkscrew curls smirked as she ran her gaze over them. 'You're awfully wet,' she said. 'Aren't they, Lionel, aren't they looking awfully bedraggled?'

The man she was addressing was very fair too, and stocky. He thrust a tea towel towards Emma and Kirsty. 'Take this, you must dry your hair before you catch cold. Come and stand by the fire. I'm Lionel Sutton, by the way, and this is my sister, Julia.'

Emma apologised for being late. 'I'm afraid we got rather lost,' she said.

Max came into the room. 'You made it,' he said. 'Thanks for slogging out here. I just went to get a torch so that I could go and look for you. I wasn't sure whether you'd come, in this weather.' He smiled at them. 'Of course, I forgot, you're used to turbulence.'

A woman wearing a floral skirt and a navy-blue ribbed jersey that emphasised her hourglass figure came to stand beside Max. 'What do you mean, darling?'

'This is Emma and this is Kirsty,' Max said. 'They work for British Caledonian. Emma and I met on a plane. I was freaking out, going over the Alps.'

Julia, the platinum blonde, said, 'Isn't being an air hostess much like being a glorified waitress?'

Kirsty gave Emma a quick raise of the eyebrows and then slipped away to sit between Andy and Phil on the sofa. Lionel said, 'Jules, honestly, you're such a snob.'

'I'm just being frank.' Julia glared at her brother. 'I mean, it is, isn't it? You shouldn't take offence so easily, Lionel. You're not offended, are you, Emma?'

'Not in the least,' said Emma.

Her gaze turned to the woman who had called Max 'darling'. Her dark brown hair was tied back in a bun and she had a broad, alert, cheerful face.

She held out her hand. 'It's lovely to meet you. I'm Bridget, Max's girlfriend.'

Emma murmured an automatic response. While Bridget explained that she lived in London and was staying at the farmhouse for the weekend, Emma ran through in her head the conversations she had had with Max. She had never asked him whether he had a girlfriend. What an idiot, she thought. Looking back, she recalled that it had been she who had invited him to Sue's party, and at the party, she who had asked him to dance. If there had been any misunderstanding, it was all on her part.

Bridget's very blue, slightly protuberant eyes fixed on her. 'You must be freezing in that frock!' she cried. 'Didn't you warn her, Max? Honestly! This place is always like a fridge. Darling, your shirt.' She adjusted his collar and smoothed down the creases. 'I shall lend you a cardigan, Emma,' she said, and bustled off before Emma could stop her.

Max asked Emma how her week had gone. Lionel poured drinks and laid the large pine table for dinner. Phil got up to tend a cast-iron pot on the Aga. While Emma told Max a story about a passenger who had tried to smuggle his toy poodle onto the plane, her mind kept flipping over to the discovery that he had a girlfriend. Really, it was nothing to do with her. It didn't matter at all.

Bridget came back into the room. 'Emma, do put this woolly on. We don't want our friends dying of cold, do we, Max?'

'I never notice the cold,' said Julia, who had perched on the edge of the table – rather in the way of Lionel, Emma thought, who was lighting the candles. 'I find a storm invigorating.'

Emma thanked Bridget and put on the cardigan. While it was true that apart from the immediate area round the open fire and the stove, the room was chilly, she didn't tend to notice cold. She had been brought up in a draughty house on the east coast, looking out over the North Sea. Cold, like turbulence, was something she was used to.

She was used to family squabbles, too. She came from a loving but disputatious family, and she'd have had to be living on another planet not to notice that Julia was annoyed with Lionel. When he began putting napkins on the table, she shrieked.

'Haven't you thrown out those ghastly rags yet?'

'They serve their purpose,' he said equably. 'They catch spills.'

'I shall drive to Guildford tomorrow and buy some new ones from Habitat.'

'You shouldn't waste your money. They'd only sit in the airing cupboard because I'd be nervous of sullying them.'

'Oh, for God's sake!' said Julia crossly. She slid off the table and seized a bottle of wine. 'If you'd only see sense, I wouldn't have to worry about wasting money. This place will fall about your ears and then we won't get a penny for it.'

Emma asked Bridget what she did for a living. 'I'm training to be a solicitor with a law firm in London,' Bridget said. 'Julia and I are colleagues. I'm trying to decide which area to specialise in. Roger – he's the senior partner – has advised me to go in for property law, but I wonder whether family law would be more rewarding. It's nice to be wanted, but you have to follow your heart, don't you?'

Phil announced that dinner was ready, and they all sat down. Emma sat between Max and Julia. Her own heart, she reflected, hadn't so far pointed her in any particular direction. She hadn't had a childhood longing to be an air stewardess, or anything like that; she had fallen into the job almost by accident. She had wanted to leave home and she had known she didn't want to be an artist, which was what her parents were, but that was about it. For more than a year she had drifted happily.

The food was delicious, and everyone complimented Phil and Lionel, who had cooked it. While they ate, two simultaneous conversations went on. At one end of the table, the talk was of the soaring rate of inflation and high unemployment figures and other political matters, while at the other end, Max and his friends discussed architecture. Andy mildly accused Phil of admiring brutalism, but then both Andy and Phil rounded on Max, telling him that he was impractical and out of touch. Max held his own and coolly fended off their friendly teasing. The dispute between Lionel and his sister, whatever it was about, flared up now and again.

35

Emma joined in both conversations, though she was distracted by the faint, sweet perfume that arose from the borrowed cardigan, which was a couple of sizes too large for her and made of an itchy maroon yarn that clashed fearfully with her brown velvet dress. She asked Bridget whether she had knitted it herself.

Bridget beamed. 'I did, yes.'

'How clever of you.'

'I knit all the time, don't I, Max?'

He blinked. 'Do you?'

'You know I do! Silly! Remember that scarf I made you!'

Max started to make a complimentary remark about the scarf, but Julia spoke over him. 'I don't have time for that sort of thing. But then I never think of myself as the domestic sort.' She fluffed up her pale curls and pouted. 'Do you think I look the domestic sort, Andy?'

Andy turned to her. 'Not much, Jules.'

'It's just a hobby,' murmured Bridget.

Emma asked Julia whether she lived in London. Julia extracted a cigarette from a packet and leaned towards Andy so that he could light it, displaying a lot of bosom in the process.

'Oh God, yes. I'd never live anywhere else.'

'But the bombs . . .' said Lionel.

'You mean the IRA? I don't let it bother me.'

Bridget mentioned the latest IRA attack in London, at Green Park Underground station. She had been in the vicinity and had heard the bomb go off.

'How frightening,' murmured Lionel. 'You should come and live here, Bridget. So much safer.'

'Oh, I couldn't live here,' said Bridget, very firmly. 'I'm a London girl, like Julia.'

36

Lionel speared a chunk of beef. 'Julia isn't a London girl. She was born here, the same as me.'

'Yes, but I grew out of it,' hissed Julia. 'That's the *point*.'

Pudding was a Black Forest gateau that Bridget had baked and transported all the way to the farmhouse. The conversation moved on to general topics – a film that Kirsty and Emma had seen, an undergraduate acquaintance of Max, Andy and Phil's who had recently and unexpectedly got married.

Phil was putting on the kettle for coffee and they were starting to rise from the dinner table when all the lights went out, plunging the room into darkness. Julia screamed. There was a loud crash as something rolled off the table and smashed on the floor.

Max said, 'Watch your feet, Emma, I think that was a wine bottle.'

'Don't worry, this happens from time to time.' Lionel's voice. 'I'll go and look at the fuse box.'

'You know I can't stand the dark!' Julia began to cry.

Emma patted her back and said soothing things, but Julia kept on weeping. Lionel had disappeared, taking a candle to light his way. By the light of the torch Max had in his pocket, Emma stooped and began cautiously to pick up fragments of broken bottle. Max helped her, while Andy and Kirsty steered Julia to the sofa. Emma was very aware of his presence so close to her. His arm brushed against hers. She noticed that though he always looked a little scruffy, he was quick and neat picking up the glass.

The lights went back on as suddenly as they had gone off. Lionel returned to the room and said cheerfully, 'Only a fuse! No damage done!' Julia had stopped sobbing and was curled up against Andy, snuffling into his shirt.

Phil made the coffee, and as Lionel began to heap up the dirty dishes in the sink, he suggested that Max show Emma and Kirsty round the house. Kirsty announced that she had been brought up in a draughty old farmhouse and would rather stay where she was. 'You don't mind, do you, Lionel? I'll give you a hand with the dishes.'

'I should have warned you about the cold,' Max said as he and Emma left the kitchen for the icy chill of the corridor. 'There isn't any central heating.'

Alone with him, she felt able to put her disappointment in perspective. Max Hooper would become a friend. She liked him a lot, but the feelings she'd had for him were only an attraction, a crush, nothing out of the ordinary. Now that she had recognised them as such, she would put them aside.

She followed him through a series of small rooms towards the rear of the building. He told her that the farmhouse had been built in the seventeenth century for a retired naval captain. Opening a door to a small, dimly lit room with a flagged stone floor, he said, 'This would have been a still room or pantry.'

'Does Lionel own the house?'

'He and Julia do. Their father died earlier in the year, so they inherited it.' He opened another door. Stone steps led down into darkness. 'The dairy was in the cellar. You'd have heard the cows lowing as you went about your work. Lionel and I were at school together. When I told him I'd got the job in Reigate, he offered me a room.'

'Is that what they're arguing about? The house?'

He gave her a frowning glance. 'Arguing? Who?'

She laughed. 'Max, you must have noticed. Lionel and Julia.'

'I wasn't listening, to be honest. I kind of switch off. I find Julia a bit . . . Well, she likes to be the centre of attention. I'd rather talk about, um . . . things that interest me.'

'Like architecture.'

'Yes.'

'Why were Phil and Andy teasing you?'

'Phil's always been keen on modernism, Andy's more of a classicist, and I don't fit into either category. I believe that what matters most in a building is the quality of the materials and the craftmanship involved. Look at this place.' He patted a huge oak beam. 'It's stood for decades. It's still good to live in. That's because of the structure, because of the fine materials used and the quality of the workmanship. It doesn't have pretensions, it doesn't try to stand out or to make a statement. It's a practical house that blends into its surroundings. I believe all buildings should do that, whether they're urban or rural.' His serious expression was replaced by an apologetic smile. 'Sorry. Phil would tell me I was getting on my high horse again.'

As they headed back through the house to the stairs, Emma told him about the Romillys' home on the Suffolk coast. 'It's all white and grey and brown. You'd think it had grown out of the shoreline. I wouldn't be surprised if I found barnacles on the walls.'

'You love it, don't you? Your eyes light up when you talk about it.'

'I wish you could see it.' She fell silent. Her big mouth. What a stupid thing to say. Why on earth would Max want to visit a tatty little house in the middle of nowhere?

'I'd like that,' he said.

They went upstairs. The sounds of dinner-party chatter were erased by the clamour of the wild weather outside.

Max said, 'Now you mention it, Julia did seem a bit off with Lionel. She wants him to sell the farmhouse.'

'Will he, do you think?'

'He won't want to. I can't imagine him living anywhere else.'

Emma asked Max how long he and Bridget had known each other. 'A year, more or less,' he said. 'We met at a party in Richmond upon Thames. I was getting towards the end of my diploma.'

'It must be difficult, living apart.'

'It's okay,' he said vaguely. 'We're both fine with it. Most weekends I go up to London or Bridget comes down here. I was in London applying to architectural practices, but then the Reigate one came up. I admire one of the partners, Peter Eisen, enormously. I'm learning so much from him.'

Emma remembered Bridget saying, *I'm a London girl.* She wondered whether Max's decision to leave the capital was a source of contention between them. Whether Bridget minded that Max had moved out of London. Whether if she had minded, he would have noticed.

They reached the foot of a narrow staircase. The lino was cold beneath Emma's stockinged feet. Max said, 'Watch out, the bulb's gone on the landing.'

The light from his torch illuminated the steps. Following him up, Emma noticed again his good proportions, that pleasing triangle of broad shoulders and narrow hips.

*Think about something else. The architecture, for heaven's sake. The weather. Anything.*

'This is my room.' He opened a door. 'See that window? I always think it looks like a porthole. I like to believe the old naval captain put it in to remind him of his seagoing days.'

On the far side of the room, a round window sketched

a frame round the full moon. Ripped fragments of cloud rushed across the face of the moon. Trees tossed their heads and a shimmering oval of light darted through the glass and danced on a worn oak floor scattered with books and papers and an overnight bag – Bridget's, presumably – from which trailed a scarf and a pair of tights. The glint of silver in Max's eyes must be a reflection of the moon, too. Emma took a step away from him, back to the landing.

Bridget's voice, calling out for Max, prompted them to head downstairs. She was in the hallway. 'Darling,' she said, ruffling his hair. 'I've missed you.'

Max and Bridget shared a slow and lingering kiss. Quietly Emma returned to the first floor, where she found a bathroom and locked herself in. She rinsed her hands and stared at her reflection in the mirror. The rain had made her hair spring off her scalp in tight curls.

She sat down on the edge of the bath. Her foot hurt. When she inspected it, she discovered that there was a puncture wound in the sole. Her tights were bloodied and ripped. She must have trodden on a fragment of glass from the broken wine bottle and cut herself without noticing it.

She told herself that it was just as well Max was unavailable. She enjoyed her work and wanted to see the world. She had only to think of her mother, Tamar, how she'd always had to squeeze her career into the cracks left by the demands of family, to know that domesticity wasn't for her, for now at least. She wasn't the sort of woman to have designs on another woman's boyfriend, so she must forget her attraction to Max Hooper. It would wear off. She had a habit of falling in and out of love quite quickly. All she had to do was to fall out of love with him, and that shouldn't be hard at all.

*

Easily, delightfully, the two households slipped into a friendship that autumn. Either the girls from the house in Horley piled into Sue's Mini and headed off to the farmhouse, or the men turned up at the Horley semi with a bottle of wine, while Emma made an enormous spaghetti bolognese and Max, her sous chef, chopped mushrooms and crushed garlic. There were nights when they didn't get round to going home, when Emma and Kirsty stayed over in a freezing little room in the farmhouse's attic, dashing off in the early hours to crew a plane. As Sue's relationship with her pilot boyfriend became more serious, she came to the farmhouse less often. Sometimes Phil and Andy slept the night in the living room of the Horley house, rolled up in blankets on sofa and floor. On those weekends when Bridget wasn't staying at the farmhouse, Max joined them.

They crammed into cars and headed to Brighton or Box Hill, and they went on long walks through the Surrey countryside. As the days grew shorter and the temperature dropped and the first frosts came, the furrows in the ploughed fields had a glassy glitter. The air was sweet with the scent of the resin of the conifers; around mid afternoon, the sun sank in a flash of pink and coral behind distant silhouetted trees. Often, when Bridget was away in London, Emma and Max ended up walking side by side, a little apart from the others. They would stop to look at something and then glance up to find that their friends were now far in the distance while the two of them were left behind, examining a gall on a rose bush, or a badger's sett dug into a sunken lane.

In early December, the men threw a party at the farmhouse to celebrate Kirsty's twenty-third birthday. Lionel and Phil cooked a four-course meal. Emma, who had to work the next day, stuck to drinking water. Afterwards, Bridget suggested they play a round of bridge. Emma didn't play bridge, so she helped Lionel with the dishes.

As the game went on, it became obvious that though Bridget was a keen and competent player, Max, who was partnering her, didn't have his mind on the game. After a couple of hands, she cried out, 'Why did you lay the seven of clubs? What on earth were you thinking, Max? You have to concentrate.'

Emma put the plates back on the dresser while the card game ground on, becoming increasingly bad-tempered. After Bridget and Max lost to Kirsty and Andy, Bridget stomped out of the kitchen. Max looked startled.

Emma left the room too, to put away a tureen. She had replaced it on the sitting-room sideboard when a sound from behind her made her spin round.

Bridget was sitting on the sofa, alone in the gloom. Emma asked her whether she was all right and Bridget gave a loud sniff.

'I'm fine.'

Emma switched on a standard lamp. She saw that Bridget's cheeks were wet with tears. 'Oh Bridget,' she said gently. 'Shall I get Max?'

'God, no!' Tears spilled from Bridget's eyes.

'A cup of tea? A tissue?'

'No, thanks. Sorry, I've had too much to drink, that's all.'

Emma closed the door and sat down beside her. Bridget delved into the sleeve of her cardigan, took out a handkerchief and dabbed her cheeks. Then she gasped, and said, 'Half the time I don't think he even notices I'm there! He can be so clueless!'

'I'm sure he doesn't mean it. He was just a little distracted tonight.'

She had noticed before how Max's introspective nature sometimes annoyed Bridget. Emma, who had grown up surrounded by artists, and who came from a family that viewed burying oneself in one's work as neither selfish nor antisocial but an essential part of the creative process, respected his intensity and drive. But she could quite see how his daydreaming might grate.

'He always has his head in the clouds.' Bridget's voice quivered. 'Sometimes I wonder whether there's any space left there for me!'

'He adores you, of course he does. Men can be so dense, can't they?'

Bridget muttered, 'I didn't want him to leave London, but I knew how keen he was to work with Peter Eisen. I knew how excited he was about it, so I didn't say anything.'

'That was good of you. Long-distance love affairs are never easy.'

'Especially with someone like Max.' Bridget put back her head and exhaled. Then she said quietly, 'I'm afraid I'll end up losing him. I'm afraid it'll just fizzle out.'

'Oh Bridget.'

She made a visible effort to get her emotions under control. 'Sorry, Emma. I didn't mean to inflict all this on you.'

'It's all right. I don't mind.'

She did, though. It was late, past one, and she now regretted not having used the excuse of work to drive back to Horley earlier. The platitudes she had just spouted echoed in her ears, an inadequate attempt to conceal a truth she had discovered while sitting in the damp, chilly room, a truth she must at all costs hide from Bridget: that she was still attracted to Max. That she had wanted him from the first moment she had seen him and had not stopped wanting him since.

Bridget tucked her handkerchief back in her sleeve. 'Do I look a fright?'

'Of course not, you look beautiful.'

'No, I don't.' The alteration in Bridget's tone and expression, and her sudden clear-eyed stare, was disconcerting. 'I'm not beautiful. You are, Emma, and so is Julia. I'm not saying I'm hideous or anything, but I'm not like you, I have to try.' She smoothed her hair back behind her ears, then said quietly, 'I thought of leaving London and coming to live here with him, but I was afraid that if I did that, I might end up losing everything – my career *and* Max. And honestly, I couldn't bear that.'

She left the room. Emma remained on the sofa. In the low light, the room seemed shabby, the furnishings and objects no longer charming in their faded elegance, but tired and dusty. What pleasure she had taken in the evening was gone. She felt sorry for Bridget and she disliked herself.

After a while, she went back into the kitchen. Lionel was folding a cloth to dry on the Aga; Phil was sitting in an armchair, drinking by himself. Max was presumably upstairs, making his peace with Bridget. Phil told Emma that Kirsty had gone upstairs with Andy. He looked sour: Emma had suspected that he was attracted to Kirsty.

She headed back to Horley alone. The temperature had plummeted, but as she drove along the narrow country lanes, she was almost glad of the risk of black ice. It forced her to concentrate on the task in hand; it stopped her thinking about anything else.

Frequently during the week that followed, Emma found herself reflecting on her conversation with Bridget. It occurred to her that not once during their long discussions

45

when walking in the countryside had she heard Max say, 'Bridget and I are saving for a deposit', or 'When I move back to London, we'll look for a place together.' Not once had he spoken of a future he expected to share with his girlfriend. It was possible, of course, that he was being properly discreet about private matters. But if he was truly in love with Bridget, wouldn't he talk about her at every opportunity? Wasn't that what people who were in love did?

Though she tried to shove these thoughts out of her head, they kept popping back. The memory of Bridget weeping in the dark stayed with her too. *Half the time I don't think he even notices I'm there.* Her own recognition of the invidious position in which she had found herself, trying to offer solace to Max's girlfriend, made her angry with both herself and Max.

On Sunday, she was on the verge of making an excuse to avoid spending the afternoon at the farmhouse, but Kirsty wanted to go and in the end Emma let herself be persuaded. Kirsty borrowed Sue's Mini. Heading out of the town and into the misty grey December landscape, Emma had to fight back a gut feeling that she was going in the wrong direction. She knew that she had agreed to come today because she wanted to see Max. And yet it was wrong of her to want to see him. Max himself would, of course, be blithely unaware of all undercurrents. It must be nice to be Max Hooper, she thought crossly; it must be nice to float through life without noticing things.

After a walk in the woods, the eight of them returned to the house. They had peeled off their coats and boots and Phil was making tea when Lionel spoke.

'I've got something to tell you all,' he said. 'I've decided to sell the farmhouse.'

'Man, *seriously?*' Phil swung round from spooning tea into the pot.

'I have to, I'm afraid. I've been racking my brains trying to think of an alternative, but I don't think there is one.'

'Has Julia been twisting your arm?'

'Andy . . .' Lionel looked utterly miserable. 'The truth is, I can't afford the upkeep. It's as simple as that. The place needs re-roofing and rewiring, and I haven't the spare cash. And there's damp in the cellar and worm in some of the beams. Yes, Jules wants me to sell, but that's not unreasonable. This house is half hers. She wants to buy a flat in London and she needs a deposit.'

'Christ, Lionel . . .'

'She's the only family I have left and I've no wish to fall out with her.' Lionel, who never raised his voice, did so now, drowning out Andy's response.

Max said, 'It can't have been an easy decision.'

'No, bloody hard.' Lionel took mugs from the dresser. 'I'll miss it more than I can say. It may take a while to sell, I don't know, but I thought I should let you all know now so that you can make other plans.'

Andy said, 'Kirsty and I were thinking of looking for a place of our own anyway.'

'You could come back to London, Max,' said Bridget. 'There's plenty of room at my place.'

'No, I think I'll hang on here,' he said. 'I'm sure I'll be able to find somewhere in Reigate or Horley.'

Phil poured tea into mugs. 'What will you do, Lionel?'

Lionel began to discuss his own plans. Emma hardly heard him. She was glancing from Max to Bridget, who had fallen silent. If Max had bothered to look at Bridget, he might have noticed her stricken expression.

47

Several minutes passed, then Bridget touched his hand and stood up. 'I've got some work to catch up on. Give me an hour or so, darling.'

'Sure. I'll bring you a cup of tea, shall I?'

'No, don't bother.' She left the room.

Shortly afterwards, Max disappeared too, a mug of tea in hand. Discussions went on around Emma while she seethed inwardly. After a while, she slipped out of the kitchen. Through the sitting-room window she caught sight of Max on the gravel area in front of the house. The bonnet of his Cortina was open and he was peering inside it.

She went outside. Hearing her footsteps, he looked up. 'Hi, Em.'

As she marched across the gravel, she said furiously, 'It's all very well not having a clue about what's going on around you, but it isn't okay, it really isn't at all, not noticing how unhappy you're making Bridget.'

'What?' Straightening, he stared at her. 'Bridget?'

'Yes, Max.' She was so angry she could hardly speak coherently. 'Your girlfriend, Bridget. Bridget, the woman who's in love with you. *That* Bridget!'

'I don't think—'

'No, I know you don't! You don't think at all, do you? You just bumble on, oblivious to everything. And if you're about to tell me that Bridget's all right, then I assure you, Max, she isn't. And I notice these things, so I know what I'm talking about. Bridget isn't all right at all. In fact, she's devastated.'

Max closed the Cortina's bonnet. He ran his oily hands down his jeans and frowned deeply. 'Are you saying that she's not all right about what I said just then, about preferring to stay here rather than go back to London?'

'Yes, Max, exactly that. Well done for working it out,' Emma added sarcastically. 'Of course, there's a whole load of other things she's not all right about too. But it would take me a while to list them.'

'But she and I agreed—'

She lost her temper with him. 'I don't know whether you're being deliberately unkind or just plain stupid.'

Her voice was ice cold and she saw him flinch. For a while, neither of them spoke. The tension between them seemed to intensify as the light dipped behind the trees, casting long shadows.

Then he said quietly, 'If I've been unkind, it was not intentional. But I see now that I may have been . . . careless. And that's no better.'

Her anger faded and all she felt was an utter weariness. 'Max, are you in love with Bridget?' she said bluntly. 'You need to make up your mind. Because if you aren't, then you should be honest with her. Because she loves you.'

She went back into the house. Through the sitting-room window she saw Max leave the car and come indoors. She waited until she was sure he had gone upstairs before going into the hall and putting on her coat. She could hear from the kitchen that the discussion about the sale of the farmhouse was still going on. She scribbled a note and tucked it into the top of Kirsty's handbag, where she was bound to see it, and then let herself out of the house.

It was a six-mile walk back to Horley, but she welcomed the distraction of movement, and besides, she couldn't bear to stay at the farmhouse a moment longer. She had been walking for half a mile when she heard the sound of a car behind her. She glanced over her shoulder and saw the Cortina, slowing as it drew level with her.

Max wound down the window. 'Emma, what are you doing?'

'I'm going home.'

'Let me give you a lift.'

'Thanks, but I'd rather walk.'

'It's raining.'

She glanced up at the charcoal sky. It was indeed raining.

He said, 'Bridget didn't want to speak to me. I can see I've been a selfish idiot. I'm going to try to sort it out.'

'Okay.' She gave him a cold look. 'That doesn't magically make it all right, you know.'

'Yes, I know.' He too looked miserable.

She shrugged, then shivered. There was a sleety edge to the rain.

'Hop in,' he said. 'I promise I won't say a word if you don't want me to.'

She stood, irresolute, then nodded and climbed into the car.

They did not speak throughout the journey to Horley. Max parked the car outside her house, and Emma said, 'Thanks for the lift,' and got out, slamming the door just a little to make clear to him that she wanted to be on her own.

For months she had rationalised her relationship with Max; for months she had told herself that they were no more than friends, and that her one-sided regard for him could not be dignified with the name of love. But now the door in her mind she had been struggling to hold shut had burst open. There was no pleasure in being with him any more, this she now saw; only desolation and loneliness. No joy, only a sense of shame she could no longer dismiss. The long conversations she and Max had when Bridget was safely out of the way in London had been wrong. Sharing their dreams and aspirations: that was a form of deceit, too, because there was an intimacy in it. You didn't have to touch someone to feel close to them.

She knew that she must do what she should have done ever since she had found out that Max Hooper had a girlfriend: she must keep away from him. An outbreak of flu among the cabin crew meant that during the weeks that followed she was able to work plenty of overtime. In what little time off she had, she kept away from the farmhouse and saw other friends. She went home to Seastone for a couple of days at Christmas, before returning to Horley.

During the dying end of 1975 and the first days of the new year, Emma felt sad that the friendship between the two households was disintegrating. Lionel had put the farmhouse up for sale. Sue and her pilot boyfriend were getting married and setting up home together. Andy and Kirsty were looking for a place of their own in Horley, and Phil planned to go back to university to study for a PhD. As for her, she must either move out of the Horley house and find somewhere else to live or begin the process of looking for new people to rent the rooms that would soon fall vacant. She could not seem to find the enthusiasm for the task, and let things drift.

One evening, returning home from work, she stopped at a small late-night supermarket to buy food. She had worked a long shift and her throat was sore and her muscles ached. She felt exhausted beyond words, which she put down to all those extra hours.

At the house, she carried her shopping bags into the kitchen. The task of unpacking her purchases and putting them away seemed almost too much. Her head pulsed as she opened the fridge door. She had spent the last weeks trying not to think of Max, but now her resistance was low and thoughts and memories crowded in on her. Though she reminded herself she should want what was best for him, because love meant caring more about the other person than yourself, those fine principles did nothing to ameliorate the ache in her heart. The realisation came to her, relentless and deadening, that she might never stop yearning for him.

She began to put away the milk and butter, but then stopped, blinking fiercely and futilely while she stared into the interior of the fridge. She had been rather dense, she thought as the tears began to fall. She liked to think herself a perceptive person, and yet she had been fooling herself over and over again.

# Chapter Three

## 1975

He brought her a cup of tea in bed. 'Here you are, Mary,' he said. 'Saturday treat.'

'Thank you,' she murmured, shuffling upright.

He put the mug on the table and sat down on the bed beside her. She forced herself not to shrink away or flinch as he kissed her. *Saturday treat* . . . He would be at home all day. While he talked about this and that, he ran his hand back and forth along her thigh, beneath the duvet.

She picked up the mug, careful not to spill any, because Jamie hated mess. 'Mustn't let it go cold,' she said.

'What shall we do today? We could go out for a drive. Go to the New Forest.'

'Yes.'

'Or Stonehenge. You've been living in Salisbury all this time, Mary, and you haven't been to Stonehenge yet.'

She could have told him she had been to Stonehenge years ago with her mother, but stopped herself. Jamie didn't like her talking about her mother.

Too late, she saw that her lack of response was annoying

him. 'I can't always be ferrying you around,' he said, standing up. 'I've work to catch up on.'

'I don't mind. Whatever you think best.'

His blue eyes darkened, as if someone had flicked a switch. It didn't take much: the wrong expression, the wrong choice of words.

He was standing between her and the door, legs apart, fists clenched. He was a big man, solid and square-jawed, handsome in a florid English way. 'I just wish you'd show some enthusiasm,' he said. 'It's like offering treats to a jellyfish. I think that's what I'll call you – jellyfish, Mary the jellyfish, because you're cold and flabby and you haven't any backbone.'

He left the room. When she was alone again, she put the mug on the bedside table and clamped her hands together to stop them shaking. Jamie hadn't apologised. After the other times, he had apologised, sort of, though he had also pointed out where she had been to blame for setting him off. That was what he called it, *setting him off*. As if he was a firework. Light the blue touchpaper and stand back.

He might return; if he did, she didn't want to be in bed in her nightie. He might force her to have sex with him, and she couldn't face it, not after last night. He would be angry if she hadn't drunk the tea, so she gulped it down. On her way to the bathroom, she paused, listening, glancing downstairs. She couldn't hear anything. She didn't know where he was and that made her nervous. She pictured him sitting in the kitchen reading the *Daily Mail*, or prowling round the living room, annoyed that she hadn't tidied up yet.

She stood in the shower, letting the hot water spray on her bruises. She felt tired and low. Even the air in the house felt tense today. *I can't always be ferrying you round*, he had said, as if it was her fault she couldn't drive. Soon after they had married, she had talked to him about letting her have driving lessons. He hadn't been keen. He was proud of his car and was afraid she would damage it because she was so clumsy.

In her imagination, her mother's voice said, *You're not clumsy at all. Think of all those beautiful clothes you make.*

*Then why do I drop things?*

*It's because you're afraid of him. We're all butter-fingered when we're nervous.*

It had been Jamie who had broken the plate last night, not her, but he had blamed her for not stacking them properly. She had been clearing up after their dinner party, after their guests – Jamie's boss and his wife, and one of his colleagues and the colleague's fiancée – had left. The plate had been part of a set given to them as a wedding present. They weren't particularly nice, and Mary didn't like them much. As Jamie had taken one from the draining board, another had slipped to the floor and smashed.

He had turned to her with that look on his face, the one she had come to know well. 'Now look what you've made me do.'

'You dropped it,' she had said. 'Not me.'

She shouldn't have said that. So you could say it was her fault. Her mother's voice again: *But it was the truth, Mary.*

She rinsed the shampoo from her hair, then turned off the water. Jamie hated hot water to be wasted, so she didn't dare spend too much time in the shower. She stepped out of the cubicle, wincing as she rubbed the towel over her bruised hip. The large red marks were starting to turn purple. She pulled on her dressing gown, then knotted it firmly so she couldn't see the bruises any more.

\*

She had met him fourteen months ago, on the train from London to Andover. It was the third carriage she had tried, and all the seats were full. Men and women in damp raincoats stood in the aisles. Mary breathed in the wet sheep smell of the Afghan coat of the young woman squashed in front of her. Her muscles were tense with the stresses of the day, and she seemed to have had a headache for months.

A hand touched her sleeve, a voice said, 'Here, take my seat.'

She looked round. He was in his late twenties, she guessed. Handsome, well dressed, nice silk tie: she noticed that sort of thing.

She said, 'That's very kind, but I don't want to trouble you.'

Reddish hair, light blue eyes and a neat, full mouth that shaped itself into a charming smile as he rose, making a sweeping movement with his hand. A bow, a gesture of gallantry. Now that he was standing, she saw that he was tall and broad-shouldered. He had a physical presence.

'I insist,' he said.

Mary thanked him and sat down. She was very tired. They fell into a conversation, which was pleasant, because it took her mind off the dreary pathways into which it had fallen these last months. He told her he worked for a building society in Salisbury. She told him about her job interview that afternoon in the fashion department of one of the big London department stores.

'But you don't live in London?' he asked her.

'No, in Andover. I've always lived in Andover.'

'And you want to move?'

'Yes.'

'Why's that?' His gaze latched on to her. 'Andover's a nice

little town. What would make a girl like you want to leave her home town?'

She was enjoying their conversation. It seemed a long time since anyone had shown an interest in her. She had felt so lonely lately. She ended up telling him about her mother, about her long illness and her death two months ago. She hadn't meant to, because she didn't want to bore a stranger with her grief, but it was never far from her mind and she found it hard to think about anything else. At home, her mother's reading glasses were still on the sitting-room mantelpiece. Her knitting bag lay on the hearth and there was a hollow in the cushion of her favourite armchair. It had been the only chair she could sit in with any comfort during her last months, and it had moulded itself to her body, as if it retained the memory of her breath. Mary herself still slept in the single bed in her childhood bedroom. Once a week she went into her mother's room to dust, but that was as much as she could bear. It wasn't that she wanted to forget, but that remembering was an unhealable wound.

As the train approached Andover, he suggested they have a drink at the station bar. Mary was attracted to him and dreaded the thought of returning to the silent house, but she didn't want him to get the wrong idea. And perhaps he understood this, because he told her that he had to catch the next train on to Salisbury. He would nip out at Andover, they would have a drink, and then he'd be off again. Perhaps – a smile – there would be more seats on the next train.

'Half an hour,' he coaxed. 'I haven't introduced myself yet, have I? I'm Jamie Canterbury. What's your name?'

'Mary Finch.'

'Mary,' he said, rolling it around his mouth as if he was tasting it. 'I like that. I like the simple, old-fashioned names.'

He had detected a vulnerability in her: this she had worked out some time ago. That was what men like Jamie did. *I insist*, he had said when he had offered her the seat. Jamie liked to have his own way. He disliked being thwarted, especially by a woman.

Mary tidied the bathroom, folding the towels and drying the inside of the shower with a cloth, then went back to the bedroom to dress. She couldn't decide what to wear. As she looked through the wardrobe, Jamie's criticisms echoed. Jeans were scruffy and unfeminine, midi skirts were frumpy, and girls wearing miniskirts looked like tarts. She settled for a black skinny-rib jumper and a camel corduroy skirt she had made herself, with a hemline two inches above the knee. She had always made her own clothes. Her mother had taught her to sew on her treadle Singer, which now occupied a corner of the spare room in the Salisbury house. The smell of the sewing machine, of metal and oil and thread, always made her think of her mother.

She swept back her hair from her face. There was a pink mark on her left temple that she covered up with foundation. Jamie liked her to look nice, but he didn't approve of women who wore too much make-up. He liked to laugh at older women who plastered it on, as he said. Who did they think they were trying to fool? Mary's hand shook too much to apply mascara. She rested her elbows on the dressing table and took a deep breath. *What shall we do today?* A part of her wanted to curl up in bed and pull the duvet over her head. And yet at the same time, the seed of resolve germinating inside her these past weeks was pushing up through the darkness, fighting for air.

She went downstairs. Jamie was outside, giving the garden

hedge a trim, so she had a breathing space. She put on the washing first so that it would have time to dry on the line. The sink was full of last night's dirty dishes, the pieces of the plate still on the floor. She got out the dustpan and brush and set to work, sweeping up every last fragment. Tiny particles glittered in the sunlight that fell through the kitchen window. Winding among them were long strands of her hair. She soaked a floor cloth beneath the hot tap and ran it over the tiles, scrubbing them clean, scrubbing away the memory.

It was only the third time he had hit her. (Only? said her mother.) She set to work collecting up glasses and cups and taking them to the kitchen to wash and dry. She polished the watermarks off the coffee table and plumped up the cushions. Then she went round with the vacuum cleaner, getting up all the specks and crumbs. Jamie liked the place to look nice. He said it was the least she could do when he kept her in such comfort. Her hip and shoulder hurt as she moved.

It was a spacious house, substantially bigger than the tiny terrace in which she had grown up, and when Jamie had shown her round the first time, she had been thrilled to imagine herself living there. Today, as she polished and tidied, she detested its claustrophobic solidity.

When the washing was finished, she pegged it out on the line. It was a good drying day, and a freshening wind lifted Jamie's shirts, tossing them up and filling them out so they looked as if a big, heavy man was inside them, his arms outstretched. She hung out the shirt he had worn last night at the dinner party. She remembered focusing on the small pale green checks, an inch or two from her vision, and suddenly felt so tired she could hardly stand. She rested her back against the wall of the house. A dog was barking in a neighbour's garden, and she could hear the rumble of the hedge trimmer.

The wind cooled her skin and her panic retreated. Her gaze lifted to the stand of ornamental trees at the bottom of the garden. Beyond them were more roads, more houses, and then, a mile or so away, the Iron Age hill fort of Old Sarum. She had walked there during the summer while Jamie was at work, round the tops of the high grassy ramparts. She remembered looking out over the Wiltshire landscape. She had imagined herself flying alone, as free as a bird, above woodland, river, and cornfields streaked with scarlet poppies, swooping like a swallow until she reached the blue-grey mist of the horizon, then soaring north over Amesbury and Stonehenge and on to Andover.

And on again, further and further, to London. London was about a hundred miles away. Far enough, thought Mary.

The events of the past year had been a succession of dividing roads between which she had consistently made the wrong choice, ending up with her in this house, with this man. First there had been her meeting with Jamie on the train. A few days later, they had gone on a date, though she had known herself to be too emotionally fragile to embark on a serious relationship. Three months after that, she had accepted his proposal of marriage. And so on, and so on, a fatal series of steps in the wrong direction.

They had married eight months ago. It rained all day, which put Jamie in a bad mood. He drank steadily. He hadn't drunk much when they were courting, just the odd glass of beer or wine. There was a sit-down meal at a hotel in Salisbury, and after that a dance. Jamie and Mary danced the first number, alone on the floor, with the guests all watching and smiling and clapping. After several dances, he went off to fetch a drink from the bar. Mary didn't know many of the other guests – they were mostly workmates of Jamie's – and felt rather self-conscious standing there on her own. Then the band struck up a slow number and the best man asked her onto the floor. As they circled the room, she caught sight of Jamie weaving through the other couples towards her. 'Sorry, Mike, but she's mine,' he said, and took her in his arms.

She had thought this romantic. She had thought he loved her so much he couldn't bear to let her out of his sight.

After a week's honeymoon on the Isle of Wight, they returned to Salisbury, to Jamie's house in Moberly Road. Several of the neighbours invited them round to welcome her to the street, but Jamie didn't want to go, and he didn't want her to go either. *I like having you all to myself. I hate having to share you. You couldn't manage without me, Mary, you know that, don't you?*

Again she told herself this was sweet, and a sign of his devotion. She accepted one or two coffee-morning invitations for politeness's sake, but he didn't let up. Jamie never let up, and in the end she gave in, because whatever it was – a cup of coffee, a hem length, a way of stacking the dishes – didn't seem worth provoking a row. And anyway, back then she had still thought herself in love with him. She had imagined they would settle down to each other and smooth things out.

Jamie didn't want her to go out to work. It was the man's role to earn money, to be the breadwinner, and the wife's to run the home. A man who couldn't support his wife wasn't much of a man at all. Would she have married him if she had known before the wedding that he held such old-fashioned views? She was horribly afraid she would have. She would have assumed she could change his mind. When she tried to explain to him how much she missed the company of her workmates, he said, 'You've got me now, haven't you?' His expression made her back off. That blue touchpaper.

She had never had a lover as attentive as Jamie. In the early days, he had sent her flowers for no reason other than to tell her he loved her. He phoned her several times a day from work, and when he came home, he wanted to know everything she had done, every tiny detail of her day. Back then, for a while, she had believed herself embraced by love, sealed up tight in its silky warm cocoon.

Jamie came in from the garden and sat down at the kitchen table. Mary put the Cona on. He was looking at the newspaper but couldn't seem to settle on any particular article, and was flicking from page to page. He was in one of his restless moods, which made her feel anxious. The hedge trimmer, which lay on the table, was black with oil. The smell mingled unpleasantly with the aroma of the coffee bubbling in the Cona.

'The hedge looks nice,' she said.

'I haven't finished it yet. There's still the back to do. What's for dinner tonight?'

'Smoked haddock.' She poured him a cup of coffee. She felt him watching her as she set out the cream and sugar.

His lip curled. 'Fish again.'

'Or I could do the sausages.'

'Or I could do the sausages.' His mimicry of her was a pathetic falsetto bleat. 'Christ, are you incapable of making up your mind about anything?'

'Sorry.' Her thoughts were shattering, splitting, scattering all over the place. She struggled to assemble them. 'Why don't we go out for lunch? We could go to that nice pub near Old Sarum. You deserve a treat after all that hard work.'

As she put the cutlery away in the drawer, she knew that the exchange might go either way. 'All right,' he said, and she let out a silent breath of relief.

After Jamie had finished his coffee, he went back out to the garden. Mary cleared up the coffee things, then went upstairs to get ready. She put her purse and lipstick in her handbag. Then she went into the back bedroom. Standing in the shadow of the curtain, she looked out of the window to where Jamie was trimming the hedge.

How easily she had given over control of her life to another! It was as if she had stepped out onto a frozen pond, believing it to be solid, while all around her cracks were widening, and by the time she noticed them, she was standing alone and isolated on a shard of ice. She wondered whether this was what he believed love was, this jealous and cloying possessiveness that had all but cut her off from other people. Love and hatred rubbed up against each other in Jamie's heart. His love for her was all-consuming. This was the trouble, she had realised after a few months of marriage: that Jamie's version of love was consuming her. This life, where she weighed every word and was always on guard, afraid that he would hurt her again, wasn't the right one for her. She yearned to walk out of it, to go somewhere new, to become a different person.

Her mother's voice whispered, *Then why don't you? Go now, Mary, don't wait.*

Three weeks ago, at the library, her gaze had latched on to a poster. She had gone to get a closer look. *Women's Aid,* it said. *Advice and shelter for battered women and their children.* At the foot of the poster was a phone number and a London address. A long time ago, in another life, Mary had read about women's refuges in newspaper articles. She had seen Erin Pizzey talk on the telly about the problem of domestic violence. At the time, she had found it unimaginable that any of this would apply to her. Before checking out her library books, she had memorised the phone number.

She took out an envelope from its hiding place behind the chest of drawers and slipped it into the zipped compartment of her handbag. For a moment her gaze lingered on her mother's sewing machine in the corner of the room. Then she went back into the main bedroom, put on her jacket, tidied her hair in the mirror and hurried downstairs.

The first time: Jamie had gone out for the evening with some of his colleagues. He had come home in a bad mood because someone had said something he interpreted as a slight. Jamie took offence easily. Mary was in the hall, on the phone, when he opened the front door. He pushed past her so roughly she whacked her head against a cupboard and saw stars.

The next morning, he apologised, in his way. He brought her breakfast in bed. He told her he was sorry if she thought he'd hurt her, but he hadn't meant to. The hallway was narrow. She must have lost her footing. She should have got out of the way. She shouldn't waste so much time on the phone, it must cost them a fortune.

He ran his thumb over the lump on her forehead, caressing the swelling. *Poor little Mary*, he murmured. *You bruise so easily, don't you?* There was a touch of malice in his smile.

Afterwards, there were things she said to herself. Jamie

had his faults, but he was a good provider. Yes, he had a temper, but he could be so sweet. She'd talk to him about his drinking when he'd calmed down.

But she never talked to him about his drinking. The truth was, she didn't dare. To embark on such a conversation would be to strike a match, to smell the burning paper.

Jamie finished the hedge and changed out of his gardening clothes. They left the house and walked up Castle Street to the pub. His mood shifted again and he was affable Jamie, chatty and self-congratulatory.

'That was a job and a half. I must have trimmed half a mile of hedge.'

'You've done a brilliant job. It looks so neat.' They were holding hands. Mary was gripping her handbag in her other hand, conscious of the envelope in the zipped compartment.

They ate their scampi and chips in the saloon bar. The spacious room was busy with couples and families. Jamie's gaze raked restlessly round the tables, settling on the women. *Jesus, would you look at her. Face like the back of a bus.*

He talked about his work. Next week he had an interview for a more senior position at the building society. 'Neville hasn't a hope,' he told her, stretching out his legs so people had to step around him. 'He shouldn't have bothered applying. And John hasn't the flair. The job's mine for the taking. Deputy manager's wife . . . you'd like that, wouldn't you, Mary? We could have a decent holiday. Go abroad. Where would you like to go?'

She had been abroad only once, to Paris, when she was eighteen, with her mother. She had loved Paris but she knew she didn't want to go there with Jamie.

She must say something, though. 'Tenerife, maybe.'

65

He grinned, showing white, even teeth. His strong fingers kneaded her palm as he spoke, pressing and rubbing. He murmured, 'Sun, sea and sex, that's what you fancy, isn't it?'

Shortly afterwards, he went off to the gents. Mary imagined being at an airport with Jamie, flying on a plane with Jamie, being shut in a hotel room for a fortnight with Jamie. And what if he didn't get the job? He never took disappointment well. Her handbag lay on the bench beside her. She pictured herself scooping it up and running out of the pub, all the way down Castle Street, across the town to the railway station. Her muscles flexed, ready to go.

Jamie came back into the bar. He said, 'What are you thinking about?'

'Oh, nothing much,' she said coolly, looking up at him. 'Whether I've got enough room for pudding or just a coffee, that's about it. What about you?'

The second time had been two months ago. She was shopping in town when she ran into Valerie, a neighbour. Valerie suggested they have a cup of tea together. Mary, who was by then fourteen weeks pregnant, thought it would be okay just this once. Jamie had been nicer to her since she'd told him about the baby. She hoped the prospect of fatherhood would steady him.

After she left the café, she went to the bus stop. She'd just missed a bus so hurried home on foot. Halfway along Moberly Road, she felt chilled to see Jamie standing on the front doorstep. He was looking out for her. The thought flashed into her head that he hadn't noticed her yet, that she could walk away and keep on walking until she had put miles between them. But then he turned and saw her.

When she reached the house, he dragged her into the

hall and slammed shut the front door. Where had she been? Who had she been with? What had she and Valerie been talking about? And why, when she had promised to return to the house within an hour, had she taken two? Each question was punctuated with a slap. The slaps, and the questions, seemed to go on for ever, and eventually Mary stumbled, lost her footing and fell to the floor. Jamie walked away.

She lost the baby that night in a flood of blood and jellied clots on the bathroom floor. She didn't dare ask Jamie to call an ambulance. She cleared up the mess as best she could and curled up shivering in the spare bedroom, a couple of towels beneath her to spare the mattress. She wept for the baby, flushed down the toilet and mopped up with an old towel, and for the loss of hope. She had longed for a daughter, a brown-haired little girl who liked sewing outfits for her dolls, as she had done. She would have called her Jacqueline, after her mother. She thought she might die of the blood seeping out of her, and the truth was, she didn't care.

In the morning, Jamie came into the room with a cup of tea for her. She told him about the baby and he said he was sorry. He took her in his arms. 'Poor little Mary,' he said. 'I was so worried about you. I was afraid you'd had an accident, that was what set me off. You mustn't worry me like that again. Promise me.'

Two days later, her temperature shot up and she was still bleeding. She went to see the doctor and ended up in hospital having a D and C. She had an infection and remained in hospital for a week while they got it under control. One of the nurses asked her about the circumstances of her miscarriage, but Mary didn't tell her the truth. What good would it have done? Jamie was her mistake and she must work out what to do about him.

It was a relief to be in a hospital bed, to be away from him. If it hadn't been for the pain, she would have enjoyed being there. People brought her trays of food, and it was good to be in the company of women who knew what it was to suffer and to mourn. She had time and space to think, and went over in her head what had happened. Vividly she recalled that sudden, powerful impulse to turn and walk away from the house. She had stayed because of the baby and because she had only a couple of pounds in her purse. That decision had cost her child its life. She hated Jamie for that, and she hated herself for being so weak.

She had no money of her own, no savings, no cheque-book. The bank account was in Jamie's name. But after that day, after she went home from the hospital, she put aside small amounts of money. Ten or fifty pence at a time, because Jamie knew the price of everything and was very exact about the amount of cash he gave her to buy groceries and other essentials. She kept it in an envelope, which she hid behind the chest of drawers in the spare bedroom. She had saved up almost sixteen pounds.

It was her running-away fund. She knew by now that it was never going to get better. She had married Jamie Canterbury because she was lonely, but she was lonelier than ever now, and it needed to stop.

They walked back to the house. Jamie sat in the living room while Mary went into the kitchen to make tea. The kettle came to the boil and she poured water on the leaves. From the adjacent room there was the scrape and flick of Jamie turning the pages of the newspaper.

Her gaze was drawn to the wall beside the fridge. She remembered the shards of plate sprayed across the floor. You *dropped it. Not me*, she had said. For once, she hadn't tried to appease him. Instead she had attempted to fight him off, pushing and clawing at him, writhing out from under his grasp. A dark veil had drawn across his face and he had grabbed her. *Don't.* He had seized her by her hair and slammed her against the wall. *Don't you dare try to get away from me.* Another blow. She would never forget the smell of him, of sweat and fury, and she would never forget the green and white check of his shirt, pressed up hot against her face, and the way her terror had made it hard to breathe.

*Shut up. Do you want me to do it again? This is what happens when you don't do as you're told. Now just shut up.*

Later, he had said to her, *I won't ever let you go, Mary. I'd rather you were dead. Remember that.* She knew those words would haunt her for the rest of her days.

She took the mugs of tea through to the living room. She pretended to look at a magazine while Jamie read the newspaper, but all the while she was thinking. She had intended to wait till she had more money, or at least for a weekday, when it would be easier because Jamie was at work. But the events of last night had changed her mind. His mood had remained volatile, and throughout the day his resentment and aggression had kept bubbling close to the surface. It might happen again tonight. He might hit her harder. He might knock her unconscious or push her down the stairs.

He looked up from the sports page. 'We could go out for a drive later.'

She forced a smile. 'A drive would be fun.'

'I'll need to check the tyres and engine oil first.'

'I've a couple of letters to post. Why don't I get that out of the way while you're sorting out the car?'

'What letters?'

'That *Woman's Own* coupon I filled in, for the paper patterns. And a note to Auntie Carol.'

'You're always writing to her. I don't know what you find to say to the boring old cow.'

'We just rattle on, Jamie.'

As she left the room and went upstairs, she struggled to remember what normal was, to recall how in ordinary circumstances she climbed the stairs or opened a bedroom door. How long it was reasonable to take, preparing to go out to post a letter.

She heard the front door close as Jamie went outside to work on his car. The green Hillman Avenger was parked on the drive. She watched from the bedroom window as he propped open the bonnet and peered inside, then she opened his drawer and took out her passport from where he kept it beneath a pile of handkerchiefs. She needed her passport, because whatever life she made for herself in the future must be full and free from fear.

Though she sensed on the edge of her consciousness a dizzy excitement and longing, she made herself think everything through carefully. She couldn't afford to make any mistakes. He might ask her why she needed her handbag when she was only going out to post a couple of letters, so she shouldn't take it. She put her passport and the envelope with the money into her jacket pocket and stared at her reflection in the mirror. The passport peeked out over the top of the pocket. She tucked it into the waistband of her skirt and pulled her jumper down over it.

A lipstick, tissue and comb went into her other pocket. She left her house keys in her handbag and put it in the wardrobe, out of view. As she went downstairs, she took a last glance round the house in which she had spent her married life. Already it was taking on an air of unfamiliarity, as if she had begun to erase it from her memory. *Never again,* she promised as she let herself out. *I will never put myself at the mercy of a man ever again.*

On the drive, Jamie was still tinkering beneath the bonnet. 'Won't be a tick,' she called out, waving the letters at him.

Would he notice the fullness of her pockets, would he read her intention in her eyes? Would he insist on going with her to the postbox? As she walked away, she longed to look back but knew she mustn't. She seemed to feel his gaze on her, burning twin bruises between her shoulder blades. Her breath came thick and rasping. She was aware of the rumble of traffic from the main road and a rustling as she waded through drifts of dead leaves on the pavement. Her heart pounded, a fast, anxious beat, as she turned the corner. Now the house was out of sight; now she looked back. A neighbour walking his dog, a couple of children playing on bikes. No Jamie. She sped up her pace, started to jog.

*Run, and keep on running. Run until you're safe. Make a new start, Mary. And never look back.*

A bus passed her, slowing as it approached the stop on Castle Street. She ran faster. It seemed to her that her future depended on catching that bus. As she hurtled down the hill, the rows of red-brick houses with their leafy gardens blurred and faded. The conductor caught sight of her and waited. A last burst of speed and she jumped onto the platform.

She spent a week in a refuge in a terraced house in Chiswick. She shared a room with a woman and three children and slept on a mattress on the floor. The curtains were made of hessian and there were beds squeezed into every inch of

71

space. There was always mayhem in the refuge. The tiny galley kitchen was crammed with women making toast or cooking fish fingers, and little boys racing Dinky cars and getting under everyone's feet. There was often someone in tears, and a husband or boyfriend hammering on the door demanding to be let in. They never were. Mary felt safe there.

She was befriended by a woman called Cathy, who, like her, was childless. When Cathy offered her a share in a room in a squat in Whitechapel, Mary accepted. Other women – women with children – needed her space in the cramped Chiswick refuge.

The squat's Georgian exterior had seen better days. The frames of the sash windows were peeling, and stucco was coming away in powdery chunks. Inside, the floor of the front room was rotten, and someone had hacked down the banister for firewood. The electricity had been cut off, so they used candles and torches.

Half a dozen people lived in the squat. Mary noticed that the women cooked the vegetarian, macrobiotic dishes they all ate and did what little housework anyone bothered with, while the men sat round the kitchen table drinking and talking politics. A guy called Terry, who had long dark brown hair and a Zapata moustache, made a pass at her one evening, winding his arm round her waist, kneading her belly. She shoved him away. She hated to be touched. Afterwards, she stayed in her room, reading and trying to get her head together.

One afternoon, she was returning to the house from Whitechapel market, having bought herself some second-hand clothes, when she caught sight of Jamie standing on the pavement outside the squat. She felt faint and had to grab the railings for support. Then she turned and walked away. As soon as he was out of view, she began to run.

*I won't ever let you go, Mary. I'd rather you were dead.*

She didn't dare go back to the Chiswick refuge. Jamie must have traced her there; someone must have told him about Cathy and the squat. She spent a cold, frightening night sleeping on a park bench. The next day she managed to talk herself into another squat, this one lived in only by women. She liked the women, who lent her *The Female Eunuch* and *The Feminine Mystique* to read, both of which opened her eyes. She found casual work at the market, helping on a clothes stall and sorting through donations. She repaired those of value, the beaded flapper dresses and Persian lamb-trimmed coats, and took them to sell in posh second-hand shops in places like Hampstead and Chelsea. Bella, who kept the stall, was pleased with her and offered her more hours.

Someone in the squat mentioned to her that a man had been asking for her, so she moved again. While she was working on the market stall she wore a floppy-brimmed felt hat and a maxi coat and kept an eye out for Jamie. Once, outside Whitechapel Underground station, she thought she saw him, so she moved house again, and then again. She kept on changing address until she was sure he would never be able to catch up with her.

Wherever she was living, she always looked up and down the street before letting herself in. An unexpected knock on the door and she'd plan her escape route. Apart from the occasional cup of coffee with a woman friend, she avoided socialising. She kept away from men. She didn't trust them.

She acquired an old Singer sewing machine that no one else wanted. She didn't sleep well, so she sewed late into the night. She made women's blouses out of second-hand men's shirts, sourced from the market stall, and refashioned old coats and mackintoshes into the narrower silhouettes of the seventies. When she found a second-hand garment of good-quality fabric – a Savile Row cotton, a fine gabardine – she felt the excitement of unearthing a treasure.

She began to make clothes from scratch, to her own design. It took her a while to show them to Bella, because there was always that voice in her head telling her that she was useless, that she couldn't manage on her own, but when eventually she did, Bella loved them. To begin with, she sewed headscarves and simple tops. The first batch sold out in a day. She moved on to smocks and tiered skirts for those customers who favoured the romantic, bucolic look. Women from all over the place began to visit the market stall to buy her garments, which delighted Bella.

Over a drink one evening, they agreed that Mary should start up her own fashion label. The name came to her as she was walking home one night. *Marissa Flint*. It was a pretty name, but it had a hardness too.

Not long after that, she cut her hair. Long brown locks tumbled to the floor. Next, in the bathroom, she applied the contents of a bottle of Clairol.

Marissa Flint looked back at her from the bathroom mirror. Her short, feathery blonde hair framed blue-green eyes and fine-boned features. She was beautiful and distant and no one would ever get close enough to her to hurt her again.

# Chapter Four

## 1976

When Emma arrived at her family home at Seastone, she found her mother, Tamar, standing at her easel in the back room, wearing one of her husband's old shirts over her skirt and jersey. Emma told her that she had had flu. She was fine now, but she had some leave due so had decided to come home for a week. Tamar didn't think her daughter looked fine at all. She looked pale and tired and thin and unhappy.

Emma put her small suitcase in the room that she and Gale had shared as children, then came into the back room and studied the canvas on the easel.

Tamar said, 'I was thinking of painting over it.'

'You mustn't,' Emma said. 'I love it. It just needs . . . *something*.'

'Exactly,' Tamar said grimly.

Shortly afterwards, Rob turned up. At sixteen, Emma's brother was tall and skinny and had an enormous appetite, so Tamar put on the kettle and sliced bread while her son and daughter talked about aeroplanes. Rob was at an age where he lurched between apathy and wild enthusiasm;

sprawled on the sofa, his eyes sparked as Emma told him about a difficult landing in the fog at Schiphol, a transatlantic flight.

Morgan returned to the house at five. He had been out for a long walk through the fields, taking their dog, Bonny, and his eyes were bright and his clothing smelled of salt and cold air. He gave Emma an enormous hug and then they both went to his studio so that Emma could see the series of woodcuts on which he was working. Tamar prepared the tea and Rob made an unconvincing stab at his homework. After they had eaten, they all went out for a walk. Morgan slung an arm round Tamar's shoulders as they headed along the shingle, against the wind.

It wasn't until half past nine that Tamar and Emma had the chance to talk properly. Morgan had gone back to his studio and Rob was in his room, listening to music. Though Emma tried to make light of it — a man she had met on a flight, they had been friends, that was all — she was unable to disguise her misery.

'You're in love with him,' said Tamar.

'Hmm. Yes. I suppose so. It's so silly, Mum!'

Tamar squeezed her hand. 'It isn't silly at all. It happens.'

Tamar made cocoa and opened a packet of biscuits because she could see that Emma needed building up. Emma crumbled a biscuit into a little heap and stirred her cocoa but left it untouched.

Tamar felt a rush of dislike towards this man, Max, who had made her daughter so unhappy. How could he possibly prefer any other woman to her Emma? How could he be too dense to see what Emma felt for him?

'Falling in love at first sight,' said Emma wretchedly. 'I thought that only happened in novels. But I felt . . . oh, that

76

there was something special between us. I know it's not reasonable, Mum, I know it doesn't make sense.'

Tamar had learned a long time ago that love had nothing to do with reason or sense. With a pang, she remembered the sudden impact of love, like a small, contained explosion.

Later, in her bedroom, once Morgan was asleep, she took out of a drawer the small blue leather box that contained the butterfly pin. Running her fingertip along a mother-of-pearl wing, she remembered.

In December 1943, in the middle of the war, at the age of sixteen, Tamar had left Cornwall for London. The Blitz was over, she had pointed out to her parents, so London was safe – or as safe as anywhere – and she was dying of boredom stuck in the middle of nowhere. She wanted adventure, she wanted her freedom. She wanted to help with the war effort, like her brothers Ellis and Gerren, who were both in the army.

It was eventually agreed that she could go to London provided she stayed with a family friend, Evelyn Carrow. Before the war, Evelyn had often been a guest at Nanpean. She was an artist, a single woman, her fiancé having died at Ypres in the Great War.

Evelyn was in her late forties and lived in a tall, thin house in Notting Hill that had been divided into three flats. She had the top floor along with the two attic rooms, which she let out to lodgers. There was a large skylight in the sloping ceiling of Tamar's room, criss-crossed with strips of brown paper to protect the glass in an air raid.

Evelyn used the sitting room as her studio, where she was a portraitist. Mostly she painted women. She told Tamar that she preferred painting interesting women to beautiful women. 'Beauty can be bland,' she said that first evening, over supper. Her sharp hazel eyes settled on Tamar. 'You, my dear, are both beautiful and interesting. Your glorious hair . . . I hope you'll let me paint you.'

Through Evelyn, Tamar found work as a filing clerk at the Ministry of Information. She enjoyed being a part of the rush and bustle of London; once she had got the hang of it and had stopped making foolish blunders, she enjoyed her work too.

The lull in the bombing of London came to an end in the latter part of January 1944. Though she never became accustomed to being woken at night by the whine of the air raid siren or shrapnel hammering against the skylight, Tamar quickly learned what to do. She got to know the rumbling thrum of the bombers and the rip of a high-explosive bomb as it plunged through the air. She became familiar with the dull crump of falling walls. She knew what a bomber's moon was and how to look out for incendiaries and how to use the stirrup pump, and how, when her route was blocked by yellow diversion notices, to navigate new ways to and from work. She knew when to leap out of bed and retreat to the landing, and when, if the raid was heavy, she should join their neighbours, the Gallaghers, on the ground floor. One particularly bad night, half a dozen of the inmates of the house sheltered under Mrs Gallagher's splendid mahogany dining table. In her imagination, Tamar sketched the scene: the six of them shoulder to shoulder and thigh to thigh, no one saying a word because of the noise of the barrage and the cannonade of ceiling plaster hammering the tabletop.

Tamar already knew some of Evelyn's friends, those who were friends of the Cotterells too and had stayed at Nanpean before the war. It was in Evelyn's flat that May that she met Morgan Romilly. She came home after work and there he was, in the kitchen, eating a flan she had baked the previous evening.

He looked at Tamar and then, suspiciously, at the flan. 'What on earth is it?'

'Mock apricot,' Tamar said, unbuttoning her coat. 'There aren't any apricots in it, I'm afraid, only carrots.'

'Christ.'

'You're Morgan Romilly, aren't you?'

He gave her a second glance, blinked, then frowned.

'I'm Tamar Cotterell,' she said. 'John Cotterell's daughter. You came to Nanpean when I was just a kid.'

Evelyn turned up at that moment and dumped on the kitchen table a shopping bag that smelled of fish. 'Mackerel,' she announced, then saw the empty flan tin.

'Have you eaten our pudding, Morgan?'

'You don't mind, do you, Evelyn darling?' He put his head to one side and gave her a cocky grin.

'Not a bit.' Evelyn hugged him. 'How long are you staying?'

'Just the one night.'

'Everyone's in such a rush these days.'

They were all waiting for the opening of the Second Front and for the battle for Europe to begin. It was hard to think of anything else. There was in the air an ache of longing and a heavy weight of dread.

Evelyn gutted the mackerel and Tamar peeled potatoes while they discussed old friends, painting and parties. Morgan talked a lot and was very sure of his opinions. Tamar couldn't decide whether she liked him or not.

It was while they were eating supper that she noticed how his hand trembled whenever he lifted his knife. Evelyn

79

must have seen it too, because she put her hand over his to suppress the tremor. 'It's so good to see you,' she said gently, smiling at him. 'Such a pleasure, my dear.'

Later, when Morgan had gone out for a drink, Evelyn told Tamar that Morgan Romilly had been injured in the desert, at El Alamein, and had been shipped back to England. It had been a serious wound and it had been thought at first that he would not recover. 'It was a miracle really,' she said as she washed a plate and put it on the rack.

Morgan had already left the house by the time Tamar got up for work the next morning. A fortnight later, the invasion began and London seemed to still, holding its breath.

The first of the V-1 flying bombs landed on the city while the Allied troops were still fighting their way out of the beachheads. It was sobering to discover, Tamar thought as she caught the drone of one of the cigar-shaped robot planes and peered upwards, searching the sky, how quickly the thrill of the news of the Second Front had faded, smothered by an apprehension that the war would never end, that Hitler would always have another horror up his sleeve.

One day she found a jewellery box in the rubble of a bombed house. Inside it was a hairpin, of the type Edwardian women used to secure their pompadour hairstyles. The butterfly's body was a pearl; its eyes were rubies, she suspected.

The following evening she went the same way home after finishing work. Someone had chalked a message on the front door of one of the houses beside the bomb site. The house looked as if a monster had bitten a chunk out of the upper storey. Half the roof was missing. Tamar read the notice. It said, *Still living here*.

A man came out, shutting the door behind him. Gingerly,

as if a slam might cause the entire edifice to collapse. He was wearing the uniform of an army officer, and he was young, tall and slim with cleanly chiselled features and straight light-coloured hair.

Tamar called up to him, 'Excuse me!'

'Yes?'

'Is this your house?'

'What's left of it, yes.'

He came down the steps. She held out the blue leather box. 'I came past here yesterday. I found this.'

His eyes widened. He was standing close enough for her to see that they were a light hazel, almost golden. 'Good Lord,' he said. 'It's the butterfly pin!' He took the box from her, opened it, then flashed a smile at her. 'I never thought I'd see that again. How marvellous. Thank you.'

'I'm so glad I found you. It was under some bricks.'

The smile became rueful. 'A great many of my possessions are under some bricks.'

'It looks very old.'

'It belonged to my grandmother,' he said. 'It was one of her favourite pieces of jewellery. She was a famous actress and I was very fond of her. Butterflies are a symbol of transformation, and my grandmother was adept at transforming herself.'

'It's very beautiful.'

His gaze moved from the butterfly pin to Tamar. 'There's a problem, though.'

'Oh dear, is it damaged?'

'No, it looks perfect. It's just that, where I'm going, I can't possibly take it with me. And I've nowhere to keep it. I doubt the house will stay upright for long. I think you should have it.'

He held out the box to her. Startled, Tamar said, 'I couldn't possibly.'

'Look after it for me. Would you, please? You'd be doing me a favour.'

A motor car drew up on the far side of the road. A blast of the horn and a masculine voice called out, 'Alexander! Stop chatting up the girls and get a move on!'

He said, 'I must dash, I'm afraid. Tell you what, I'll meet you at the Lyons on the corner of Tottenham Court Road at three in the afternoon a year from today. You can give it back to me then. Can you do that?'

Tamar promised.

'Thank you.' He smiled at her. 'This wretched war must be over by then, God willing.'

Somehow the blue jewellery box was back in Tamar's hand. As he – Alexander – crossed the road to the car, he called back to her, 'You must wear it! It'll look magnificent with your red hair.' He touched his cap in a lazy salute. 'Wish me luck!'

He climbed into the car. Tamar looked down at the butterfly pin, nestled in her palm. She wanted to call him back, to ask him his surname, to find out everything about him, to prolong the vivid pleasure of being in his company – the sudden impact of love at first sight. She stared back up the road, but the car had already disappeared.

A few days after Emma's return to Seastone, she went out after lunch for a walk, heading north along the beach. Her mother offered to accompany her, but Emma said she would be fine on her own. She knew Tamar wanted to get back to her painting. Inside the house, her canvases were stacked behind chairs and propped on shelves. Her paintings were like a conversation with the sea, ongoing and inconclusive.

Bonny ran beside her, now and then making futile forays at passing seagulls. Emma's route took her past two Martello towers, part of the chain that stood along the east coast, looking out over the North Sea, sentinels poised to fend off invasion. The cold, fresh air washed away the fog of tiredness that had settled over her since she had fallen ill. She knew that her exhaustion was compounded by unhappiness. She would have liked to have been able to walk that away, too.

The afternoon was still and grey, and by the time she headed back to Seastone, the sun had shrunk to a muzzy white circle in the cloud. A storm the previous week had scattered the shoreline with flotsam and jetsam. She kept an eye out for sea glass and shells, stooping now and then to pick up a treasure.

The beach curved in a shallow arc; once she had rounded the low-lying headland, the hamlet's half-dozen houses, scattered in higgledy-piggledy fashion along the top of the shingle ridge, came into view. As she drew nearer, she saw that a man was heading down the bank towards the beach, moving in the lurching plod necessitated by walking on shifting pebbles. Her heart began to thud.

A flash of blue caught her attention and she crouched to prise a fragment of sea glass out of the wet, rippled sand. Sapphire-coloured, it was in the shape of a teardrop. She turned it over in her hand and then looked up.

Max was walking towards her. She waited until he had come within earshot, then called out to him, 'What are you doing here?'

'I came to see you.'

83

'You're an idiot, Max Hooper!'

'I know,' he said humbly.

She looked away, back to the sea. 'You should have left me in peace.'

He came to stand beside her. The air seemed to reverberate with all the misunderstandings and unvoiced feelings between them.

'There are things I need to say to you.'

'I don't know if I want to hear them.'

They walked back to the drier land.

He said, 'You were right about Bridget.'

'Of course I was.'

'We've split up.'

She glared at him. 'What am I supposed to do – congratulate you?'

They had reached the nearer of the two Martello towers. He dug at a patch of sandy soil with the toe of his boot. 'I let it drift on. I knew it wasn't going anywhere, but I let it drift on. We wanted different things, Bridget and I. I've hurt her badly and I regret that very much.'

'Is she all right?'

'No, I don't think so.' He sounded grim. 'But she's a strong woman, and no doubt in time she'll find someone else, someone better suited to her than me. Someone who isn't a mistake.'

Gulls whirled into the salt air, startled by something, their cries raw and alarmed. The sun, burning low through the cloud, flashed a white phosphorescent light on the sea.

'Maybe I'm making another mistake,' he said. 'I don't feel sure of anything. The only thing I know without doubt is that I've fallen in love with you, Emma.'

Her heart gave a loud thump and the scene altered, as if

with the twist of a kaleidoscope. But an instant later, her anger returned, and she rounded on him.

'And what am I supposed to do with that? What, Max? How dare you come here and suddenly tell me you've fallen in love with me! How dare you decide to change your mind whenever it suits you!'

He took her in his arms, and she let her head rest against his shoulder. She had wanted to do this for months. A few tears leaked out, but beneath all the turmoil she discovered a sense of rightness, a conviction that here, at last, she might find solace. They stood for a long time, wrapped in each other's arms. When she put up her face, he kissed her forehead. His mouth brushed against hers, then they kissed more deeply.

'Be dark soon,' he said. 'I should go.'

She watched him walk away down the bank, towards the field. Dusk was falling; soon the shadows would swallow him up.

And then she was running after him, and the soles of her feet were striking the frozen ruts in the track as she hurried to catch up with him. He looked back and, seeing her, came to a halt.

She called out, 'Don't go! Wait for me!'

'Emma?'

Gasping for breath, she grabbed his hands. 'Oh Max, I can't think why, because you're impossible, but I love you.'

'Do you?' Tenderly he touched her cheek, then he drew her close to him and they stood face to face in the fading light. 'Emma, you are all I care about. This and this alone I'm sure of, that you are in my heart.' And happiness flooded through her.

# Chapter Five

## 1978

Though she adored parties, Bea wished they were not giving one that evening. Visits to his parents' home in Surrey invariably put her husband in a bad mood, but that afternoon, driving back to London, he was incoherent with rage. As soon as they reached their Islington house, he went down to the damp, low-ceilinged cellar, emerging a few minutes later with a couple of bottles of red wine.

Bea fed fourteen-month-old Alice, then bathed her and settled her in her cot. When she went downstairs, Clive was lounging against the sink, smoking a roll-up.

'We can cancel if you like,' she said. 'I'll phone round, I don't mind.'

'Hell, no.' He sloshed wine into his glass and gulped it down. 'I could do with some company.'

'You've got me.'

'Thank God. What would I do without you? I love you.' He hugged and kissed her. He was a head taller than her, strong and rangy, and she always felt safe in his arms.

'I love you too.'

He said bitterly, 'A measly couple of thousand, Bea.'

*A couple of thousand* . . . She looked up at him. 'That's a lot of money, darling.'

'He can afford it.'

'I didn't realise—'

'Do you know what he said?' Clive's fists were clenched. 'He said he wouldn't consider lending it to me without seeing my bank statements first. I told him he was being bloody insulting.'

It crossed Bea's mind that even had Clive been prepared to let Kenneth, her father-in-law, inspect his bank statements, he might not have been able to find them. But it wouldn't help to point that out.

She began to scrub the remains of the scrambled egg Alice had had for tea from the high chair. Neither of them were tidy people and nor were they good with paperwork. Bills and bank statements were mislaid or forgotten or crumpled up and put in the bin by Alice, who was going through a phase of putting everything in the bin. The discovery that they had so badly lost track of their financial affairs that Clive needed to borrow two thousand pounds shocked her.

She said, 'Will we be able to manage without the money?'

'Yes, of course. The restaurant will pick up, I'm sure of it. Businesses often make a loss in the first couple of years.'

Bea had always taken for granted Clive's competence in handling their finances. He spoke of his business ventures with such confidence. Two thousand pounds, though. It was a frightening sum.

She wondered whether he was angry because he was worried about money or because he interpreted his wealthy father's refusal to help him out as a further withdrawal of affection. His relationship with his parents had always been difficult. Kenneth Cornwell had a senior position within the civil service. Philippa, Clive's mother, had been a civil servant too, but had since retired and now raised money for children's charities. Clive's elder sister, Melanie, who was married with two daughters, still lived in the same small Surrey village in which she had been born. The Cornwells admired the virtues of steadiness and caution. Clive hadn't a cautious bone in his body.

'You didn't tell me, Clive,' she said.

'I didn't want to worry you.'

'We have to share things. Maybe there's something I can do to help. I could try to cut down on our spending.'

'There's no need for that. Look, Bea, I lost a few bob selling the Hampshire house, that's all.' He lit another cigarette.

They had lived in an old house with an acre of land in the Hampshire countryside for a year. Alice had been born there. Both of them had missed the city, so they had sold up and returned to London seven months ago.

He said, 'It wasn't a good time to sell. I made a packet on the other houses I renovated because of inflation. I assumed it would be like that again. I'll be more choosy about when I sell this place.'

'Sell it?' She stopped scrubbing and stared at him. 'Clive, I don't want to move again.'

'Not this minute, I wasn't suggesting anything like that. We'll talk later, darling. Do we need to do anything?' He glanced at his watch. 'I'll sort out the drinks. What time is everyone coming?'

'Eight thirty, I think. Could you wash up some glasses?'

Bea was three and a half months pregnant. The day had been long and exhausting. The kitchen was in a state because they had been in a rush to get out earlier that day, and the sink was still full to the brim of that morning's breakfast things. Bea had had to fit in a dash to the baker's to pick up the order of French loaves for the party before leaving for the Cornwells' house. Clive's parents abhorred lateness.

'I need to get ready,' she said. 'I look a mess.'

'You look beautiful.' He smoothed back her hair from her forehead and kissed her again. 'You always look beautiful.'

'I'd better go and check on Alice,' she said.

Upstairs, she quietly opened the nursery door. Alice was a light sleeper. In the cot, she lay humped up on her front, her face turned to one side, bottom in the air. She was fair, like Clive, and had a cloud of adorable silver-blonde curls. Clive had beautiful hair too, a ripple of gold and brown. Alice took after her father in other ways, too. She was lively and mercurial, interested in anything and everything, always on the go. Gently Bea tucked the cot blanket round her.

In her bedroom, she opened the wardrobe. Not long ago, when she had been miserable with morning sickness, Clive had bought her a couple of dresses to cheer her up, gorgeous colourful, floaty garments from Zandra Rhodes that she would be able to wear long into her pregnancy. Clive was surprisingly good at choosing clothes for her. He had an unusual mixture of talents, which was why, Bea thought, he found it hard to settle to a career.

Now, running her gaze along the rail, much of her pleasure in the new clothes evaporated. They must have been very expensive, she thought. It had not until then occurred to her that they should economise. During the three years of their marriage, they had spent freely and lived well. The house was spacious and furnished in a modern style, and she had an automatic washing machine and a freezer. Clive, who adored cars, ran a fast, up-to-date model, and they entertained lavishly. Surely he must have had an inkling by the time he bought the dresses that money was tight? Though she loved him for his generosity, perhaps he should have treated her to clothes from Richard Shops rather than Zandra Rhodes.

But she herself was little better, she reflected guiltily. She hadn't a clue how much she spent each week on groceries. She always meant to keep a running total on her chequebook stubs, but then forgot and mislaid the receipts. She left checking the bank statements to Clive. Whenever she asked him for cash, he gave it to her. She tried to tot up in her head how much money they must have spent on tonight's party. Clive had got in crates of wine and kegs of beer, and Bea had bought the cheese and olives in Harrods Food Hall. The sums muddled her and she gave up, but she was left with the uneasy suspicion that the evening's entertainment might have cost more than they could afford.

She changed into one of the dresses Clive had given her, a scarlet chiffon that hid the slight swell of her belly. When she had been pregnant with Alice, she had been as flat as a board for months before ballooning out in her last trimester. In this, her third pregnancy, she had begun to show already.

She sat down at the dressing table to touch up her make-up. That morning, on the Surrey visit, Clive had told his parents about the coming baby, in the hope, Bea suspected, that it would soften them. If so, it had been a misjudgement. 'I would have thought you'd want to get your financial affairs on a more even keel before bringing another child into the world,' Kenneth had said pompously. The conversation had taken place in the Cornwells' chintzy drawing room, while they were having a pre-lunch drink. Clive's sister and her husband had been invited too. Both had shot an apprehensive glance at Clive. The day had deteriorated from that moment.

When she was ready, she went downstairs to the kitchen. The saucepans were still in the sink and the wine glasses unwashed from the previous night. 'Eight Miles High' was issuing from the front room, which meant that Clive had abandoned clearing up for his favourite party task of choosing LPs. Bea washed the glasses and scrubbed the table, then put out food and filled ceramic bowls with olives and crisps. She shoved the dirty saucepans into a washing-up bowl, which she dumped in the cellar.

Coming back up the steps, she heard voices in the hall. Clive's was welcoming and full of bonhomie. It had just gone eight, so perhaps she had told their guests to come at eight rather than eight thirty. As she rushed to dry glasses and crockery, she found herself looking forward to the evening. A party would cheer Clive up. The two of them might not be any good with money, but they were very good at parties.

Within a short space of time, the downstairs had filled up with guests and there was a high, steady hum of conversation and laughter. Wandering from room to room, stopping to chat to friends and make sure everyone had a drink and company, Bea forgot her worries and began to enjoy herself.

On the night of the party, Alice woke at half past one in the morning. Bea comforted her and gave her a drink. Once her daughter was back in her cot, she went to bed herself. Clive would stay up with stragglers for hours.

She had expected to fall back to sleep instantly, but Clive's words – *a measly couple of thousand* – came back to her, troubling her. Though he had turned down the volume of the music, she still seemed to feel its vibration through the floor, as if the structure of the house was less secure than she had allowed herself to admit.

In the morning, Marissa discovered that she had left her silk shawl at the Cornwells' house. She decided to go and retrieve it before starting work. She often worked on a Sunday.

She was living in a flat in Hoxton, which also functioned as her business premises. The rent was low, and because it was on the top floor, the light was good. Much of the living room was taken up by her cutting table, on one end of which stood her sewing machine. The sofa pulled out to make up into a bed at night. On a pinboard she had stuck photos, newspaper cuttings, sketches and fabric samples. Seagrass baskets containing buttons, trims and spools of cotton were arranged on the shelves. The small kitchen area housed a sink and a two-ring hob, and she had made enough space in a corner for a table large enough to hold a second-hand typewriter and notepaper and pens. This was her office, where she kept her accounts.

Since the summer of 1976, Marissa had been working at Liberty, in Regent Street, first in the stockroom and later on the shop floor, in the fabric department. It paid the rent, but the downside was that she could only design for Marissa Flint in the evenings and at weekends. She was planning to give up the job at Liberty shortly so that she could concentrate solely on the business she was building up. It would be risky, but exciting.

It was a fine day, so she walked the mile and a half to the Cornwells' house. Her ring of the doorbell was answered by Bea Cornwell, who had a toddler propped on her hip.

At the party the previous night, Bea had been wearing a red evening dress; now she had on a short cotton dressing gown knotted over pyjamas. Marissa wondered whether she should have left it another hour or two.

'I'm sorry to bother you,' she said. 'Is it too early? I can come back later if you like.'

'Not at all.' Bea peered at her. 'You were at the party, weren't you? Weren't you with Tom Harper?'

'I was, yes.' Tom Harper was Marissa's boyfriend. He was a friend of Clive Cornwell's. 'I think I left my shawl here.'

'Come in.' Bea stood aside. 'I'm awfully sorry, but I've forgotten your name.'

'It's Marissa Flint.'

'I haven't had a chance to tidy up, I'm afraid. It's impossible to do anything much while Alice is up.'

Marissa's gaze settled hungrily on the baby. 'She's gorgeous,' she said.

'Isn't she? Just as well, isn't it, sweetheart?' Bea planted a kiss on her daughter's head. 'She was up before six.'

'How old is she?'

'Alice is fourteen months, aren't you, darling? I was just about to put her down for a nap, then I can give you a hand finding your shawl. Do go through to the sitting room and have a hunt round.' A wave of a hand towards the open doorway. 'I'm sorry it's in such a state.'

Bea went upstairs. Fourteen months, Marissa thought. Her own baby, had he or she lived, would have been two years old by now.

She stood on the threshold of the sitting room. The walls were a soft olive green, the large sofa upholstered in cream and charcoal stripes. Coloured light filtered through high stained-glass windows onto the varnished floorboards. It's *in such a state.* This wasn't an exaggeration. Books had been pulled from the shelves – by Alice, Marissa supposed – and a sofa denuded of its cushions, presumably by party guests making themselves comfortable as they sat on the floor. There was an ashy smell, and the roaches of joints nestled among cigarette ends in a saucer on a high shelf. Splinters of French bread scattered the magnificent Indian rug in the centre of the room, and someone must have spilled a glass of red wine, because it had bled onto the cream-coloured tufts.

Marissa felt awkward. She had turned up too early and had interrupted the Cornwells' family day. As so often when she was ill at ease, she itched to tidy up. She would have liked to fetch a cloth from the kitchen to soak up the wine from the rug, but that would be intrusive. There were some tissues in her handbag; crouching, she began to blot.

'Oh gosh, it's pretty frightful, isn't it?' Bea was in the doorway.

Marissa sprang to her feet. 'Sorry . . .'

Bea gave a raucous crack of laughter, a surprisingly loud sound, Marissa thought, from such a petite woman. 'Goodness me, I should be the one saying sorry. What a tip.'

'This is just surface mess,' Marissa said comfortingly. 'It's such a lovely house. I like the colours you've chosen. I'm guessing you decorated it, not Clive?'

'I wouldn't let him go near a paintbrush. He'd paint the walls black and purple. He leaves all that to me. Would you like a cup of tea, Marissa? Or coffee?'

Marissa was about to refuse – all that paperwork to catch up on – but then, surprising herself, she said, 'Yes, please, coffee would be great.'

\*

In the end, she stayed to help Bea clear up, having retrieved her shawl from behind an armchair. Clive had gone out for the day, racing cars round a track somewhere – which was, Marissa thought with a private and silent snort of derision, ridiculous and selfish when there was so much to do. Bea was pregnant ('I can't drink coffee. It makes me sick. Such a bore'), and Alice never napped for more than an hour, she said, which meant she had to rush around. So it would have seemed mean to walk out.

The kitchen was even more chaotic than the living room, though Marissa noticed that someone – Bea, she suspected – had collected up the glasses and cutlery and put them towards the back of the work surface so that the child couldn't reach them. While Bea washed up, Marissa had a go at the rug with Fairy Liquid and white vinegar. Once she had got out the stain, she tackled the big pine kitchen table, removing the purple wine rings from the surface with salt and then baking powder.

'How do you know how to do all that?' asked Bea.

'My mother was a cleaner.' Straightening, Marissa had a good look at the table. 'I used to go and help her in the school holidays. We got through it quicker when there were two of us. Mum knew all these ways of making things look as good as new.'

'Gosh. How clever.'

Bea spoke with a smart upper-middle-class clip; Marissa imagined her mother to be the sort of woman who employed a cleaner, rather than the sort who cleaned for other people. Marissa dried plates and glasses and Bea put them away. By the time they had finished, Alice had woken up.

Bea brought the baby down to the kitchen and put her in her high chair. 'Could you keep an eye on her while I dash upstairs and get dressed? I feel such a slob, still in my PJs while you look so smart.'

Marissa was wearing Levi's and a pale grey linen top. She said, 'I loved that Zandra Rhodes dress you were wearing last night.'

'Isn't it fabulous? How clever of you to recognise it.'

'I'm a dress designer, so knowing about that sort of thing is my job. You go. Alice and I will get to know each other.'

She sat down at the table beside the high chair. Alice regarded her with beady curiosity and crumbled her biscuit in her fist. Marissa picked up a small morsel and held it out to her. Carefully Alice took it from her and peered at it.

'Bikkit,' she said.

'That's right, love. Biscuit. Clever girl.' Marissa offered her another piece. This time Alice ate it from Marissa's fingers. Then Alice picked up her two-handed sucking cup and banged it on the high-chair tray so that drops sprayed out. She looked very pleased with herself. Her smile melted Marissa's heart. With the back of her forefinger she stroked the child's petal-soft cheek.

Bea came back into the room wearing a coral-coloured dress, and kissed the top of her daughter's head. She refilled Marissa's coffee mug. 'So when you say you're a dress designer . . .'

'I design and make a range of women's clothing. It's called Marissa Flint. This is one of mine.' Marissa touched her grey linen top.

'I love it. Such a gorgeous colour.'

'I do shirts and jackets, and trousers too. Trousers are difficult because women are such different shapes, but a good pair is such a boon. I like making practical clothes. I want a woman to be able to put on one of my pieces in

96

the morning and feel great about herself and then forget about it.'

The clothes she made were easy to wear and subtly enhanced a woman's figure. If there was room for a pocket, she fitted in one or two, because pockets were useful. She liked soft, pliable fabrics that were easy to wear and colours that were beautiful and flattering. She might be diffident and modest about a lot of things, but where her work was concerned, she conveyed confidence. If she didn't believe in herself, no one else would, and anyway, she knew herself to be talented, hard-working and ambitious. What she needed now was a stroke of luck, that magic ingredient that would take her to the next level.

Fashion was a highly competitive world, and designers failed far more often than they succeeded. Marissa strove hard for success because it would give her what she wanted: money, recognition and the ability to live her life on her own terms. Success would mean that she could buy a house as nice as Bea Cornwell's, and then she would no longer be at the mercy of unscrupulous landlords and noisy neighbours. It would allow her to escape her background and the lifetime of scrimping and insecurity that her mother had endured. Success would mean she need never again be dependent on another person. Then she would be safe.

'I was going to make a sandwich,' said Bea. 'Would you like one?'

'I don't want to put you to any trouble.'

Bea put her head to one side and considered her. 'Marissa, you've just cleaned Clive's precious Indian rug. He'd have gone spare if he'd seen it. Cheese or ham?'

'Cheese, please.'

Bea buttered bread. 'Do you have your own shop?'

'Not yet. I intend to, though, as soon as I can.'

'How do you sell your clothes?'

'I have a number of private clients who buy from me regularly. And half a dozen boutiques have taken my garments.' Most were on a sale-or-return basis, which wasn't ideal, though much better than nothing.

'A friend of mine, Trisha, owns a boutique in Richmond,' said Bea. 'She sells the most gorgeous clothes. Everyone loves her stuff. Would you like me to speak to her on your behalf?'

'Yes, if you would, that would be great.' Marissa burrowed into her handbag. 'Here's my card.'

Alice was straining against the reins, trying to stand up in her high chair. 'Shall I . . .?' said Marissa, rising.

'Please.'

She unclipped the reins and lifted the child out of the high chair. For a moment Alice relaxed in her grasp, and she revelled in the warmth and weight of the baby. Then, spying a yellow plastic duck on the floor, Alice pulled away. Marissa put her down by the toys, holding her soft, pillowy little hand until she got her balance.

She sat down cross-legged on the floor beside Alice. Bea gave her a plate of sandwiches and another cup of coffee. Marissa asked Bea what she had done before she was married, and Bea told her she had been an assistant to a photographer. She had been very good at arranging a room, she said. 'You wouldn't believe it now, would you?' That raucous laugh again. She and Clive had been married for three years. They had met at a party in Pimlico. At that time, he had been earning his living by renovating dilapidated houses in unfashionable parts of London and selling them on for a profit. The first place they had lived in, they had camped out in the kitchen for months because the rest of the house was uninhabitable. She described a subsequent failed attempt at rural self-sufficiency in deepest Hampshire in terms that made Marissa laugh.

Then Bea asked her whether her relationship with Tom Harper was serious. Marissa told her that it wasn't. She didn't say that though she enjoyed going to bed with Tom, and though she liked his company and he was a decent man without a touch of Jamie's entitled resentment, she would rather have flown to the moon than embark on a serious relationship with him. Or indeed with any man.

By the time she left, it was getting on for four and they had sorted out and vacuumed the downstairs rooms. They looked tidier, Bea said, looking round admiringly, than they had for months.

She didn't usually accept spontaneous invitations, Marissa thought as she said goodbye and headed home. On the whole, she kept assiduously to the timetable of tasks she always had in her head, yet today she felt relaxed and happy. She had liked Bea a lot. She sensed that she might become a friend.

She told herself not to get too excited about Bea's offer to introduce her to Trisha, who owned the boutique in Richmond. People said things like that and then the boutique turned out to be a dire little provincial establishment selling gaudy polyester evening dresses and mother-of-the-bride outfits. Anyway, Bea had a lot on her plate, and with such a young child and a husband like Clive Cornwell, she would probably forget.

But Bea didn't forget. A week later, she phoned Marissa and asked her if she could get together some garments to show Trisha. Marissa didn't drive – she couldn't yet afford to run a car, so there was no point – so Bea offered to give her a lift. Marissa sat in the back of Bea's little Fiat with Alice on her knee while Bea negotiated the roads of west London.

The clothes in Trisha's chic shop bore no resemblance to the polyester horrors of Marissa's imagination. Trisha herself was in her early sixties, slim and elegant, her hair cut in a silver-grey bob. She examined Marissa's samples with silent thoroughness, which was nerve-racking, and then said, 'I love them all. Thank you so much for showing them to me. I know they'll sell like hot cakes.'

Coolly she reeled off an order so sizeable it made Marissa's heart pound. Bea, who was standing behind Trisha as she cuddled a cranky Alice, beamed at her and gave her a thumbs-up. On the way back to Hoxton, it seemed to Marissa that she might have come across that all-important stroke of luck. That Bea Cornwell might have found it for her.

# Chapter Six

## 1978–1979

The removal men had gone at last. In the kitchen, skirting from one box to another, her nineteen-month-old daughter balanced on her right hip, Emma was searching for a saucepan.

Her mother, who had offered to help with the move, held up a frying pan. 'I'll scramble an egg in this.'

The pair of them were wearing their coats. It was October and chilly, partly because the front door had been open for a long time while the removal men carried in the furniture and boxes, but also because Emma had not yet worked out how to turn on the central heating. Max would do it instantly, it was the sort of thing he was good at, but something had come up at work and he had had to go into the office.

She wondered whether she had left all their saucepans behind. Whether the couple who had bought their flat in Reigate would find them at the back of the kitchen cupboard. Emma was seven months pregnant and had crawled off to bed early the previous night, tired from the packing. With this second baby, she felt rotten in the evenings rather than the mornings – which made a change, she supposed.

Pregnancy made her forgetful, too, and it was all too possible that she had intended to pack the saucepans in the morning and in the rush and excitement of moving they had slipped her mind.

They hadn't yet put together the high chair, so she sat her daughter on her knee and fed her. Lucienne batted the spoon away and screamed, arching her back. Emma glanced at her watch. She hoped Max would come home soon. After a while, she gave up with the egg and made a bottle of milk. Her daughter curled into her, sucking the bottle, the tantrum averted.

They had moved to Cambridge because Max had gone into partnership with Peter Eisen, his colleague from Reigate. Peter had relocated to Cambridge nine months ago so that he could be near his grandchildren. Woken early that morning by the fish-like squirming of her unborn baby, Emma had felt a thrill of anticipation at the thought of a new house, a new city, a new life. She had seen the house only once before today, moving day, because Lucienne wasn't good in the car. Everyone said babies slept on car journeys, but her daughter didn't, and it was a long way from Reigate to Cambridge. She hadn't been able to face the trip a second time, so Max had gone on his own to measure up and work out where their furniture would go.

The house was Victorian and had four bedrooms and two bathrooms. They had been able to afford it because it was, as the estate agent had pointed out, unimproved, having belonged to an old lady who had died. Ivy had got a stranglehold on the paved area glimpsed from the kitchen window; the windows of the sunroom tacked onto the back of the building were peeling and rotten. *We'll take this down*, Max had said as they had stood in the sunroom on the day they had viewed the house. *We'll extend this back room and make the far wall of glass. Just think of it, Em. We'll be able to fit both our families in here at Christmas.*

On the day he had come to Seastone and told her he loved her, they had agreed to take it slowly. Emma had shared a flat with another British Caledonian stewardess in Horley while Max had moved to Reigate. Because every time she tried the Pill she experienced one dire side effect or another, and because they were both disorganised and busy, she quickly fell pregnant. They were married in September 1976. Emma wore an antique Edwardian wedding dress and her mother's butterfly pin in her hair. In the photos, she looked wan but joyful.

After the wedding, they moved into a two-bedroom flat in Reigate. Lucienne was born on the first day of the following March. Motherhood came with a piercing love and an instant and drastic rearrangement of priorities. A year later, Max won an award for a house he had designed, and not long afterwards, Peter Eisen made his offer. And now here they were, starting a new life in Cambridge.

With her daughter in her arms, Emma went outside to the garden. Trees and shrubs cast long black shadows in the fading light. The rain that had fallen relentlessly throughout moving day had stopped at last. She breathed in the autumnal tang of dead leaves and damp earth. A high brick wall gave the garden a feeling of seclusion; beyond, the gleam of a street lamp and the rumble of traffic hinted at the city waiting to be explored.

A narrow, mossy brick path wound between overgrown trees and beds of straggling chrysanthemums and drooping Michaelmas daisies. Raindrops rolled from curled wet leaves.

Lucienne said, 'Daddy,' and Emma looked back.

Max swept up his daughter in his arms. 'Sorry I'm so late. Peter's away and a client was having a panic attack.'

She kissed him. 'Which client?'

'The musician, Silas Parish.'

'The Dunwich house?'

'Yes. He was getting cold feet, talking about something more conventional. It was a bit of a battle, but I think I've got him onside again.' Max had shown Emma the plans for the house, which would look out over salt marsh and shoreline.

She said, 'The boiler . . .'

'I've done it. The radiators are warming up.'

'And I can't find any saucepans.'

He put an arm round her. 'I'll go and hunt for them. Have a rest. I'll sort this one out.' He rubbed his nose against his daughter's belly, and she laughed.

Max looked out at the garden. 'It's like something from *Sleeping Beauty*,' he said.

'Or an Arthur Rackham illustration.'

In the wet, dusky light, jasmine and clematis snaked blackly up the brick walls. Fronds of bramble, heavy with rain, arched above them, their thorns barbed. Emma imagined living in the house, getting to know it, making it theirs. Their two girls – she was sure this baby was another girl – playing in the garden. The four of them happy, safe and content.

Tamar left Max to greet his wife while she went upstairs to the room in which she was to sleep.

She made up the bed, unpacked her toiletries and hung tomorrow's blouse and cardigan on the back of a chair. She took off her shoes and lay down on the bed. The ache in her back, which she had been trying to ignore, eased. She opened The Magus, but after a couple of pages put it down and closed her eyes.

She, like Emma, felt relieved that Max was home. He was a practical man and would quickly fathom the boiler. Tamar was very fond of her son-in-law. She smiled to herself as her thoughts wandered back to Emma and Max's wedding day. Emma had looked so beautiful in her ivory lace gown, which had complemented her striking colouring. Copper-coloured tendrils had framed her finely drawn features, and the loose bun on top of her head had been secured by the butterfly pin.

Deliciously drowsy, Tamar lingered for a while between wakefulness and sleep, drifting back through the decades. The butterfly pin . . . In June 1945, a few weeks after the war had ended and a year to the day since she had met Alexander on the bomb site, she had waited for him in the crowded Lyons Corner House in Tottenham Court Road. She remembered the knot of anxiety and longing beneath her ribs, and how she had looked up every time a customer had entered the restaurant. But none of them had been Alexander, and disappointment had seared through her. After a couple of hours, she had gathered up her handbag, in which the butterfly pin nestled safely in its box, and left the café.

Babysitting for the Cornwells and struggling to stay awake on their comfortable sofa, Marissa overheard as the front door opened both the tail end of an argument and its making-up.

Bea's voice. 'The trouble with you, Clive, is you only ever remember the good bits.'

Then Clive's, conciliatory. 'You're right, I know, sweetie.

105

Look, we won't make a decision until after the baby's born, I promise.' A silence, presumably filled by a kiss.

Marissa sat up, stretched, and picked up the Michael Moorcock paperback she had been reading, which had fallen splayed on the floor. The front door closed as Bea came into the house. 'Sorry! I'm letting in the cold.' In the hall, she unwound her long knitted scarf. 'Has Alice been all right?'

'Not a peep,' said Marissa. 'I had a look at her a few times, but she was out for the count.'

'I'll go and check on her. Won't be a minute.'

When Bea came back downstairs, Marissa said, 'Where's Clive?'

'He's gone down the road to have a drink with Jerry.' Bea made a face. 'We had a bit of a row. Do you have to dash off?'

Marissa could tell she wanted to talk. 'A cup of tea would be nice.'

In the kitchen, Bea dropped tea bags into mugs. She said, 'Clive's talking about selling the house.'

'Selling it . . . Why? Where are you going?'

'This is our fourth home in three and a bit years,' said Bea, rather tremulously. 'I really don't want to move again.'

'If you told him how you felt . . .'

'It isn't even finished!' The kettle whistled and Bea poured boiling water into the mugs. 'And then, Marissa, he said why didn't we go and live in India! He seems simply to forget that he was awfully ill when he lived there. Does he seriously think I'd take Alice to India? And a newborn baby? So he said okay, Wales then. But I don't want to go and live in Wales!'

'Why does he want to move?'

'Oh . . .' Bea stirred the tea vigorously, as if taking out

her annoyance on it. 'He's always been a restless person. And we're rather short of money.'

Marissa would never have made such an admission. She would have seen it as humiliating, an acknowledgement of failure. But then Bea's openness was one of the things Marissa liked about her.

Marissa babysat now and then for the Cornwells. She liked the big, comfortable house, and once Alice was settled, it was easy to get on with her work and made a nice change from her bedsit. If Alice woke, she soothed her back to sleep. It gave her a warm feeling to know that the little girl knew and trusted her.

She was surprised to hear that the Cornwells were short of money. To Marissa, their lifestyle seemed enviably luxurious. When Bea and Clive went out to dinner, they invariably ate at a smart restaurant such as the Gay Hussar or Veeraswamy. They were always either planning to throw a lavish party or else recovering from one.

She said, 'It's rather a drastic solution, selling the house.'

'I've been trying to economise. I'm not awfully good at it, but Clive's even worse.'

'How's the restaurant doing?'

'Not very well.' Bea sipped her tea and brooded. 'I think he thought it would be like giving a party every night. I've been trying to help him with the paperwork, but there's Alice, and by the time she's settled in the evening and I've made dinner for me and Clive, I'm too tired.'

Clive had celebrated his thirtieth birthday six weeks ago. Marissa couldn't help feeling he should have found his niche by now. She was careful to keep from Bea what she honestly thought about Clive – he was, after all, Bea's husband and Marissa could tell that she loved him very much. And he had his good points. He was generous and kind and good fun. You'd need to have a heart of stone to fail to warm to him.

But he was the sort of person Marissa found exasperating. Clive Cornwell had everything – looks, charisma and intelligence, and he had been born with a silver spoon in his mouth – yet he would behave like a sullen little boy when something didn't work out as he wished. Marissa knew that if you loved something, whether it was a restaurant or a fashion business, and you wanted to make a success of it, then you had to live and breathe it. You had to work every hour God sent, and you had to get everything right. If you were half-hearted, you would fail. She wondered whether Clive knew that too. If the restaurant was in trouble, why wasn't he there tonight, *making* it work, instead of dining out with Bea and his friends?

She said, 'He just needs to decide to stick at something.'

'All I've ever wanted was to be settled, to have a safe, comfortable home for me and my children.' Bea paused, then said quietly, 'Alice wasn't my first baby. I had another baby before her, a little boy, but I had to give him away. I was still at school when I got pregnant, and only just eighteen when my baby was born, and I didn't have a job or any money, so I couldn't keep him. Clive seems to think I'll just go and live wherever the mood takes him, but I won't, because I have to give my children a proper home. That's the most important thing in the world to me.'

'Oh Bea . . .' Appalled, Marissa sat down beside her. 'I had no idea. How sad for you.'

'It's all right. I don't mind now. I've got used to it.'

Marissa thought it typical of Bea that *she* was trying to reassure *her*. Bea was a very unselfish person. 'That doesn't mean it doesn't hurt,' she said.

'No. But it's better now, honestly it is.' Bea twisted a cuff button between finger and thumb. 'For ages afterwards I used to wake up in the morning and for a second I'd feel all right, and then I'd think about my baby boy, about Patrick, and have a cry. I had a breakdown, I suppose, after he was born. I could hardly even get out of bed, I missed him so much.'

*I know exactly how you feel. I know what it is to lose a child.* The words formed in Marissa's head, but she didn't say them aloud. To wade in with her own grief at that moment would be tactless and egotistical.

She said, 'You're so brave, Bea.'

'If I was brave, I'd have found a way of keeping him.'

Bea was still twisting the button. Marissa was afraid she would pull it off. 'You were very young,' she said gently. 'I don't suppose you had much choice in the matter.'

'You too?'

She realised that she had said more than she had meant to. For a moment she wondered whether she could confide in Bea. Could she tell her about her marriage, about Jamie? What a relief it would be to be able to talk to a sympathetic friend about what had happened to her!

But Bea had begun to speak again. 'I still miss him,' she said. 'I don't suppose I'll ever stop missing him.'

'Do you know anything about his adopted family?'

She shook her head. 'Not really. They were a young couple who couldn't have children of their own. Everyone said it was for the best. Everyone said I wouldn't have been able to take care of him properly, and I'm sure they were right.' Marissa thought Bea sounded as though she was trying to reassure herself.

'What about your boyfriend, the baby's father? What happened to him?'

'Ciaran? He was my first boyfriend. When he found out about the baby, he went away.'

'Good God,' said Marissa. 'What a creep.'

Bea shook her head. 'He wasn't. He just had a lot more to lose than me.'

Bea told Marissa about Ciaran. He had been the same age as her, seventeen, and had come from an impoverished Irish family. He had been a grammar school boy, the first in his family to have the opportunity to go to university. He had known he had one chance to make a better life for himself, and when he had found out about the baby, he had run away, back to Ireland. They had both been so ignorant, Bea added. Neither of them had really known anything at all.

'I hated him for quite a long time,' she added. 'But now I don't, not any more. I can see why he did it.'

Marissa understood why Bea was making excuses for this boy who had let her down so badly. She remembered that it had taken her a shamefully long time to see what Jamie truly was. It was hard to admit to yourself, let alone to anyone else, that you had made a terrible mistake. It was hard to recognise that you had been so clueless about the destructive power of love.

'Hatred's rather exhausting,' she acknowledged. 'And you can't change the past.'

'I loved him so much, Marissa. When I was with Ciaran, nothing else mattered.'

Once more Marissa felt an urge alien to her, a sudden, irrational yearning to share the past and so puncture its power. This time the words began to form on her lips. *Sometimes we make mistakes. I lost a baby too, and for a long time I blamed myself.*

But a cry from upstairs broke the spell. 'I'll be back in a minute,' Bea said, and hurried out of the room.

In Bea's absence, Marissa's customary defensiveness reasserted itself. To tell anyone, even her closest friend, about Jamie could be dangerous. Tell one person, and that person might tell another, and then everything would fall apart. She had never regretted the decision she had made three years ago to transform herself into Marissa Flint. In colouring her hair and changing her name by deed poll, she had put the past behind her. She had cut off contact with everyone she had known before that day, had started again from scratch and taken drastic action to enable herself to feel safe. She had given up a lot to reinvent herself; she must not throw away the gains she had made.

If there was guilt in lack of frankness and dishonesty in silence, and if a part of her longed to reciprocate Bea's confidence in her, still she could not regret having kept her counsel. She hadn't run away from mousy, vulnerable Mary Canterbury only to allow her back into her life. The person she had once been repelled and humiliated her. She didn't want Bea to know that person. She didn't think she would like her.

Marissa tidied away the mugs, then put on her coat. By the time Bea came back downstairs, she was waiting in the hall.

'Sorry about that,' Bea said. 'She's fine now. And sorry for keeping you talking for so long.'

'Nonsense.' Marissa gave her a big hug. 'Thank you for telling me about your baby. Thank you for trusting me.'

'There was never any question.' Bea smiled at her. 'I'll call you a taxi.'

\*

111

The taxi dropped Marissa outside her home in Hoxton. As was her habit, she looked up and down the street before she let herself into the building. A flicker of movement in the shadows and she paused, rigid, staring into a place where darkness pooled. But it was only a cat, pattering along the pavement.

In her bedsit, she switched on the light, locked and bolted the door and took off her coat. She ran the back of her hand over the length of soft oatmeal-coloured Yorkshire tweed that lay on the table. You might have been able to fit her bedsit into the Cornwells' house four or five times over, but this was her home, and she had made it clean, light and comfortable. It gave her a space where she could be what she wanted to be.

She was Marissa Flint, who preferred to own a few nice things – a Margaret Howell shirt, a Le Creuset dish – to having cupboards crammed with belongings. She was Marissa Flint, whose modest fashion business was prospering in spite of the economic storms that were battering the country. Who enjoyed reading Muriel Spark and Iris Murdoch, but who also had a sneaking affection for the improbably heroic characters of fantasy fiction. Who loved visiting art galleries and would have chosen any day to browse an exhibition over an elaborate meal in a restaurant. Who treasured her few close friends but hated to be in a crowd. Who never allowed herself to fall in love.

Sometimes the gains she had made felt precarious. Her unease stemmed from that evening's conversation, from the revelation that Bea had had a baby son who had been adopted. Mixed in with the pity and affection she felt for her friend had been a less creditable emotion. She envied Bea, who in spite of her losses had a child of her own to love. She herself had no one.

She brushed the thought away. During the years that had passed since she had walked out of her old life, she had found ways of keeping her turbulent emotions in check. She poured herself a glass of wine, sat down on the bed-settee and wrapped herself up in the duvet. Be content with what you've got, she told herself sternly. Love your friends' babies, love little Alice. Children and careers don't mix, not for women anyway. How many women manage to have a career and a family without feeling they're failing at one or the other . . . or both? She would never marry again, so babies were simply not on the cards.

A noise from outside the door caught her attention. She sat up, heart beating fast, listening. Someone was climbing the stairs. Hearing men's voices, Marissa rose silently and went to stand by the door. A thud as something was dropped on the landing outside. A voice called out; another answered it. She did not recognise either voice, and some of the tension drained from her. The room adjacent to hers was unoccupied – or at least it had been until now. New tenants must be moving in. Suddenly Status Quo's 'Rockin' All Over the World' resounded through the floor, and she flinched. Her room seemed to reverberate to the beat. She tensed again, but this time with anger.

When the footsteps died away, she cracked open her front door. On the shared landing was a heap of cardboard boxes and carrier bags. Grubby-looking clothing, tins of food and bottles of beer spilled out onto the floor. It looked, she thought, like jumble left outside a church hall for a sale. The door to the bedsit opposite was wide open.

She went back inside her own room and locked the door

113

from the inside. Unable to relax, she did some ironing and cleaned the little kitchen area. Someone hammered on the door of her new neighbour's bedsit and angry words were exchanged. The music stopped as suddenly as it had started.

Now her room was quiet, and all that intruded was the memory of fear. Sometimes, still, she thought she heard his voice. *Where have you been? Who have you been with?* She understood what had happened to her better now. Jamie had cut her off from family and friends not because he had desired her, nor even because he had wanted her for himself, but because he had believed her to be worthless. Her survival had been dependent on making a complete break with the past. He remained the embodiment of a nightmare, and that was another reason why she would never tell anyone, not even Bea, about him: because to do so would bring him back to life.

She took out her sketchbook. There was joy in creating beautiful things, in helping women feel good about their bodies and enabling them to reinvent themselves. Two months ago, she had taken the plunge and resigned from her job at Liberty so that she could concentrate on building up her business. She was taking an evening class in tailoring to improve her skills, and had already completed a book-keeping correspondence course. In a couple of days' time, she had another appointment with Trisha, Bea's friend who owned the boutique in Richmond. She planned to show her Marissa Flint's latest designs. The first pieces Trisha had taken had sold out within a fortnight.

The last time they had lunched together, Trisha had told her that it was time to think about renting her own premises. 'You remind me of myself at your age, when I was starting out,' she had said. 'It was more difficult for women back then, before the war. Don't hold back, Marissa, don't wait. As soon as you see an opportunity, grab it with both hands. Just go for it, that's my advice.'

Clive closed down the restaurant in the early January of 1979, after the lorry drivers went on strike and the petrol stations shut for lack of fuel. 'No one's coming out to eat anyway,' he said. 'Too bloody cold.'

The baby was due at the end of January. It was only now that Bea remembered that there was a stage in pregnancy where her swollen womb grew in all directions at once, outwards and sideways, pushing up against her ribs to accommodate the maturing infant. Freezing rain clattered across the country, exquisite and deadly, encasing tree branches and telegraph wires in ice. Blizzards blocked the roads and piled up snow against walls and hedgerows. Bea's mother, Vivien, visiting, told her not to go out in case she slipped on the icy pavements. Bea hid from her what had really happened: that she and Clive had had an awful row, after which Clive had gone away to stay with a friend in Wiltshire, leaving her and Alice alone in the house. They had rowed about money again. Their rows were always about money. Their lack of it, his spending of it. Clive was now marooned in the snow somewhere near Trowbridge.

When she ran out of milk and bread, Bea shuffled to the newsagent, walking on the compacted snow with a crablike gait, Alice's hand in hers. Because the refuse collectors were on strike, she had to skirt round black bin bags and wet cardboard boxes, fearful of slipping over. Friends arrived with gifts of food and provisions, thawing themselves in her kitchen and spreading their hands over the warm hob of the Aga while they related their adventures. A skid on

115

black ice, a stranded car, an epic expedition from shop to shop because everywhere had run out of butter or eggs. Marissa trudged over to Islington with a bag of shopping for her. In her Cossack boots and long black coat, tendrils of ash-fair hair showing beneath a fake-fur hat, she looked, Bea thought, like a Russian princess left to fend for herself after the Revolution. She did not regret telling Marissa about her baby son. She never found it easy to speak of Patrick, and yet if she hadn't, she would have felt her secret standing between her and her friend, walling them off from each other.

The train drivers downed tools too, but then the trains weren't going anywhere anyway because of the iced-up rails. Some of Bea's friends told stories of bodies unburied, stacked up in hospital freezers, in those parts of the country where the gravediggers were on strike. Not that you'd need a freezer in this weather, they added, with black humour. In Leicester Square and the great London parks, dark ribbons of rats streamed across the snow to feast on the mountains of rubbish. 'That big,' one of her visitors said, spacing his hands a foot apart.

Bea didn't waste her time worrying about politics. It would sort itself out, or it wouldn't, and there was nothing she could do about it. Her world had compressed to caring for Alice and waiting for her baby to be born. She remembered how much labour hurt, and felt afraid. She hadn't felt afraid before Patrick because she hadn't understood what she was in for back then. Always the optimist, she had assumed with Alice that it would be easier second time round. Now that her third child was about to be born, she knew that labour was never easy. Fear came when she was alone, when her daughter was in bed and no one was in the kitchen with stories of snowdrifts and shortages. She was afraid that something would go wrong or something would be wrong with the baby. A small, dark part of her felt she deserved it.

Now their quarrel seemed unimportant and she yearned for Clive to come home. She needed him to be with her while she gave birth, needed the solace of his big, solid presence. She imagined him making his way back from the south-west, abandoning his car in a blizzard, perhaps, and hitching a lift on a tractor or ploughing on through the snow on foot. The ambulance drivers, too, had gone on strike. She was afraid that she wouldn't reach the hospital in time and would give birth to her baby at home, alone.

Clive turned up on the evening of the second to last day of January, shaking snow from his coat, filling up the hallway.

'Oh, thank God you're home!' Bea cried. Relief washed through her, and their quarrel was forgotten as he wrapped his arms around her. Pools of water trailed from his boots onto the tiles; he smelled of winter.

'Forgive me, darling Bea, please.' He held her close, careful of the baby bump between them. 'I'm so sorry. I should never have gone off like that. I'll never do it again, I swear. I was afraid I'd be too late.' Light kisses traced the shape of her brow, cheekbones and jaw, then found her mouth.

Clive was home, and fear shrank to a manageable thing. She went into labour later that night. Her second daughter, Rachel Beatrice, was born at five the following morning, a quick and easy birth, as births went. In years to come, Bea always told her daughter that she had hung on, not wanting to come into the world until her father was home.

Vivien stayed for a week to help out with Alice and the housework. When Marissa visited with a gift of exquisite

French baby clothes and a wooden caterpillar on a string for Alice, Bea asked her if she would like to be Rachel's godmother. So good for a girl, she thought, to have an elegant and capable godmother. Marissa was a dependable person who would remember to take Rachel out to lunch on her birthday. Perhaps she would make up for the more capricious people in Rachel's life. Seeing the sparkle of tears in Marissa's eyes as she accepted, Bea struggled not to cry herself.

After the first few chaotic weeks, Rachel turned out to be a contented, easy baby. Unaccustomed to an infant who slept soundly between feeds, Bea peered at her in her Moses basket, a finger lightly balanced on her ribcage to check the rise and fall of her breath. Days started early and ended late. She was always behindhand, frantically sterilising bottles or running out of clean dungarees for Alice. The kitchen was a muddle of washing-up and baskets of nappies that needed laundering or folding and putting away. Caring for two children seemed three times the work of looking after one.

At night, when Rachel's cries dragged her out of a deep sleep, Bea would pause for a moment, perched on the edge of the bed, half deranged with tiredness. *Please let her go back to sleep, please. Just for another hour until I can think straight. Please let her start sleeping through the night, because I can't do this any more.* Fighting not to doze off, she breastfed her daughter in the nursery. Desperate, noisy sucking to start with, and then Rachel settled down to a rhythm. The dark blue eyes opened, fixing on Bea's face. A milky smile, and Bea felt a rush of love so powerful it almost knocked her off balance.

Joy came unexpectedly, in the most mundane of circumstances: when she was pushing the pram home from the park, or when she was sitting on the sofa reading Frog and Toad to Alice, the baby curled like a comma against her chest.

In a former incarnation, the shop in Margaret Street had sold kaftans and throws, joss sticks and brass incense holders. Inside, the fragrance of sandalwood and frankincense lingered.

While the letting agent pattered on, Marissa let her gaze roam round the interior, picturing what it could become. Clothes rails along either side of the shop. On the counter, the cash desk and rolls of tissue paper, paper carriers on a shelf beneath. To one side of the cash desk a chair, so that a husband or boyfriend could sit and read a newspaper while his wife or girlfriend tried on garments. Good lighting, mirrors, and spacious changing rooms that ensured privacy.

She explored the warren of cupboards and cubicles to the rear of the premises. The letting agent was talking about the desirability of the shop's West End location on the border between Fitzrovia and Marylebone, close to the smart retail outlets of Great Portland Street and Oxford Street.

Marissa ran a fingertip over a skirting board, then a shop fixture. It came away black. 'It'll need a lot of work,' she said. She itched to roll up her sleeves and scrub the place clean, to paint a subtle off-white over the hippy horoscope signs daubed on the walls, to sand and varnish the wooden floor.

Boutiques and dress shops went to the wall daily, leaving their owners in debt, sometimes for thousands of pounds. Renting this shop would mean taking out a loan from the bank – only a small loan, but she shrank from the prospect of indebtedness. Her mother had never borrowed a penny in her entire life. Yet Marissa knew in her heart that she could make it work, that she could make a success of it. It was the logical next step, one that she had been planning for years.

They went outside. As the letting agent locked up, Marissa took another look at the frontage and was unable this time to suppress a smile. One or two mannequins in the window, no more. A leather bag or a piece of jewellery to complement the outfits. Sage-green or petrol-blue paint on the woodwork. And her name, *Marissa Flint*, printed in simple black lettering across the top of the window pane.

A letter arrived from the bank, addressed to Clive. He hadn't come home the previous night, so Bea slit open the envelope. Phrases sprang out of the typed sheet of paper: *overdraft limit reached . . . £300 overdrawn . . . insufficient funds . . . cheques unable to be honoured*. Feeling sick inside, she examined the returned cheques the bank manager had enclosed. They were to the gas board, the post office, Clive's wine merchant.

Alice pulled at her cardigan, and Rachel, who had been napping in the pram, started to whimper. While she fed Rachel and played with Alice, Bea's thoughts skated away. Had Clive stayed out overnight because he was afraid to tell her they had run out of money? Why hadn't she, when warning bells had rung nine months ago on that visit to Clive's parents, insisted on checking the bank statements?

Friends were coming round for a small get-together that evening, so she scraped up cash from bags and pockets before leaving the house to buy food. If she wrote a cheque, it might bounce.

At half past five, she heard his key in the lock. Clive came into the hall. His clothing was crumpled and he had a day's growth of copper-coloured beard. It was Rachel's grizzly time of day, and Bea had propped her against her shoulder.

She said in a whispery screech, 'Where were you?'

'I stayed over at Jerry's.'

'Didn't you think I might wonder where you were?'

He slung his jacket over the banister. 'Sorry.'

'Sorry?'

He gave her a cold look. 'I didn't think I needed to ask permission to have a night out.'

Because of the baby, she suppressed her rage. 'Oh, for God's sake, Clive, grow up,' she said coldly, and went back to the kitchen to sit with Alice, who was having her tea. Clive came into the room, ruffled Alice's hair and kissed the top of her head. Then he went upstairs.

While the water was running for Alice's bath, Bea fetched the bank manager's letter and dropped it on Clive's desk. She went downstairs to the bathroom and stripped off Alice's clothing. In the bath, Alice poured bubbly water from one plastic beaker to another.

Clive came into the room. 'I shouldn't have said that.'

'I was worried,' Bea said flatly. 'All you had to do was phone.'

'Yes, I'm sorry. Let me take her.' He settled the baby over his shoulder.

'You have to face up to things. Running away won't help.'

Bea was addressing herself as much as him. Until now, she had not considered the possibility that Clive's restlessness, which she had assumed he would grow out of, might be his defining characteristic. He might never change, and what would that mean for her? For the first time, she was afraid that in falling in love with Clive, she had repeated the same mistakes she had made with Ciaran. Her yearning for romance, her lack of realism and her fatal need to see the best in people meant that she veiled the objects of her affection with a deceptive golden glow.

He looked away. 'We'll talk later, love. I'll go and get things ready for the party.'

He left the room. From the kitchen, the sound of running water and clattering pots. Bea put Alice to bed, then fed Rachel and settled her in her cot. Her anger had evaporated, and she felt frightened instead. It was hard to see which way to turn. Dressing for the party, applying make-up, she felt as if she had dropped off to sleep and opened her eyes to find a disaster unfolding.

She went downstairs. Clive was drying tumblers. He said to her, 'The restaurant lost me money. It was a lousy time to get it going with all the strikes and such a hard winter.'

A fortnight ago – a day ago – she would have kissed him, tousled his hair, agreed that he had just been unlucky. But something had changed. She said, 'You stopped going there in the evenings. Even before Christmas. You left it to Martin.' Martin was Clive's business partner.

'It's not really my thing, spending every evening buttering up customers and making sure the chef doesn't drink himself into a stupor.'

'Why not?'

He looked at her, startled. 'What do you mean?'

'Why isn't it your thing?'

'I don't like routine, you know that, Bea.'

She chucked a grubby tea towel down the cellar stairs, then shut the door. 'What if I decided I didn't like the routine of looking after a toddler or feeding a baby?'

'That's different.'

'Is it?'

'Of course it is. I'll sort it out, I promise. I'll find something that suits me.'

'You could get a job. A proper job that pays a regular salary. Then we'd know where we were financially. You could ask your father to help you find something.'

'What, me, work in the City?' Predictably, he laughed. 'With some idiot of a boss telling me what to do? Nine to five in an office with all the other drones? Bea, I'm never going to fall into that trap. Hey, come here.' He wrapped his free arm round her and she let herself relax against him. She breathed in the familiar scents of his sweat and Paco Rabanne's Pour Homme. 'I love you,' he murmured. 'I love you so much.'

The doorbell rang and Bea let in the first of their guests. Though she welcomed the distraction of music and talking, tonight a portion of her seemed to stand apart. When she looked at Clive, topping up drinks, the perfect host, handsome in his Paul Smith shirt and Levi's, she seemed to see him more clearly. He was still the attractive charmer who had swept her off her feet, and she still loved him. But she knew that he did not feel as she did, that they were teetering on the edge of a cliff. In fact, she suspected he had already forgotten their conversation.

# Chapter Seven

## 1979

Max looked after Lucienne and Elizabeth while Emma had a day out on her own in London. She was, she had explained to him one evening, going slightly spare. She had forgotten what the outside world looked like.

Going out, even for only a few hours, demanded a huge amount of organisation. Emma expressed milk and made sure she had washed enough nappies. She did her hair and put on make-up and found smart clothes that fitted, more or less.

London was bliss. She meandered round some of her favourite places and had lunch in a café on Wigmore Street. During a spare three quarters of an hour between visiting an exhibition of botanical art and heading off to King's Cross to catch the train back to Cambridge, she explored the area around Great Portland Street, looking in the windows of the smart little shops.

One of the shops was called Marissa Flint. Emma's eye was caught by a garment displayed in its window, a black linen jumpsuit. She itched to try it on. It was, of course, completely impractical. If she breastfed when wearing it, she would have to get more or less undressed. And it probably cost a fortune.

She went inside the shop. The slim, fair-haired woman at the counter smiled and wished her good afternoon. A customer was browsing the rails and there was another in a changing room. Oh, the bliss, Emma thought as she leafed through silk blouses and boxy pinstriped jackets, of being able to take her time looking at lovely clothes. She hadn't realised how hungry she was for such pleasures.

She asked to try on the jumpsuit. When she stepped out of the changing room, the saleswoman looked up and smiled. 'Fabulous. It really suits you.'

'I adore it.'

'Is it for a special occasion?'

Emma shook her head. 'Dinner with friends. The mother and toddler group disco. That sort of thing. I live a wild life.'

'You have children?'

'Two little girls, Lucienne and Elizabeth.'

'What gorgeous names.'

'Lucienne's after Lucienne Day and Elizabeth was named after my grandmother, who wove textiles. She wasn't famous or anything, but I have a few of her pieces and I love them.'

'I always feel that sort of craftsmanship is very underrated.'

Emma gave the saleswoman a closer look. She was around her own age, and her fair, feathery hair framed a delicately pretty face. Her slenderness was emphasised by the simple, narrow navy-blue dress she was wearing.

Emma turned back to the mirror. 'I was afraid it wouldn't fit. I've put on a few pounds.' She patted her waist. 'Ah, but it's so heavenly! I'll take it.'

'The hems could do with being taken up an inch or so. I could pin it for you now, if you like. Where do you live?'

'Cambridge.'

'I'll put it in the post.' The saleswoman took a pincushion out of a drawer. As she knelt on the floor to measure the hems, she asked Emma whether she was enjoying her day in London.

'I've just been to an exhibition in Wigmore Street.'

'The botanical art exhibition?' A pin was placed. 'Isn't it wonderful? I've been three times. There was a watercolour of a blue hydrangea that I fell in love with. I've been searching for a silk that shade ever since. I more often go for neutrals, but I'm obsessed by that colour. Just think, a shirt in sand-washed silk the colour of blue hydrangeas. How could any woman resist that?'

Emma went to the counter to pay for the garment. She was getting her purse out of her handbag when the saleswoman said, 'May I ask where you bought your necklace?'

Emma's hand flew to her beads. 'This? I made it. It's just papier mâché.'

She had been making model animals for Lucienne and there had been some papier mâché left over. She had had the idea of making beads that resembled pebbles, and had ground up one of Lucienne's chalks and added the dust to the pulped paper mixture to make it last longer. She had lost track of time, absorbed in the task.

'I was trying to make them look like shingle,' she said. 'After the sea's washed over it.'

'May I look at it?'

Emma unclasped the necklace. The saleswoman ran a thumb over the beads' hard, varnished brilliance. 'The colours are so subtle. You've achieved the illusion of solidity. Would you think about making some for me?'

Emma stared at her. 'Not seriously?'

126

'I'm perfectly serious. I've been looking for strong, attractive costume jewellery to set off my garments for quite a while, but so much of what's around is garish or flimsy. My name's Marissa Flint, by the way.'

Emma shook Marissa's hand. 'Emma Hooper.'

'If you're interested, I would initially commission half a dozen. I'd send you swatches of material so you could match the shades I'm using. We could discuss size and length, though to me this looks about right.' Marissa took a card out of a drawer and offered it to her. 'Think about it. If you'd like to go ahead, give me a ring and we can discuss terms. It would be great to work with you, Emma.'

On the Cambridge train, Emma reflected on her conversation with Marissa Flint. She felt a little dazed. It seemed ridiculous to think that anyone might want to buy a necklace made of mushed-up paper, of beads that looked like pebbles. That Marissa had seemed truly serious only opened the door to a whole host of other problems. How would she find the time to make papier-mâché necklaces to order? There weren't enough hours for all the vital tasks, like remembering to buy food or mop the kitchen floor. Every moment of her day – and some of the night, too – was taken up with one thing or another. She was on the mother and toddler group committee, she hosted coffee mornings for the National Housewives Register, she shopped for an elderly neighbour. People came to stay: old friends, Max's parents and his brother, Adam, Tamar and Morgan and Gale and Rob. There was no slack in her life.

She had never intended to be an artist – she had, in fact, tried quite hard not to be one. When she looked back to her childhood, it seemed to her that Tamar had often been worn thin. As the eldest child, it had been Emma's role to help, to keep an eye on her younger siblings, to conciliate and smooth things over. Why choose to go down the same rocky, poorly rewarded route as her mother? Women artists were not taken seriously. They had to try twice as hard as men. She remembered all too clearly the economies and humiliations of her upbringing, the jumble-sale clothes and the home-grown veg with bits cut out where a rabbit or slug had taken a nibble. The chaos and disorganisation and the pretending that being poor didn't matter, that it was a badge of pride.

And yet the prospect of taking on the commission excited her. She had liked Marissa Flint, had felt an instant rapport with her. She enjoyed creating things. Since Marissa had made her unexpected request, Emma had run through in her mind endless shapes and colours of beads: creams and greys and sage green and the soft violet-blues of hydrangeas.

Clive's father, Kenneth, stipulated as a condition of paying off his debts that they rent out the Islington house for a year and move into a smaller property to save money. One of Clive's friends, a man called Mitch Fraser, offered them the loan of a cottage in the grounds of his house at Hazewell, near Great Chesterford, on the Cambridgeshire–Essex border.

Bea and Clive moved into the cottage in early May. Though Hazewell was less than half an hour's drive from Cambridge and only an hour from London, Bea felt as if she had plunged into another world. The cottage dated from the 1920s. The roof was low and mossy and the bathroom was tacked onto the back of the building and accessed from an outside door. There was no mains gas and the living room smelled of coal dust and Cardinal floor polish. No phone, either, so Bea wrote a lot of letters. Once a week she pushed the pram to a telephone box a quarter of a mile away to call her mother, her mother-in-law and Marissa.

Marissa's visits, every couple of weeks or so, were like a breath of fresh air. Marissa mentioned that she had recently commissioned half a dozen papier-mâché necklaces from a woman who lived in Cambridge. 'She's called Emma Hooper. She's lovely, Bea, I think you'd like her. I'd love you to meet her.'

Bea adored the cottage garden, which melted into woodland. On fine days, sunshine filtered through the tall trees. A froth of pink and white hawthorn blossom was succeeded by festoons of dog rose and honeysuckle. Beneath the beech trees was an earthy, flickering darkness.

Mitch was a record producer. He had bought the Hazewell estate two years ago. Hazewell House itself was an imposing red-brick Georgian building, which stood on top of a shallow hill and was reached by a long driveway that meandered through parkland. Mitch was in the Bahamas, and the house was currently empty, so with Rachel in a sling on her front and Alice scampering beside her, Bea explored the grounds. Whenever the weather was fine, they packed a picnic and spent the entire day outside. Earth-shaking events were taking place – the election of Britain's first woman prime minster, Margaret Thatcher; the trial of the former Liberal leader, Jeremy Thorpe, for attempted murder – but Bea felt happily distant from all that.

She felt distant from Clive, too, which troubled her. As a further condition of his father loaning him the money, Clive had taken a job with an insurance company, which meant that he was away in London during the week, staying with a friend. After less than two months working for the company, he had walked out of the office one morning and never gone back. He had remained in London, though, returning to the cottage only at the weekends. He was looking for work, he told Bea. He was in discussions about going into business with a friend. He was thinking of setting up a comedy club or moving to the Lake District and breeding sheep.

Or he was getting plastered in the pub. Bea had no way of knowing. She didn't think he was having an affair. There was no lipstick on his collar, no lingering, alien scent. But perhaps she was being naïve. What she knew, what she had belatedly come to understand, was that Clive felt entitled to his freedom. *I didn't think I needed to ask permission to have a night out.* Though he had apologised for saying that, and though she believed he sincerely regretted angering her, she knew that deep down he had meant it. Since the early days of their marriage she had tolerated him staying out for the occasional night. She remembered her mother grilling her father after he had returned home late, and her father's wounded resentfulness. She wanted her own marriage to be different. Trust was so important. She and Clive both believed that married couples should give each other space, that they should each be able to do their own thing. Anyway, that was what she had said to herself.

But she put up with his absences now because she knew that nothing she said would make any difference. Which worried her. In the long, quiet evenings at the cottage, she had plenty of time to think. She and Clive were from a similar echelon in society, though the Meades were less affluent than the Cornwells. The difference was that Clive had a feeling of entitlement that she herself lacked. Perhaps the raw pain of losing Ciaran and her baby had punctured her self-confidence, or perhaps it was different for girls, who tended to know themselves to be inferior, destined for a supporting role. Clive felt he had the right to the best of everything: to eat out in good restaurants, to buy expensive clothes, to holiday abroad whenever he wanted to. The problem was, he didn't think he should have to work in a dull job to pay for these things. He was capable of hard work, but only on his own terms. She hadn't stopped loving him, but she saw his faults.

The impossibility of getting anything much done at all while looking after a toddler and a baby, let alone creating six – six! – papier-mâché necklaces to a standard that would satisfy a discerning woman like Marissa Flint, led Emma to sweep the girls into the car and decamp to Seastone, to stay with her mother for a week.

They fell into a routine. The weather was fine and sunny, so Tamar took Lucienne and Elizabeth out to play on the beach in the mornings, leaving Emma free to work. As promised, Marissa had sent her swatches of fabric so that she could match the colours of the beads. Absorbed in her task, the hours seemed to fly by. Morgan joined them for lunch, which they ate in the garden, and then returned to his studio while Tamar worked. Emma spent the afternoons with the girls, searching for shells among the shingle.

On her second-to-last day, she was washing up when she looked out through the kitchen window and caught sight of a man walking along the path through the fields, heading towards the little row of houses. As he drew closer, she saw that he had longish receding brown hair and was wearing a yellow shirt, a brown leather jacket and dark trousers. He was limping.

'Mum,' she said. 'Do you know him?'

Her mother came to stand beside her. She shook her head.

'Hmm. London clothes, don't you think? Maybe he's a journalist. Or maybe he's writing a book about your father, something like that.'

'Shall I get rid of him?'

'Please, love.' Tamar picked up Elizabeth, who was grizzling in her carrycot.

Emma peeled off her rubber gloves and went outside. She noticed how the stranger's smooth-soled city shoes slipped as the earth path rose up to the bank.

He called out, 'Hello! I'm looking for Mrs Romilly.'

'Tamar Romilly is my mother.'

Panting, red-faced, his brow sheened with sweat – he was forty-ish and a portly man – he reached the top of the rickety earth and wooden steps.

'My name's Nick Lauderdale,' he said when he had got his breath back. He offered Emma his hand.

'Emma Hooper.'

'Please forgive me for turning up uninvited. I wrote to Mrs Romilly, but my letter can't have got through. I would have phoned, but . . .'

'I'm afraid my parents don't have a phone.'

He took a card out of his wallet and handed it to Emma. 'I'm from the Rochester Street Gallery.'

She said politely, 'Unfortunately, my father's working just now and can't be disturbed.'

'Actually, it was Mrs Romilly, your mother, I was hoping to talk to.'

Emma looked at him more closely. 'You'd better come in.'

Nick Lauderdale followed her into the house. Emma introduced him to Tamar.

'It's such a pleasure to meet you,' he said as he limped into the room.

'Have you hurt your foot, Mr Lauderdale?'

'Call me Nick, please. I turned my ankle in a rut. I've left my car on the road. I wasn't sure whether the track was suitable for vehicles.'

'It isn't,' Emma said. 'Do sit down. I'll get you a bag of frozen peas to put on your ankle. That'll help keep the swelling down. Would you like a cup of coffee?'

'Oh *yes*. Thank you.' He sank onto the sofa with a sigh of relief and began to loosen his shoelace.

Emma put the kettle on. She heard Nick Lauderdale explain to Tamar that he had come to Seastone because he wanted to talk to her about her father, John Cotterell. It was quite likely, Emma thought as she spooned ground coffee into a jug, that his letter hadn't got through because Tamar had stuffed it behind the clock on the mantelpiece without opening it. She had a habit of doing this with official-looking letters – a hangover, Emma assumed, from the years when they had contained unpayable bills. And Morgan never looked at the post.

She put some biscuits on a plate. From the living room she heard Tamar say, 'The Rochester Street Gallery . . .'

'We represented your father from the mid fifties.'

'I remember. The gallery that originally represented him was destroyed in the war, wasn't it?'

Emma took the plate into the back room. Mr Lauderdale, in his socks, had risen from the sofa to look at the painting on the easel. 'Is this one of Morgan Romilly's?'

'No, it's mine,' said Tamar. 'It's not finished yet.'

'I didn't know you were an artist too.'

'Didn't you? Well, then. I've been painting all my life, Mr Lauderdale.'

The irritation in her mother's voice was audible to Emma.

She handed Nick Lauderdale the bag of frozen peas. 'Here, you should rest your foot. Put this on it.'

Lauderdale sat down and flinched as he draped the icy bag over his ankle. Perhaps he too had picked up on Tamar's exasperation, because he said quickly, 'Let me explain why I'm here. I took over the management of the gallery four months ago. Not long past, I was approached by a gentleman offering to sell us his collection of works by twentieth-century British artists. It would be a substantial acquisition and really rather fine. It includes half a dozen paintings by John Cotterell. I've been an admirer of your father's work for a long time, Mrs Romilly. He has perhaps been a little overlooked in the past couple of decades, but that's often the case, I'm afraid. There's a certain cycle, a fashion, to art.'

'My father didn't complete a lot of work in the later years of his life,' said Tamar. 'And he pretty much stopped painting in the fifties.'

'He turned to relief-making, didn't he? But then his paintings always had a sculptural quality.'

Emma liked Nick Lauderdale better then, because she saw that he had some understanding of her grandfather's work. She put the tray with the jug and mugs on the table.

Tamar poured the coffee. 'I don't think my father ever really recovered from my elder brother's death in the war. He was killed at the battle of Arnhem.' She passed Nick Lauderdale a cup. 'And then, in the fifties, my other brother emigrated to Australia. We'd been a close family, and suddenly Ellis was on the other side of the world while poor Gerren was gone. My mother died in 1967. My father stayed on at Nanpean. We visited him as often as we could, Morgan and I, in the last five years of his life, but he must have been lonely. Nanpean was such a busy place between the wars.'

134

'Perhaps painting, for John Cotterell, required a certain amount of joy.'

'Perhaps it did.'

'Does it for you, Mrs Romilly?'

Tamar considered. 'No, I don't think so. For me, painting is more of an interrogation, a process of working something out.'

'That's one of your father's, isn't it?' Lauderdale nodded to a large painting over the fireplace.

'It is, yes. That's Nanpean farm.'

'It's magnificent. I've seen reproductions, but never the real thing.' He got up and limped across the room to examine it more closely. 'What a privilege to see it at last.'

'My father was never very prolific. It might take him a year, much longer sometimes, before he decided that a work was complete. I'm afraid I take after him.'

'Do you have others?'

'I own around a dozen of his paintings and a couple of reliefs.'

Lauderdale sat down again. He dipped a Rich Tea into his coffee. 'Forgive me, Mrs Romilly, but I was speaking of your own work.'

'Oh, yes,' said Tamar, sounding flustered. 'Quite a few.'

Tamar's paintings, her seascapes, landscapes and self-portraits, were propped against walls and stacked behind armchairs. Or they were gathering cobwebs in a cupboard in the old boat shed in which Morgan worked. Emma's childhood memories were of her mother working in a corner of the sitting room at the back of the house. Over the years, the balance had changed. Since Rob had left home, much of the remaining portion of the room had been swallowed up by Tamar's studio.

135

'They're wonderful,' Emma said to Lauderdale. 'You should have a look at them.'

'I would very much like to.' Nick Lauderdale helped himself to another biscuit. 'May I ask who represents you, Mrs Romilly?'

'No one does. There was a gallery after the war, in the late forties, but it never came to much. And then I got married and Morgan and I moved to Suffolk and we had a family, and that takes up time. I've had some exhibitions locally, in Ipswich and Aldeburgh . . .' Tamar's words trailed away.

Emma filled the ensuing silence by offering more coffee. Then Lauderdale leaned forward, clasping his hands.

'I would consider it an honour if you would allow me to see some of your paintings, Mrs Romilly. However, I came here today because I would like very much to stage a retrospective of your father's work. Would you be prepared to consider loaning the gallery those pieces that you own? I believe it's time for a reassessment of his standing. I'm afraid there's no way of putting this that doesn't sound brutal, but after an artist dies and a certain length of time has passed, there can be a renewal of interest. I believe we're reaching that moment. It would be interesting to show John Cotterell's progression from oil painting to reliefs and then to the late pen-and-ink sketches and watercolours. The exhibition would place him in the context of his times and demonstrate the influence of the Cornish landscape on his development as an artist. It might be fascinating, also, to explore his relationship to the wider circle of artists who stayed at Nanpean . . . and perhaps to the St Ives group as well. I promise you, Mrs Romilly, that I would do my utmost to do justice to him.'

After Mr Lauderdale had left, and once they had finished lunch, Emma and her mother walked to the village so that Emma could call Marissa from the phone box to tell her that the necklaces were almost finished.

Tamar was pushing the pram. She said suddenly, impatiently, 'Why did I feel I had to try and justify myself to him? Why did I feel the need to tell him about that silly little exhibition in Ipswich? It was the sort of thing an amateur would say – a woman who dabbles.'

'Mum, he loved your work.'

Tamar, frowning, turned to look at her. 'Do you think so?'

Before Lauderdale had left, Tamar had shaken the dust off several of her paintings to show them to him. Emma had noticed the seriousness with which he had examined them, and the excitement in his eyes.

She squeezed her mother's shoulder. 'He loved them, Mum. He absolutely adored them.'

It was funny, thought Bea, how the moment she entered Emma Hooper's Cambridge house, she felt at home. Emma's baby daughter, Elizabeth, was asleep in her pram in the garden, so Bea offered to keep an eye on her and the older children while Emma showed Marissa the necklaces she had made. Bea fed Rachel while Alice played with Emma's elder daughter, Lucienne, in the sandpit.

In the garden, there was a terrace and children's playthings and a great many roses, scrambling over the wall and the overgrown shrubs. Fragments of conversation drifted through the open doors of the old sunroom tacked on the back of the house. *I love this colour, Emma, this soft turquoise. Wow – so gorgeous.* Now and then Bea caught a glimpse of Emma's husband, Max, who was at the far end of the garden, pruning

137

a tree. A flash of dark hair, an upraised arm, and then the creak and snap of a branch falling to the ground.

A phone rang, the doorbell chimed. It was a busy household, but Bea sensed a peacefulness here nevertheless. She pushed away the thought that the Hoopers possessed what she and Clive had never quite found: comfort and serenity. Rachel was falling asleep at the breast, and the part of Bea that had been on edge since she had discovered how deeply they were in debt seemed to relax a little. She would have liked to doze off too, but she remained awake, sitting in the flickering shade of the garden, watching the children.

Marissa and Emma came out of the house. Marissa said, 'The necklaces are beautiful. Emma's agreed to make me half a dozen more.'

Emma crouched down beside Bea. With the tip of her forefinger, she gently stroked Rachel's cheek. 'What a poppet. May I hold her? Marissa said you're living in Great Chesterford just now. Would you like me to drop round one morning, if you're not too busy? The girls seem to be getting on so well, don't they?'

In July, a procession of cars and vans heading up the drive announced that Mitch Fraser had returned to Hazewell House. The following afternoon, Bea and Clive were invited for drinks. Mitch was short and dark, in his late thirties, deeply tanned from his months in the Bahamas. He came from a northern working-class background and was ambitious and very successful. Along with Hazewell and the place in the Bahamas, he owned a house in Chelsea.

Mitch introduced the Cornwells to his girlfriend, a tall, blonde, athletic-looking Australian woman called Sandra.

Sandra had a son, Wolfie, a pale, temperamental child who was a year and a half older than Alice. No one seemed to keep much of an eye on him, neither Sandra nor the au pair, a slight young French girl called Paulette. Bea took the little boy to the cottage to play with Alice, where he shocked her staid daughter with his habits of putting pebbles in his mouth and stripping off all his clothes. Neither Bea nor Clive knew whether Mitch was Wolfie's father. It wasn't a question either of them felt they could ask.

There was a terrace at the back of Hazewell House, made of crumbling flagstones bordered by a balustrade topped with mossy urns. There, Sandra, wearing shorts and a halter top, stretched out on a sunlounger while her pair of sleek Afghan hounds draped themselves elegantly on the lichened stone steps.

Mitch and Sandra's guests were businessmen, pop stars, actresses and models. In conversation Mitch liked to provoke and to challenge. He was a hard drinker and contemptuous of any man unwise enough to turn down the offer of a drink. Bea and Clive had a standing dinner invitation, and most afternoons they wandered up to the house, pushing the girls in the pram. By the time they arrived, guests would be lounging on the terrace and Mitch mixing himself a Scotch and water. The French doors would be open so that *Parallel Lines* or the Velvet Underground could flood out onto the terrace. Some warm late-summer afternoons, Bea heard a distant rumble of thunder, as if someone was flexing a sheet of metal.

Eventually one of the guests would drive off to Saffron Walden to buy wine, and Paulette would go to the kitchen to chop onions and wash lettuce. At Hazewell House they ate late, after nine, so Rachel slept in the pram to the side of the terrace while Bea tucked up Alice on a sofa in a nearby room. Bea took the girls home at eleven, but Clive usually stayed on until the early hours of the morning. They were indebted to Mitch, who was allowing them to live in his property for free, so perhaps Clive felt the least he could do in return was to offer his company.

Though Bea admired Mitch's generosity, his abrasive personality made it hard for her to feel at ease in his company. She felt happiest at the cottage, when Marissa or Emma came to visit. Sitting in the garden with her friends, drinking coffee and chatting, the intractable problems of her marriage slipped at last into the background.

As the summer wore on, the grassy parkland became flecked with papery seed-heads and the leaves of the horse chestnuts turned a dusty brownish green. Mitch spoke of finding Clive a role in the record company. The two men shared a love of fast cars and liked to race each other around Hazewell's grounds, Clive driving his Lancia, Mitch a Lotus.

It was Clive who had the idea of making a racing circuit on the estate. Over drinks on the terrace, he and Mitch talked about turning the track into a business, hiring it out by the day to people who enjoyed driving fast cars. The men spent their days constructing the circuit, stripped to their waists, their torsos conker brown as they scythed down ragwort and felled saplings. The sun bleached the swaying grass to the colour of hessian, and the quiet of the Essex countryside was obliterated by the whine of car engines and the screech of tyres. Even Sandra detached herself from her sunlounger long enough to stand by the makeshift finishing post with the other guests, cheering the drivers on.

*

Leicester Square Underground station was packed with commuters. Marissa was making her way to the Embankment, to a party at the Tate. The hot, dry August weather had boiled up into a thunderstorm, so she dived into the station to escape the downpour.

A train slowed as it approached the platform. Searching for a route through the throng, she saw him: Jamie Canterbury, her husband, standing ten or fifteen yards away from her. Her heart gave a violent, painful lurch, as if it was trying to force its way through her ribcage.

She was afraid to look at him again, yet knew that she must. After all, she might be mistaken. This had happened before. She had thought she had seen him more than a dozen times during the four years that had passed since she had walked out of the house in Moberly Road. This man had Jamie's stocky build, reddish hair, florid face and neat, conventionally handsome features. He was standing in that restless, nervy way Marissa remembered so well, rocking on the balls of his feet, his gaze darting from side to side. As his head turned in her direction, she looked away, pulling up the hood of her raincoat, making herself still and small.

*I won't ever let you go, Mary. I'd rather you were dead.*

Passengers surged round her as the train drew to a halt. The thunderous beat of her heart was loud in her ears. Out of the corner of her eye she watched Jamie, the man who might be Jamie, shoulder his way into a carriage. In a rush of dusty air, the train pulled out of the station and disappeared into the black tunnel.

Marissa looked along the platform. Only a scattering of people remained. Frightening possibilities sprang into her mind. He might have looked out of the carriage window and recognised her. He might have got off at Charing Cross and already be on a train back to Leicester Square. A vision of Jamie's green and white checked shirt, rammed up against her face, leapt into her mind. She could smell his sweat and his anger. She had to get away, she couldn't stand the dark, enclosed space any longer, but in her rush to leave the platform, her high heel slipped on the wet surface and she tripped awkwardly, dropping her briefcase and handbag.

A woman helped her gather up her belongings. 'You all right, love?' she said. 'I hate it when it's as busy as this. I'd rather wait for another train, wouldn't you?'

Marissa couldn't speak. She stumbled towards the exit. Outside, rain was still pelting off the pavements. She tipped back her head, letting the water beat against her face. The fear that she might faint or be sick in front of strangers retreated. She was sweating beneath her trench coat, so she loosened the belt and buttons. Then she began to walk. Though she tried to tell herself that it hadn't been Jamie, that she had been imagining it, she couldn't be sure.

At the Embankment, she rested her forearms on the concrete wall, trying to catch her breath. Every muscle in her body ached with tension. She looked out over the grey, dappled blur of the river and tried to think clearly, to draw on her excellent visual memory. The man on the platform had been more heavily built than Jamie, but then he could have put on weight – he had always liked his food. Anxiety gave her imagination wings. He might be working in London now; he might have moved here. She pictured him promoted to work at the head office of the building society – successful Jamie, rich and prosperous, in command of everything he had always thought should be his. A cheap mortgage from his employers so that he could buy a flat. He might be living an Underground stop away from her . . . he might be living a street away.

He might have seen her. The thought wormed its insidious way into her mind. He might have followed her here. She scanned the surrounding area, checking off the passers-by. She couldn't see him. She looked again to make sure, pressing her knuckles against her teeth until she drew blood.

She hated to think of him, hated to picture him, hated to dismantle, if only temporarily, the barricades she had so meticulously erected against him. And yet slowly, as the rain began to ease off at last and she breathed in cool, fresh air, she seemed to come to her senses. Though the man she had seen had looked a bit like Jamie, it probably hadn't been him. More than likely she had conjured him up because she'd had a long day and because travelling on a crowded Underground train always made her feel anxious.

She couldn't face the party. She couldn't cope with more crowds, and anyway, her hair was sticking to her head in clammy tendrils, her shoes had let in rainwater and her tights were holed from her fall. She must look a sight, she thought.

She flagged down a taxi. Sitting in the back of the cab, cold, clammy and shivering, every stitch of her clothing soaked, she murmured a numbed agreement to the driver's monologue as the vehicle stopped and started, caught up in slow traffic.

His voice calmed her. Soon she would be safe at home. She would have a hot shower and she would put on warm, dry clothes. She would pour herself a glass of wine and phone Emma for a chat. Later, she would work out what she was going to take with her tomorrow when she travelled to Hazewell to visit Bea.

She had remembered who she was. She was Marissa Flint, a successful dress designer, the owner of a profitable boutique. That other woman had gone. She no longer existed.

'Someone needs to buy some more bloody booze,' Mitch roared over the hum of music and conversation on Hazewell House's terrace. 'Damned cellar's empty.'

A dozen guests were basking in the late-afternoon sun. 'I didn't know you had a cellar, Mitch,' said a young woman in a pale blue tube top. 'So posh.'

Mitch hauled himself out of his deckchair. Ash dripped from his cigarette. 'Right now, there's nothing in it but bats. So unless you all want to go teetotal, one of you needs to shift their arse and do some shopping.'

'Christ,' someone drawled. 'Call this a party . . .'

Mitch wheeled round. 'Fuck off back to London, then.' He had a short fuse and had been drinking all afternoon. Mitch was a mean drunk.

Clive was sitting beside Bea on the stone balustrade. He stood up. 'I'll go,' he said, and Mitch, heading into the drawing room, swivelled to look back at him.

'I thought you were broke,' he said unpleasantly. 'I thought that's why you were sponging off me.'

Clive's eyes narrowed. 'On one condition. We'll have a race tomorrow, you and I, twenty laps. Whoever wins buys half a dozen cases of wine.'

Mitch shrugged. 'Okay. You're on.'

The other guests began to lay bets. Sandra, who was wearing a bikini under a crocheted tunic, along with knee-length tan leather boots, perched on the edge of her sunlounger and noted the wagers down. When Mitch reappeared brandishing a bottle of Glenmorangie, there were scattered cheers. He clapped Clive's back and poured him a measure.

Alice was playing on the lawn with Wolfie; Rachel was asleep in her pram to one side of the terrace. Bea went to check on her. She stood in the shadow of the wing of the house as Mitch and Sandra's guests milled around. She felt separate from them. If she walked away, would anyone notice? Wolfie was putting stones in his mouth, so she went down to the garden and prised them out. 'Don't do that, honey, you'll give yourself tummy ache.' She stroked his tangled hair.

On the terrace, Sandra's arm was draped round Clive's shoulders. Her voice floated back to Bea. 'I'm putting my money on you, darling. Mitch is losing his edge.' Bea's gaze moved from one man to the other, from Mitch's snarl to Clive's sleepy, heavy-lidded gaze. 'Pale Blue Eyes' was playing on the record player. Bea loved the song, but it was about betrayal, and today it made her feel troubled.

She took Clive's hand and pulled him away from the others. 'I don't want you to do it,' she said.

'What?'

'The race.'

'Why not?'

*Because it's stupid and dangerous.* But she knew Clive, knew that wouldn't work. Recklessness was ingrained through him.

'I want to go back to London,' she said. 'I've had enough of it here.'

'We will, sweetie.' Beneath her blouse, he stroked her waist. When he kissed her, he tasted of wine and cigarettes. 'I'm sick of the bloody countryside too. Soon, Bea, I promise.'

'I want to go *now*.' She heard the whine in her voice, like a child begging for an ice cream, and knew she had lost his attention.

His expression altered. 'I can't just drop everything. I promised Mitch I'd help him get the racetrack going.'

'Clive. You heard what he said just now, about you.'

'He was winding me up, that's all.'

'He meant it.'

'For Christ's sake, Bea, these are our friends.'

'Are they?' When she looked back at the other people on the terrace, it seemed to her that she hardly knew them at all. She grabbed Clive's hand again as he began to move away. 'Let's go back to London, darling,' she coaxed. 'We'll find another house to do up, it doesn't matter where. Don't you remember our first house, what fun it was?'

'Bea, I can't just cut and run,' he said. 'Not after everything Mitch has done for us.'

'I'm going back to the cottage.' Her grip on his hand tightened. 'I want you to come with me. It's ages since you put Alice to bed. Marissa's coming tomorrow and I need to sort things out. I could do with some help.'

'I'll be with you in half an hour.'

'Now, Clive.'

'My God, Bea, when did you turn into such a nag?' He shook her off and walked away.

Bea collected Alice and put her on the pram seat. When she looked back, she saw that Clive was crouched down beside Sandra's sunlounger. As she pushed her daughters back to the cottage, her head ached and the horse chestnuts in the park blurred with her tears. She almost wished Marissa wasn't coming to visit. She could tell her friend anything, but to tell her that she was afraid her marriage was falling apart would make it unbearably real.

Perhaps she was a nag, or perhaps marriage had turned her into one. She thought of her wedding, which had taken

146

place in a small jewel box of a chapel in the Surrey countryside, near the Cornwells' home. Clive had been to the pub before the ceremony and had had too much to drink. So had his best man, who had tripped over a pew and knocked over both a floral arrangement and the smallest bridesmaid, who had burst into tears. Perhaps the failure of her marriage had been written even then, on her wedding day, though she had been too much of an optimist to see it. She knew that they wouldn't renovate another London house, because Clive was bored with doing up houses. Besides, you couldn't live in a kitchen when you had two small children.

But she had made up her mind. If Clive wouldn't come with her, she would leave Hazewell on her own. Next week she would take the girls to London to stay with her parents. It wasn't that she was planning to leave him, and it wasn't that she didn't love him any more, but if, for a change, she was the one who went away, perhaps he might understand that she was serious about making a fresh start.

While she was in London, she would look for work. Though it would be hard to find anything to fit round caring for Alice and Rachel, she knew that she must. Her French was fluent, so perhaps she could tutor teenagers for their exams, or her mother might agree to babysit a couple of evenings a week while she waitressed. She saw now that it had been a mistake to allow herself to become financially dependent, and foolish to be swept along so by another person. She must take control of her life.

Clive came home very late that night. They hardly spoke over breakfast, and he headed back up to the house as soon as the meal was over. At midday, Bea picked up Marissa from Great Chesterford station. They had a picnic lunch in the cottage garden. Afterwards, Marissa lay in the shade beside Rachel, who sat on a blanket chewing a pink rubber pig. Bea fetched Alice a washing-up bowl full of water, and her toy tea set.

The relentless whine of the cars racing round the track made Bea think of a mosquito trapped in a room. The engine noise rose in volume whenever a car sped past the cottage. Still, it was good to be with Marissa, good to escape her worries and talk about different things, about Marissa's shop and London life. Bea wished she was more like Marissa; that she, like her friend, had an orderly, sensible life. Marissa never rushed into things; she was calm and measured, and Bea admired that. It seemed to her that she had spent so much of her life rushing into things.

Patches of light flitted across the grass. Alice watered the dandelions with her miniature plastic teapot. Rachel hauled herself onto her hands and knees and began to crawl off the blanket, onto the lawn.

A loud *whump* made the air tremble. Rooks rose from the beeches, cawing, ragged black specks against a pallid sky. When the sound died away, the silence was filled by the thudding of Bea's heart.

Alice stared at her, mouth open, teapot in hand. Bea stood up, shivered, and looked out over the trees. Then both women ran towards the side gate. Alice began to wail.

Marissa said, 'I'll go.'

'No. Look after the girls.' Bea was already hurrying away from the cottage.

As she ran up the drive, she saw that to the far side of Hazewell House a thick column of smoke was scrawling in charcoal across the forget-me-not-blue sky. She caught sight of Sandra at the top of the slope, sprinting down the road towards her. Bea didn't know whether it was Clive's car that had crashed or Mitch's, but when Sandra tried to stop her running on towards the plume of smoke, she knew in her heart that it was Clive's. Shoving Sandra aside, she tried to gather speed as she ran, but all the time the air, which was acrid and tasted of oil, kept catching in her throat, so that she felt as if she had forgotten how to breathe.

# Chapter Eight

## 1979–1980

'The most awful morning. Kenneth and Philippa turned up. I wasn't expecting them, and the house was such a mess.' Bea hauled the pushchair and children into Marissa's flat.

'Poor you,' said Marissa sympathetically.

'I had to ask them for money. I hate doing it, it's so humiliating, and I know I ought to be able to manage on my own, but there's an electricity bill, and something's gone wrong with the car – shock absorbers, the man at the garage said. I can't ask Mummy and Daddy again.' Bea unbuckled Rachel and lifted her out of the pushchair.

'Any news on the house?' Marissa was unzipping Alice's raincoat.

'Not yet. You don't mind, do you, us turning up out of the blue? You're not in the middle of something?'

'Nothing that's urgent.' She gave Bea's arm a comforting pat. 'Emma's going to call in. She said she was meeting her mother in town.'

Angie, who was Marissa's part-time assistant, appeared with mugs of coffee, biscuits, and orange squash for Alice and Rachel before retreating to the kitchen table and the accounts.

Marissa took the baby from Bea. 'Hello, beautiful. How's my gorgeous god-daughter? How did it go with Clive's parents?'

'Kenneth has made a chart for me. He's written all my financial things on it.'

'How helpful,' Marissa said with irony.

'Philippa did the washing-up. I didn't *ask* her to, she just did it.' Bea wiped Alice's nose. She had tried to pay attention while her father-in-law was explaining the columns on the chart, but since Clive had died, two months ago, she'd found it hard to concentrate on anything much and could not now remember a single thing Kenneth had said.

'Where are they now?'

'They've gone to Peter Jones, thank goodness, to buy Kenneth new socks.'

Marissa snorted. Bea sat down on the sofa and Alice clung to her. Rachel would have no memories of her father. These days, Alice refused to let Bea out of her sight. Bea knew her daughter was afraid that she too might slip off when she wasn't looking.

'They *blame* me, I know they do!' The words burst out of her.

'Your in-laws? I'm sure they don't.' Marissa hugged her. 'Bea, they're grieving too. Maybe they're just trying to be useful. Maybe that's all they can think of to do to help.'

Bea wiped her eyes. She hated Kenneth's lengthy lectures about financial probity, she resented Philippa tidying up her kitchen without even asking, and she was exhausted by her own churning emotions and her constant anxiety about the future. It wasn't that she didn't understand her situation: she understood completely that she was on her own now, the sole parent of two very small children, and that she had hardly any money. She was also aware that one of the reasons she was angry with her in-laws was because the person she really wanted to be angry with was Clive, for dying at the age of thirty in such a stupid and pointless way. But you couldn't be angry with a dead person.

Clive had left her with shock, grief, guilt and a heap of unpaid bills. To be fair to Kenneth, he must have spent a considerable amount of time trying to disentangle the knotted net of his son's debts. Bea had had no alternative but to put the Islington house on the market – but that would be another grief, leaving the home she had loved from the first day they had moved into it, the home in which she and Clive had given their fabulous parties and nurtured their children. But she couldn't afford to continue to live there now. She was a single parent, responsible for her daughters' well-being, and she alone must compensate for what they had lost and make decisions about a future that felt frightening and precarious.

If only she could rewrite the script, if only she had found the words on that last evening at Hazewell to persuade Clive to agree to return to London. It seared her that she had been planning to leave him on the day he had died. Not leave him for ever, not properly, but still. Had he had an inkling? Was that why he had driven so fast, taken the corner too tightly and skidded into a tree? It tormented her to think that her coldness towards him might have made him angry and reckless. She tiptoed round her memories of that day as if they would burn her.

In the immediate aftermath of the tragedy, it had been Marissa who had comforted her. Bea had tried to hold on to something Marissa had said to her that afternoon. 'Clive was an adult. He made his own decisions. What happened wasn't your fault, Bea. You loved him and he loved you. I saw that. It was as plain as day how much you loved each other.'

Bea's mother had said much the same thing, only more impatiently. 'For heaven's sake, how can you possibly blame yourself? Clive was a sweet man and I was very fond of him, but he always did exactly what he wanted. Men generally do, Bea. Haven't you learned that yet?'

Clive hadn't left her only grief and debts. Though Kenneth Cornwell's calculations revealed the messy turmoil of her marriage, they demonstrated none of its delights. She had two beautiful daughters to treasure, and she had the memory of the years she and Clive had been together. She missed him more than she could possibly express, missed the touch of him, the smell of him, the taste of him. Sometimes she even missed the aspects of him that had infuriated her.

The front doorbell rang. Marissa rose to answer it. Bea's memory darted back to the evening many years ago when she had first met Clive, at a party in a basement in Chelsea. They had talked for hours, and then, later that night, they had driven to the coast. She remembered their midnight journey to Whitstable and the beach where they had kissed. The crystalline sparkle of the stars, the hush of the waves and the warmth of his arms. She was trying to hold on to that too.

Emma arrived at Marissa's flat with her mother, Tamar. Introductions were made and Marissa thanked Emma for the necklaces she had brought with her, which were exquisite, as always. Emma was talented and inventive and had the

153

gift of understanding what was wanted, sometimes even before it was completely clear in Marissa's own mind.

While she talked to Tamar Romilly, Marissa cuddled Rachel, who was dark, like Bea, and plump, with bracelets of chubbiness at her wrists and ankles. Marissa wanted to eat her up, but confined herself to kissing the baby's head. Emma was chatting to Bea. The tragedy of Clive's death had brought the three of them closer together. Thank God, Marissa thought, that Bea had the friendship of a warm, kind woman like Emma.

Emma and Tamar had come straight from a gallery in Rochester Street, where they had been discussing an exhibition that the gallery planned to stage the following year. It was to feature the work of the artist John Cotterell, who was Emma's grandfather and Tamar's father, as well as paintings by Tamar herself.

'Emma told me about the exhibition,' said Marissa to Tamar. 'She's thrilled about it. You must be so excited.'

'It's like a dream. I keep having to pinch myself.'

They talked for a while about the exhibition. Tamar had the same red hair and blue eyes as Emma. Like Emma, she was a striking and attractive woman, but she lacked her daughter's dress sense. During their conversation, Marissa found herself distracted by the awfulness of the older woman's outfit, an ensemble of bright prints. The badly cut, unflattering swathes of fabric swamped her height and slenderness. Where on earth would you even buy such a hideous ensemble? The grimmer recesses of a charity shop, Marissa assumed. The leftovers from a jumble sale.

She said, 'Have you thought what you'll wear for your private view?'

'Not at all.' Tamar gave herself a vague downwards glance. 'Would something like this do, do you think?'

'Certainly not,' said Marissa firmly. 'Come to my shop and I'll help you pick out something lovely. Let me give you my card.'

Tamar went to talk to Emma and Bea. Marissa ground more coffee beans. The decision she must make, which had been preoccupying her for days, kept bobbing to the forefront of her mind. Increasingly, excitement bubbled through the layers of anxiety. She sensed that she was on the verge of a breakthrough. She had only to hold her nerve for her life to be transformed.

Two days ago, she had been in the Margaret Street shop when the phone rang. The person on the other end of the line had introduced herself as Georgina Simmonds, an editor for *Vogue* magazine. Georgina had explained that *Vogue* would like to feature the Marissa Flint label in a piece they were running about up-and-coming young British designers. 'Someone mentioned you,' she said. 'So I sent my assistant to have a mooch round your store, and she absolutely *loved* your stuff.' A shiver ran down Marissa's spine.

The hitch that had prevented her committing there and then had been the magazine's insistence that they publish a photo of her along with the article. 'Surely the clothes should speak for themselves,' she had ventured, rather feebly, but Georgina had brushed that off. 'Our readers like to put a face to the name. The story of your clothes is your own story, Marissa. You are reflected in your label.' All of which sounded reasonable unless you knew the truth: that she was an invention, self-created, a figment of her own imagination.

During the days that had passed since the phone call, she had tortured herself with an image of Jamie flicking through a magazine in that twitchy, restless way of his. He might glance through a discarded copy of *Vogue* on a train. Jamie liked to look at a photo of a pretty girl. In her imagination, she saw him stopping at the feature, his eye caught by her image and putting two and two together. The life she had constructed for herself would disintegrate; her hard-won security would be gone for ever.

And yet she was slowly reasoning herself out of her fear. Everything was going so well for her now. The shop was profitable, and she had moved again, this time out of the bedsit into a small flat. She delighted in her tiny kitchen and separate bedroom. She could have afforded a bigger place, but she was always careful with money and mindful of the future.

The prospect of a feature in *Vogue* was both tantalising and irresistible. It would boost her reputation to a different level altogether, and was such a huge and unexpected seal of approval she couldn't possibly turn it down. As she put on the kettle, Marissa reasoned with herself. What were the chances that Jamie would even bother opening a fashion magazine? He despised such things.

She looked different now. She had changed her name; she had become a different woman. She would insist on wearing dark glasses and a wide-brimmed hat when her photograph was taken. Mary Canterbury was so far behind her, she had diminished to a pinpoint. She wasn't that person any more.

Emma said to Bea, 'Any luck with the house?' and Bea shook her head.

'Not yet. The estate agent told me that a young couple were interested, but they haven't made an offer yet. Clive and I, we never really finished it. The bathroom's such a mess. I keep thinking that's putting people off.'

In the aftermath of the car crash that had killed Clive Cornwell, Marissa had rung Emma, and Emma had driven to Hazewell and taken Alice and Rachel back to the Hoopers' house while Marissa remained with Bea at the cottage to speak to the police and doctor. In the late evening, once the dreadful formalities had been completed, Max had picked up the two women from Hazewell and taken them to Cambridge. Emma remembered how Bea had sat on the sofa in the back room of the Glisson Road house, her expression dazed, vibrating like an over-tightened string.

She was much the same now. She kept picking up her mug of coffee and putting it down without drinking from it. Her gaze constantly darted from one of her daughters to the other, as if afraid that they too might vanish.

Bea said, 'And everything's so fearfully expensive. Even the smallest flat or terraced house seems to cost a fortune.'

'Do you need to be in London, Bea?'

'I suppose not. I sometimes think . . .' The words trailed away.

Tamar said gently, 'Would you consider moving elsewhere?'

'I don't know. I can't decide.'

Bea broke off to gather up Alice, who was crying. The child looped her arms round her mother's neck and buried her flaxen head in her chest. Bea rocked her and murmured comfort.

An autumnal light fell through the window, onto the cutting table. Marissa brought in the coffee mugs and sat down cross-legged on the floor with her friends. Rachel sat on her lap, playing with a string of plastic beads. Alice hid her face in her mother's cardigan. Emma scrabbled in the debris at the bottom of her handbag – biscuit fragments, a dummy, a bottle cap, a biro – and unearthed a Mr Men book. After a few pages, Alice squirmed towards her and listened as Emma read the story.

The phone rang and Marissa got up to answer it. What

would she do, wondered Emma, as she hugged Alice, if something were to happen to Max, leaving her with two infant daughters to look after? Even to think of such a catastrophe seemed dangerous, tempting fate. Would she choose to stay in a place that was familiar to her, or might it be imprinted with too many painful memories?

She said to Bea, 'Mum and I have been talking. We wondered whether you'd think of moving to Cambridge.'

'It was just a thought,' said Tamar. 'Houses are cheaper there, so you'd get more for your money.'

'It's only an hour to London by train; you'd be able to keep in touch with your family and friends. There's a lot going on – theatres, cinema, museums.'

'Good schools, too.'

'Cambridge . . .' repeated Bea.

'Come and stay with us for the weekend.' Emma patted her arm. 'I'll show you round and then you can see what you think. We could go and look at some houses if you like. I love looking round other people's houses. Honestly, Bea, you'd be more than welcome.'

'Think about it.' Tamar gave Bea a warm smile. 'Take your time. See how you feel.'

The conversation moved on. They chatted about the John Cotterell exhibition. Nick Lauderdale wanted to entitle it 'Father and Daughter', which both Emma and Tamar disliked. Many of the exhibits would be seascapes and landscapes. Sitting there in Marissa's flat, they played around with titles, trying to find one that worked.

Tamar said, 'Girls, you'll come to the private view, won't you? Marissa? Bea? It's not for ages, not till next year, but I'd love it if you would both come.'

*

158

After Nick Lauderdale's visit to Seastone in June, Tamar hadn't heard from him again for weeks. Recalling how he had limped around inspecting her paintings, and how she had felt ashamed for the poor neglected things, shut away from human gaze for years, some of them, she had assumed he had had second thoughts and had abandoned his idea of staging an exhibition of her father's work. He had shown an interest in her dusty daubs out of politeness, that was all.

Then, six weeks later, another letter had arrived. Nick Lauderdale had indeed had second thoughts. He was no longer proposing to put on a solo exhibition of John Cotterell's work; instead, he had offered to show her own paintings alongside those of her father.

It was a shock. She was used to bumping along the bottom. It was hard to take in such a change of fortune. She had walked away from the London art world years ago and had become accustomed to pottering. Taking part in the occasional small show in Ipswich, that was her level. The possibility that her career might blossom, that she might unexpectedly achieve success so late in the day, felt jarring. It might be disruptive, she thought. It might knock her off course.

It was eventually settled that the exhibition would be entitled 'Shorelines', which Tamar liked. Three quarters of the pieces were to be by John Cotterell.

'Don't read too much into that,' Nick said to her when they had lunch one day in London. 'I want you to enjoy yourself, Tamar. It'll be an opportunity to introduce you to some useful people. The exhibition will get you noticed, and it'll prepare the ground for your first solo event in a year or so, when you'll take centre stage.'

Tamar felt sometimes as if Nick Lauderdale was talking about some other woman entirely. The sort of woman who thought nothing of exhibiting her work in a London gallery, the sort of woman who was accustomed to dressing in a beautiful outfit by Marissa Flint. On a damp February afternoon, she made her way to Marissa's shop in Margaret Street. After Marissa and her assistant had coaxed her into trying on almost every garment in the store, she purchased a small, elegant capsule wardrobe. 'These should see you through every possible occasion,' Marissa had said to her as the clothes were wrapped in tissue paper and placed in a smart paper carrier. Marissa had made it fun, and the shopping had been less exhausting than Tamar had anticipated. And afterwards they went to the pub, where they drank gin and tonic and went on discovering how much they enjoyed each other's company.

London was too full of memories. The row of shops in which Bea had bought the French bread for their parties, the street in Earls Court where they had lived in the derelict house before they married.

*Think about it. See how you feel*, Tamar Romilly had said to her. The Islington house sold at last, and Bea knew she needed to make a break with the past. Packing up to leave the city, she felt as though she was dismantling the life that she and Clive had made together. Vivien helped her sort out his clothing and personal effects, folding garments for the charity shop and picking out items for Bea to keep – his watch, a gold cigarette case, a tweed jacket. Pressing her face into the soft fabric, she breathed in the familiar scents of Paco Rabanne and Player's cigarettes.

She yearned for the door to open and for Clive to walk into the room. For the past to peel itself away, for everything to be all right again.

\*

The private view was in March. Morgan had a slight cold and at the last minute refused to come, so Tamar travelled to London on her own. Their quarrel was mild, a mere shadow of what they had once been capable of. Their marriage had always been stormy, crashing waves interspersed by patches of glorious sunshine. She would do perfectly well without him, she said to herself. She was to stay in a hotel overnight – oh, the bliss of someone else cooking her breakfast and making her bed!

And now here she was, at the gallery. Emma and Max had arrived, and so had Gale and Rob. Marissa and Bea turned up shortly afterwards. They hugged and congratulated her.

Nick had walked her round the gallery before the event opened. It moved Tamar to see her father's work so beautifully displayed, and there were moments when she fought to keep her emotions under control. Her own paintings seemed, in this austere setting, to take on a life of their own, separate from her, as if she had scarcely been involved in their creation.

Glasses clinked and the chatter was pierced by peals of laughter. After an hour or so, Tamar felt the need to retreat to a quiet corner of the room. She had been introduced to dozens of people, and though it was wonderful to know that so many guests appreciated both her own and her father's work, her face had begun to ache with smiling and her brain was buzzing.

To one side of the gallery, a narrow slice of window revealed a garden in which brick paths, flurried still with half a dozen wet leaves from the previous autumn, wound between ferns and silver birch.

She was looking out of the window when a voice from behind her said, 'I like the way in which the window frames the scene. It makes the garden itself a work of art.'

'So it does.' She turned round. He was around her own age, tall, handsome and distinguished-looking.

He said, 'I believe we've met before, a very long time ago.'

She scrutinised him. 'I don't think so. I don't come to these functions often at all.'

'I'm afraid I go to a great many of them. My name's Alexander Rainsford.'

'Tamar Romilly.' She shook his hand.

'Tamar . . .' He quoted from the Bible. '"A woman of fair countenance." So this is your exhibition then. Congratulations.'

'Thank you, though I would say that it's mostly my father's. And actually I was named after the river, the one between Devon and Cornwall.'

'I see.' He frowned, then said, 'I'm pleased to see that my butterfly pin suits you every bit as well as I thought it would.'

Tamar's hand flew to her hair. Her heart hammered. She gave him a hard stare. Was it possible? 'Alexander?' she said disbelievingly. 'You're *that* Alexander?'

'I am, yes. And so you're Tamar. What an utter idiot I was back then not to ask you your name.'

She laughed, delighted by it all. '*Alexander*. How extraordinary! After all this time!'

Studying him, she was able to make out traces of his hazily remembered younger self, like a pencil outline beneath a painting, from their meeting on the bomb site in 1944. She remembered that he had had fair hair then. Now it was silver-grey. His eyes were a mixture of gold and hazel, and they were clear and amused.

'I recognised you the moment I saw you,' he said. 'Before I saw that you were wearing my grandmother's pin.'

She did not believe him, and said so.

162

'It's true. You haven't changed a bit.'

'You're very flattering, Alexander.'

'You were dressed differently then. A white blouse and a grey skirt, something like that. And you were wearing your hair down.'

'What an excellent memory you have.' It seemed a miracle that they had found each other at last, after thirty-five years.

He said, 'I've only just arrived – I'm afraid I was later than I had intended – but I've had a brief opportunity to look at your work and I think it's remarkable.'

'Thank you, that's so kind.'

'I'm not being kind, Tamar. I've ended up serving on a lot of boards and committees, so I'm obliged to show up to this sort of thing now and then. Depressingly often the work is competent but nothing out of the ordinary. But I see such life and passion in your paintings. I see how you express emotion through your brush, and that's a rare gift.'

His sincerity raised her spirits. Her confidence had always ebbed and flowed. She murmured more thanks.

His smile broadened. 'How marvellous it is to see you again.'

She remembered how, when she had been so young, not yet twenty, she had come to the conclusion that he couldn't have made much of an effort to find her. She had assumed that their encounter outside his bomb-damaged house had not meant as much to him as it had to her. For three years in a row she had sat in the Lyons Corner House, watching the hands of the clock creep round and avoiding the bored glare of the waitress, impatient to clear the table.

And maybe he guessed that she was remembering this, because he said, 'Back then, in 1944, I was posted to France. My battalion fought all the way through to Germany. I was caught in crossfire a few days before the end of the war, which meant that I was rather out of it for a while.'

'I'm sorry. Were you badly hurt?'

'A bit bashed about,' he said, making light of it, she suspected. 'But you recover quickly, don't you, when you're young? I felt bad about having stood you up, Tamar. Though to be honest, I thought you might have forgotten. Or found something better to do.'

'Not at all. I'd promised to take care of the butterfly pin for you, and I did. Were you in Germany for long?'

'Until 1947. After I was discharged from the army, I went back to London. I waited in the Lyons Corner House on the last day of June, as we'd arranged, on the off chance that you might turn up. I knew it was a forlorn hope; that you might understandably have given up on me.'

'But I did go!' she exclaimed. 'That was the last time. I was late, I think – yes, I remember that I was late. Oh Alexander, perhaps we missed each other by moments!'

Again he smiled. 'I bet you were fed up with me, sitting there on your own, eating cake. Tell me what you did after that.'

'I got married.' She had married Morgan in 1948. Theirs had been a passionate courtship, full of heart-wrenching break-ups and glorious reunions.

'Congratulations. How did you meet your husband?'

'I met him in London, during the war.' She remembered coming into the kitchen of Evelyn Carrow's flat and finding Morgan there, eating the mock-apricot flan. 'And then a couple of years after the war had ended, when I was studying art, we came across each other again in Kingston upon Thames, at a party. I was dressed as a lobster, by the way. It was one of those parties.'

'I wouldn't know, I'm afraid. I was never a student. I went from school to the army and then to work in a bank.'

'It was rather hot and cumbersome, being a lobster.'

Her twenty-year-old self, with its mixture of flair and gaucherie, seemed both enviable and foreign to her now. Sometimes she could hardly remember her. 'We had an argument that night, Morgan and I.' She furrowed her brow. 'Figurative art versus abstractionism, something like that. Morgan has always disapproved of the abstract.'

'Morgan . . .' She saw him making connections. 'Are you married to Morgan Romilly?'

'Yes.'

'And your father was John Cotterell?'

So now Alexander knew about her relationship to those twin luminaries of mid-century British art. Perhaps he would ask her to introduce him to Morgan – perhaps she would have to explain that her husband had used a mild cold as an excuse to avoid accompanying her to this event.

But he said, 'Do you mind?'.

'Mind?'

'Fame's a funny thing. It has an effect on those people who are close to it. My grandmother was an actress called Edie Rainsford. I was very fond of her and she always had time for me. The butterfly pin was made for her. There's a painting of her by John Singer Sargent, costumed as Titania and wearing the pin in her hair. She had a great many lovers. Whenever she came into a room, everyone's eyes turned to her, even when she was in her seventies. My mother was a sweet and selfless woman, but she once told me that Edie made her feel invisible. I'm sure it wasn't intentional on my grandmother's part. It was just what she did.'

'Sometimes I've lived in their shadow,' Tamar said. 'My father's and my husband's.'

'I can't imagine you being overshadowed by anyone.'

She felt herself flush – the champagne she had drunk, she assumed. She was long past the age when she blushed at compliments. 'And you, Alexander? Tell me about yourself. Do you have a family?'

'I have a wife, Caroline, and a son, Sebastian. He's twenty-seven and lives in New York.'

'So far away. You must miss him.'

'All the time. Do you have children?'

'Three. Rob's in London, doing this and that. Gale's a midwife at St Thomas's. My eldest, Emma, is married and has two daughters, so I'm a grandmother now. Lucienne and Elizabeth are dear little things.' Tamar caught herself before she could bore him by taking a photograph out of her bag and relating to him incidences of her granddaughters' beauty and cleverness. Talk of grandchildren was permissible only in the company of other grandparents, who understood.

'Is your wife here?' She explored the crowds. She imagined Caroline Rainsford to be dark, sparkling, beautiful.

'She had another engagement. Caroline does a lot of charity work. I haven't seen any of Morgan Romilly's work for a while. Does he still paint?'

How lightly he said this! She felt herself draw back from him then. How little he understood, he with his presumably affluent and perhaps untroubled life. Tamar had a sudden yearning to be back in Seastone. She had remembered how tiresome private views were, how exhausting she found the chit-chat and opinions of strangers.

Because Alexander Rainsford was, after all, a stranger. She didn't know him at all. She could almost touch his aura of comfortable privilege. She had nothing in common with him. Perhaps she never had.

'Morgan's moved on,' she said lightly. 'He's concentrating on prints now.' Morgan's war injuries had left him with intermittent tremors. He was no longer capable of the fine and much-admired detail of his early paintings. He had cut himself off from the art world so that he might find equilibrium, which even now sporadically deserted him.

She put her hands up to her hair, to the butterfly pin. 'Let me give this back to you.'

'Not at all, I wouldn't dream of it.' His fingers brushed against hers, preventing her from unclasping the pin. 'I hope you've worn it often. I hope it's given you pleasure.'

In an instant, her hostility faded. 'I've always loved it. I remember you told me that butterflies were a symbol of transformation. I wear it when I want my life to change.'

'Do you want it to change now?'

'I don't know. I'm not sure. Perhaps.' She looked back at the crowds in the gallery and caught sight of Nick Lauderdale carving a route towards her, a dignitary in tow. 'Alexander, forgive me, but I'm afraid I have to go.'

Again her hand went to her hair, but he smiled and said, 'Give it back to me some other time. We'll see each other again, I'm sure of it.'

# PART TWO

# FRIENDS AND FAMILY

# Chapter Nine

## 1980–1983

After the Islington house was sold, and after Bea had paid off Clive's remaining debts, she bought a two-bedroom terraced house in Cambridge, in Sedgwick Street, a short walk from where Emma and Max lived in Glisson Road.

Once the boxes were unpacked, the Sedgwick Street house began to look like a home. There was a small amount of cash left over from the sale of the London house, and both Bea's own father and Kenneth Cornwell paid into her bank account each month a sum of money to help with the children. So as long as she was careful, she could manage. She found work teaching French in a language school two evenings a week. Emma babysat when she was working, and in return Bea looked after Emma's children, Lucienne and baby Elizabeth, two mornings a week, so that Emma had time to make her papier-mâché necklaces for Marissa. Whenever she was free, Marissa joined them all for Sunday lunch at the Hoopers' house.

Both Bea and Emma were at that stage in their lives when they were busy all the time. There was always a child to be fed or changed, food to be bought and cooked, washing to be done, activities organised. Work must be fitted with ingenuity and forethought into narrow slivers of the day. Conversations were snapped in half by a child who needed their attention. They talked while they were pushing their buggies across Parker's Piece, while they were watching the girls on the slide and while they were running across the grass to stop Rachel investigating a discarded cigarette packet.

They were always in and out of each other's houses, picking up the threads of the previous day's conversation. The Hoopers' house was large and untidy and welcoming. On the sofa were heaps of books and toys or ironing that must be moved if you wanted to sit down. The table in the back room was covered with art projects – lumps of papier mâché in various stages of construction, a painting Emma was halfway through, an architectural drawing of Max's and the girls' splodgy, colourful daubs. Tamar and Morgan or Max's parents might be staying, or Emma's brother Rob or Max's brother Adam would turn up and join them for the evening meal. A neighbour returned something borrowed, a woman from playgroup dropped off a cake for a bring-and-buy sale. A mug of tea in the afternoon turned into a supper of fish fingers and baked beans, until eventually Bea ambled home and put Alice and Rachel to bed.

Marissa remained the person to whom Bea could say anything. Every Saturday evening, no matter how busy she was, Marissa took the train to Cambridge after the Margaret Street shop closed. She stayed overnight in Sedgwick Street and looked after the girls on Sunday morning so that Bea had a break. Most weekday evenings, the two of them talked on the phone. It was Marissa who comforted her when she was low, who gave her encouragement when she was doubting herself and who told her funny anecdotes about her customers to make her laugh. Marissa was the backbone of her life, the person to whom she could open her heart. Bea might not herself have an ounce of Marissa's ambition, and Marissa might not really understand Bea's compulsion to escape stuffy middle-class conformity, but they were close to each other and they shared everything.

Grief trailed after her, grabbing at the hem of her coat to catch her attention. A gesture of Alice's that so perfectly mirrored one of Clive's. A man glimpsed on the other side of the road who had Clive's height and his confident bouncing walk. She would go into a Mill Road health food shop frequented by students and breathe in aromas of turmeric and paprika, and remember Clive picking out vegetables from a market stall, and Clive standing at the stove in the Islington house, cooking one of his enormous curries or goulashes that would last them the week.

She was managing, just. But she was tired, so tired. And perhaps Tamar noticed that, because it was she who made the suggestion when Bea was at Emma's house one Saturday and the three of them were clearing up after supper.

'Why don't you come and stay with us at Seastone for a weekend? I'll ask Marissa too. You could bring the girls if you wanted to, or you could see if your parents, for instance, could look after them. You wouldn't have to do a thing. You need a break, Bea. You've had a tough time.'

Tears stung Bea's eyes, but she managed to hold them back. She imagined walking along a beach, breathing in salt air. Sun warming her skin and two whole days with no washing, cooking or cleaning.

'I'd like that,' she said. 'I'd like it very much.'

*

She waded out of the tear-shaped lagoon that had formed within the shingle spit at Seastone, then hauled herself up the slope, costume dripping, bare feet sludging into the pebbles.

Emma passed her a towel. Bea sat beside her on top of the bank and rubbed her hair. The sun warmed her and melted away some of the stresses of the past year.

She and Emma had arrived at Seastone the previous afternoon. Seastone wasn't like Whitstable or Bournemouth, seaside towns with which Bea had been familiar since childhood. There were no cafés, no pier or arcades, no golden sand. Just a vast shingle bank and a little row of houses and a big sky. Tamar and Morgan's house was at the end of the row. On first sight, Bea fell in love with the peeling weatherboarding and the poppy-red door and window frames. When she looked out of the window in the back room, she saw a distant silver ribbon of sea.

Her parents were taking care of Alice and Rachel. It felt strange not having the girls with her, but they adored their grandparents. Marissa had joined them for supper on Saturday evening, after driving from London once the shop had closed. After the meal, the four women sat and talked into the small hours. Bea and Marissa slept in Rob's old room, where Airfix planes dangled from the ceiling and pencil sketches of seabirds were sellotaped to the walls. The house was crammed with paintings and drawings and shells and sea glass, and it had an immense and restful charm.

This morning, Bea didn't wake until almost ten. Emerging heavy-limbed and bleary-eyed, she couldn't recall when she had last slept so deeply. Tamar made her toast and tea, which she took out to where Emma and Marissa sat on the beach. There was a huge sapphire sky and a calm sea and not a great deal else. Strange fleshy-leaved plants grew in the shingle.

The sun dried off the beads of moisture that speckled her limbs. Bea had the oddest feeling. It was as though while she had been swimming in the lagoon, a weight had slipped from her and sunk into the depths. As if she had stepped out of the still, tepid water a slightly different person from when she went in. She wasn't okay yet, she thought, but she was getting there.

The following summer, they went back to Seastone. They took all four girls with them that time, because Jack and Vivien were cruising on the Rhine and Max was away in Scotland, working on a project. Picnics in the garden and outings to Aldeburgh and Southwold, and a mad afternoon when they searched for large pebbles and piled them into towers, which grew out of the shingle like stalagmites. A sudden violent shower of rain sent them all running for the house, laughing and shrieking. The asphalt roof on Morgan's studio flapped in the gale, making a sound like the beat of an enormous drum.

Two years had passed. Grief was a familiar companion, but it had become quiet and soft now, licking like a wave at Bea's toes, impossible to ignore but more bearable. In the early summer of 1982, while the Task Force was sailing across the Atlantic towards the Falkland Islands, Rachel began to attend a local playgroup. By then, Alice had been attending primary school for two terms. On her first child-free morning, Bea mooched around. She stopped to talk to a friend, bought a *Guardian*, and then sat in her long, thin garden, taking her time over a coffee. She skimmed through the newspaper and gave a mental shudder as her gaze ran over a photo of warships and a map of South Georgia. There were things you could protect your children from and events over which you had no control whatsoever.

She folded up the newspaper and put it aside. She felt as if she'd been sprinting for ages and now, at last, could take a breath. She didn't think she'd done too badly. They had a home, they were solvent, more or less, and Alice and Rachel were happy and healthy. She loved them so much it sometimes hurt, but oh God, the pleasure of a morning off.

Bea didn't *deliberately* start giving parties again. She happened to mention to a few friends that she was at home on Friday evening, then opened a couple of bottles of wine and put out cheese and crackers, and people just seemed to *gather*. Emma and Max and Marissa, of course, and maybe a boyfriend of Marissa's now and then, though they never lasted long, poor dears. And then there were Bea's neighbours and the mothers she met outside Alice's school, with their husbands in tow. They danced in the back room to Dexys Midnight Runners or David Bowie, the volume turned down low because the girls were asleep and the walls of the house were thin. When the weather was fine, they spilled out into the garden.

She invited the people she'd met at the language school, too. By then, she had known her colleague Francis Lockwood for more than a year. Francis was in his mid thirties, a fluent French speaker who taught during the day at a boys' prep school in Cambridge. His eyes and hair were light brown and he was slim and lithe and of medium height. His expressive face had an impish look, Bea thought, and when he smiled, which he did a lot, his mouth tilted up at the corners and his brows rose into little peaks and his eyes widened as if he found everything funny as well as delightful. Because Bea was invariably in a rush to get the girls fed and settled before she set out, she often arrived late at the language school. Francis always had a mug of coffee ready and waiting for her. At three minutes to seven, he would rinse his own mug under the tap, give her his quirky smile, then say, 'So, onwards and upwards!' before heading off to the classroom.

One of the other teachers told Bea that Francis was divorced. 'Apparently Deborah was a complete nightmare,' she confided. 'The dramatic sort, always picking quarrels and storming off.' Bea felt sorry for him and suggested they meet up at the weekend. She and Francis fell into the habit of seeing each other on Sunday afternoons, after Marissa had headed off for the London train. She liked that he was neither bored by small children nor clueless with them.

One day, after an hour at the playground on Jesus Green, he invited them to his home in Portugal Place, a stone's throw away. Portugal Place was a pretty pedestrian alleyway that led through to St Clement's Church and Bridge Street. A camellia in a pot flourished by the blue front door of a whitewashed terraced house, and a window box hung from iron railings. Francis ushered the three of them through to a room attractively decorated with apple-green Laura Ashley wallpaper, at the back of the house. French doors looked out onto a courtyard garden. Rachel explored, stroking a dusty pot plant, pressing a piano key. Bea sprang up to stop her, but Francis said, 'No, no, I don't mind at all, a piano should be played.' Alice stood aside, looking on, her thumb in her mouth. Francis found her paper and pencils and she knelt on the floor to draw.

'I'll make us some coffee,' he said. 'What would Alice and Rachel like to drink?'

Bea followed him into the kitchen to help. Francis took mugs out of the cupboard.

'I'm afraid it has the look of a bachelor's home,' he said.

'Not at all,' said Bea, though it did. There were no vases of flowers, and a stack of old copies of the Times yellowed on the dining table. She pictured Francis leafing through one while he ate alone. The air in the kitchen was stale and she wondered if he ever thought of opening a window.

'It's a charming house,' she said. 'I love the wallpaper.'

'Deborah chose it. She was so clever at that sort of thing. I haven't a clue about cushions and rugs.'

'She had good taste.'

'But a cold heart.' He gave a theatrical shudder.

'When did you two break up?'

'Two years ago. It was horrendous. I hadn't realised what she was like before we married, so jealous and overemotional. There were some appalling scenes. I can't bear scenes. It took me months to recover.' He peered in a cupboard, then said doubtfully, 'There is some orange squash, but it may be rather old.'

'A little milk will be fine. You must have found it hard to get used to being on your own again.'

He gave her a sympathetic glance. 'I shouldn't complain. So much worse for you, Bea, such a tragedy. To tell the truth, it was in some ways a relief when Deborah left, so much more peaceful, though of course I was desperately sad that it hadn't worked out. When she went out of the front door that last time – when she slammed the door – I'm afraid I breathed a little sigh of relief.'

'Where is she now?'

'Trumpington.'

'Trumpington?' Trumpington was on the other side of Cambridge. Bea had pictured Deborah flouncing off somewhere further afield.

Francis put a hand to his heart, as if suppressing palpitations. 'Occasionally I catch sight of her. I always run a mile.'

'How awful for you. Clive and I, we had rows too.'

'Bea, show me a married couple who don't quarrel now and then.'

Bea thought of Emma and Max. She had never heard them argue. It didn't seem helpful to say that to Francis, yet she felt compelled to be honest about Clive.

'It was more than now and then, I'm afraid.'

He had picked up the tray; he put it down then, and said seriously, 'Do you think it's possible for a man and a woman to live together amicably?'

'I do, yes. But then I'm an incurable optimist. Do you?'

'Oh *yes!* I'm absolutely sure of it. It's just a question of meeting the right person.'

Francis opened the French doors, put the tray on the table in the courtyard, realised he had forgotten to bring teaspoons and hurried off to fetch them. Someone had made an effort here, Bea noticed as she looked round at the bright pelargoniums in blue glazed pots, the yellow rambling rose and a terracotta trough planted with herbs. She wondered whether Francis or Deborah had done the gardening.

He returned with the teaspoons. 'I took the job at the language school after Debs walked out,' he said. 'I needed something to do on my spare evenings. I have choral society on Monday and madrigal group on Wednesdays. I was a chorister when I was a boy, at Lincoln Cathedral, but then my voice broke. I'm a passable tenor, no more, but I do love to sing. Music is my passion. I play squash a couple of nights a week, so that only leaves Sunday evenings here on my own, and I have my marking to keep me busy then.'

He glanced over his shoulder at Alice's drawing. 'What's that, Alice? Is it a lion? Did you know there's a lion living in my garden?' He dropped down onto his hands and knees and prowled round the courtyard, an unthreatening lion, roaring mildly and pretending to nibble the plants. Alice looked on, amazed, then began to laugh.

Bea poured the coffee while Francis was being a lion. She had tried to be both mother and father to her daughters but didn't feel she made a good job of it. Clive had been better at the rough-and-tumble play. It was depressing to think that she was usually too busy or too tired to pretend to be a lion.

Before they left half an hour later, she mentioned to Francis that she had invited some people to her house the following Friday. 'Do come along if you'd like to,' she said. 'Though I know you must have things to do.'

'Nothing that can't wait.' He beamed at her. 'So long as you haven't had enough Francis for one week.'

She laughed. As the three of them set off for Sedgwick Street, she thought about Francis and Deborah. It sounded as though Deborah had been attention-seeking, given to raising her voice and criticising, which Francis, who was a gentle soul, must have hated. She sensed that he was lonely. She had learned that there were different kinds of loneliness. She remembered him prowling leonine round the paving slabs and thought of his strong shoulders, narrow hips and fluid movements, and of the way his softly curling nut-brown hair brushed against the collar of his shirt. When he had

180

raised his head to roar, she had seen that his profile was perfectly, classically Grecian.

She had been to bed with a man only a couple of times since Clive had died. Both times had been, frankly, rather disastrous. It wasn't that she didn't feel desire, and though pregnancy and childbirth hadn't done her figure any favours and a flabby bit lingered annoyingly round her middle, men made it clear that they found her attractive. But nothing had worked out. She had come across men who thought a widow must be desperate for sex on any terms, and men who made a hasty exit as soon as they discovered she had two small children. Or worse, who regarded Alice and Rachel as a nuisance. 'Isn't there anyone who'll take them off somewhere for a while?' one would-be boyfriend had moaned, thus sealing his fate.

Risk-takers, thrill-seekers and spendthrifts, she had ruled them out too, for obvious reasons, not to mention gorgeous Irish boys who ran for the hills as soon as things became difficult. She mustn't make another mistake. She had loved Clive, but they hadn't been perfectly suited; she had come to accept that had he lived, their marriage might not have lasted. She had loved Ciaran too, but it had been a wild, rash sort of love, and she had no desire to experience that ever again. Any future affair of the heart must be rational and thoroughly considered. She no longer looked for passion: friendship and security and sexual compatibility would do.

She must protect her daughters and set a good example to them, so no one-night stands, no ill-judged involvements she might later regret. Falling in love too easily was one of her faults. A pair of blue eyes, a walk on a moonlit beach, and there she was, head over heels. She had learned too well how love hurt. Letting herself fall in love again would

181

be like running the tip of a knife over her skin and waiting for the blood to bead.

On Friday evening, after she'd put the girls to bed, she changed into her favourite red Zandra Rhodes dress. She always thought of Clive when she wore it. It was, after all, Clive who had taught her how to throw a party.

She was putting out deckchairs on the lawn when the first of the guests rang the doorbell. Francis turned up an hour later, wearing a flamboyant buttercup-yellow shirt. People sat in deckchairs or sprawled on grass that had gone thin and straw-coloured this warm summer of 1983. Now and then, while she was topping up wine glasses, her gaze turned to Francis. She had known him for more than a year, yet only recently had she felt physically attracted to him. Or perhaps it was only recently that she had allowed herself to be attracted to him.

She found it hard to tell what he thought about her, because he seemed to treat everyone with the same genial good nature. They had not so much as held hands, let alone kissed. A friendly pat on the shoulder as he stood aside to let her go first down the narrow stairs at the language school: that had been the extent of their contact.

She went to sit beside him. 'Reminds me of the south of France,' he said.

Everyone was saying the same thing: how marvellous it was to sit out past nine o'clock in an English summer without feeling cold. 'I remember once,' she said, 'when I was in Provence with my grandmother, me and my cousin stayed awake all night, it was so warm.'

'You have family in France?'

'My mother's mother is French.'

'That's why your accent is so good. So much better than

182

mine. I'm envious.' He gave her his amused smile, then scrutinised her in the fading light. 'I can see it now that you say it. You have a French look about you. Your dark eyes and dark hair. I'm as dull as ditchwater, drearily English through and through.'

'Francis, you're anything but dreary.'

'I'm glad you think so.' Lightly he touched her hand.

When night fell, the remaining guests retreated into the back room. A friend had made a party tape and couples danced to it. Bea wanted Francis to ask her to dance, but he didn't. She could ask him, yet she was reluctant to. Perhaps he felt sorry for her, a widow with two small children, or perhaps that fleeting touch of the hand, which had seemed to jolt her awake, making her feel whole and alive again, had been an affirmation of friendship. Friendship should be enough for her, she said to herself sternly.

The last of the stragglers left, murmuring regrets about babysitters as they retrieved bags and jackets from the hall. Bea went upstairs to check on the girls. When she came down, only Francis remained.

'It was just Rachel,' she said, 'making noises in her sleep.'

'Dance with me, Bea.'

They went into the back room, where Soft Cell's 'Tainted Love' murmured seductively on the cassette player. He took her in his arms and she rested her head against his shoulder. The room, with its clutter of Barbies with missing limbs and handle-less mugs containing coloured felt tips, receded. First his cheek brushed against her hair, then his mouth. She couldn't kid herself any longer that she wanted Francis Lockwood merely as a friend, because the warmth of his arms and the scent of his skin were intoxicating to her. His palm, tracing the curve of her waist and hip, stirred up a hunger inside her that she had repressed for too long, and she tilted her face up to kiss him. The kiss obliterated all her usual preoccupations: the children, work, money. She was lost in the cool, soft touch of his lips and the heavenly sensation as he stroked the nape of her neck.

When the track finished, Francis murmured, 'You know that I'm madly in love with you, don't you, Bea?'

It was as if he had chucked a bucket of icy water over her. She took a step back.

'Well, I am. You don't mind, do you?'

She shook her head. She thought he was going to say something more, but then he seemed to change his mind. All she wanted was to hustle him outside, to shut the door behind him, to be on her own again.

She mumbled about it being late. In the hall, they kissed again and then she almost pushed him out of the front door. She sat down on the stairs, feeling exhausted and confused. Francis falling in love with her wasn't part of her plan. She had thought she might be ready to embark on another relationship, but she wasn't. She had more or less got her life under control and wasn't going to mess it up again. Better to stick to writing her shopping lists, to adding up her cheque stubs and marking her students' exercises and making sure Alice and Rachel brushed their teeth.

That night, she had the dream again. The dark corridors of the deserted Underground station were familiar to her, though that did nothing to lessen their menace. She searched the dusty floors and tiled passageways for her baby son, peering under benches and into litter bins as if he might be hidden there, like a terrorist's bomb. As always, she had the feeling that she had been negligent and had somehow mislaid him. Dragging herself awake, she was sweaty and shaking and her face was wet with tears. Knowing she would find no easy route back to sleep, she went downstairs and made herself a cup of tea. Wine glasses from the party stood on the work surface, to be washed in the morning. Oh my God, what on earth are you doing, Bea Cornwell? she muttered to herself as she ferreted around looking for a clean mug. Letting yourself feel attracted to Francis Lockwood . . . what an *idiot* you are!

Eventually she slept. Waking in the morning, she found herself thinking about Francis. Prowling round his garden on all fours, pretending to eat the plants. How he had put Alice at ease. The countless mugs of coffee he had made ready and waiting for her when she arrived at work. The sensation of his slim, lithe body against hers.

She thought of calling him but did not. She knew she wasn't being fair, that she was doing to him what Ciaran had done to her, running for cover because she was afraid of emotional involvement. If she was frightened of love, it was likely that he, who had been through a divorce, felt the same. In telling her that he loved her, he had been brave and honest.

She spent Saturday at the Hoopers' house, only returning to Sedgwick Street when it was time to put the girls to bed. Marissa arrived while she was arranging the bunch of yellow roses she had found propped up against her front door. She would cool it down, she said to Marissa later, over a glass of wine. She would make it clear to Francis that she was only interested in friendship. Not that there was much to cool down, only a kiss or two.

'Do you like him?' asked Marissa.

'Yes.'

'A lot?'

'I think so.'

'Do you trust him?'

'He's a good man. Gentle. Considerate. But Marissa . . .'

Marissa, who was looking stunningly elegant in blue jeans and a white silk shirt – a rash choice in a household of biscuit crumbs and felt tips left in crevices in sofas – gave her a clear-eyed look.

'You're thirty, Bea. Do you mean to avoid intimacy for the rest of your life?'

This was a bit rich, Bea thought resentfully, coming from a woman who rarely turned up with the same boyfriend twice.

And Marissa must have read her mind, because she grinned and said, 'I know . . . pots, kettles and all that. But we're not the same, you and I. I'm not looking for a long-term relationship. I'll never marry, you know that. All I'm saying is, maybe go on a date with him. See what happens. See what he's like. And if it doesn't work out, or if you're not sure, then . . .' She shrugged and smoothed back her short fair hair. 'Then you can drop him, can't you?'

After her lesson finished on Tuesday evening, Francis was in the corridor, waiting for her. He asked if he could walk her home and they headed out of the building.

The hot late-summer air was like a warm flannel over her face. As they turned the corner of Norfolk Street onto East Road, they both spoke at the same time.

'I'm sorry . . .'

They laughed, which broke the tension. He offered her his arm and she tucked her hand through it. He said, 'I didn't mean to be pushy.'

'You weren't.'

'Bea, I messed up. You can say so.'

'No, you didn't, honestly. It's me.'

Francis had eyes like a robin's, brown and darting, and just now there was a wounded expression in them. 'I don't mean that I'm not very fond of you,' she said kindly. 'It just took me by surprise, that's all.'

He was silent for a while. Perhaps he was trying to gather his thoughts. Then he said, 'This isn't a whim, Bea. The first time I saw you, I was swept away. It was like a thunderbolt. God, what a cliché, but it's true, I looked at you and I just knew. When I heard about your husband, obviously I held back. I wasn't going to go blazing in like a bull in a china shop. But I love you, Bea, and I'm going to go on loving you. For me, this is it.'

They cut through the park on the corner of Mill Road. The leaves on the trees drooped in the heat, black and limp. A handful of teenagers sprawled on the swings, scuffing their shoes on the tarmac as they swung back and forth. The smoke from their cigarettes made clouds in the darkening air.

She felt a mixture of fear and excitement. 'I've found it . . . safer, I think, not to get fond of anyone.'

'I've no idea of what you've been through, Bea. I can't have. Only someone who's lost a partner can know. But I do know what it's like to fall in love, madly and deeply, and then for it to go all wrong. I know what it's like to find yourself on your own, to have to start again from scratch. I'm not in love with you just because you're beautiful, if that's what you're thinking. I love you because you're kind and sweet-natured . . . and so, so sensible as well.'

She stopped, turned to face him and gave a bark of laughter. 'Sensible? Oh Francis, if only you knew! I'm anything but. If you had any sense, you'd run a mile.'

'You shouldn't talk about yourself like that, Bea. You're amazing and you're wonderful and I absolutely adore you.'

Cross with him, she snapped, 'Be quiet. Don't say anything at all, I can't bear it. Please listen.'

As they walked past the Turkish cafés and wholefood shops, she told him about Ciaran and her baby boy. In the years that had passed since Patrick had been born, she had told her story to only a handful of people. Francis wasn't a gossip and she trusted him not to be judgemental.

Finishing, she said, with a small laugh, 'You needed to know about my awfully chequered past.'

'Oh, a great many of us have one of *those*,' he said feelingly.

'Not to the same degree.'

'No, of course not, I wouldn't compare—'

'I'm not trying to score points, not saying my problems are worse than yours, anything like that. But if you mean what you say, you need to know how lousy my judgement's been in the past. I wouldn't want to . . . Oh dear, this is coming out all wrong. I can see you're a kind person, Francis, a good person. And I'm attracted to you. But I find it hard to trust myself. I've been a soft-hearted idiot too often.'

'It's not idiotic to fall in love.'

'Isn't it? When it leaves such *wreckage*?'

'It takes . . . Falling in love takes . . .' Light from a street lamp poured shadows beneath his cheekbones and hollowed out his eyes. His features were delicate for a man, she thought. Oh dear, she wanted to kiss him again.

'Is one ever ready for love, Bea? Don't you think it takes a leap of faith? It's not something you can work out in your head, is it? You have to feel it *here*.' He clenched his fist and put it to his chest.

'Was that how you felt about Deborah?'

'Oh yes! I was so much in love with her. It was only later I realised she could be hurtful and cruel.'

They hopped off the pavement to make way for an old man with a carrier bag of laundry. Bea said with a sigh, 'When I was younger, I thought love was the answer to everything. That if only I could meet The One, I'd be happy, I'd feel grown up and my life would be sorted out.'

'You're a romantic, Bea. There's nothing wrong in that.'

'There's a great deal wrong with it. It's stupid and naïve and people end up getting hurt.'

They walked over the railway bridge. A train clattered through the darkness, breaking the quiet between them and leaving in its wake a hot, dusty, metallic tang.

Francis said bitterly, 'Have I ever told you how long my marriage lasted? Eighteen months. Eighteen piddling, pathetic months. Afterwards, I met someone on the rebound. That didn't last either.' At the top of the arch, he looked down to the track. 'One feels such a fool. You say *you're* hopeless, but Bea, I can be my own little disaster area.'

Bicycles sped along the road, bringing with them flurries of cooler air. They passed the rich, spicy scents of a curry house, then the oilier aromas of a fish and chip shop.

'I can't afford to make another mistake,' she said. 'I have to think of the girls.'

'I *completely* understand. Naturally you must put them first. They are such delightful little creatures. Deborah didn't want children, and I felt the same way, but Alice and Rachel are adorable. Bea, you've had such a tough time, and my God, you must be a strong person to have gone through all those horrors without ending up bitter or broken. I wanted to shut myself in a *cupboard* after Debs left and never open the door again. But one has to battle on, don't you think?'

'I suppose so.'

'I promise I'll never try to rush you. I promise I'll never ask you for something you don't feel able to give.'

Beneath her turmoil, Bea was aware of a smouldering excitement. She liked him, she wanted him. Did she dare to try again? *All I'm saying is, maybe go on a date with him.* Perhaps Marissa was right. She felt her resistance faltering.

They turned into Sedgwick Street. Here, the pavement was narrow, so to walk side by side they must huddle up to each other. Francis put his arm round her and drew her closer. Behind the front window of a house, a parrot dozing on a perch opened its eyes and ruffled its feathers as they passed.

They reached her house. Francis said, 'I won't ask if I can come in. I know you need time to think about it. And if you'd rather we went on being just friends and colleagues, then that's fine with me. What I couldn't bear is if you were to shut me out of your life. I love you, Bea, I love you so much. And the truth is, whenever I look at you, my heart sings.'

Could she trust him? Could she trust herself not to make another mistake? It came to her that she could never be sure, that it was impossible to be sure. As Francis had said, love took a leap of faith.

She unlocked the door. Taking his hand in hers, she led him into the house.

# Chapter Ten

## 1985

When she came out of the Harley Street consulting rooms, it was drizzling. Looking up, Marissa was surprised to catch sight of Tamar Romilly walking ahead of her on the other side of the road. She recognised her instantly because of her height and her red hair, but though she squinted, she could see only the back of Tamar's tall, silver-haired companion.

She thought of hurrying to catch up with them, to say hello, but dropped the idea. She knew she would not be good company. Tamar's friend put a protective arm around her, steering her through the crowds.

Marissa raised a hand and a taxi drew up. 'Floral Street, please,' she said.

Her appointment had taken longer than expected. There was still so much to be done at the new shop, her second Marissa Flint shop, in Covent Garden, which was opening in less than four weeks' time, though just now that seemed an impossibility. Her manager, David Johnstone, had sounded tense when they had spoken on the phone that morning.

David was a Scot: quiet, clever, efficient and brooding, emotionally contained.

Angie met her at the door of the shop. 'David's in the back room,' she said.

'How bad is it?'

Angie was one of the calmest people Marissa knew. It was a bad sign when she pursed her lips, which she did now. 'It's a bit of a mess,' she said.

'Has the shelving turned up? And Conrad? Has he called?'

'I've just been on the phone to the manufacturers about the shelving. They've promised to get back to me this morning. We haven't been able to track down Conrad yet.'

'Where on earth is he? How can he be so flaky?'

'David's chasing him up, Marissa. He'll sort it out.'

You could have fitted the tiny Margaret Street shop into the new premises half a dozen times over. Looking round the area that would become the showroom, Marissa saw that progress had been slight since she had inspected it the previous morning. Only one wall was painted, and the floorboards were still scuffed and spattered with plaster. There was the smell of dust and paint. Planks of wood, to be assembled into a framework for changing rooms, made a tower that she skirted round.

She greeted the workmen, then went through the changing area to the room at the back of the building, which would eventually become her design studio. David had phoned early that morning to tell her that when the builders had taken down the panelling, they had found damp. The three of them, Marissa, David and the foreman, Guy, stared at the patch of grey bloom. Angie brought her a cup of coffee and Marissa drank it gratefully. She hadn't had lunch, but she didn't feel hungry.

There were days when she could clearly see in her mind's eye what this echoing, chaotic place would become, days when she could believe that a spacious showroom, with her clothes hanging on uncluttered rails, and chairs upholstered in soft gold corduroy, sourced from her supplier in Lancashire, would spring up and create a harmonious whole. Days when she could picture the one or two attractive pieces of furniture her interior designer would find and the exquisite ceramic bowls that would set them off. The area behind the showroom was to house the comfortable private changing rooms and fitting area. Behind that – and whenever she thought about this, she felt a zing of excitement – there would be a large, high-ceilinged, well-lit studio. This would house cutting tables, drawing boards and desks for Marissa and her staff. There would be a mood board, rolls of fabric on shelves, and baskets containing trims, buttons and buckles. She was going to create a workspace that would inspire her and her team.

And yet today it was hard to hold on to her vision, and her investment seemed rash. A long time ago she had worked out that the only cure for anxiety was action. Tackle the most important problems. Smile, remain even-tempered and cheerful. You can get through anything, she reminded herself as she set to work. You've done it before.

This afternoon, she had other concerns, but she put them aside to be looked at later. She spoke to Guy about the damp, and together they pinned down a schedule of repair. David would track down Conrad Wright, who was handling publicity for the new shop. At mid afternoon, Marissa and Angie escaped to a nearby café, where, over a pot of coffee, they compiled a long to-do list.

The builders left at four, after Marissa had extracted a

promise from them to finish the plastering the following day. By six, Angie had tracked down the glass shelves that had been lost en route between Frankfurt and London and had rearranged delivery. David was still trying to get in touch with Conrad.

At eight o'clock, Marissa thanked her staff and told them to go home. At the door, Angie asked her whether she would like a drink.

'Thanks, but I've a date.'

Angie blew her a kiss. 'Enjoy.'

In the lavatory at the back of the building, Marissa touched up her make-up and coaxed her hair into place. She was wearing a black jersey Marissa Flint skirt and jacket over a sand-coloured fine-knit short-sleeved jumper that she had had for years and had repaired several times. The clothes she designed would take a woman from work to a dinner date. What woman in the mid eighties had time to go home, shower, redo her hair and make-up, and change? She put on her coat and left the premises.

She met her boyfriend, Ed Sykes, in a curry restaurant in Brick Lane. They had bumped into each other – literally; he was rather clumsy – four months ago, in the Crush Room of the Royal Opera House. They had seen each other several evenings a month since then. Ed lived in Battersea and did something clever with computers, for which he was paid a lot of money. In manner, he was easy-going and unhurried, funny and absent-minded, and Marissa found his taut, wiry body desirable. Though she could have helped him dress better, could have picked out shirts and a jacket for him, she didn't. It would have implied too much of an investment.

The two of them liked to talk politics, where they were largely in agreement, both being rather left-wing, and they shared a relish for the more wildly imaginative science fiction and fantasy novels. For all his scruffy appearance, Ed was, like her, fiercely ambitious. Their tastes were sufficiently different to be interesting. He loved the cinema but was restless when he accompanied her to an art gallery. Marissa tended to doze off during a long art-house film.

Over poppadoms and pickles, they enjoyed sharing their pleasure in the news that Labour was at last ahead of the Conservatives in the polls. The food was good, and Marissa's appetite returned. But after a while, she seemed to run out of steam. There was Ed, venting his disgust about the miserable, long-drawn-out end of the year-long miners' strike. She had seen the television footage of Grimethorpe Colliery miners marching under their banners back to the pits, the brass band playing. Yet her mind veered off elsewhere.

Away from the frenetic pace of her work, all she could think of was the Harley Street consulting room and her gynaecologist's diagnosis. What would Ed say if she tried to share her feeling of desolation with him? He would attempt to be kind, but he would be out of his depth. She knew that this relationship would go the way of all her other ones, because there wasn't enough between them to sustain it. She and Ed liked each other, they were attracted to each other, but they would never love each other. Soon one of them would face up to that, and then it would end.

Once or twice in the past she had thought about going to see a therapist so that she could talk in confidence to a professional about what had happened to her. But even the idea of it made her feel simultaneously bored and edgy. She didn't want to dig all that up, and anyway, she hardly needed a therapist to point out to her that whenever she suspected herself of growing emotionally close to a man, she dropped him. As for marriage, that was not a possibility. She didn't know whether Jamie had divorced her for desertion. She hoped he had. Whatever steps he had taken, the institution of marriage repelled her. Though many years had gone by since she had last looked down a crowded Underground platform and imagined she saw Jamie Canterbury, and though nowadays months passed in which she did not think of him at all, that time in her life had left its legacy.

After the meal, she made an excuse not to go home with Ed and instead took a taxi back to Tufnell Park. There she poured herself a large glass of wine and tidied the kitchen, putting away the breakfast things, cleaning the work surface and buffing the stainless-steel sink until it shone. In the living room, she plumped up the cushions on the navy-blue corduroy sofa. It was from Heal's and had been an extravagance, a present she had given herself when four years ago she had moved into this larger rented flat. At first it had seemed strange to have so much space to herself, but she had become used to it and now revelled in it. She was still trying to get used to other accoutrements of middle-class London life, to not worrying about the cost of taking a taxi and not feeling guilty about paying for ridiculously expensive cups of coffee in restaurants.

Five years had passed since *Vogue* had published their article. In it, Marissa Flint had been described as a prominent up-and-coming young designer. The accompanying photograph, in which she had been wearing a white dress, a cream-coloured linen jacket and a floppy hat that shaded her face, had been attractive and atmospheric. It could have been of almost any young woman. Elegance and simplicity combined with a touch of romance: that was the look she and the *Vogue* stylist had been aiming for.

If she would never enjoy personal publicity, and if photographs and interviews still left her feeling exposed, the fear she had had all those years ago, that Jamie might see the image and recognise her and track her down, had proved baseless. The *Vogue* article had given her business a huge leg-up. Since then, newspapers and magazines had regularly featured Marissa Flint garments. Women of the moment – actresses and TV presenters of the more serious shows, successful writers and a scattering of female politicians – called in at the Margaret Street shop.

As soon as the Covent Garden shop opened, she and Angie would move into the design studio, although Marissa would always keep a workspace at home. If the shop ever opened. She gnawed a fingernail, a bad habit. If the building work was ever finished.

She poured herself a second glass of wine and opened her notebook. But her thoughts intruded and she put down her glass and screwed up her eyes in an effort to stem the tears. Hunching up her knees, she wrapped her arms around them as she rocked back and forth. Her imagined child faded and then vanished.

The phone rang. It was Bea.

'It's not too late to call, is it?'

Marissa cleared her throat. 'No, of course not.'

'How's it going?'

'The shop? Oh . . . fine, it's fine.'

'Marissa?'

But she was crying now, the tears flowing down her cheeks. She grabbed a handful of tissues and scrubbed at her face. She heard Bea say gently, 'Marissa, what is it? What's happened?'

'Nothing. I mean—'

'*Marissa*,' said Bea firmly. 'Tell me.'

So she took a shuddering breath and said, 'I went to the doctor this morning.' Then more tears, because she couldn't speak, because she was back in the large-windowed white room where her gynaecologist, a kind, matter-of-fact older woman, had conveyed to her the results of the battery of unpleasant tests she had undergone the previous week. She looked up at the ceiling, blinking, trying to get herself under control.

She heard Bea say, 'Are you ill?'

'No, nothing like that.' She gulped another breath and ran her sleeve over her face. 'I can't have a baby, Bea. Not ever.'

There, she had got it out. The specialist had told her that there was damage to her uterus, cervix and one of her fallopian tubes. *I'm afraid I think it's unlikely that you'll be able to bear a child, Marissa.* Then she had said, *Is there anything you'd like to talk to me about?* And Marissa, remembering Jamie's blows and her subsequent miscarriage and infection, had said, 'No, nothing.' But she couldn't tell Bea about that.

She heard Bea say, 'Oh Marissa, how awful, I'm so sorry.'

'I mean, it's not as though I was thinking of having a baby . . .'

'That's not the point. It's so sad for you.'

'It's just the shock. But it shouldn't have been a shock. I've been a bit careless sometimes and nothing's happened.' Tears were oozing from her eyes again.

'Sweetie, this is such a huge thing to have to come to terms with.'

She was thirty-two years old. Her longing for a child of her own was undiminished, and her loss lay inside her like a stone, dark and heavy and unyielding.

She blew her nose. 'You'd think I'd have got used to the idea of never being a mother.'

'Marissa, love . . .'

'It would be so silly and impractical to have a baby now. Just when my career's going so well. I know how hard it is for single mothers. I saw you, I saw how hard it was for you before you and Francis married.'

'It's not a rational thing. It's a part of us, wanting to have a baby. Not all women, no, but an awful lot of women.'

'I have so much . . .'

'You can't reason yourself out of feeling sad. Not about something like this.'

Her voice sank to a whisper. 'I'll always be alone. I'll never have a family.' Her father had died when she was very young, only a baby, too young for her to remember him, and she had been in her early twenties when she had lost her mother. It wasn't fair, she thought. Why should she always be condemned to solitariness?

But Bea said robustly, 'Well, that's utter rot. Of course you have a family. You've got me and Francis and you've got Emma and Max and Tamar. You've got Alice and Rachel and Lucienne and Elizabeth and baby Ben.'

'What I meant was—'

Bea spoke over her. 'And think of all the other people who love you. Think of Angie and the gorgeous David. And Trisha . . . and whatshername who writes for *Vogue* . . .'

'Georgina.'

'And what about all those people who weave your stuff in their cottages or whatever?'

'Bea, it's not the eighteenth century.' But Marissa laughed, and that was an achievement, and she was thankful for that. She added quietly, 'I love you too. You're not family, though.'

'Aren't we?'

She found she couldn't answer that. She made a point of speaking in person at one time or another to all the people who worked for Marissa Flint, from the cleaners, part-time assistants and office typists to her managers, accountant and assistant designers. She put a great deal of effort into sourcing the right fabrics, preferred to use natural fibres and visited weaving sheds and factories to make sure those who made her garments were properly paid and had decent conditions. Her look was timeless but quirky and flattering to all ages, and her clothes were designed to last. Properly cared for, a Marissa Flint cashmere could be worn for a decade or more. None of this would have been possible without all the people she depended on. Perhaps Bea was right; perhaps she did have a family.

She said, 'You and Emma, I couldn't manage without you. I really, honestly couldn't.' She was afraid she was going to cry again, so she changed the subject and asked after the children.

They talked for a while longer. By the time she ended the call, Marissa had agreed to take the train to Cambridge that Saturday after work, no matter how dire the progress of the shop renovation. Bea told her to call whenever she wanted to talk and Marissa said she would, though as she put down the phone, she knew she would never bring up the subject of her childlessness again. She would tidy it away, as she had tidied away the plates and mugs in the kitchen, because that was what she did.

She thought of pouring herself another glass of wine, but decided not to. She rinsed out the glass in the sink. The phone rang again.

She blew her nose, then answered it. This time it was David Johnstone. She said, 'Have you found Conrad?'

'Tracked down the wee bampot to a club in Soho. He was off his face, but I reminded him that we existed. He's promised to phone tomorrow morning. Sounds like he's got some cracking ideas.'

Marissa thanked David, then hung up. She felt drained by the intense emotions of the day. On the wall above the sofa was a corkboard with pinned fabric samples, ribbons and sketches. She had had a mood board like this in all the rooms and flats she had lived in since she had become Marissa Flint. Her gaze ran over the photos and scraps. She stroked a taffeta ribbon, touched a wisp of angora yarn. She reminded herself that there was always a point in any big project – a new collection, a new shop – when it seemed unfeasible that it would ever be finished. But they would get there in the end, she knew they would, and one day the Floral Street premises would be everything she hoped for, a bright, airy space that would realise her vision and attract women from all over London and beyond. Marissa Flint would move from being a small fashion label, loved by those in the know, to being a brand familiar to many.

Perhaps Bea was right. Perhaps she had been mistaken in thinking she was alone. Perhaps she did have a family, though it was not a conventional one. Her friends were her family, and so were her colleagues and the loyal customers who had bought clothes from her since the earliest days.

Her thoughts drifted to the moment earlier that day when, coming out of the doctor's surgery, she had looked down the street and seen Tamar Romilly. Tamar visited Marissa's Margaret Street shop twice a year or so to purchase clothes. Marissa made sure to be there in person to help her pick out dresses, shirts and trousers that were both useful and flattering. Afterwards, they always went out for a drink to help Tamar recover from shopping, which she loathed.

And then there were their summers at Seastone. Each year, one weekend in July or August, whenever the three of them could manage it, they stayed with Tamar and Morgan in their house on the shingle beach. It had become a tradition. There had been the summer of 1983, when Emma had been pregnant with Ben and had felt unwell and had lain on a sunlounger much of the time, dozing in the heat. Then there had been the summer of 1984, when almost the entire back room of the house had been filled by an immense canvas of Tamar's, whose first solo exhibition the previous year had been a success. Marissa looked forward enormously to their weekends and made room for them in her diary, no matter how busy she was. She needed that space, she needed the company of her friends, and always drove back to London feeling revived and comforted.

She was very fond of Tamar, who was warm, funny and talented and never took herself too seriously. She never complained about her husband, though he was a complex and sometimes difficult man. During their summer weekends at Seastone, he stayed in his studio most of the time, working.

Morgan Romilly was broad-shouldered and stocky, with thick, greying dark hair. He had the look, Marissa often thought, of a swashbuckling pirate. The man she had seen Tamar with that morning had been tall and slender, with fine, straight silver hair. She decided that when she next saw Tamar for a fitting, she wouldn't mention having seen her. In fact, she would forget all about it.

\*

Emma and Max ran through the rain from Glisson Road to the station and caught the train by the skin of their teeth. In the corridor of the carriage, Emma leaned against Max, laughing, catching her breath, slipping off her high heels and flexing her feet.

'God, Max, can't you ever be on time?'

'I'm sorry. A client phoned.'

He had been hideously late; they had meant to catch a train an hour earlier. But she kissed him, then smoothed down the shoulders of his jacket, and they pressed on through the carriages until they found seats. She felt carefree, travelling to London with Max to the gallery in Rochester Street, where the private view for her mother's second solo exhibition was to take place that evening.

Reaching the gallery, she saw in the window the huge painting of Orford Ness that her mother had taken more than a year to complete. Beside it, a poster: *Works by Tamar Romilly: The Sea and the Sky*. A quick glance through the window told her that the event was in full swing.

Inside, a young woman took their raincoats. Tamar was with Nick Lauderdale, a few metres from the entrance to the gallery, greeting new arrivals. Emma hugged and congratulated her and shook Nick's hand.

Her father was standing by a pillar, a few paces back. He said to Emma, 'People never come to these affairs to look at the paintings. They're only here to show off how cultured they are.'

'Mum's work looks amazing, doesn't it, Dad?'

'It's hard to tell. Too many bloody people in the way.'

Her sister Gale joined them, a short, thickset man in tow. Gale handed Morgan a glass of water and introduced them to her friend, who was called Gareth. Gareth struck up a conversation with Morgan. Max wandered off to look at the paintings. Half a dozen invitees poured through the gallery door and clustered round Tamar, congratulating her.

Gale steered Emma away. 'At least Dad's not wearing his painting trousers,' she said. They both snorted: a family joke.

'Thank God. We'd meant to catch an earlier train, but Max couldn't get away and Ben went down late for his nap. He gets grumpy if I have to wake him up.'

Emma's son, Ben, was fourteen months old. He had been born a month early, at the end of 1983, on 15 December. Their surprise early Christmas present, Max said.

Gale gave her a sideways look. 'He'll be fine, Em, staying at Bea's, honestly. The girls will make a fuss of him.'

Emma smiled. She always worried, though. 'I know. Who's Gareth?'

'He's a nurse at the hospital. He's just bought a caravan. I thought he could talk to Dad about caravans, keep him busy.' Their father detested private views and rarely attended them.

'Cunning,' said Emma. 'Where's Douglas?' Douglas was her sister's fiancé, solid and sensible and caring, like Gale herself.

'He's away up north, tarting up the wee but and ben.' After they married in a month's time, Gale and Douglas were to move to the Highlands of Scotland, to a cottage on the outskirts of Braemar. Gale had already organised a community midwife post for herself there.

While Gale described the improvements Douglas was making to the house, Emma scanned the rapidly filling gallery, looking for their brother.

'No sign of Rob?'

Gale shook her head. 'Not yet.'

'He said he'd come.'

'He'd better get a move on then. Useless twit.' Gale scowled. 'Oh bloody hell,' she said under her breath.

Emma followed her sister's gaze to the gallery entrance. She saw that Morgan was heading through the front door.

'Nipping out to buy a packet of Polos, do you think?' said Gale sarcastically. 'Come on.'

They wove through the crowds to Tamar. Emma said, 'Where's Dad going?' and Tamar said in a small, tight voice, 'To Liverpool Street, to catch the train home.'

'It's ten past *seven*, Mum.'

'So it is.' Tamar's face was set hard, like stone.

Emma went outside. Light glittered on the wet pavements. She caught sight of her father striding away from the gallery, and ran to catch up with him. Too much running in one day, she thought. She should have worn plimsolls.

She called out to him, and he looked back and waited for her. In his mid sixties, he remained an imposing figure, broad-shouldered, his stance confident. The rain scattered beads of moisture on his silver-streaked curls.

'Dad, you're not leaving, are you?'

Stupid question. The warmth in his eyes cooled a degree or two. He said, 'Go back to the gallery, you'll get soaked.'

'I'm all right. I'll walk with you. Where are you heading?'

'Victoria, to catch the Tube.' He set off again.

She scuttled along beside him. 'Won't you change your mind? For Mum?'

'She won't mind.'

She couldn't let him get away with that. 'She does, Dad. She minds.'

'There's a train at a quarter to eight. That's late enough.

There won't be any buses from Woodbridge. If I leave it much longer, there won't be any taxis either, and then I'll have to walk.'

'I thought you and Mum were staying overnight in a hotel.'

Morgan scowled. 'I made it perfectly clear to your mother that I had no intention of doing that.' They were heading down Rochester Row. After a while he said, 'You know I hate these things. I don't even go to my own.'

'I know, Dad. But if you could put up with it for just a little longer . . . just another hour. Please.' Emma knew, too late, that she had taken the wrong tone. Morgan never responded well to pleading.

'I have to get a move on. I'll miss my train.'

He darted across the road without saying goodbye. His quick stride and uneven gait, the legacy of his injury during the war, were familiar to her. She watched him disappear into the crowds and the rainy darkness. Her pleasure in the evening had vanished. She understood that her father disliked leaving Seastone, but she also understood how hurt and humiliated her mother must feel. If they had been at home, her parents would have had a blazing row.

They often argued. Mostly their disagreements were short-lived and fiery, like an afternoon thunderstorm, but there had been times when Emma had seen her mother deeply upset. Morgan could be hot-tempered and Tamar sharp-tongued. Neither was keen on compromising, though when compromises had inevitably to be made, it was always Tamar who made them. There had been times when Emma and Gale were children when they had both worried that their parents might get divorced. They had grown up trying to smooth things over.

Tonight she felt furious with her father and her heart bled for her mother. She walked back to the gallery. Max met her halfway.

She said, 'How could he?'

'To tell the truth, I was surprised he'd come at all.' He put his arm round her as they walked back to the studio.

'Max, what he's done is *worse*. To walk out on Mum like this, on her private view! I tried to persuade him to come back, but he wouldn't listen.'

'I can't remember anyone ever changing Morgan's mind about anything.'

Max was right. Morgan resented demands being made of him and went out of his way to resist them. She said, 'Your father would never do something like that.'

'No,' he conceded.

'I feel so sorry for Mum.'

Max didn't say *she's used to it*, or *she's tough*, though both those things were true. Instead he said, 'We need to make the best of it. Make sure she has a good time.'

'Is Rob there yet?' He shook his head.

Inside the gallery, Tamar was talking to a smartly dressed older couple. The man was admiring the exhibition and Emma overheard him broaching the possibility of commissioning a work. She touched her mother's arm and gave her a smile, then wove through the crowds looking for Nick Lauderdale.

She asked Nick if she could use his phone. He showed her to his office. Closing the door so that she had privacy, Emma excluded the noise of the gallery. There was a desk in pale wood and a sleek leather chair and a tall, thin window that looked out onto a serene and elegant garden. Emma felt a moment of deep envy for Nick Lauderdale's workspace.

She imagined sitting at that desk and sketching the green and dripping garden.

She dialled Bea's number. Bea reassured her that the children were happy and well fed. The girls were almost asleep, and Ben was out for the count. Bea and Francis were going to tidy up, then have supper and get an early night. Emma mustn't rush to pick up the children in the morning.

Emma thanked her and put down the phone but did not yet go back into the gallery. She worried about Ben more than she had ever worried about Lucienne or Elizabeth. She didn't feel able to share with anyone how she truly felt. Max had enough on his plate just now; Peter Eisen had suffered a stroke three months ago, and though he was making a good recovery, his illness meant that Max had had to take on a lot of his work at the architectural practice. He was also supervising the extension and alterations to their Glisson Road house, a long-delayed project that had become urgent as soon as they had discovered that there was a third baby on the way.

She could never have told either Bea or Marissa that since Ben's birth, there had been times when she had felt trapped and erased by family life. How could she complain of her all-too-easy facility in conceiving a child when one friend had had to give her infant son away and the other was unable to have children of her own? Her third pregnancy had been a miserable marathon of morning sickness and high blood pressure, her son's premature birth a frightening ordeal. The anxieties of that day had not yet left her. Max had been in London, giving a speech at a conference. Bea had been teaching. Emma had been bundling Elizabeth into her pushchair to set off to pick up Lucienne from school when her waters had broken, four whole weeks too early.

Somehow she had managed. A friend had taken Lucienne home with her, a neighbour had cared for Elizabeth until Max had arrived home. Tamar had thrown some belongings into a bag and caught a train from Woodbridge, arriving in Cambridge that evening. Emma had loved her tiny son from the moment she had set eyes on him. And yet some of the blankness and panic of that moment persisted, like a distant echo. She hoped it would go away, this feeling that nothing was safe any more.

She went back to the gallery. Nick Lauderdale came to stand beside her. 'Was everything all right?'

'Oh yes, thank you, Nick, everything's fine. Who's that man Mum's talking to?' Tamar was conversing with a tall, distinguished-looking silver-haired man.

Nick followed her gaze. 'That's Alexander Rainsford. Good that your mother knows him. He's very influential, has a lot of useful contacts.'

He told her that Rainsford was well known in the arts world, that he served on the boards of several galleries and foundations. Her mother was looking more cheerful, Emma thought. The butterfly pin gleamed in her red hair.

They went to join Max, who had found a plate of canapés. They were to have dinner with Tamar and Nick at Tamar's hotel, but that was more than an hour away and Emma was ravenous. Nick made a short speech, then Tamar thanked her guests for attending and everyone applauded. The crowds were thinning by the time Rob came through the door, looking wet and dishevelled.

Gale was eating the last of the vol-au-vents. Rob was talking to Tamar, explaining his lateness, Emma supposed. Tamar embraced him.

Gale said softly, 'Have you ever wondered what it must

be like to have a normal family? We joke about Dad turning up in his painting trousers, but didn't it make you feel a little bit sick to think that he might actually do that? There's a part of me can't wait to go and live in Scotland. I won't have to look at Dad and try and judge what sort of mood he's in. I won't have to worry about whether Rob's going to get round to showing his face or not.' She brushed pastry crumbs from her jumper. 'There are the sensible Romillys and there are the dramatic Romillys. You know which category you and I fall into, Em.'

'I'll miss you,' Emma said forlornly, thinking of Gale living hundreds of miles away. She waved to Marissa, who was talking to Max.

'I'll miss you too,' said Gale, as Marissa and Max came towards them. 'You must come and stay as often as you like. You'll love it there, honestly you will.'

After dinner, after she had seen her family off to the railway station, Tamar went to sit in the hotel bar. She was relieved to be on her own; the strain of continuing to pretend she was all right had told on her. Her head ached and a muscle beneath her right eye flickered and twitched.

She had chosen the hotel because it was a quiet, modest establishment, a ten-minute walk from the gallery. She had thought Morgan would prefer it to some glass-and-concrete palace. *Ha*, she said to herself. What a fool she was!

The bar room was pleasant, the brown leather chairs comfortable and occupied by a scattering of guests. The waiter came to her table and Tamar ordered a drink. Sipping her whisky, the sense of hurt and humiliation she had felt when Morgan had walked out on her in front of family and friends and the people she was supposed to be trying to impress still reverberated through her. She should be used to it, she told herself, but found that she resented that too – that she had taught herself to expect so little of him. She did not think he had made his demonstration of disloyalty out of jealousy, but others may have believed so, and that was deeply mortifying. As Nick Lauderdale had said to her the first time they had met, there was often a cycle to artistic success, and just now, her star was in the ascendant while Morgan's had taken a dip.

The need to be fair made her acknowledge that Morgan had never been one of those male artists who believed that anything created by a woman must necessarily be inferior. Though he had never made it easy for her to work, either. The children, the shopping, the housework and gardening had always been her responsibility. But she knew him well, knew that his behaviour was fired not by envy but by his overpowering arrogance. Morgan had been born in a pit village near Wakefield. He had learned to draw first at school and then at evening classes put on by the miners' union. He would have laughed if anyone had accused him of having a sense of entitlement. But he had his own brand of it. He had always been certain of his superiority to lesser artists and uncompromising in demanding for himself the time and space to create. She did not believe he felt any shame at all for walking out on her. The humiliation was all hers.

The whisky warmed and soothed her. She decided not to think about Morgan any more and to make the most of the pleasure of being on her own in civilised surroundings. When the waiter stopped by her table to ask her if he could get her anything else, she told him she would like to make a phone call. She was directed to a booth in the lobby, where

211

she dialled Alexander Rainsford's number. If his wife answered, she would put the phone down.

'Alexander Rainsford. Hello?'

Her heart gave a flurry of fast beats. 'It's me,' she said. 'Tamar.'

'Where are you now?'

'In my hotel, having a drink in the bar.' She hesitated, then said, 'My family has gone home.'

'Ah. Then may I join you?'

Her mood lifted and she felt a rush of excitement. 'Can you? Would you like to?'

'I can, yes, and I should like to very much. Give me fifteen minutes.'

Tamar went back to sit in the bar. A few weeks after she had met him at the Rochester Street gallery, five years ago, Alexander had written to her. On a trip to London to buy art supplies, she had had lunch with him in a restaurant off Sloane Street. She had taken the butterfly pin with her, in its blue leather box, but again he had refused to take it. 'Keep it,' he had said, 'and then I'll go on having an excuse to invite you to lunch.' Since then, they had met up on the two or three times a year she came to London to buy painting supplies or to talk with Nick Lauderdale about plans for the future. Her first solo exhibition had been a modest success. Alexander had helped make it so by encouraging his friends in the art world to attend.

She had briefly mentioned Alexander to Morgan, who hadn't seemed interested. London restaurants and moneyed upper-middle-class Londoners like Alexander Rainsford fell into the substantial category of things of which Morgan was scornful. As she had come to know Alexander better, Tamar had felt herself draw closer to him. She had learned that his work bored him and that he loved his son, Sebastian, very much and was saddened that he had settled so far away, in New York. He had talked a little to her about Caroline, his wife, and though he had not said so, Tamar suspected the marriage was not happy. Alexander was a restless person who had his own insecurities and dissatisfactions. Tamar assumed that he viewed their lunches as she did, as a treat, an opportunity to discuss common interests.

Yet she knew, as she sat that night in the bar, reeling from the shortcomings of her own marriage, that she was lying to herself. As time had passed, she and Alexander had spun out the hours they spent together by adding on a visit to a gallery or a stroll in the park. A lunch was no longer enough for them. He placed his hand on the small of her back to steer her through the door of a restaurant. She took his arm when they darted across a busy road. She felt at ease with these gestures, but there was a tension in them too. She tried not to think about him when she was at Seastone. She liked to tell herself that he was nothing to do with that part of her life, that he was her separate, urban, joyful pleasure, slotted safely away in the narrow expanse of her London existence.

She caught sight of him in the doorway and rose. Her gaze lingered on his features, his high forehead and prominent cheekbones, his heavy-lidded eyes.

He crossed the room and kissed her cheek. 'I didn't get the chance to tell you how stunning you're looking tonight,' he said.

She had chosen for the private view a short-sleeved navy-blue Marissa Flint dress, the waist of which was delineated by a wide self-coloured sash. 'Thank you,' she said. 'I'm afraid I've interrupted your evening.'

'Your interruption was very welcome. And I'm always in the mood to see you, Tamar. One never gets the chance to talk properly at gallery functions. What are you drinking?'

'Glenfiddich.'

He went to the bar. *I'm always in the mood to see you,* she thought.

When he came back, he sat down beside her. He said, 'It went well, didn't it? I knew it would. Did the Coopers commission a painting?'

'Yes, they did.'

'Congratulations.' He raised his glass in a toast.

A journalist had promised to write a profile of her, and there had been a scattering of red dots on the captions by her pictures. And yet what clawed at her was the hurt and dismay she had felt when Morgan had told her he was leaving. Even though Alexander was here, she kept returning to that moment.

She said bitterly, 'I always hope it'll be different, and it never is. I wish I wasn't so irrational.'

'You're one of the most rational people I've ever met.'

'Walking out in the middle of it – everyone saw him. I feel so humiliated. I expect all the guests thought we'd quarrelled. He has a reputation, you know, for being difficult.' The words spilled out; she put up her fingers to suppress the twitch below her eye.

'It must have been so upsetting for you.'

She turned to him, frowning. 'I'm not *upset*, I'm *furious*. I don't mind going to dinners and parties by myself. I expect to. I know he hates all that. He loathes London and he despises private views and polite parties. He even makes a point of despising canapés! He hates being told what to do and he hates being expected to conform. But this was my

214

most important exhibition so far. Goodness me, I went for thirty-five years with *nothing*! Tonight *mattered* to me! Couldn't he have just for once forgotten about his wretched likes and dislikes and principles?' Her hair had come out of the style the hairdresser had tortured it into that afternoon and she swept it away from her forehead. 'Why should his thought-lessness and selfishness still take me by surprise? Let me tell you what makes me angriest. He'll assume I'll forgive him. He'll assume I'll go home and we'll have a row, and then I'll forget about it.'

His gaze settled on her. 'Will you?'

'I don't *feel* as though I will.' She splashed water into her drink. 'But he knows I'm in the habit of forgiving him. Do you think there's only room in a marriage for one rule-breaker? That if one partner does as they please, the other feels obliged to make up for it?'

He didn't respond, and she wondered whether she had overstepped the mark. Perhaps what Alexander Rainsford wanted from her was a pleasant and sophisticated lunch companion. Perhaps he was repelled by the complaints of an emotional middle-aged woman. Confession and intimacy could be off-putting. At their lunches, they spoke of paint-ings they had seen, books they had read. They shared similar tastes.

But he said gently, 'Forgiveness isn't necessarily a bad thing, is it?'

Before tonight, she thought, they had skated round emotional closeness, but now at last they were letting down their guard. She considered what he had said to her. She found it impossible to think rationally about her marriage to Morgan. It was like trying to judge the strength of the wind when you were up to your neck in rough water. 'I'm afraid I've given him too much leeway,' she said bitterly. 'I adapt to his needs no matter how inconvenient they are for me. What happened tonight made me feel stupid. And it's stupid enough, isn't it, imagining one might become successful at the age of fifty-eight.' She dug a tissue out of her bag and blew her nose.

A smile turned up the corners of his mouth and warmed the gold of his eyes. 'But you are, Tamar, you *are* a success, so it can't be stupid.'

'It won't last.'

'Now you're fishing for compliments.'

She too smiled, recognising that he was teasing her. 'Maybe I am. Maybe I've been starved of them.'

'In deepest Suffolk?'

'Yes, in deepest Suffolk.'

'What made you decide to go and live there?'

'Morgan wanted to, not me. My career was just starting to take off. We were married and living in a dire little room in Fulham.'

'After I left the army, in '47 or so, I shared a place in Holborn with a couple of other men. What a dump. We didn't have a dining table, so we found an old door on a bomb site and put it on top of the bath and ate off that.'

They smiled at each other, complicit, both recalling the battered, shabby city of the post-war years, with its bomb sites and shortages.

She said, 'I'd finally managed to complete my window series. They're portraits – self-portraits, actually – of a woman looking out of a window. A gallery in London took the lot of them. I was so excited. Nothing came of it. You know how it is. They're gathering dust in lofts by now, I daresay. Anyway, I went to Seastone because of Morgan. Because I was in love with him. He thought living by the sea would be better for him.'

'That was good of you, Tamar. Did it help?'

'He still has depressions, but they're not as severe as they once were.'

'The quiet . . .'

She laughed. 'It's anything but quiet. Have you ever stood on the North Sea coast in a gale?'

'I haven't, no. But in the spring, when we're at our Hampshire house, I'm always woken early by the birds. Of course, I don't mind, it's delightful.'

'How long have you had the house?'

'Fifteen, sixteen years, since Caroline's parents died. It was her childhood home.'

'A friend of Morgan's who was living at Seastone told us there was a cottage to rent there. I imagined we'd stay for six months or so, until Morgan felt better, and then we'd go back to London. But we've ended up living there ever since. After some years, we were able to buy the house.'

'What happened with the London gallery?'

'I think they rather forgot about me. That's what happens when you're not around to remind people you exist. And then the children came along. I was always a slow worker, but once I had babies, it would take me a year − two − to complete a painting. By the time I'd finished one, fashions had changed.'

He touched his glass against hers. 'Looks like they've changed again, and in your favour.'

Being with Alexander Rainsford always cheered her up. In his company, she saw herself differently. Change and trans-formation seemed possible. She said, 'At first I felt trapped in Seastone. I'd escaped from a remote part of Cornwall only

217

to end up in an equally remote part of Suffolk. But in time I discovered that it had a beauty of its own. And it saved Morgan. It gave him the chance to recover. I don't regret it.'

The waiter came to their table and Alexander ordered more drinks. He said, 'It was tough starting again after the war. Caroline helped me get back on an even keel.'

She sensed the gaps between words, things unsaid, evaded. He glanced at his watch, and she thought he was about to tell her he must leave, but instead he said, 'I feel we've grown apart. Caroline has her world, her charities and her garden and her friends, and I have mine. We don't quarrel, but we don't talk, either. I would say that our lives run along on parallel lines. Caroline and Sebastian are very close. I have felt . . . distant from her for a long time.' He swallowed some whisky. 'My own parents were divorced when I was nine years old. I had no wish to inflict such misery on my son. Also, Caroline is a Roman Catholic, as am I. So we limp along.' Frowning, he said quickly, 'Don't feel sorry for me, Tamar. I don't deserve it.'

He ran his palm over his short hair. 'Is Morgan faithful to you?'

'Yes, I believe so.'

'I shouldn't have asked. I'm sorry, forgive me.'

Oh, she thought, in their silence. 'Is Caroline faithful to you?'

'Yes, I'm sure she is faithful.' He paused, then said, 'I feel I can talk to you. But one is ashamed of these things.'

Half a dozen people came into the bar, talking loudly and laughing. The women were wearing glossy, wide-shouldered frocks and they wore their hair with heavy fringes swept to one side, like Princess Diana. They sat down at the table behind Tamar and Alexander.

'Caroline is a remarkable woman,' he said. 'It's me who's changed, not her.'

She thought he sounded weary, tired of it all. One of the men at the table behind them rose and stumbled against her chair. 'Watch what you're doing,' Alexander said sharply, and the man murmured an apology.

Alexander drew his chair closer to Tamar's, forming a barricade. He raised his glass in a toast. 'To success. I always knew you had it in you. I saw it that first time, at the bomb site.'

'Such rot you talk,' she said, though she was flattered. 'I was such a drab little thing then, in my grey clothes and dusty shoes.'

'That's not what I thought of you at all. I thought you were remarkable. I thought there was a wildness in you.'

She turned away, plucked another topic of conversation out of the air. She was on edge and yet she was exulting too.

When they finished their drinks, they went outside to the street. Tamar breathed in the cool air. There was a fine drizzle, and the headlamps of the cars cast bright zigzags on the wet tarmac.

They talked on. There was so much they needed to say to each other. Though she protested that she never felt the cold, which was largely true, he insisted on taking off his jacket to keep the rain from her. It felt like an act of intimacy as he wrapped it round her. She breathed in his scent, which was elusive and expensive. He was saying she must capitalise on the success of her exhibition. Oh, but she needed to paint, she told him. She must go home and focus and paint.

'I hope it's not too long before you're back in London, buying linseed oil or whatever. Will you be all right?'

She didn't want him to go. She wanted him to stay with her. She wanted him to hold her.

Suddenly he spoke again. 'So much depends on chance, doesn't it? The course of our lives . . . who we meet and when we meet them. If I'd come out of my house that first evening a few minutes earlier, you and I could have talked for longer. I would have asked you your name, and when I came back to London, I'd have found you again.'

She pressed his hand in hers, then drew it to her mouth, kissing his strong brown knuckles. He embraced her and they kissed some more. Neither of them spoke, because it was a serious and beautiful thing, their kissing, and it made her feel alive and excited and youthfully optimistic again. After a while, they went back inside the hotel and up to her room.

In the middle of the night, he woke. His voice was soft in her ear.

'Caroline is a good person,' he said. 'I am not such a good person, Tamar. I have betrayed her before, but it wasn't like this. I promise you it was never like this.'

Later, while he slept, she carefully disentangled herself and went to the bathroom. Returning with a glass of water, she sat down on the edge of the bed. Her head ached – the whisky, and a day so overly long and filled with violent emotion it felt as if it had lasted far longer.

She knew this to be love, and that was both wonderful and sobering. What had happened between her and Alexander tonight was not the product of dissatisfaction with her long marriage, and nor was it a crude attempt to get even with Morgan. The truth was that she had always loved him. Love had happened in an instant, forty-one years ago on a bomb site, in the turn of a head and the flash of an eye. Because she had loved him, she had waited in the café for him. She had rung him tonight to ask him to join her for a drink because she had remembered that she loved him. She and Alexander Rainsford had loved each other for a very long time. Love had just been buried, like the butterfly pin under the rubble.

# Chapter Eleven

## 1986

A tall, toothy young woman, who was pushing a pram, came to stand beside Bea. She said, 'Do you know if this is where the infants come out?'

'That door across the playground.' It was three fifteen, and Bea was among the huddle of mothers waiting outside the primary school. 'You're Yvonne, aren't you, from the madrigal group?'

'That's right. My sister's got a migraine. I had the day off work, so I said I'd pick up Liam for her. It's Bea, isn't it? How's Francis?'

'He's fine.' Bea found it slightly odd that Yvonne was asking after Francis when she must have seen him at the rehearsal yesterday evening. Perhaps Yvonne had missed the rehearsal.

Then Yvonne said, 'Isn't it awful about Keith?'

'Keith? Madrigal group Keith?'

'Mmm. I broke my leg a couple of years ago and it was so painful. It sounds like a bad break, too. He could be out of action for weeks. Charlie Lewis is trying to find someone to fill in so we don't have to cancel any more rehearsals. You know, with the concert coming up and everything.'

Bea's mind was ticking over wildly. Yesterday had been Wednesday, so Francis had been out singing with his madrigal group. Bea had asked him how the rehearsal had gone, and he had told her that it had been fine. Yet Yvonne was implying that it had been cancelled.

The door across the playground opened to let out the smallest children. Some ran, others dawdled, trailing bags and coats. Bea thought about Keith, who was the musical director of the madrigal group, and his broken leg.

She said casually, 'Francis didn't mention to me how Keith did it.'

'Knocked off his bike, outside the Catholic church.'

'Oh no, how ghastly. When did it happen?'

'Monday night. Oh look, there's Liam. Good to talk to you, Bea. Tell Francis I might give him a ring. He may be able to think of someone who could take over for a month or so.'

They had been married for two and a bit years. Because Francis's house was the larger one, they had agreed that Bea should sell her Sedgwick Street home and the three of them move into Portugal Place. She adored the house for its city-centre location, its prettiness and quirky charm. There were three bedrooms, so as Alice and Rachel preferred to share, that left a spare room for guests. Francis had been happy for Bea to redecorate the sitting room. Though she hadn't consciously tried to erase the ghost of his ex-wife, Deborah, she had stripped off the Laura Ashley wallpaper and painted the walls a soft blue-green, set off with white woodwork. An Indian rug, some old prints and china jugs, bought for a song in junk shops, completed the transformation.

Their first summer as a family, they had gone on a three-week touring holiday in France, the girls in the back of their VW Beetle, meandering round the narrow roads of the Dordogne and staying in sweet little hotels and *pensions*. They visited villages perched on high rocky outcrops and picnicked on baguettes and pâté in fields scattered with wild orchids. It was all utterly blissful and Bea couldn't have been happier. Francis carried Rachel on his shoulders when she tired during their walks and amused the girls on the choppy ferry sailing home when Bea was feeling frightful.

It was only when the holiday was over and they were back in Cambridge, and Alice and Rachel had returned to school and Francis had started teaching again, that Bea wondered whether living in a household with two small children was proving more demanding than he had anticipated. Not that he ever lost his temper or snapped at anyone, but it had surprised her a little that he continued to carry on with the same routine he had had before they married. Choral society on Monday, madrigal group on Wednesday, French society once a month, a squash session or two during the week and the part-time work at the language school. All of which meant that he was rarely at home in the evenings. When she suggested he drop the language school so that he had some free time, he earnestly reminded her that he was putting his salary into a savings account. The money would come in useful if, for instance, they decided to educate Alice and Rachel privately or if the girls needed music lessons. Bea had noticed that Francis was very careful with money, which was a relief after Clive. He wasn't stingy, not at all, and that he was thinking of her daughters' futures touched her deeply, so she dropped the subject.

She had altered her own working hours so that she now

taught in the afternoons. She told herself that she needed to give Francis time and space to adapt to being part of a ready-made family. It had been so good of him to take on another man's children and it was only reasonable that he should continue to pursue his own interests. She mustn't mind that she seemed to spend almost as much time on her own as she had when she was a single mother living in Sedgwick Street.

Francis had his routines, but Bea didn't realise how much he disliked being required to abandon them until one afternoon in early March, when Vivien phoned to tell her that her father was in hospital. Jack had suffered a heart attack and was undergoing emergency surgery. When Francis came home from work, Bea was in their bedroom, throwing items of clothing into a holdall. She told him about her father's illness and asked him to take care of the girls while she stayed with her mother for a few days.

She had expected him to say yes, of course, whatever I can do to help, but instead he had looked alarmed. He had a habit of tugging at his hair when he felt anxious, and quite quickly his light brown locks were standing up in tufts. 'I'm so sorry about your father, darling,' he said. 'How frightening. Of course I'd *love* to take care of the girls, and you *must* be with your mother, but the thing is, my job, I can't just *drop* it, it's impossible.'

Bea reminded him that Alice and Rachel were at school during the day, so he need only make arrangements for the latter half of the afternoons and the evenings. Couldn't he adjust his timetable? But he was adamant, and eventually she phoned Emma and asked her to take the girls.

Early the following morning, Francis drove them all to Emma's house to drop off Alice and Rachel and their suitcase and school bags before continuing on to the railway station with Bea. Saying goodbye to him, queuing in the ticket hall, she felt, for the first time, a slight coolness towards him. In the railway carriage, as she sped towards the capital, fighting to keep her anxiety for her father under control, she reasoned with herself. Her father's illness had been a huge shock for them all. Francis wasn't a person who coped well with sudden changes of plan. And it was true that it was hard for a teacher to take time off during the term, so perhaps it had been unreasonable of her to expect him to do so.

And yet. The incident bothered her. Francis's parents were both dead, but Bea knew she would have dropped everything to support him if their circumstances had been reversed.

She stayed with her mother for six days, sharing hospital visits. She returned to Cambridge when she was confident that her father was on the road to recovery. The girls had a lovely time with the Hoopers, and she was touched to discover that Francis had not only hoovered the entire house in her absence but had also restocked the pantry. The first evening she was home, he cancelled his squash match and cooked dinner for the two of them: moussaka, which was one of his specialities, with a green salad.

But it wasn't long before they slipped back into the old routine, with Francis going out most evenings and Bea staying at home with the girls. She reminded herself of all the advantages of her marriage. She had needed to make a fresh start, and in marrying Francis, whom she loved, and moving into his delightful little house in Portugal Place, she had achieved that. As Mrs Beatrice Lockwood, she had a financial security she had never known before. Plus, they were good together in bed, she and Francis, and he was an easy man to get on with on the whole, and never moody, as Clive had been. He was invariably kind and attentive with the girls, though she suspected he found them tiring. Most importantly, Alice and Rachel adored him. A voice in her head now and then meanly whispered that of course they did, because Francis was a source of treats. He was the one who bought them sweets and ice creams and played silly games with them. It wasn't his job to badger them into tidying their rooms and cleaning their teeth. But she was being unfair: Alice and Rachel loved Francis because he was, well, lovable.

She had noticed that he looked at other women. Not in a nasty, lecherous way, but in an interested, appreciative way. A second glance at the pretty waitress serving their coffee in a restaurant, a turn of his head towards an attractive female guest at the dinner table. He enjoyed the company of women. Well, that was fine; the last thing she would have wanted would be to have found herself married to one of those men who desired women but didn't actually like them, so she tried to push away her recollection of the conversation the two of them had had when she had first visited his Portugal Place house. He had described Deborah as jealous and overemotional. *Jealous*. Now and then, Bea found herself wondering whether Deborah had had something to be jealous about.

It shamed her that such a thought should cross her mind. She had a bad habit of expecting the men she loved to be perfect. But they weren't, because no one was perfect, and life wasn't all picnics in flower-filled meadows. She must learn to be more hard-headed; she must get a grip.

She said, 'I ran into Yvonne Pritchard outside the school today.'

They were in the kitchen, clearing up the supper things.

Bea was drying and Francis was putting the china away. 'Oh yes?' he said. 'How was she?'

'Fine, I think. You didn't tell me Keith was in hospital.'

'I didn't want to upset you. It's rather grim.' His back to her, he stacked tea plates in the cupboard. 'Smashed his leg to pieces, poor blighter.' He shut the cupboard door and turned towards her. 'A few of us went to the pub instead, to drink his health.'

So that was all right then. Relieved, Bea put down the tea towel, kissed him and ruffled his hair. He put his arms round her and held her tightly until Alice came in, crying that there was a bee in the room.

Morgan was making coffee. He and Tamar were discussing a mutual acquaintance, an artist who had been living at Seastone when they had first moved there in 1951, and who had since decamped to the south of France.

'Connor says Hester has a dodgy liver.' Connor was a Seastone neighbour who made sculptures out of odds and ends he found on the beach. Morgan poured boiling water on the ground beans. 'All that red wine, I expect.'

Tamar said, 'She always liked a drink.'

'True.'

She was perched on the windowsill. Her gaze flicked to the painting on the easel, a commission on which she had started work two months ago, a large coastal scene. She had completed a quarter of it, perhaps a third, and so was past the excitement of the initial phase yet nowhere near the satisfying final stages of completion.

Morgan put the mug of coffee beside her. He said, 'Hester was a better painter when she lived here.'

'She was younger then.'

'So were you, and you're doing your best work now.' Standing beside her, he took a mouthful of coffee. Morgan liked his coffee black and scalding. 'No, it's probably the booze.'

'Poor Hester.'

He put a hand on her shoulder. 'Do you know where you're going with it?'

He was talking about the painting. Tamar shook her head. 'I'm plodding on, but I keep running up against the buffers. It makes me question myself.'

'It's going to be great. One of your best, I think.' He squeezed her shoulder. 'It's not there yet, but it will be. It has a real power.' Then he said, 'Tamar, have a look outside.'

She squirmed round in her seat and followed Morgan's gaze out to sea. She saw that in the brief length of time since she had last glanced out, a mist had wrapped itself round water and land.

'Let's go and see, shall we?' he said.

They went outside and stood side by side on top of the shingle bank. A sea haze had muted the landscape to bands of grey and lavender, and the light was coral-coloured and diluted. Unusually for Seastone, there was no wind.

'It's never the same, is it?' he said. A smile turned up the corners of his mouth. 'You never get fed up with it.'

'No, never.' She liked the damp, fresh chill of early May.

Morgan said, 'It's a question of holding on to your vision.'

'What if my vision is false?'

'It won't be. Whatever's at the heart of it, that's what you've got to dig up. So work out how best to do that. Recognise when you've headed off in the wrong direction and find a way of putting it right.'

Mist beaded his tight spiralling curls. He needed a haircut, she thought. She said fondly, 'Why is it you hate teaching when you're the only person I've ever met who's always given me decent advice?'

'Because it's you,' he said with a widening of the eyes. 'Isn't it obvious?' He touched her hand, interlacing his fingers with hers.

Looking up, she saw how the sky appeared still and clotted, almost solid, its beauty tinged with menace. The previous evening she had phoned Emma from the kiosk in the village. 'I'm afraid to let the children play out in the garden,' Emma had told her, sounding upset. Newspaper reports were carrying diagrams of the radiation cloud from the damaged nuclear reactor at Chernobyl as it spread over Europe, a vast, deadly, invisible growth in the sky. Emma had gone on, 'I called Henry last night to ask him whether the radiation might get into milk.' Henry, Max's father, was a physicist. 'I need to know if it's safe to let the children drink milk.' Tamar had tried to reassure her, but life seemed fragile indeed when the very air they breathed and the food they ate held a threat.

She went back inside the house. Morgan remained on the shingle bank, looking out. They had got on better recently; there was less friction between them. Perhaps that was because, having sold several of her paintings, money was less tight, or perhaps they were both relieved that Rob, who had just turned twenty-six, had at last found a job he seemed to enjoy as well as somewhere to live.

You would have said her marriage was ticking along nicely, were it not that every little while she travelled to London to see her lover. It made her uncomfortable to think that happiness might have made her less touchy, that perhaps it was not Morgan who had mellowed, but her. Perhaps her love affair with Alexander had given her a safety valve. At sixty-eight, Morgan remained complex and multifaceted. Looking outside, Tamar saw his bulky silhouette charcoal grey against the murky, eldritch light. He turned and headed for his studio. He still had the same fast, upright walk she had noticed the very first time she had seen him, a child looking through the window of her family home of Nanpean farmhouse. Guilt waxed and waned according to her mood, but it never went away.

Though he would never apologise, she suspected that Morgan knew he had overstepped the mark at her private view. She had always known that both his powerful self-assurance and his insistence on cutting out for himself the time and space to paint were essential to him. He could not have escaped his impoverished upbringing had he not possessed both self-belief and talent. He might infuriate her, he might sometimes hurt her, but still, she understood him, she always had, and that, she thought, made her betrayal of him all the worse.

During her visits to London, she always stayed in the same hotel in Paddington. She tried to get the same room each time, because it was spacious and not overlooked. She had grown fond of the ugly, dark, old-fashioned furniture and slippery satin eiderdown; she felt it gave them good luck. Alexander laughed at the pre-war decor and elderly clientele. 'You have a Puritan streak,' he said to her. 'You're a successful woman, my darling. You've no need to stay in a dump like this.' Tamar teased him about his predilection for glamorous haunts, but the truth was that the obscure and frankly dingy establishment seemed to her a wise choice. The Rainsfords had influence and social standing. Both Alexander and Caroline came from old and moneyed families; both were public figures, known for their extensive charitable work, and there remained the ever-present possibility that one of their large circle of acquaintances might see her and Alexander together and ask questions. Some might enjoy the frisson of danger that was part of a love affair, but Tamar did not. Relying on their good fortune holding out felt precarious.

One day, having bought a copy of the *Times* to read on her train journey home from London, she came across a photograph of Alexander to illustrate an article about arts funding. In the picture, he had been entering a Mayfair hotel to attend a function. His wife had been in the background, a little shadowy, but Tamar had been able to make out that she was a head shorter than Alexander, full-figured, smiling and attractive, her dark hair cut in a flattering feathered, gamine style. She had always tried to resist the temptation to slot Caroline Rainsford into the role of the dull, no longer suitable wife, unaware and careless of her husband's unhappiness, and the vibrant woman in the photo had finished off any possibility of doing so. She left the newspaper on the train.

If she and Alexander had only the slivers left over from her life and his, then so be it. The stolen hours were magical, and they nourished her. On one occasion he had less than an hour to spare between one meeting and the next. Alexander was a busy man. He was always heading off to a board meeting, dinner or reception. Walking through Hyde Park, she caught sight of him beneath the skeletal winter trees. She revelled in the delight of seeing him again after a long parting. He offered to take her to a café, but she said that she preferred to be alone with him, and so they walked by the Serpentine, huddled in coats and scarves. In an hour, they caught up on a lifetime of memories. They marvelled at their similarities of taste – a shared fondness for Welsh rarebit and the thrillers of Eric Ambler and Hammond Innes; a loathing of oysters, canned music and litter louts. Their birthdays were a mere few days apart, though he was five years older. When he was a boy, Alexander had holidayed yearly at Perranporth, a few miles along the Cornish coast from Nanpean. There were little coves they both remembered, a particular cliff path, a shop that sold ice creams. He said to her: 'This is the conversation we should have had in 1944.'

The last time she had seen him had been just before Christmas, when they had come across each other by chance at a party at a gallery on the Strand. Tamar had glimpsed him across the room. The lights on a Christmas tree had turned his silver hair once more to gold, and an occasion that had been a chore for her became a joy. As if he had sensed her gaze, as if it had weight and substance, he turned and smiled at her. 'I believe that it's because I've been thinking about you all day,' he murmured when they were at last able to speak alone. 'I believe that what we feel for each other draws us together, like magnetism.'

Later that night, she sensed a darkness in him as soon as he shut the door of the hotel room behind him. Their lovemaking was gentle and quiet, and afterwards he cradled her in his arms. When she asked what was troubling him, he said, 'Nothing. Nothing important. A wretched disagreement at work, that's all.' He lit a cigarette one-handed, then seemed to make a conscious effort. 'Actually, we've had some wonderful news. Sebastian's wife, Lynette, is expecting a baby. It's early days yet, of course, but Caroline and I are thrilled.'

In the spring, Morgan had had flu, rather badly, followed by an episode of depression. Tamar had sat with him during the worst weeks, and then, when he was getting better, they had walked for miles each day along the beach. The medicine the doctor had prescribed for him helped shorten the episode, and in time the shadows had lifted. When she had next been able to go to London, Alexander had been out of the country, skiing. Now, not having seen him for months, she yearned for him.

She stood at the window, looking out. The mist was thinning. Air and sea seemed to shimmer, caught between one mode of being and another as the sun burned away the haze. The sky was the blue of forget-me-nots, the surface of the sea alive with light.

She looked back at her painting. At last she was able to see clearly the image that was struggling to emerge from the void. Excitement coursed through her as she squeezed dabs of oil paint onto the palette, working them together to make soft shades of mauve and taupe, the colours of the sea mist. Then she began to paint over the harsh reds and blues.

Marissa met him at Trisha's seventieth birthday party in Kingston upon Thames. He was French, and his name was Gabriel Vernier. He was tall, slim and well dressed, forty-ish, and had close-cropped chestnut curls. His face was long and slender with the fine, sculptured jaw of a medieval prince, and his eyes were a deep olive green. Marissa had always liked green eyes. There was kindness in them, and she liked that too. Talking to him, he struck her as a grown-up, assured sort of man, rather than a work in progress.

When he took her out to lunch the following Friday they

spoke, to begin with, about their businesses. Gabriel imported floor tiles, terracotta and ceramics, for kitchens and conservatories. His business, Turquoise and Azure, was based at an old farmhouse in the Berkshire downland, not far from Hungerford. 'Quite derelict,' he told her, 'when we bought it ten years ago. Better now, though. At least we have a bathroom.' His smile was bright and beguiling. 'One day I want to have my own manufacturing plant,' he said. 'I want to be able to design my own tiles. I'd like to be able to do bespoke designs to complement a fabric or a wallpaper.'

His daughter, Isabelle, was thirteen years old. He and Isabelle's mother, Justine, who was English, were divorced. Isabelle boarded weekly at a school in Chelsea and spent most weekends at the farmhouse. 'She sees her mother now and then,' Gabriel said. 'Justine doesn't like to be tied to a routine.' Marissa sensed a painful history encapsulated in that comment. Gabriel's summers were passed at his childhood home, the Verniers' house in Normandy, in which his mother and sister still lived. Marissa noticed the warmth in his eyes when he spoke of it. 'People often drive quickly through that part of France on the way to the south,' he said to her. 'They assume it's all farms and battlefields. Where we live is very beautiful. There's an old watermill and you can walk in the woods for miles.'

Marissa told Gabriel what she told everyone. That her upbringing had been humble, that her mother had taught her to sew. That she had started small and built up the business over a decade. That she was unattached and childless and very much focused on her work. Her business was her baby; her friends and employees her family.

She mentioned to him that she was looking for a couple of terracotta pots to put on her balcony. She had bought the flat, which was in Battersea, five months ago. Her accountant had advised her to invest her savings in property, and that had been all the prompting she had needed. Leaving rented bedsits and flats behind her had been a long-cherished dream. Since the red-letter day she had moved into her new home, the keys gripped in her hand, it had become her haven, her citadel. The flat was on the top floor of a four-storey block; she liked that it was brand new and that she was the very first person to live there. There were two bedrooms, so she could have friends to stay, and a large L-shaped living room. Sliding glass doors led out to the balcony, with which she had fallen in love when she had viewed the flat for the first time. The brochure had claimed a riverside outlook, and between the surrounding buildings she could see flashes of brown Thames water.

'You'll think it's silly,' she said to Gabriel, 'but I haven't had time to furnish it properly yet. It's rather sparse. I've been meaning to buy a table and a couple of large pots for the balcony. I could employ an interior designer, but I don't want to. I want to choose everything myself. I want it to be perfect.'

'Come to Blackthorn Farm,' he said as they rose to leave the restaurant. 'I've picked up a few nice terracotta pots on my travels. You could have a look at them if you like. What about Sunday? You can meet Isabelle and I'll cook lunch. I'm a good cook.'

She felt a thrill of pleasure, but said, 'I can't this Sunday. I'm taking my god-daughter out.'

'You have a god-daughter?'

'She's called Rachel and she's seven years old and completely adorable.' Mentally Marissa flicked through her diary and cancelled a couple of existing appointments. 'I'm free the Sunday after, though.'

He kissed her cheek before they parted, Marissa to return to Floral Street and he to pick up his daughter from school. His lips were cool and dry, and their fleeting touch made her want more.

A week later, she drove to Blackthorn Farm. The deeper she headed into the countryside, the more familiar the landscape became. She recalled how, when she was a girl, she and her mother had taken buses out to the North Downs and picnicked on the grassy slopes. A long, chalk-white track trailed upwards through scrubby hawthorns. A breeze gusted, making the leaves dance.

As she neared the top of the hill, she caught sight of a low, gabled red-brick house surrounded by several outbuildings, one of which was an enormous thatched wooden barn. She parked her Audi on the gravel forecourt beside a battered Jeep and a large sign that read: *Turquoise and Azure*. Two girls' bicycles were abandoned on the gravel. A black cat dozed on top of a wall, soaking up the sun.

She got out of the car. Here the air smelled fresh and clean; not far away, a lark spilled its liquid song into the sky. Hearing the crunch of footsteps on gravel, she turned to see Gabriel coming out of the house.

'Love the apron!' she called out to him.

'You see, I'm very domesticated.' He was wearing a dark blue canvas apron over jeans and a white shirt. There was a dusting of flour on the apron. 'Hello, Marissa. I'm so glad you're here.' His lips brushed against her cheek.

She offered him her gifts of a punnet of strawberries and a bottle of wine. He thanked her and asked after the drive.

'I enjoyed it,' she said. 'It's good to get out of London, and I've always loved this part of the country.'

'Come inside. Come and meet Isabelle.'

Marissa followed him indoors, into a spacious beamed kitchen. Inside were pine dressers and painted cupboards, and a large table laid for lunch, with two reclaimed church pews for seats. Delicious smells rose from the pans on the Rayburn.

Two girls were sprawled on a window seat, poring over a magazine. The dark-haired one looked up as Marissa came into the room, her eyes half hidden by an overlong fringe.

'Isabelle, chérie, come and meet Marissa,' said Gabriel. 'And this is Isabelle's friend Kate, who's staying with us for the weekend.'

Kate, a lanky blonde, bounded up and offered Marissa her hand. After a second or two, Isabelle slid off the seat to do the same. Then she said to her friend, 'Let's finish the quiz,' and both girls went back to giggling over the magazine.

Gabriel made a coffee for Marissa. She asked him whether she could do anything to help. 'Not at all,' he said. 'Sit down. You've had a long drive. Relax.'

Marissa sat down. She wasn't much good at relaxing without a drink, and she wasn't drinking because she must drive back to London later that afternoon. She was better at doing than relaxing, she thought; she was accustomed to occupying every moment of her day. And yet, as her gaze moved from the stack of recipe books, some in French and others in English, on a high shelf above the fridge, to the jug of wild flowers in the centre of the table, and then to Gabriel himself, standing at the stove, his back to her, his shirtsleeves rolled up as he stirred a pan, she felt some of the stresses of the week unwind.

Lunch was roast lamb, followed by apple crumble. Gabriel was, as he had claimed, a good cook. He made sure the lunchtime conversation flowed smoothly and easily but did not appear to feel obliged to fill every silence. Though Marissa tried to talk to the girls, it was mostly Kate who replied. Isabelle answered her questions only in monosyllables.

After lunch, the two girls ran off to get lollies from the freezer and then to go out on a bike ride. Marissa helped Gabriel clear up. Once they had finished, he offered to show her round the tile warehouse.

They crossed the gravel courtyard to the thatched barn she had glimpsed earlier. Inside, Gabriel showed her hand-made terracotta tiles from Spain and plain ceramic English ones in peacock blue and a soft pea green. Marissa couldn't help but run her fingertips over their cool, shiny surfaces.

She asked him how he had started up the business. He told her that he had studied design at college, and then, in his twenties, had worked with floor-covering companies, first in Paris and then later in Birmingham. When the Birmingham firm went bankrupt, he decided to work for himself.

'After Justine and I got married, she took a break from her work – she's an interior designer. We had an extended honeymoon travelling round Europe for six months. It was a pilgrimage, almost. I wanted to meet the craftsmen who made the tiles, and I was looking for inspiration too. I was trying to get clear in my head what it was I wanted to do.'

'You wanted to find your style, to get your eye in,' she said.

'Exactly that. We went to the towns and villages where the great artists had lived – Cézanne and Braque and Picasso and Van Gogh. When Justine became pregnant with Isabelle, we moved back to my childhood home near Bayeux. I started the business there, selling terracotta tiles to our neighbours.

I still have a small outlet in Normandy. I hope one day to expand it and to open a shop in Paris.'

At the rear of the showroom, he showed her into an outside area paved with flint, on which stood half a dozen large terracotta pots. As she inspected them, he leaned with lazy grace against the wall of the barn.

'A couple of these might do for your balcony. They're Catalan, antique, originally used to store olives.'

'Oh Gabriel, they're beautiful!' Smiling, Marissa ran her palm over the flaking greenish-white surface of a large, bulbous pot.

'You could plant olive trees in them.'

'Perhaps I will. I'm not much of a gardener, though. I kill off my house plants. May I take them home with me?'

'You live in a flat, don't you? They'll be too heavy for you to haul up in a lift. I can bring them round the next time I'm in London.'

The suggestion was offered lightly; she answered equally easily. 'Make it an evening and I'll cook you a meal.' There it was again, that ripple of excitement at the thought of seeing him.

They left the warehouse and walked round the house to the back garden. Gabriel made coffee and brought it out to where Marissa was sitting on the terrace. She asked him how long he had lived at Blackthorn Farm.

'We bought the house when Isabelle was three.' He frowned as he poured the coffee. 'She doesn't mean to be impolite. You mustn't be offended by her.'

'Gabriel, I'm not. I thought perhaps she was shy.'

'She lacks confidence, it's true.'

'Thirteen's not an easy age for a girl.'

'It's been hard for her.' He passed her a cup. 'She was

only four when Justine walked out. I woke up one morning and she'd gone.' He shrugged. 'She left a note on the kitchen table telling me that the marriage was over. That was how I found out that she'd fallen in love with someone else.'

Pouring cream into her coffee, Marissa looked up at him. 'I'm so sorry, Gabriel. How awful.'

'In part I blame myself. That first year we came here, I was working all hours. I knew Justine wasn't happy. I was trying to get the business going and the house was a wreck. I'd be up at six repairing a wall or laying a floor, and then I'd be out all day getting in orders, making sure the deliveries were going smoothly.' He gave a crooked smile. 'In the evenings, I'd fall asleep over the paperwork. Not much of a husband.'

Marissa couldn't stop herself saying, 'But to leave her *daughter* . . .'

'Perhaps she was trying to be realistic. Generous, even. She knew she couldn't look after Isabelle properly on her own.'

Marissa suspected that he had spent years rationalising those events, years of lurching between self-blame and anger. He would have had to rein in his resentment for his daughter's sake. Whatever her failings, Justine was still Isabelle's mother.

She said sympathetically, 'It must have been very hard.'

'It was.' He looked grim. 'I was the sole parent of a very confused and unhappy little girl. I couldn't let the business go under because it was my only source of income. At that stage, half of the house was still uninhabitable. We managed, Isabelle and I, but only just. My sister, Andrée, came over to help out in the early days, after Justine left. I couldn't have coped without her. But my mother's unwell and in a wheelchair, and she needs Andrée at home, so after a couple of weeks she had to go back to Normandy. Andrée looks after the French side of the business too, and it was important to keep that going. We needed the money, you see.'

Marissa looked round. The old house cast a shadow over the garden, with its rambling roses. 'You've done a brilliant job,' she said. 'It's heavenly here. And Isabelle seems a delightful girl.'

He rubbed a hand across the back of his neck. 'It took a while. You have to find people you can rely on, don't you? People you can have faith in. Kevin took over the estimates and the contracts a couple of months after Justine left. He still works for me. Then I found Diane, and she gave me a hand with Isabelle. She still comes over a couple of times a week to help with the housework and shopping.' He glanced away. 'And I found a good lawyer, because I had a divorce to go through, and I worked whatever hours I could to keep us going, until midnight if necessary.' His green eyes came to rest on her. 'I think you'd do the same, Marissa. I think you're like me. You know what you want and you'll do whatever it takes to make it happen.'

She remembered the early years of growing the business, fitting it round her job at Liberty, sewing late into the night in whatever grotty bedsit she was renting at the time.

'It wasn't easy,' she acknowledged. 'But I didn't have to juggle looking after a small child as well.'

The sound of voices told them that the girls had returned to the house. Rising, Gabriel said quietly, 'Isabelle is supposed to see her mother every other weekend during term time. She was meant to see her this weekend.'

'What happened?'

'Justine found something better to do.' Marissa saw anger

crease his brow as he dripped the dregs from the coffee pot onto the rose bed. 'She's an impulsive person. She likes to think of herself as a free spirit, to do whatever she wishes, when she wants to.' His lip curled. 'I found this charming when I met her. She was . . . *enchantant* – how do you say it? – bewitching. She still can be, when she puts her mind to it. Not to me, though.'

'I'm so sorry. How difficult for you.'

He put the cups on the tray. 'I know how I sound, Marissa – the bitter ex-husband – but if we are to get to know each other better, I'd like you to understand how things stand.'

She felt a thrill of delight at his words, that he, like her, hoped that their relationship would continue. She squeezed his hand. 'Thank you. Thank you for having confidence in me, for trusting me.'

'It's natural that Isabelle should crave her mother's love. It's natural that she should go on hoping that in the future things will be different. But she's been hurt so often, and I hate to see it.'

'You love her, Gabriel. You want to protect her.'

Isabelle came out into the garden. She shot a look at her father and Marissa. Marissa let go of Gabriel's hand.

'Papa,' said Isabelle. 'I need you to help me with my maths homework.'

Marissa left soon afterwards. As they said their goodbyes outside the farmhouse, Isabelle clung to her father's side. Gabriel raised a hand in farewell, and Marissa put the car into gear and headed down the track.

# Chapter Twelve

## 1986

Max had invited his new trainee, Damien Harrison, and Damien's girlfriend, Tara, to dinner. Tara peered at the chicken liver pâté starter that Emma had put in front of her.

'I can't eat that. I'm a vegetarian.'

'Oh dear, I'm so sorry. Let me find you something else.'

'I can't eat onions, either. And I'm allergic to shellfish. I don't want to be a pain. A piece of plain bread will be fine, so long as it isn't shop-bought.'

As well as Damien and Tara, their dinner guests that evening were Max's brother, Adam, and his fiancée, Helena, who were staying with them for a few days, and Bea and Francis. Emma had asked the Lockwoods to come because Max had mentioned that Damien was quiet and reserved. As Adam too had his taciturn side, she had been afraid that the men might sit in silence. Bea and Francis were good at keeping a conversation going.

Emma whisked away Tara's plate and took it into the kitchen. A cry from the upper reaches of the house and she dashed upstairs to soothe Ben. Before he had come along, they had used the fourth bedroom as a guest room, but now it was Ben's. Max was drawing up plans to convert the attic so that they had another bedroom, but until that was completed, they put the girls in together when guests were staying.

Emma knelt on the floor beside her son's bed. She had been up since six – Ben was an early riser and liked to wake them first thing. It was Friday, a school day; Saturday was their usual evening for a dinner party, but Damien and Tara hadn't been free on Saturday.

Once Ben was settled, she went back to the kitchen and began to slice tomatoes. Max came in to fetch another bottle of wine. Emma hissed at him, 'You didn't tell me Tara was a vegetarian.'

'Didn't I?' He looked vague.

'Did you remember to ask?'

He uncorked the bottle. 'Probably not,' he admitted.

'For God's sake, Max.' She rummaged in the fridge and found half a mozzarella. She tried to slice it neatly. 'Keep them talking. Top up their wine glasses while I sort this out.'

When he returned, she said, 'Are they all right?' She cocked her head towards the back room.

'Fine, yes.'

'Bea's being really off with Francis.' Emma arranged the sliced cheese and tomatoes on a plate. 'I don't think she's said a single word to him since they arrived.'

'D'you think he's noticed?'

Emma wasn't sure. It was possible that he hadn't – Francis wasn't a particularly observant person – but also possible that he had noticed and was pretending he hadn't, in the hope that Bea would forget about whatever it was that was annoying her. Max, who rarely criticised other people, had once commented that Francis lacked depth. Emma understood what he meant. Francis was likeable, good-looking, charming, and clever at putting people at their ease, but there was something superficial about him. She wouldn't have wanted to be married to Francis Lockwood. She wouldn't have felt there was anything solid to hold on to.

'Here, take this through.' She scattered basil leaves, then handed Max the plate. She was afraid that the mess of tomatoes and mozzarella looked unappetising.

She checked on the main course, a boeuf bourguignon that Max had put together the previous evening, then went back to the dining table.

'This is such a fabulous room,' Helena was saying.

They had knocked down the dilapidated sunroom and extended the back of the house into the garden. In the summer, they opened the glass doors and the scents of rose and lavender floated into the house.

'Damien and I are trying to find somewhere in Cambridge,' said Tara. She twisted a lock of her heavy dark hair round a finger. 'I've told him that I simply must have a garden. I can't live without one.'

Francis beamed at her. 'Oh yes, you must. I have only the tiniest little courtyard, but I adore it. I love to potter round.'

'You never do a thing in the garden,' said Bea sharply. Emma thought it was the first time that evening that she had addressed Francis directly.

Francis, looking wounded, said, 'I do! I water the pots!'

'Once a fortnight, if that. The poor plants would all be dead if I didn't remember.'

Emma said, 'I love your garden, Bea. It always feels like an oasis.'

'You're a keen gardener, aren't you, Emma?' said Helena.

'Theoretically I am. There's still a part at the far end that

I haven't sorted out yet. God knows what's living there. A family of tigers, perhaps.'

The laughter broke the tension. Bea was very pink in the face, either because of the red wine or because she was angry. Francis seemed to have finally taken on the fact that he was in the doghouse, because he gave her an anxious glance.

Like many married couples, the Lockwoods bickered. Emma had never seen them have a full-blown argument, though. Bea looked strained and unhappy. Emma caught her eye and gave her a reassuring smile.

In the kitchen, as she scraped the starter plates into the bin and drained vegetables for the main course, rain rattled against the window. Max had extended this room into the concreted area at the side of the house, which meant that it was twice as big as before.

He took the casserole dish out of the oven. Emma said to him, 'It'll have to be an omelette. I can't think of a quick vegetarian main course that isn't an omelette.' She ran her gaze over the mess of used pots and pans and packets of flour and suchlike. 'How can we still run out of space?'

He kissed her. 'Because we're hopelessly disorganised, you know that. Don't worry about it, I'll clear up later. I'll go ahead and serve this.'

He left the room carrying the casserole. Shortly afterwards, Bea appeared. 'Can I do anything?'

'If you could just clear the decks a little to give me a bit of room.' There was a limp bunch of parsley at the bottom of the fridge; Emma selected the best bits and chopped it for the omelette. She said, 'What's happened?'

'What do you mean?'

'*Bea*. You and Francis. What's going on?'

247

There was a silence. Then Bea said, 'I think he's having an affair.'

Emma swung round. Bea's eyes were pink and shiny.

'Are you sure?'

Tight-lipped, Bea shook her head. Max came back for the green beans and Helena brought in the water jug to refill. By the time they had both gone, Bea had got control of herself.

She said, 'He's been a bit funny lately. Out all the time – I mean, he always is, but even more than usual.'

Emma cracked eggs into a bowl, then dropped a knob of butter into a pan. 'Have you said anything to him?'

Bea shook her head. 'I can't. What if . . .' Her voice faltered.

'Oh Bea.' Emma hugged her. 'You have to talk to him. It's probably nothing. I expect he's doing overtime, something like that.' The butter sizzled.

'His choral society gave a concert last night. I went along. Francis sang a duet with one of the sopranos.'

'Was it good?'

'It was heavenly. I could have sat there listening to them for ever.' Bea's dark eyes were wide. 'But afterwards, in the pub, I saw the way he looked at her.'

'The soprano?'

Bea nodded. 'She's younger than me. So pretty, and so talented, of course. She's called Daisy Wynyard.' Her lip curled. 'I always think of Daisy as a little girl's name, don't you?'

'Maybe Francis was on a bit of a high after the concert. I don't expect it means anything.'

The doorbell rang. 'I'll get it.' Bea left the room.

Emma poured the egg mixture into the pan. Was Francis capable of cheating on Bea? She couldn't be sure, and that realisation made her feel uncomfortable. Her attempts at reassurance felt facile to her. A short time ago, at the dinner table, while they had been talking about gardens, Francis had said, *I have only the tiniest little courtyard* – as if the Portugal Place house was still entirely his, as if Bea and the girls were merely staying over, some kind of long-term house guests.

Recognising her brother's voice in the hallway, she frowned and abandoned the omelette. Rob was standing at the foot of the stairs and Bea was draping his parka, the shoulders of which were dark with rain, over a radiator.

'Hello, Em.'

'I thought you were in London.'

'Bloody flat fell through.' He hauled off his rucksack. 'Trevor's brother came back from Australia, so I had to move out.'

'What about your job?'

'It didn't work out.'

'I'll go and check on the omelette,' said Bea.

Emma hissed, 'Rob, we're halfway through a dinner party.'

'Sorry. Sorry. Just for one night, Em. I'll sleep on the floor if you like.'

He pushed back his wet hair from his face and gave her a charming smile. Emma had been familiar with that expression since he had been a little boy, eyeing the last biscuit when their mother had sent the three of them outside with a packet of custard creams so she could have some peace to work. Her resistance always crumbled.

'God, you are a nuisance,' she said exasperatedly. 'Sling your rucksack in here.' She opened the study door. 'You can sleep on the couch. Have you eaten?'

'A Mars bar and a couple of beers on the train. Is it a good dinner party?'

'It's been the dinner party from hell so far, frankly.' She let out a sigh. 'An unexpected vegetarian, and Bea and Francis are hardly speaking to each other. I keep reminding myself that I was once capable of quietening a planeload of passengers during a rocky landing at Schiphol.' She patted his back. 'Go in and join the others. Max will get you something to eat.'

'Thanks, Em.' He hugged her. He smelled of the rain. He headed for the back of the house.

Emma went into the study and cleared books, Lego and Max's rolled-up architectural plans from the couch. Earlier that day, while the girls had been at school and Ben had been having a nap, she had escaped from the cooking and cleaning and started on a watercolour of a bearded iris. She remembered how, as soon as she had sat down and picked up her brush, she had forgotten everything else. When she was painting, she felt most like her true self.

She went upstairs. Ben was moving restlessly in his bed, neither properly awake nor deeply asleep. His fine brown hair clung damply to his forehead. Emma touched his face. She thought he felt hot. She murmured to him and stroked his cheek until he quietened.

Back at the dining table, Max was dishing out the casserole and Bea, bless her, had served Tara the omelette. Helena was talking about her work in an animal shelter and Adam and Damien were discussing an article they had read in *New Scientist*. Francis was telling Tara about the concert. Rob wolfed down his plate of food, washing it down with red wine.

Pudding was an apple pie and a chocolate mousse. Bea came into the kitchen while Emma was whipping cream.

'If you give me a cloth, I'll tidy up the dining table a bit.' She disappeared for a few minutes. 'There,' she said, returning.

'It looks much nicer now.' She rinsed the cloth under the tap. Then she said, her voice low, 'A couple of days ago, I met Deborah in Robert Sayle.'

'Deborah?' Emma, grating chocolate on top of the mousse, turned to look at her. 'Francis's ex-wife Deborah, do you mean?'

Bea nodded. 'I was buying light bulbs in the basement, and I just saw her there.'

'I didn't know you knew her.'

'I recognised her from a photo in an album of Francis's. She's very striking, rather like Isabella Rossellini, but fatter. I wasn't absolutely sure it was her at first, I was afraid I was making a fool of myself, but it *was* her. So I introduced myself.'

'What was she like?'

'Perfectly pleasant. I'd always imagined she'd be . . . I don't know, *brassy*. Would you like me to wash some forks?'

'Please. What on earth did you say to each other?'

'Oh, all sorts of things.' Running a bundle of forks under the tap, Bea sounded evasive.

'Bea?'

Bea turned off the tap. As she dried the tines of a fork, she said, 'I asked her whether Francis had been unfaithful to her when they were married.'

'Oh God, Bea.'

'And she told me he was.' She aligned the forks neatly on the work surface. 'They'd only been married a year when Deborah found out he was cheating on her with the art teacher at his prep school. That's why she walked out. I'd thought it was *her*, that she was unreasonable and jealous, but it was *him*, it was Francis.'

Max came into the room. Emma handed him the apple

pie and the jug of custard and asked him to take them through to the dining table.

Bea murmured, 'Deborah said . . . she said that Francis falls in love with a woman every two or three years. And then once he settles down, he kind of gets bored and moves on. We've been married for two and a half years. Maybe he's gone off me.'

'Oh *Bea*.' Emma put her arm round her friend. 'Even if what she said was true, it doesn't mean it applies to you. It'll have been different with her. She can't have been right for him.'

'Do you think so?' Once more there were tears in Bea's eyes.

'You have to talk to him, Bea. You can't let this fester.'

Bea was silent as she placed the last two forks at the end of the row. She said suddenly, 'I don't know what to think any more. Sometimes I think I'm imagining it, and I hate myself for having such awful thoughts. But there are other times . . . oh Emma, there are times when I'm afraid that everything's going wrong all over again.'

Morgan was sitting at the kitchen table dismantling the clock, which had stopped working. He looked up. 'Postman,' he said.

Tamar went outside. She met the postman halfway down the wooden steps. She glanced at the letters as she returned inside the house. 'Electricity bill,' she said, peeling off the top one.

Morgan grunted as he adjusted a cog with a tiny screw-driver. Tamar's heart missed a beat as she opened the other letter and saw that the signature was Alexander's.

'What's that?'

'It's from Eunice, that's all.' Eunice was a friend of hers whom Morgan disliked. She shoved the letter into her trouser pocket. 'More tea?'

'Please.'

She made the tea and put a mug beside him. Alexander rarely wrote to her. It jolted her to receive a letter from him. She rang him at his office when she was in London, that was their arrangement, and if he was free, they met up. The letter seemed to burn a hole in her pocket.

After he had reassembled the clock, Morgan placed it back on the mantelpiece, then kissed her and headed off to his studio. When he was out of sight, Tamar took Alexander's letter out of her pocket. She hated that she had lied to Morgan. *Recognise when you've headed off in the wrong direction and find a way of putting it right.* She remembered him saying that to her. She had gone so far in the wrong direction she hardly knew how to get back. She hardly knew who she was any more. This intermittent, future-less affair with Alexander Rainsford had sent her off course. She was despicable.

Yet as she read the letter, something melted inside her. Alexander had written to ask her to have lunch with him. *There's something I need to talk to you about.* The thought of never seeing him again was unbearable. It would tear her in two.

Too unsettled to work, she took the dog out for a walk, striding along the beach past the jutting shingle bank and the Martello towers. Someone had bought the furthermost tower, and the grass that surrounded it was now strewn with rubble, while a spider's web of scaffolding crazed the old and austere brown walls. Here, the rush of sea and wind was disturbed by the sound of voices and the chipping of chisels.

Once she was out of earshot, she sat down on a concrete

groyne and looked at Alexander's letter again. The same sentence stood out. *There's something I need to talk to you about.* Turning it over in her mind, she felt uneasy. Mentally she scanned the weeks and months ahead, searching for a time when she would be free to go to London. She and Morgan were to go away in a few days' time, to visit Gale in Scotland. Gale was expecting a baby. They would stay in Cambridge on their way home with Emma and Max and the grand-children. Not long after that, she was to give a lecture at East Anglia university, on John Cotterell and his coterie of artists. The invitation was both flattering and terrifying. She felt that her life was running away from her, slipping out of her control, and sometimes found herself yearning for the routine she had known before the unexpected success of her career, before Alexander.

And yet she remembered, too, a night when he had come to her at the Paddington hotel. Her wild elation, her joy in his touch, her delight in the sound of his voice. Her deep sense of peace as she had lain in his arms, drifting in and out of sleep.

She walked down to the water's edge, where she tore both letter and envelope into tiny pieces and scattered them on the waves. There was a heavy sea with an outgoing tide, and before long, the small white fragments had disappeared.

She might hate what Francis had done, sleeping with that stupid, silly girl in the choir, but she didn't seem to be capable of actually hating him. There was something about him that ruled out hatred, which wasn't fair when you thought how much he had hurt her. In the aftermath of him eventually admitting to her that he had, in his words, made a mistake, they stayed up late a lot, drinking too much wine, engaged in arguments that went round in circles. They wept and yelled at each other, but quietly, so as not to wake the girls. Nights would end with Francis promising to be a better husband and Bea either refusing to speak to him or sobbing bitterly or having sex with him, depending on her mood. But it was always there, that fissure in her heart, the damage brought about by the knowledge that he had chosen to betray her. That he hadn't thought her worth constancy.

It was during one of those late-night drunken conversations that he said, 'I'm so sorry I hurt you, Bea. I'll never do it again, never, ever, I swear. It didn't mean anything, I promise.'

'So why did you do it?' They had had this conversation before, word for word. He couldn't seem to see that telling her the affair had been meaningless made it worse, if anything. Why break her heart by committing an act that had been, according to him, trivial?

It had happened when she had been away with Alice and Rachel, staying with Clive's parents. Which meant that through all those interminable meals with Kenneth and Philippa, while she was trying to stop Alice eating with her mouth open and Rachel getting down from her chair and running about in the middle of dinner, Francis had been alleviating his boredom, his solitude, by letting Daisy Wynyard into his bed. She had found an earring caught in the duvet cover, a cheap nickel-plated hoop with a star dangling from it. He had tried to tell her it belonged to the cleaner, but their cleaner didn't have pierced ears. Bea noticed things like that.

He said, 'I love you so much, I really, really do, and for goodness' sake, you've been through enough already, what with the baby and Clive and everything.'

She said coldly, 'I can't see what the baby and Clive have got to do with it. Even if I'd had the most lovely, perfect life, it wouldn't excuse you sleeping with that woman.'

'No, no, of course not, you know I didn't mean . . .'

She didn't, that was the trouble. She didn't feel she knew anything any more. She squeezed the last drop of red wine out of the bottle, though she felt a headache starting. They were sitting at the kitchen table and it was gone eleven. Washing-up was distributed round the room, because neither of them was capable of getting on with the dishes while they were quarrelling. Francis was picking at the lumps of wax that had dripped from the candle onto the duck-egg-blue oilcloth tablecloth.

He looked up. 'Have you ever thought of trying to get in contact with him?'

'Who?'

'Your son.'

'Of course not,' she said irritably. She suspected him of trying to change the subject away from his infidelity. 'I couldn't.'

'Do you know that for sure? Maybe you should find out whether it's possible, at least.'

He stood up. Even when he was drunk – and he was – he moved in a neat, graceful way. He dropped the wine bottle in the bin, then gathered up dishes and put them in the sink. He said, 'I could have a word with Melody, if you like.'

Bea gave him a suspicious glare. 'Who's Melody?'

'She teaches part-time at the school. She's in her fifties. I told you, it's not going to happen again, love, honestly, not ever. Melody was a social worker and then she threw it in and retrained as a biology teacher. I'll talk to her if you'd like me to, and find out whether she knows about adoption, what the rules are.'

She chewed her lip. A part of her wanted to tell him not to bother. She saw this as his way of trying to worm himself back into her good books, and anyway, she'd very likely find out that tracing Patrick was impossible and all it would do would be to dig up the hurt all over again.

But in the end she said, 'You mustn't tell her it's for me. Say it's to help out my cousin or something.'

'Bea, it isn't the 1950s. But I'll be discreet, I promise. Let me do this for you.'

He would, she knew. Francis wasn't an insincere person, or even, really, an unreliable one. Just an unfaithful one. Bea watched him as he turned on the tap to fill the sink. Her gaze strayed from his nice broad shoulders to his neat hips. Perhaps she believed his promises of future constancy. Perhaps he had learned his lesson. It would be all right, they would be absolutely fine, she and Francis, if only she didn't keep remembering with what unthinking rapidity they had gone from a first kiss to declarations of love. It would all be absolutely fine if only she could stop thinking about his ex-wife, illuminated by department store table lamps and spotlights, saying, *What you need to realise is that for Francis, it's the falling in love that matters. He does it every couple of years or so. He likes the thrill of the chase, you see.*

She hadn't told the girls all that much about Patrick, just the bare bones: that they had a brother who had another mummy now, because she, Bea, hadn't been able to look after him. They were so young – Alice was nine and Rachel only seven – and she tended to get tangled in knots when she spoke about Patrick. How could she properly explain

257

why she had given him away without also telling them about Ciaran? How could she tell her little daughters that while she had still been at school, she had been fooling around with a boy? Just to think of Alice or Rachel messing up their lives like that made her feel cold inside. Sometimes, now, she could almost sympathise with her parents.

Alice was an imaginative little soul, given to having nightmares and currently rather obsessed with death. An elaborate funeral had been conducted for a dead bird found on the terrace, and a recently deceased hamster had been given a Viking burial on the Cam. Bea was afraid this was because of Clive, because Alice had lost her father when she was just two years old. She had wondered whether she should take her to some sort of therapist, but hadn't in the end. There were photographs of Clive and the girls in Alice and Rachel's bedroom in Portugal Place. They went to stay with their Cornwell grandparents regularly in spring and summer. She knew how important it was to cherish memories of their father.

Bea abandoned the helping-out-the-cousin ruse at much the same time as Melody Jones lowered herself into one of the seats in the Portugal Place terrace garden. It was mid August, and the Virginia creeper had begun to turn crimson, and there was something about Melody that inspired trust.

'How old is your son now?' She smoothed down her coral and white dress. Her hair had the blue-black sheen of a magpie's wing and her skin was a soft, coppery brown.

'He was fifteen in April.'

'When he's eighteen, he'll have the right to apply for a copy of his original birth certificate. He'll also be able to find out which agency arranged his adoption.' When Bea did not respond, Melody spelled it out for her. 'Which means that if he wishes, and if it's feasible, he'll be able to get in touch with you.'

In three years' time, Patrick – he wouldn't be called Patrick, of course; his adoptive parents would have chosen another name for him – might be able to trace her. She repeated, 'He'll be able to contact me?'

'Yes. You didn't know?'

Bea shook her head. 'Do people do that?'

'Yes. The law was changed in 1975. Bear in mind that adopted children don't necessarily begin the process straight away, at eighteen. They frequently leave trying to trace their birth parents until their late twenties or thirties. There can be all sorts of reasons for that. It takes courage. It's a difficult emotional journey. They may be concerned about upsetting their adoptive parents.'

'I'm afraid he'd resent me. Or hate me.' She had never voiced this fear before. Not to Emma or Marissa, nor to Clive or Francis, but she found that she could bear to say it to Melody. 'I gave him away,' she said.

'You were very young, Bea. Not much more than a child.'

She had been seventeen when she had become pregnant with her son. Only eight years older than Alice.

'Do you know whether your baby was adopted through an agency or whether it was a private adoption?'

'I've no idea. My parents arranged it.' Bea reached out to pour the coffee, but her hand shook visibly.

Melody said, 'Let me.' As she poured, she said, 'Tracing a birth parent tends to be more straightforward if the adoption was done through an agency. On the whole, they're likely to have better records. If the adoption was privately arranged – by a family doctor, for instance, or a vicar, or perhaps through a nursing home – the documents can be harder to find. It can still be done, though. Mmm.' She took a deep, appreciative breath. 'Delicious coffee.'

Bea blew her nose. The breeze ruffled the tall grasses growing in the border.

'As the birth mother,' said Melody gently, 'you don't have the right to trace your child. You would have to wait for him to get in touch with you. It's hard, I know, but you should try to remain hopeful.'

Ten days after her visit to the farmhouse, Gabriel drove the terracotta pots to Marissa's flat. He hauled them up one at a time to the top floor in the lift; when the second pot was in place on the balcony and he had mopped the sweat off his brow, she handed him a glass of Chablis. They stood back and admired the pots and chatted about their day. It had begun to rain, and the green-white glaze gleamed in the pearl-grey dusk.

She said, 'I'll get on with supper, then.'

'No.' He put down his glass and drew her to him. The rain fell as they kissed. He ran his thumb up the nape of her neck and she put her head back, closing her eyes as he pressed his lips against the hollow at the base of her throat. She looped her hands round his waist and they kissed some more.

She never cooked supper that night. The lemon sole stayed chilling in the fridge, the Waitrose raspberry tart lay neglected on the work surface. Sometime in the early hours of the morning, she thought he might be hungry, so she got out of bed and fetched a tray of cheese and crackers. They ate the lot and then they made love again, and she didn't even notice the crumbs.

# Chapter Thirteen

## 1986

That morning, over toast and coffee, Morgan had offered to come with her to London. He wouldn't mind a trip to buy some art supplies, he said, and he'd enjoy a couple of days out with her. Tamar fended him off by reminding him that she had a full day: an interview with a journalist in the afternoon, and later, a dress fitting with Marissa. Morgan had never made such an offer before; it knocked her off balance, and some of the sweating panic of that moment persisted as she let herself into her room at the Paddington hotel.

Today, she noticed its shabbiness. Inspecting herself in the mirror, she saw that she had snagged her tights. She hadn't brought a spare pair, so she took them off and went barelegged. She was tanned from her walks on the shore and she had, thank God, remembered to shave her legs. She was wearing the navy-blue Marissa Flint dress Alexander had admired when they had first become lovers, more than a year ago. She applied some lipstick, but then, thinking it gave her a tawdry, mistressy air, scrubbed it off. She took the butterfly pin, which she always wore when she was going to see him, out of its box and tucked it into the loose knot piled at the back of her head. In the mirror, she saw how the butterfly's eyes glittered crimson against the white streaks in her hair. *Woman Going to See Her Lover*, she thought: that's what I would call the image if I were to paint it.

Alexander was waiting at the table when she arrived at the restaurant in St James's. He rose and kissed her cheek. There was a flurry of starched napkins and menus. The waiter hovered, pencil poised to take their orders.

Alexander ordered drinks, a red Graves for him and a gin and tonic for her. Tamar ran her gaze round the high-ceilinged room. The dozen tables were widely spaced and occupied by men in business suits. An oil painting, a blood-thirsty hunting scene, hung above the heavy, elaborate fireplace. Though the tasselled brown curtains were drawn back, their bulk excluded the sunlight, so that the diners ate and drank in a dim Victorian gloom. The pudding trolley creaked as it was wheeled to a table.

Alexander took her hand. 'How are you? You look wonderful, by the way. I hope it was all right, my writing to you. I was afraid I sounded peremptory.'

'Not at all. It was so good to hear from you.'

'This place is impossible, a relic of the past, but I can reliably get a table here. And it's discreet, and one has the space and quiet to talk properly. How is Morgan?'

'Much better, thank you. Working again. And your family? Your daughter-in-law? You must have a grandchild by now.'

'I have a granddaughter, Edith Margaret, Edie for short.' He took a photograph from his wallet and showed it to her. Tamar admired the picture of the baby. 'So adorable.'

'Caroline's in New York at the moment, helping out.' Then,

frowning, he said, 'Tamar, I've been offered a new job. It's for an arts foundation. Charitable, quite well off and influential. I've been invited to head up the board of five trustees.'

She thought it sounded right up his street. She knew that for some time he had longed to move on from a purely financial role.

He knew most of the other trustees, he told her, and they were decent and talented people. Whoever took on the role would have the opportunity to set the direction the foundation would take in the future.

She said, 'Are you going to accept it?'

'It would mean moving to the States.' His long fingers touched the stem of his wine glass, but he did not pick it up. 'The foundation's based in New York.'

Tamar looked away. This was why he had wanted to see her, she realised with a shock, to tell her that he was going abroad, that it was over. Perhaps she had half guessed that he had difficult news to break to her; she remembered that she had felt melancholy leaving Suffolk earlier that day.

'The States, so exciting!' she exclaimed. Her voice sounded high and artificially bright. 'Caroline must be delighted.'

'Yes, very much so. It would mean we'd be near our family.' He paused. In the silence, the footsteps of the waiters, the creaking of the trolley seemed unnaturally loud.

He said, 'Caroline would have liked more than one child. She wanted to have half a dozen, but it didn't happen for us.'

An emptiness was accumulating inside Tamar. She longed to leave the restaurant there and then, and it took an act of will to remain seated at the table. She could quite see that to Caroline Rainsford, this job offer must seem heaven-sent. If Alexander relocated to New York, she would be near her son and daughter-in-law. She would be close to little Edie

263

instead of condemned to the dissatisfactions of being a long-distance grandmother.

'There's no question, you must take it.' Men like Alexander Rainsford didn't stay still for long, Tamar told herself. She felt numb; the pain had not yet set in, but she was already trying to rationalise it away.

'If it means losing you,' he said quietly, 'I'll turn it down.'

She gave him a sharp look. 'You mustn't say that. I love you too much. I want the best for you. I'd never hold you back.'

The waiter returned to replace her cutlery with a fish knife and fork. She was relieved at the interruption, which allowed her to recover her composure. When they were able to talk again, she said, 'I'm not going to claim your decision doesn't affect me, because plainly that wouldn't be true. If you were to go away, I would miss you more than I can say. But you mustn't limit your future because of what can only ever be a very part-time love affair.'

'But you see, my love, the thing is, you mean everything to me.'

'Don't, please,' she said softly. 'Darling, I need you to make this easy for me.'

In the silence, she heard the tinkle of cutlery and glass, the murmur of talk from the other tables. She envied the rest of the diners their conversations, which could not possibly be as painful as hers.

'It doesn't have to be part-time,' he said.

'Alexander . . .'

'*We* don't have to be part-time. I haven't been able to think of anything else since they made me the offer. It's made me realise what's most important to me. And that's *you*, Tamar. I want you. I want to be with you all the time.'

Shaken, she looked away, over the wash of shimmering light on the floorboards, to the pudding trolley, with its colourful edifices of sponge and meringue, as it began once more its stately trundle across the room. She felt a little nauseous – she was afraid she wouldn't be able to eat at all.

'I'm tired of us meeting like this,' he said. 'I hate it, that this should be all we have. Restaurant lunches that only escape dreariness because of your company. That grim little hotel I find myself longing for because it's the one place we can be alone. It's undignified. It's unworthy of us.'

'It's better than nothing. Yes, the hotel is pretty ghastly, but I've never minded.' She forced her voice to remain steady.

Beneath the table, he squeezed her hand. 'We could have more, you and I.'

'Darling, you know that's not possible.'

'But don't you find this impossible too?' he said vehemently. 'Tamar, we have to make a choice. I can't turn down this job without good reason, because Caroline won't accept that. Because of the baby, because of Sebastian . . . because of everything.'

She understood then that he had a streak of recklessness, of ruthlessness. No, more than a streak – it was integral to him. She felt as if she was standing on the beach at Seastone, looking out to where a wave surged towards her, about to carry her off to some unknown place. She disliked being put in such a position; it made her feel resentful.

'You mustn't ask me to leave Morgan,' she murmured. 'This is just . . . it's indulgent. It's a fantasy and it's hurtful. I won't do it.'

The waiter was threading his way towards them again, carrying two plates, smoked salmon for her and thin slices of salted beef for him. The plates were put in front of them.

The waiter refilled Alexander's glass, then went off to fetch another gin and tonic for Tamar.

She said gently, 'Are we having our first quarrel, do you think?'

'I hope not.'

'I could never quarrel with you. You're not quarrelling material. You're far too considerate and generous.' She looked away. 'It's my fault, I'm in a wretched mood today.'

She found that she could eat a little after all. At first they ate in silence, though his expression remained thunderous. At last he spoke, his voice low.

'This is how I see it, Tamar. It was the war that drove us apart. Along with fate, or chance, or destiny – whatever you choose to call it. Is it reasonable that we should have to pay the price for that our entire lives? Why shouldn't we be allowed some happiness? Haven't we waited long enough?'

She put her hand on his sleeve. 'Please, let's not talk about it now. Let's enjoy our time together.'

After the meal, they took a taxi to her hotel in Paddington. Sitting in the back seat, she felt the comforting weight of his hand on her thigh. As the taxi crawled past Hyde Park, she watched people going in and out of the gates. Again she envied the apparent simplicity of their lives – but that was unreasonable of her, she thought. Wasn't everyone's life muddled and complicated?

She had first met Alexander Rainsford in the sea of destruction that had been London in June 1944. She had never forgotten the flash of joy and yearning she had experienced during their encounter. There had been times since when she had tried to pass that off as unimportant, or even self-invented. And yet she had felt the same attraction when they had met again at the gallery, many years later. How would her life have turned out if the two of them had exchanged names and addresses, then and there in the rubble? Or if his lift had been delayed – or if he had dodged the bullet in Berlin? Or if he had waited just ten minutes longer in the Lyons café? She considered the struggles of her married life to Morgan, the quarrels and the financial insecurity and her fight for self-expression. If she had married Alexander, what sort of person might she have been? She would have been another woman entirely.

They reached the hotel. In the foyer stood vases of gaudy chrysanthemums, petals browning at the edges. The staircase smelled of floor polish and gravy. In her room, they undressed. She had never felt ashamed of exposing her fifty-nine-year-old body to his gaze, and she did not feel shame today. And yet, looking down at herself, she seemed to see the story of her life inscribed on her skin. The stretch marks on belly and breast wrote of the three children she had given birth to. The veins on her legs reminded her of the countless hours she had stood at the kitchen stove and the seasons she had walked through the fields to shop and school. The oil paint ingrained in her nails and in the whorls on her fingertips told another tale.

She had made her decision. It hadn't been hard to reach, but it would be dreadfully hard to tell him.

After they had made love, she lay in his arms. A fly buzzed against the window pane; somewhere in the street below, a man was singing drunkenly at the top of his voice. She felt a sudden longing to be at home, to have nothing more to think about than what she would cook for tea or the boredom of starting the ironing.

'You're very quiet,' he said. 'Tell me what you're thinking. I don't think I want to hear it, but tell me anyway.'

'Alexander, I can't leave Morgan. I'm sorry, but I can't.'

'And yet he makes you unhappy.' His voice was rough.

'Sometimes, yes. But still, I won't leave him. Nor do I want to be the woman who breaks up your marriage, who makes you act against your conscience.'

'My conscience is my own affair and my marriage was in a poor enough state before I met you. I'd make sure Caroline was comfortably settled.'

Kneeling up, she kissed the blade of his shoulder. His brown skin was warm and tasted of salt. Caroline wouldn't want the move to the States if she didn't still love Alexander. This conclusion pressed against her heart, a heavy weight of guilt and confusion.

'You're an honourable man,' she said gently. 'If you walked away from your family, you'd end up hating yourself.'

'Perhaps. But I'll hate myself more if I walk away from you.'

'I can't leave Morgan. He needs me.'

'I need you.'

She shook her head. 'No, I don't think you do, not in the same way.'

Morgan might have the look of a freebooter, but a home and stability were essential to him. She herself had often been restless and unsettled, but in time she had discovered that there was a part of her that needed to be anchored. As for Alexander, he was an adventurer at heart.

'And there are my children,' she said. 'I know they're grown up now, but if I were to leave Morgan, it would break their hearts, and I can't do that. I don't believe you could either. I don't believe you're capable of choosing to inflict such hurt on Sebastian. And I would never ask it of you.'

'Sebastian's an adult now. He ought to be able to understand that two people can grow apart.' Yet she sensed his certainty weakening.

She tugged a brush through her tangled hair. 'My darling, I couldn't live the sort of life you live. It's too public, too busy, too full of committees and dinners and smart parties. If I tried to live like that, it would destroy me.'

'But I don't have to live that life.'

'You couldn't live the sort of life I must have. You fill every moment of your day, and I . . . I need quiet and space to paint.' The brush snagged on the butterfly pin; she had forgotten to take it out before they had tumbled into bed. Looking at it, she felt a sharp pang.

'I need Morgan and I need Seastone. They are a part of me. Without them, I can't be what I want to be.' Tenderly she kissed him, running her fingertips over the ripple of scars that circled his torso, a legacy of the war. Morgan had scars like that too. 'You have so much to look forward to. A new country, a new job . . . and the baby, a new life.'

'What is that worth if I can't be with you?' His voice was anguished.

Lying face to face, they clung to each other. Always, she had known it would end in this way. Always, she had tried to think that they might have one day, and then, if they were lucky, perhaps another one after that. But it would not last.

She felt the pressure of his fingers on the nape of her neck as he kissed her, roughly and hungrily. She felt the heat of his skin and the hardness of his body, and she closed her eyes. She wrapped her legs round him, and as the slight roughness of his chin brushed against her jaw, she threw her head back, stifling a cry.

Afterwards, they dressed. 'You won't change your mind?' he said.

'I'm sorry.' She held up her crumpled frock against her like a shield.

'Then if this is truly what you want, I won't see you again. I can't stand dragged-out farewells.' His voice was cold.

She pressed her hand against her mouth and went into the bathroom. She ran her hands under the cold tap, then pushed her fingertips hard against the skin round her eyes to stem the tears. By the time she went back into the room, he had dressed and was standing at the window, smoking a cigarette.

'When are you to go to New York?'

'They've asked me to start in a month's time.'

'You'll have a lot to do.'

'Oh yes, it'll keep me busy.'

They could have been two acquaintances, she thought, trying to strike up a conversation after some minor difference of opinion. But then he took her in his arms and for a long time held her close to him.

Breaking away, she took the butterfly pin from the bedside cabinet and offered it to him.

'No, keep it.' He gave her the ghost of a smile. 'I want you to have it. Think of me a little when you wear it. Here, let me put it in your hair.' His fingers brushed against her head, then he stood back. 'I was right that day, wasn't I? I always knew it would suit you.'

The door closed behind him. Tamar glanced at her watch. She was late for her interview at the gallery. She did not know how she would string a sentence together. She did not know how she would get on the right train. She opened her handbag, but her hotel key wasn't inside it. She searched, flinging aside cushions and pillows, peering under the dressing table, feeling hot and desperate.

She found the key on the windowsill, behind the curtain. Grabbing it, she left the room and hurried along the corridor, hoping she might catch up with him, or at least see a final glimpse of him on the street outside.

But he was gone, and the sun blinded her, and she stood on the pavement, her heart hammering. She had no feeling of having done the right thing in breaking off the affair; all she felt was muddle and despair and a desire not to make a fool of herself by weeping in the street. She dashed her hand over her eyes and hurried to the station.

Marissa kept her circle of friends small and carefully chosen. She disliked speaking in public, and still felt in her heart that the clothes she created should speak for themselves. She was choosy about which invitations she accepted and rarely stayed long at a party. The success of her career allowed her to get away with such foibles. That she avoided occasions others vied to attend only increased her mystique, adding to the perception that she was different to other people. She knew that some thought her to be a bit of a recluse, though a beautiful and fascinating one.

That evening, at half past five, she took a taxi to Margaret Street. The last customer was leaving the premises as Tamar turned up. The shop manager and her assistant went home shortly afterwards, leaving Marissa and Tamar on their own.

Tamar looked tired, Marissa thought. She made coffee in the tiny back kitchen while Tamar began to try on the outfits she had picked out for her. She carried the tray through to the changing area. Tamar came out of the cubicle wearing a pair of dark red trousers and a cream flannel shirt.

Marissa studied her. 'Fabulous colours on you. The fit isn't bad, though I might adjust those hems just the tiniest bit. How was your day?'

'Oh, you know. And you?'

'Lots going on, but that's always good.' Marissa walked round Tamar. 'Let me see you from the back. Oh, you're wearing that gorgeous pin! It's rather loose – I'm afraid it'll fall out. Shall I . . .?'

But Tamar had taken the butterfly pin from her hair. She stared at it as it lay on the palm of her hand, and then she began to cry.

Marissa found her a chair to sit on and handed her a wad of tissues. Giving Tamar's shoulders a comforting rub, she said, 'Let's leave this for another day. I know how much you hate it.'

'It's not the clothes! Oh God, I'm sorry, how awful of me!' Closing her eyes, Tamar pressed her palm against her mouth to stifle the heaving sobs.

'Everyone has bad days,' Marissa said soothingly, though she guessed that what had upset Tamar was more than a run-of-the-mill bad day. Tamar wasn't the bursting-into-tears sort.

Eventually she was able to blow her nose and wipe her eyes. 'So sorry, Marissa. I thought I was actually going to manage to get through today without falling apart. It must be the last thing you need.'

'Don't be daft. You'd be surprised how often my customers tell me their troubles. And some of them have a little cry. Drink your coffee. Is everything all right? Your family, your work . . .?'

The tissue was a damp little ball. 'It's not that.'

'Then . . .' She gave Tamar a discerning glance. 'Do you want to tell me about it?'

Tamar pressed her hands together. She had beautiful hands, elegant and strong, an artist's hands. 'I'm afraid I'll burst if I can't talk to anyone. Would you mind?'

'Not a bit.'

'Don't you need to get on home? I'm sure you have better things to do than listen to me maundering on.'

'Honestly, I don't.'

'Then thank you.' Tamar gave a loud sniff. 'Goodness, how I wish I still smoked! We all did in the war; it was how we got through it. It was a filthy habit, though.'

'I've a bottle of gin. I'll get it.'

Marissa went to the stockroom. David Johnstone had brought the gin round a few evenings ago, when they had had to work very late. Returning to the changing rooms, she said, 'I can nip up the road for some tonic if you don't like it neat.'

'Neat is fine. You're a kind person, Marissa.'

Marissa poured the gin. She knew that people were divided in their opinion of her. On the whole, her staff appreciated her, she thought, and she was a loyal friend. She suspected that more than one of her discarded lovers thought her as hard as nails. Gabriel . . . Her thoughts turned, as they so often did nowadays, to Gabriel. What did he truly think of her, what did he feel about her? He had a certain reserve, so she sometimes found it hard to tell.

After blowing her nose, Tamar said, 'I had to say goodbye to someone today.' She looked up at Marissa and caught her eye. 'Not Morgan, I mean.'

'I assumed not,' Marissa said, a little drily. As she passed her friend a glass of gin, a memory flashed into her mind from more than a year ago, of Tamar walking down Harley Street on the arm of a tall, silver-haired man.

Tamar was still holding the butterfly hairpin. She looked down at it. 'Years and years ago, during the war, he gave me this.'

'Did you know him before you knew Morgan?'

'Oh no.' Tamar shook her head. 'No, I met Morgan first.' She looked upset again and took a deep, wobbling breath.

To give Tamar a moment to gather her composure, Marissa took out the till roll and began to tuck change into small plastic bags. 'I should imagine you'd feel a strong bond with the people you'd known in the war. You'd feel only they could understand what you went through.'

'I've wondered whether that's a part of it.' Tamar ran her thumb along a mother-of-pearl wing. 'You could say that I've known him for ages. But if you look at it another way, we've hardly known each other for any time at all. If we added up the hours we've spent together, it would come to a couple of days, maybe three.' She was tearing a tissue to shreds. 'I feel such a fool. How can I be in pieces so, at my age?'

'I'm not sure age makes a difference.'

'Well, that's an awful thought, that I might still be breaking my heart when I'm ninety.'

Marissa laughed. One of the reasons she liked Tamar was because she was frank and open. She didn't try to put on a veneer of sophistication or cleverness, and she wasn't afraid of admitting failure or disappointment.

She said, 'Where did you meet him?'

'In Bloomsbury, not so far from here. And then, years later – thirty-four, thirty-five years, something like that – I met him again. But I never forgot him, Marissa. All those

274

years, I kept the butterfly pin safe and I remembered what he'd said to me.' She bit her lower lip, then said softly, 'He wouldn't let me give it back to him this afternoon. I should have insisted.' She held out her glass. 'Is there a drop more?'

'Here.' Marissa topped up both glasses.

'When we met again, a few years ago, he told me that he recognised me straight away. You'd think he was trying to flatter me, but I don't believe he was. Sometimes you think your younger self is almost a stranger to you, that you've grown so far away from it you wouldn't even recognise yourself. But he saw me, Marissa, he knew me.' Tamar's voice faltered. She took another mouthful of gin. 'And at first it was fine, we were just friends — or at least that was what I told myself. But then . . .'

Marissa said gently, 'But then it turned into something more.'

'Yes.' Tamar opened her handbag, took out a jewellery box and put the butterfly pin inside it. 'Sometimes I've found it hard to know that I missed a life I could have had, perhaps by moments. But then I wouldn't have married Morgan.'

'Do you regret that?' As soon as she said it, Marissa wondered whether she should have asked.

But Tamar shook her head and said, 'No . . . no, I don't, not at all. It would have been a different life. An easier one, in some ways, perhaps.' She snapped shut the jewellery box. 'Morgan and I don't have the perfect marriage. Really, it's anything but. But then I don't believe any marriage is perfect.' She ran her fingers through her hair to tidy it. 'Is that why you haven't married yet, Marissa?' She made a face. 'Ugh, sorry, that's the gin talking. I should shut up. You're so young. You have so much time. I only meant I can see you like everything just so, and family life is never, ever just so.'

'Do I?'

'Marissa!' Her name was an amused squawk. 'Just look at you!'

She was going through the rails of garments, making sure the hangers were the exact four centimetres apart she liked them to be. She stood back, slightly embarrassed. 'It looks nicer like this,' she murmured. 'And it's easier for the customers to see the clothes if they aren't all jammed together.'

'There's nothing wrong in keeping up high standards.' Tamar gave a throaty laugh. 'Now there's an admission from the woman who wears a dress till it falls apart and who rather too often resorts to giving her husband a dinner of a boiled egg and toast.'

Marissa sat down on the floor opposite Tamar and hunched up her knees. 'If everything's neat and in good order, it makes me feel better.' She kept her flat immaculate. 'When I'm *really* upset, I clean the oven.'

'Good Lord. I can't remember when our oven last had a clean. I chip away at the black bits now and then.'

'And I have a drink,' Marissa said honestly. 'Or two.'

'Oh, there was a time when I used to do the same.'

Marissa could see that Tamar was concentrating on keeping the tears at bay. She wanted to give her a hug but wasn't sure it would help. Tamar was a proud woman who disliked giving in to strong emotions.

Tamar summoned up a wry smile. 'I used to think of myself as the bohemian type – you know, wild at heart – but the truth is, I've seen too many friends wreck their health and their marriages with alcohol. Morgan used to drink, when he was younger, but he stopped some years ago. We don't go out often, but when we do, he drinks water.'

'Do you think it goes with the territory, with being an artist?'

'I've known artists who claimed that. Or they used it as an excuse. And it's true that when you're going through a dry patch, there's the temptation to have a few drinks in the hope that it fires you up and gives you inspiration.' She let out a long breath. 'It's funny, isn't it, how you can change. I hated Seastone when I first went to live there, but now I need it. My inspiration comes from the landscape, from the fields and the sea. And though Morgan and I have had our ups and downs, I need him too. The truth is, though you might think me old-fashioned, when it comes down to it, I think marriage is for life.'

Marissa looked down at her glass. 'But when it's a bad marriage . . .?'

'If you mean cruelty or violence or neglect, then no, absolutely not.' Tamar stood up and began to unbutton the cream-coloured shirt. 'In London, after the war, there was a woman I knew – she was an artist too – whose husband used to lock her in a room when he was fed up with her. He'd rip up her paintings as well, after he'd had a few drinks. He was an absolute brute.'

'I hope she left him.'

'She did eventually, yes, though it took her a while.'

Tamar was of a tougher generation, Marissa thought, one accustomed to putting aside all sorts of horrors. 'I hope she was all right,' she said.

'She was, more or less. He remarried, but she never did. I remember visiting her at her cottage on the Sussex coast. She did some marvellous work. There are a couple of her pieces in the Tate. You and I, we should go and see them.'

'I'd like that.'

Tamar retrieved her navy dress from where it had slithered to the floor. 'The thing about Morgan, for all his faults – and believe me, Marissa, he has a great many – is that he's never tried to change me. I can be myself with him. And that's what I think about marriage, that it should give both partners the chance to be themselves. The balance between joy and pain, that matters too. But sometimes love is painful. It just is.'

Gabriel was different to the half-dozen other men she had dated over the past few years. Marissa knew there were risks in letting herself get close to him, hurdles to be overcome. He came with a history, a difficult divorce and a shy and fragile teenage daughter – he came with *baggage*. But then surely that was the case for most men of his age. Still, Tamar's words made her feel uneasy. *Family life is never, ever just so.* Gabriel's family arrangements were complex, and if their relationship was to continue, all sorts of problems might spring up. It would be understandable if Isabelle resented her. She might seem to the girl an interloper, intruding on her close relationship with her father and a poor substitute for her mother.

And those concerns came before you even considered the fact that she and Gabriel were both so busy they struggled to find time to have lunch together. Gabriel and Isabelle were shortly to leave for France, for his family home near Bayeux. He had told her they always spent August there. Though Marissa's summer was crammed full of appointments and work trips, she couldn't help but feel that apart from the planned weekend at Seastone with her friends later that month, August loomed bleakly. Which was ridiculous. She loved her work. You've so much to do, she reminded herself sternly. It will pass in a flash.

Tamar was searching for something in her handbag. Items spilled out – a pencil, some crumpled scraps of paper, a lipstick without a cap. 'A woman has to be resilient,' she said, stuffing the lot back in the bag before drawing out her purse and checking her train ticket. 'Especially if she wants to have a career. My career has been such a mess, so hopeless, all fits and starts, and I didn't even begin to get anywhere until I'd pretty much stopped caring about success. I'm full of admiration for you, Marissa. Look at what you've achieved. You should feel so proud of yourself.' She looked at her watch. 'I think I'll head back to Seastone this evening after all. I don't think I could bear that hotel for another night. I just want to go home.' She gestured to the clothes. 'Shall I take these with me? I can always adjust the hems at home.'

'Not at all, I'll do it. I'll post them to you.' The thought of Tamar's botched, rushed stitching on the soft dark crimson wool was unbearable to Marissa.

Marissa reflected on her conversation with Tamar as she travelled home that evening. Tamar had loved two men with conviction and passion. Before Marissa had met Gabriel, she had kept herself emotionally distant from every man she met. The man she had felt closest to was David Johnstone – and he was gay and had a partner. He was safe, in other words.

She let herself into her flat, dropped her bag and briefcase on the coffee table and changed into jeans and a silk top. All the rooms were immaculate and nothing was out of place. *I can see you like everything just so*: Tamar had been right about that. Her livelihood was dependent on her capacity for rigor and perfection, and it bled over into her private life.

Yet she knew she was different when she was with Gabriel. With him, she was able to relax, to let go. And anyway,

Gabriel had high standards too, which made her love him all the more.

Love. The word startled her. She stood at the window, looking out to the balcony and the terracotta pots that Gabriel had given her. Was she falling in love with Gabriel Vernier? She felt shaken: she rather thought she might be.

She picked up the phone and dialled his number. Gabriel answered. He was cooking supper, he told her. Sizzling sounds and the clunking of saucepans in the background. Now and then, as they talked, he put down the receiver so that he could drain potatoes or rinse lettuce.

After he had slid the steaks onto a plate to rest, he spoke to her of the journey he and Isabelle were to take to France the following day. Their suitcases were packed; they would cross the Channel on the Portsmouth ferry.

Then he said, 'Come and stay with us.'

Her heart missed a beat. 'Gabriel?'

'Come to France, Marissa. Come and stay with us at my home, at the manoir. Just for a few days, if that's all you can spare, but please do come. I want you to meet my family. I want us to have time for each other. I want to show you the house I love. I want to walk in the woods with you, my darling, and I want to spend a day on the beach with you. You'll love it there, I promise. And I will love you being there.'

# Chapter Fourteen

## 1986

Driving onto the cross-Channel ferry to Caen, Marissa had a moment of doubt. It seemed incautious, this trip to France. She rarely permitted herself to be impulsive. She had so much work to do . . . and what if Gabriel's family were hard to get on with?

Her worries faded away as the ship pulled out of Portsmouth. She stayed on deck throughout the sailing. The sky was the blue of harebells, the sea calm. She watched a group of small boys playing tag and listened to the conversation of the older couple sitting opposite her, who were poring over the *Times* crossword, while the papers she had brought with her remained untouched in her bag. It felt heavenly just to sit, for there to be nowhere she must rush to, nothing she must do.

She longed to see Gabriel again. She longed to feel the warmth of his arms and the touch of his lips. She yearned for her journey to be over so that she could be with him. She had never been to Normandy before; the only part of France she had visited had been Paris. She had travelled there on that long-ago trip with her mother, when she was only eighteen, and more recently for the fashion shows.

After disembarking at Caen, she negotiated the spider's web of roads that surrounded the city. As she headed deeper into Normandy, she ran through in her memory the directions Gabriel had given her by letter. The name of his family home was the Manoir Sainte-Gilles. She followed his instructions meticulously, turning off the main highway not long after Moulins en Bessin. Now she was in peaceful countryside, heading along single-track lanes palisaded by high hedgerows. A half-timbered farmhouse, a herd of cattle in a field. Half a dozen ducks, crossing the road in stately fashion. A gap in the hedge that revealed fields of golden corn.

Tall trees cast a deep, flickering shade as she plunged down into a valley. A stream ran sparkling beside the road and small brown butterflies danced in the gloom. Then she was heading uphill once more, and after a while the trees parted and she was back among fields and copses.

She caught sight ahead of a pair of wrought-iron gates and swung the car through them. A narrow, unsurfaced driveway took her between undulating meadows dotted with willows and silver poplars. She passed a brightly glinting stream and a sculpted, blackened tree trunk that had been struck by lightning.

The Manoir Sainte-Gilles was mirrored in the glassy surface of the circular pond in front of it. As Marissa slowed to park the car on a gravelled forecourt, she admired the graceful building with its red-tiled roof and square, half-timbered turret. She climbed out of the car. And there was Gabriel, walking through a green archway cut in a hedge, raising a hand in greeting as he came towards her.

'You made it,' he called out.

'It's glorious! Like something out of a fairy tale!'

He was wearing a navy-blue shirt and jeans and he looked tanned. Her heart melted at the sight of him. When he hugged her, she closed her eyes, breathing in the scent of his skin and revelling in the warmth of his embrace.

'You didn't tell me,' she said as he took her bags out of the boot and they went into the house. 'You didn't tell me that you lived in a chateau.'

'It's a very modest chateau.' He looked down at her, smiling. 'Rather a dilapidated one. I've missed you so much.' He put down her bags in the cool black-and-white-tiled hallway. 'Darling Marissa, I'm so glad you came.' And then he kissed her.

A tall arched window at the top of the stairs framed a green landscape beyond; the room that Gabriel showed her to on the first floor, with its pale gold wallpaper so faded that the birds and flowers imprinted on it seemed on the verge of vanishing, delighted her.

Marissa changed into a white linen dress and they went outside, to the garden at the back of the house. Isabelle was sitting with two older women in the shade of a copper beech tree. That Isabelle greeted her without having to be prompted by her father gave Marissa a warm glow of pleasure. Gabriel introduced her to his mother, Jeanne, and his sister, Andrée. Jeanne was small and slight, and she had her son's slender face and fine features. She was able to stand long enough to take Marissa's hand and kiss her cheek as she welcomed her to her home, then she sat back in her wheelchair. Andrée was tall and slim, brown-skinned and athletic-looking in her denim shorts and sleeveless striped blouse. Her eyes were grey and sharp, her nose long and aquiline, and her shoulder-length brown hair was swept carelessly back from her face.

Andrée fetched tea, coffee and cakes. Jeanne spoke no English, so the conversation moved between the two languages, with Gabriel or Andrée translating when necessary. Marissa noticed that Gabriel and Andrée teased each other a lot. Andrée told Marissa stories about Gabriel when he had been a boy. When she thought her daughter was going too far, Jeanne gently intervened. Isabelle knelt down on the grass beside her grandmother and Jeanne stroked the girl's silky dark hair.

Afterwards, Jeanne went indoors to supervise the dinner preparations and Andrée offered to take Isabelle to the swimming pool in Bayeux. Gabriel and Marissa went for a walk in the grounds. He told her that his father had bought the *manoir* in the early fifties, that he had fallen passionately in love with it, though there had been swifts nesting in the bedrooms then, and the staircase had been on the verge of collapse.

'For years, the four of us lived on the ground floor,' he said. 'My father did most of the work himself. Andrée and I tried to give him a hand, as soon as we were old enough. He died fifteen years ago, and my mother thought she might have to sell the house. It was his life's work, and we all hated the idea of losing it. In the end, we managed to find ways of holding on to it. I use the old stables for my business, and we rent out land to local farmers. Andrée and Michel are restoring some of the outbuildings to let to summer visitors.'

They were heading across a tussocky field towards a band of trees. Marissa said, 'You love it here.'

'I do, yes.'

'But you chose to move to England.'

'Justine wanted to. We lived here for a while, soon after we were married. Isabelle was born here. But then Justine decided that she wanted to go back.'

Her awareness of his proximity made every cell in her body vibrate with longing. Her attention was seized by the angle of his smile and the easy grace of his movements; his hand was warm in hers.

He said, 'When I was in my late teens, I spent a month travelling round Provence, trying to find a match for some beautiful old terracotta tiles we'd uncovered at the back of the house. It's funny, isn't it, how something can take you over. How something . . . or someone . . . enchants you and you can't get them out of your head.' They had reached the shade of the trees. They embraced, and he ran his fingertips along the hollow of her spine.

They walked on. A broad path, rutted by wheels and indented with the crescent shapes of horseshoes, ran through the forest, cutting it in two. Mosses gave the gnarled bases of the trees a green velvet covering, and lichens frilled the branches. Here the air was cool and windless; here there was silence.

She said, 'When I'm designing a garment, there's often a moment when I know it's just right. I can't tell you how I know. I can't say exactly what it is that pleases me. I'm not so good with people. I'm a pretty lousy judge of character. I like someone, and then it seems to fade.'

A shadow crossed his face. 'Is that what you feel?'

'Not with you.' She seized his hand and pressed it against her heart. 'If you'd asked me to come and stay in a shed with you, Gabriel Vernier, I'd still be here.'

His lips touched hers and she closed her eyes, losing herself in his kiss. No kiss had been like this before, no kiss had made her want a man so much. He pressed another kiss against her throat, then her breast. In the cool, dark solitude of the trees, he undid the small pearl buttons that ran down the front of her dress and then slipped it from her shoulders.

Bea said, 'What's in here?' and her mother said, 'China. Jack's mother's set, with the forget-me-nots. I don't know whether to bother unpacking it. We never use it.' They were sitting on the floor of the front room, going through boxes. Bea's father and Francis had taken Alice and Rachel to the beach, while Bea had stayed behind to help her mother. A month earlier, her parents had moved to Boscombe, near Bournemouth, the move prompted by Jack Meade's retirement and his long-held desire to live by the sea.

Bea unwrapped newspaper from a cup. 'It's pretty.'

'Take it home with you then.'

'Are you sure?'

'I have three sets of china. We don't know anyone here, so it's not as if we'll be entertaining.'

She looked at her mother. 'You don't regret moving, do you, Mummy?'

'No, of course not,' said Vivien briskly. 'Your father's making lots of friends at the golf club. No doubt some of them will be bearable.'

They shared a smile. Bea wrapped up the cup and put it back in the box. 'If you're sure, then. I've always loved these.'

'Francis won't mind?' Vivien bent over a box and extracted a crystal brandy glass. 'Cluttering up that pretty little house.'

'I shouldn't think so.' Francis wouldn't dare mind. Francis remained on his best behaviour.

'Still no baby, then?'

Irritation surged through her. They had had this conversation before. 'I told you, Mummy, Francis and I have decided not to have children. We have the girls, and we're completely happy with them.'

Her mother sat back on her heels. 'Are you absolutely certain Francis is happy, Bea?'

'Yes, of course,' Bea said furiously. 'Anyway, I don't want any more children, and I'd hardly have a baby just to please him.'

That hadn't come out as she had meant it to. Her mother peered at her over her reading glasses. 'Is everything all right between you two?'

'It's fine,' she snapped. 'Of course it is.'

'You have to work at a marriage, darling. You can't expect it just to tick by without any effort on your part.'

Bea hauled another box into the centre of the room, ran the tip of her scissors along the tape, then dug in the blades viciously and tore open the box. Though she constantly tiptoed round her mother's sensibilities, Vivien seemed to think it acceptable to poke her nose into the most sensitive of matters. Bea knew that her usual reaction was to gloss over conversations like this, to keep the peace, yet something had hardened inside her this past difficult year. Her instinct to please, to appease seemed no longer as strong as it had once been.

Annoyance gave her the courage to embark on the conversation she had been putting off for some time, and she said, 'I wanted to ask you something, Mummy, about the baby, mine and Ciaran's baby. How was the adoption arranged? Was it done through an agency?'

'Why do you want to know?' Her mother removed a blue and white bowl from the packaging.

'Because he's my son.'

'It was such a long time ago.' Vivien's face was turned away. 'Why dig up all that again?'

'When he turns eighteen, he'll have the right to try and contact me.' Bea ran her sweating palms down her jeans.

Vivien stared at her, frowning. 'Are you sure? I didn't think that was allowed.'

'They changed the law.'

Vivien looked bewildered. She pulled at one of the striped straps of her sundress. She had lost weight, Bea thought. Her collarbones were clearly visible beneath her tanned skin, and the once rounded prettiness of her features had become a series of sharp planes and angles. Neither of them looked at each other properly. Neither of them wanted to acknowledge how the other had changed.

Some of her resentment crumbled. Her mother had always seemed to her both ageless and indomitable, and it disturbed her to realise that Vivien had her own vulnerabilities. She must have found the move exhausting. She was very much a London person and might not have wanted to move to Boscombe at all. In all likelihood, she had agreed to it for Bea's father's sake, because his health, following his heart attack, was still poor.

'The adoption was arranged privately,' Vivien said, and Bea's heart sank. 'Dr Wilton organised it for us. You remember Dr Wilton, don't you?'

She recalled the consulting room and their family doctor's contempt of her as though it was yesterday. *You've been a silly little girl, haven't you . . . ?*

'Does he still practise? Are you in contact with him?'

'I'm afraid he died some time ago. His liver, apparently.' Vivien's mouth pursed. 'Neither Jack nor I had him down as a drinker. It just goes to show, you can't always tell. He offered to arrange the adoption for us and it seemed the easiest way. Does it matter?'

'Someone told me that birth parents can be more difficult to trace if the adoption was privately arranged.'

Marooned in a sea of objects, many remembered from her girlhood, Bea tried to absorb her disappointment. Outside, beyond the bay window, sunlight flashed on the sections of sea visible between the houses on the other side of the road. A family trailing buckets and spades ambled along the pavement. Gulls wheeled, dark flicks against the clouds that were boiling up in the sky.

She took a pair of carved wooden candlesticks from the box. 'What about these?'

'We bought them in India, on our honeymoon.' Vivien held out her hand for them. Closing her eyes, she took a deep breath. 'When I brought them home to England, they still smelled of spices, of Kashmir.'

'They're beautiful.' Bea put the candlesticks on the 'to keep' pile.

Vivien was silent, smoothing out a tissue-paper wrapping on her thigh. Then, suddenly, she said, 'The only thing we've ever wanted is for you to be happy, Bea. Everything we did, we were only ever trying to do our best for you.'

Shortly afterwards, her mother went upstairs for a lie-down. Bea tidied up, then went outside to the back garden. It was large, with a grass tennis court and an ornamental pond and deep herbaceous borders. He might never be able to trace her, her boy, even if he wanted to. He might be understandably loyal to his adoptive parents and think it wrong even to try. He might not even want to know her name. He might never think of her at all. Tears blurred the stands of lupins and delphiniums. When Bea shut her eyes, his face, her son's face, crumpled and perfect, came into her mind's eye, as clear as it had been on the day she had given him away.

For the first time in years, she allowed herself to think of Ciaran. She was older now, and found it easier to understand why, faced with the prejudices of her family and his own, he might have run back to Ireland. He had been seventeen, like her. Just a boy. If only he had written, though. If only he had said goodbye.

What she had always wanted, what she yearned for, was love, a love that was powerful and lasting. As she walked out to the front of the house to see whether her father, Francis and the girls were on their way back yet, she found herself wondering whether everything that had happened to her since, for good or ill, had been the legacy of that sharp, sweet love affair with Ciaran O'Neill. It seemed to her that her life had been made up of disparate pieces, mismatched beads on a necklace that never sat right. So many of her choices had been in reaction to one crisis or another.

There they were, coming round the street corner. She waved, then walked along the pavement to meet them. Her gaze settled on Francis, on his neat, well-proportioned form and graceful stride. He was just the same, she thought. It was she who had changed, she who saw things differently now.

Marissa offered to help Andrée prepare dinner. She was standing at the kitchen sink peeling potatoes, while Andrée inserted sprigs of rosemary into slits she had made in a leg of lamb. Gabriel and Isabelle were outside in the garden, playing tennis.

Andrée said, 'Where did you go this afternoon?'

'To the beach at Arromanches. It was glorious.'

'I adore it there.' Andrée clipped more rosemary sprigs from the branch. The resinous, oily perfume pervaded the kitchen. 'Gabriel adores you, you know.'

'And I adore him.'

'Then that's good.'

Though Andrée's voice was light, Marissa sensed a warning in it. She put down the peeling knife. 'He's a wonderful man.'

Andrée made a scathing sound and smacked her hands together, then picked up the roasting tin with the lamb in it and slid it into the oven. 'He's an idiot, like most men. He fell for that stupid Justine.'

'What was she like?' Marissa couldn't resist asking. They had skated round the subject of his first wife, she and Gabriel. She wondered whether he retained a certain loyalty towards her. Justine was, after all, the mother of his child.

'She was a cow,' said Andrée briskly. 'And she was a cheat and a liar.'

Marissa stood aside so that Andrée could rinse her hands beneath the tap. Andrée gave her a sideways look. 'I say this to you, Marissa. I wouldn't say it to anyone else – to Michel, yes, but he never listens to me. He says I go yap, yap, yap, like a little puppy.' She made a mouth opening and closing gesture with her hand. Michel was Andrée's boyfriend, a composed and burly man who, along with Andrée herself, did a lot of the practical work in the house and grounds. 'My mother will never talk about Justine. She hates that she broke Gabriel's heart. And I must be very polite about her when I'm with Isabelle.'

'Of course.'

'Gabriel and Isabelle stay here every summer, but it always takes me a while to get to know Isabelle again. When she first arrives here, every time she is . . .' Another flap of her hand.

'Unhappy?'

'Yes, and . . . *de mauvaise humeur*.'

Marissa's understanding of the French language was rudimentary, but she could work that one out. 'Moody,' she said.

'Yes. Then she settles down and has a great time. It's because she has to recover from being with that woman.'

'Gabriel told me that Isabelle is supposed to see her mother once a fortnight, but she sometimes cancels.'

Andrée snorted. '*Often*, Marissa. She *often* cancels. Which means that poor little girl is upset *before* she goes to see her mother, because she's afraid that at the last minute Justine will call it off. Here.' Andrée dropped a bunch of carrots, earth still clinging to them, into the large enamel sink. 'You scrub them, please. Do not peel them.' She began rapidly and expertly to slice the potatoes Marissa had prepared. The knife made clipping sounds on the wooden board. 'Justine forgets about Isabelle for months, and then, *pouf*!' She spread her fingers. 'She remembers she has a daughter. She invites Isabelle to stay and makes a fuss of her. She buys her new clothes and handbags and takes her to restaurants, maybe to a musical. And then Isabelle goes home to Gabriel, and she is *de mauvaise humeur* because she misses her mother and has been spoiled. And because she's afraid Justine will forget her again. Which she does. She always does.'

'Gabriel said that Justine likes to think of herself as a free spirit.'

Andrée's lip curled with contempt. 'Oh yes. She is a flower child, a hippy. That's her excuse for the way she treats Isabelle.

You understand, Marissa, why I say she is a cow.' She lifted down a large dish and began to butter it.

Marissa said, 'Is she beautiful?' A part of her didn't want to know, and yet, again, she was compelled to ask.

'Very. Black hair and brown eyes. Very pretty and very spoiled. Her father is an English lord. This is how Justine looks, Marissa.' Andrée turned her mouth down at the corners in an exaggerated fashion.

Marissa laughed. 'Sulky.'

'Yes. She sulks if she doesn't get her own way. When Gabriel didn't give her what she asked him for, she used to cry. I wanted to crack her on the head.' Andrée waved a jug in a threatening manner. 'You don't mind cream? Sometimes I make this with stock, but cream is better.'

'Cream is fine.'

'You're so slim. Englishwomen are always dieting,' Andrée added, giving Marissa a disdainful look.

'I never diet. I often don't have time for lunch, that's all, and I forget to buy food. And I'm always busy.'

'You're not a cook?'

'My mother taught me to cook, so I can, but to be honest, I don't bother very much. You don't always feel like cooking when you live by yourself.'

Andrée poured cream into the sliced potato dish. She rubbed the last drip from the lip of the jug with her fingertip and licked it. 'Mmm. Delicious.' She leaned against the kitchen table, her gaze resting on Marissa. 'Did Gabriel tell you that it was Justine who persuaded him to go back to England?'

'He did, yes. I wondered whether she was homesick.'

'Uh-uh.' Andrée shook her head emphatically. 'That's what she *said* to him. She told him that she missed her family and her friends. But it wasn't true. She was seeing someone in London.'

Shocked, Marissa looked up from scrubbing the carrots. 'Justine was having an affair?'

'Yes. So Gabriel packs up and they all head off back to England. My stupid brother, he spends all hours working at his business and making that house into a home for her, and guess what? She is already planning to leave. She told him so after they split up. She told him because she wanted to hurt him.' Andrée shrugged. 'Perhaps he'd already guessed. He can be stupid, my brother, but maybe he isn't *that* stupid. Have you finished the carrots?'

Marissa handed her the cleaned vegetables. Andrée opened the fridge and took out a bottle of white wine. She filled two glasses and gave one to Marissa.

'Gabriel cares for you,' she said. 'It's a long time since I've seen him like this with a woman.' She opened the oven door and put the potatoes beneath the roasting lamb. Hot air wafted into the kitchen.

She stood up, rubbed her hands on a tea towel and hung it on a hook. 'He cares for you,' she repeated. 'I hope you feel the same for him, Marissa.' The warning note had returned to Andrée's voice. 'Because if you don't, then it would be better if you went back to England now. If you're just passing the time with him. Do you understand? Gabriel's my brother and I don't want to see him hurt again.'

'I'll never hurt him. I love him.'

Marissa went to stand in the doorway. Looking out into the garden, she saw that Gabriel and Isabelle were heading back to the house. The sounds of cooking, the bubbling of pots and Andrée's crashing of pans, receded into the background as she let her eyes rest on him, this man she felt so much for. There, she had said it, a truth she had been half afraid of admitting even to herself: that she had fallen in love with Gabriel Vernier.

On Marissa's last afternoon in France, the three of them went to the beach. They all swam in the sea. A breeze lifted, ruffling the waves. Gabriel remained in the water while Marissa and Isabelle returned to the bags and towels.

Isabelle was shivering. 'Come here,' said Marissa. Isabelle scowled, but then went to sit beside her. Marissa wrapped a towel round the girl's thin shoulders and began to dry her hair. Isabelle didn't say a word. But she didn't move away either.

When Isabelle's hair was drier, Marissa ran a brush through it. 'You have such beautiful hair,' she said. 'When I was a girl, I used to long to have dark hair like yours. Mine was mousy brown. If you like, I could trim your fringe for you.'

The frown returned. 'I hate it when it's too short.'

'I won't cut it too short, I promise. I'm good at cutting hair. I always do my own.'

Isabelle chewed her lip, frowning. 'Okay.'

Isabelle changed into shorts and a T-shirt. Gabriel emerged from the sea, dripping water. Father and daughter went for a walk along the beach. While they were away, Marissa thought of the girl's fragile neck and bird-like collarbones, and how, eventually, she had agreed to let her cut her fringe.

Gabriel and Isabelle came back with ice-cream cones. They all sat on the sand to eat them. Afterwards, Isabelle wandered along the shoreline, looking for shells.

Gabriel waited until she was out of earshot, then said, 'You're good with her. You know when to hold back and when to step forward.'

'She's a sweet girl, Gabriel, and I'm fond of her.'

He shot her a glance. 'I know it's a lot to ask, getting to know someone else's child.'

She looked away, out to sea, to where the sun cast a soft silvery light on the water. 'Gabriel, I can't have children of my own.'

'Chérie . . .' He took her hand, pressed it to his lips. 'Are you sure?'

'Yes, I'm afraid so. So you see, if I can borrow your child for a while, that feels like a privilege.'

'Do you mind very much?' His voice was gentle.

'At first I did, yes. But you get used to things.' She gave a small laugh. 'You fill up your life so there isn't time to notice what's missing.'

'You make time in your life for me, Marissa.'

'Not enough. I wish I could stay here longer.'

'So do I.'

The angle of the sun had lowered. She tipped the wide brim of her straw hat forward so that it shaded her face and said, 'Perhaps sometime you'd like to stay over at the flat. For a few days . . . or for a weekend.'

'I'd like that very much.'

She licked her lips, which tasted of salt. 'I want you to feel at home when you're at my flat. I want you to think of it as another home.'

The hush and scrape of the waves on sand; chatter and laughter from the clumps of people on the beach. She waited, the low sun warming the skin on her calves, for his response.

He said, 'After Justine, I did not think I would ever fall in love again. But I was wrong. I love you, Marissa.'

'I love you too.' Their lips touched and she thought her heart would burst with happiness.

He put his arm round her and she leaned her head against him. 'So what should we do about this, you and I, Marissa?'

'I don't know.' She laughed. 'It so impractical. Do we even have time for each other? It always seems such a fight to find time just to have coffee with you, let alone . . .' She stopped, afraid that she was moving too fast and assuming too much.

But he finished the sentence for her. 'Let alone live together.'

'And I don't want to get married, Gabriel.' Again she knew that she was jumping the gun, but this was another hurdle she needed to get over.

'Ah.'

'Not because I don't love you very much,' she added quickly. 'Not because I don't believe we're going to last. I can't imagine ever loving anyone except you.'

'Then you dislike marriage . . . you dislike the institution of marriage?'

She might still be legally married to Jamie. She didn't know. He might have divorced her for desertion, but he might not. Which meant there was no possibility of her marrying Gabriel. But even if she had been able to put that glaring omission to one side, she had reservations.

'Marriage always seems to come with a loss of control, of autonomy,' she said. She thought of Tamar, weeping in the changing room. She thought of Bea and Francis, bickering over this and that. Even Max and Emma – everyone always said they had a good marriage, but Marissa had observed that it was Max's career that had flourished, whereas Emma scrabbled around, never finding time or space to do much. Marriage so often seemed to involve compromise, usually by the woman.

She said, 'I value my independence. I love my flat. I've worked so hard to be able to afford it and I don't want to lose it. But none of that means I love you any the less, my darling.'

Isabelle was walking towards them, her cupped hands full of shells. 'I have no wish to marry again,' Gabriel said. Gently he ran the back of his forefinger along Marissa's cheek. 'We'll manage. We'll find a way. I want to be with you, Marissa. That's what I want. I want to share my life with you.'

The day's warmth lingered into the evening. The three of them were late back at the house, and Jeanne, Andrée and Michel had already dined. Gabriel cooked supper for Isabelle. Shortly afterwards, tired from the long day on the beach, the girl went to bed early.

Gabriel made a simple meal of steak and salad, which he and Marissa ate outside, on the lawn beneath the copper beech tree. The citronella candles on the wicker table made darts of light. When she looked up through the branches, the stars were like silver threads against the black sky. The air was perfumed with the scents of the roses by the terrace. Gabriel brought out an old battery-operated record player and put on a disc of Charles Trenet songs. When the lyrics of 'La Mer' drifted towards them, he held out his hand to her and she rose to her feet, and they danced barefoot on the grass. Beneath her silk shirt, his hands caressed her. His body was warm and strong against hers. She closed her eyes and gave herself up to the perfection of the moment.

She woke suddenly and sat up in bed. Her heart was hammering; she wondered what had roused her. An alarm, perhaps, or something falling. When she glanced at the clock, she saw that it had just gone five in the morning. Gabriel lay beside her, deeply asleep. Too agitated to doze off again, she pulled on a cashmere jumper and a pair of leggings and left the room, softly closing the door behind her. Padding downstairs, she wrapped her arms round her as if she were cold, as if she needed to be held.

She let herself out through the glass doors at the back of the house. In the murky grey dawn light she saw the copper beech, the wicker table, the patch of lawn where she and Gabriel had danced. 'La Mer' played through the back of her mind, its melody insistent. She felt the chill dew beneath the soles of her feet as she crossed the grass, leaving a dark pathway behind her. She would have liked to walk for miles, to walk until the unease that weighed upon her went away.

She had told Gabriel that she could not have children. She had told him that she would never marry, and he had accepted that. And yet there remained a hidden piece of her past she had not shared with him. She had not told him about Jamie Canterbury, she had told him nothing of her marriage or the abuse or her miscarriage or her eventual escape to the refuge in London. She had pushed all that out of her mind because it did not belong here. This was a place of happiness, and she could not bear those memories to intrude. She thought of how, the previous evening, she had trimmed Isabelle's hair, and how Gabriel's daughter had sat still, trusting her. She thought of their afternoon on the beach. She remembered making love in the forest, dancing with him on the lawn.

She had not been honest with him. It was a big thing not to mention: a marriage. She recalled Andrée saying that Justine had been a cheat and a liar. She knew that though she herself had not lied, she had left a lot out. She should go to him now; she should wake him and tell him the truth.

But she remained standing on the lawn. Rays of sunlight made jewelled colours sparkle in the dew. She and Gabriel could have a future together. Jamie had stolen so much of the future she might have had. There was pleasure in being with Emma and Bea and their children, but there was pain too. She had taught herself to stifle the envy she felt, seeing her friends with their families, but that didn't mean it didn't hurt. With Gabriel, she would become part of a family. Didn't she deserve that? Why throw away a chance of happiness because of a mistake she had made years ago? Jamie would never trouble her again. She had erased that episode in her past; it did not concern anyone else, not even Gabriel. There was no reason to share it and every reason not to. She had put it behind her.

Besides, it was already too late. If she had intended to tell him the truth, she should have done it months ago. To do so now would be to risk losing him. She had stitched up her life too neatly to attempt to unravel it again. Dig up those sour old memories and everyone would think differently of her – her friends, her colleagues, even the journalists who wrote articles about her in newspapers and magazines. But most importantly, Gabriel, the man she loved – he might see her differently, and that possibility was unbearable to her.

No, she had made her decision years ago, on the day she had cut her hair and changed her name, and had never regretted it. The sun was rising, bright on the horizon, bathing the scene in a pink and gold light. Marissa's sense of dread shredded and dispersed as she walked back to the house.

*

300

Bea, Emma and Tamar were in the back room at Seastone. It was late, almost midnight. The window was open, and a salty breeze ruffled the blades of grass in the garden outside. They had shared a bottle of wine and talked about anything and everything.

And now they were talking about Francis.

'When I look at him,' said Bea, 'what I feel most of all is disappointment.'

Sometimes she felt quite cold about it, almost callous. It surprised her that she could view this man whom she had once thought she loved so dispassionately.

Tamar put a tray of tea things on the table. She said, 'Do you think that will change?'

'I don't know.' Bea considered. 'I don't think so.'

She was trying to be more honest with herself. She knew she had a bad habit of seeing the best in people. She ran her gaze around the familiar, beloved shabby room, which smelled of oil paint and the sea. She had needed time to think and had found that, as always, at Seastone.

She didn't know whether Francis was capable of being the man she wanted him to be. She wished she could tell herself that things were getting better between them but did not think that was true. He had let her down so casually. How could she live with a man she felt permanently disappointed in?

Emma said, 'Do you still love him?'

'Not as much as I thought I did.' This was a hard realisation to confront. It made her question how strong her feelings for Francis had been to begin with.

She went to stand by the window. She watched the ragged pennants of cloud sweep across a half-moon, high in the night sky.

Tamar said, 'You don't have to do anything, love. You must think it over. But in the end you have to listen to how you feel. And if you don't love him – if love isn't there any more – then perhaps it's time for a change.'

Tamar was right, she knew that. Sometime in the future, not too far away, decisions must be made. Lately, the thought had crept into her head that she might leave Francis. She had pushed this idea away. She was too familiar with the hardships of being a single parent, too familiar with loneliness. Yet she knew she might have to find the courage to take this step.

In the distance, waves crashed on the shingle. The wind was getting up, the air growing colder. Tamar put a comforting hand on Bea's shoulder, then closed the window, shutting out the sound of the sea and the hint of a change in the season.

# PART THREE

# THE BUTTERFLY PIN

# Chapter Fifteen

## 1989

Tamar was walking along the shingle bank. A high spring tide had forced the sweeping outcrop of pebbles into a raised ridge. Behind was a pond in the shape of a teardrop; ahead of her the grey churning sea.

She was remembering the day she and Morgan had moved to Seastone, in the early fifties. A friend had offered him the house to rent and he had made up his mind to take it, in the way that Morgan did, without consulting her, and she had gone along with it. She had seen the cottage for the first time on the day they had moved in. Morgan had hired a van to transport their belongings from London, and they had squeezed into the front seat beside the driver. Suffolk became emptier and flatter as they approached the coast. Morgan was reading the map. 'Here we are,' he said, and as they turned off the tarmacked road onto a track, the plummeting of Tamar's heart seemed audible to her, like the whoosh of a lift going down.

The weather had been much like today's, raw and grey. The marshes, the creeks of slick brown water, and the long, flat shoreline with its scattering of houses beneath a wide, heavy sky had oppressed her, though she had tried to disguise her disappointment. She remembered that the driver had worried about his wheels getting stuck in the mud; they had carried their boxes and sticks of furniture the last quarter of a mile. Later that day, Morgan had made pencil sketches of their exodus. He and the driver lugging a table up the grassy incline. Tamar, suitcase in hand, picking her way between the puddles, her hair blown about by a fierce breeze.

That first evening, Hester Freedman had invited them to supper at her house, a short way along the beach. All the neighbours had turned up. A supper invitation had turned into a party to celebrate their arrival. Hester's back room had smelled of oil paint and turps; someone had made cheese on toast, and glasses of beer had been passed round. They had at first talked about their work, and then the discussion had slipped, as it so often did, into whether so-and-so was producing anything of note, and whether old Angus was still hitting the bottle. In company, Morgan had come alive. The shadows that fell on him in the depths of winter had lifted, and he had told stories and made them all laugh. Tamar had begun to think she might be able to bear it, living there.

She trudged up the shingle rise. Today the walk, which she must have taken thousands of times, was hard going. Shading her eyes from the late-afternoon sun, she made out in the distance a conical stack of stones and headed towards it.

The winds and tides continually redrew the shape of the shingle beach. Two years ago, the hurricane of 1987 had reduced Morgan's boathouse studio to matchsticks, scattering shards of wood and strips of roof felt along the shore. Not even he had been able to put it back together again. He had

306

had the foresight to bring his paintings and prints into the house the evening before the storm, so his work, at least, was saved. For the last eighteen months, the two of them had worked amicably together in the back room. Morgan had shared the household tasks, had even cooked lunch when Tamar was busy. They had had coffee together mid morning and had gone for walks in the afternoon. They had found a rhythm, a peaceful equilibrium.

She reached the cairn, a round structure of white stones. Their neighbour, Connor, a sculptor, had made it to mark the spot where, twelve days ago, he had found Morgan lying on the shingle. He had told her that at first, when he had glimpsed him, he had thought Morgan was sleeping.

There had been generous obituaries in the *Times* and the *Guardian*. Tamar had received dozens of letters and cards, and that morning, a long procession of old artist friends, some of whom she had not seen for decades, had filed into the small honey-coloured country church where the funeral had taken place, to pay their respects. Afterwards, they had had lunch in a hotel in Woodbridge. By now, Tamar's head ached and her brain fizzed with the effort of maintaining her composure. She longed for cold and fresh air and solitude.

Kneeling beside the cairn, surrounded by the soft in-and-out breath of the waves, she took out of her pocket the items she had brought with her and tucked them between the stones. A jay's feather, gathered on one of their last walks together, a flash of iridescent blue. A dried flower from her wedding bouquet. A small yellowed sketch that Morgan had done years ago, during the war. She had thought of placing the butterfly pin in the cairn too, but she knew that not even the highest tide was powerful enough to assuage her guilt and regret. Besides, she did not feel the pin was hers to give.

She sat back on her heels and wept for his passing and for all that she had lost. Soon the wind would blow her fragile mementos away. The cairn itself would vanish with the next storm. Nothing lasted for ever. In losing Morgan, she had lost a large part of her past. She murmured a farewell to him: her husband, the father of her children, her friend, her mentor. The man she had loved passionately, the man who had often hurt her, and whom she had betrayed.

It was growing dark, and she headed back towards the house. Light gleamed in the windows, beckoning her home.

Bea had come to the funeral. Emma was glad of her support. Marissa hadn't been able to attend because she was in Paris for the fashion shows, but she had sent Tamar a huge bunch of spring flowers. The small house was bursting at the seams. Emma had thought the mourners might begin to trail off after lunch, but they hadn't; most of them had come back to the Romillys' place and were now sprawled on the sofa and chairs or sitting cross-legged on the rug, reminiscing, loud-voiced and expansive with the relief of having got through the most difficult part of the day, the funeral service and interment. Max and Rob were topping up whisky glasses and Gale was somehow succeeding in amusing all five children at once, her two and Emma's three, while Douglas, her husband, was in the garden, chopping wood so that they could keep feeding the fire.

Emma and Bea made themselves responsible for the teas and coffees. They kept running out of mugs, though the neighbours had lent theirs. There was a continual loud hubbub of conversation. It was the sort of friendly, relaxed occasion her father would have loved, Emma thought, and tears burned her eyes. She had sobbed in Max's arms after Tamar had phoned to break the news of her father's death, but since then it had been like this: the tears seeping slowly through, like a dam weakening. It had become her natural state to be continually on the edge of tears.

Bea was making coffee. Emma said, 'How's Miles?' Miles was Bea's boyfriend, good-looking and self-satisfied.

'He's fine. He sends his condolences.'

'Please thank him for me. And Alice and Rachel?'

'Oh, they love staying with Francis and her.' This was Bea's usual way of referring to Daisy, Francis's current wife. As though her name had a bitter taste. She added, 'They'll love it even more when the baby comes.' She gave a rather spiteful grin. 'Imagine Francis coping with night feeds.'

Maybe Daisy had Francis's number, thought Emma. She said, 'When's it due?'

'Another month or so. Somewhere around the middle of April.'

Bea handed Emma a mug. They leaned against the sink drinking coffee. Emma saw that Tamar had come in from her walk and was peeling off her scarf. Her face was blotched with cold and her eyes were red. Gale went to take her mother's coat from her.

Emma found it impossible to picture Tamar without Morgan. It was literally unimaginable. She looked round the room until she found Max, who was talking to two of Morgan's ancient artist friends. Since her father had died, everything felt precarious.

Tamar sat down on the rug with Gale and the children. Even in these circumstances, she managed to smile. This was another thing Emma did not want to imagine: how her mother must feel now. It hurt too much to do so. Gale was trying to persuade Tamar to move house, to Cambridge perhaps, where she would be closer to her children and grandchildren. 'You can't possibly stay here in the middle of nowhere now that you're on your own,' she had announced over breakfast that morning, with immense lack of tact. Emma knew that it was far too soon for her mother to think about moving house. She suspected that for now, Tamar felt life to be like a canvas with a blank patch in it. She would have to look at it and think about it, and work out what to do.

Gale, with a baby propped on her hip, came to join them. 'He was a contrary old bugger,' she said, 'but I'll miss him. I'm afraid we'll all be so much duller without him.' Her eyes too glittered with tears. Emma took her nephew from her and kissed him.

If Morgan's spirit lingered anywhere, it was here in this remote place on the border between land and sea. A part of Emma still expected her father to walk through the door, red-faced from the cold, wild curly hair blown about by the wind, talking about something he had seen, drawing everyone's attention. It felt wrong that he wasn't here. Yesterday, crouching on the shingle to sketch the strange dried plants that rattled in the breeze, she had felt him standing behind her, looking over her shoulder, helping her, giving her the confidence to go on.

In a few weeks or months, his ghost would have shredded like the sea mist and vanished to wherever such presences went. While he remained here, she found some comfort. She was sure that Tamar felt the same.

# Chapter Sixteen

## 1989

The photography session was sprung on her late in the day. Marissa disliked having her photo taken and wished she could have cancelled, but the images were for the *Sunday Times*, who had promised to show samples from her hugely successful latest collection in their colour supplement, along with an interview with the founder of the Marissa Flint brand. It was a fabulous promotional opportunity, and Conrad Wright, who handled publicity for her, was thrilled to have secured it.

For the session, Marissa wore a duck-egg-blue skirt and a classic white shirt, open at the neck, with a simple gold chain necklace. She had a brief disagreement with the stylist, a girl called Sasha who looked little older than Isabelle, who wanted to sweep back her hair from her face and forbade her to wear dark glasses. 'Your eyes are your best feature. Such a stunning colour.' This said in a lackadaisical drawl, as if she could scarcely be bothered getting the words out. In the end, for the sake of speed and her own sanity, Marissa let Sasha do what she wanted.

When the session was over, she went home. The way she

and Gabriel lived, splitting their time between her Battersea flat and his farmhouse in Berkshire, might seem unconventional to others, but it worked for them. Marissa spent Monday to Friday in London so that she could be close to her business; Gabriel joined her there when his work obligations permitted. Weekends they both preferred to be at the farmhouse, providing their schedules allow it.

Her life was pretty much perfect, Marissa thought. She was financially secure and had become successful beyond her wildest dreams. She had friends she loved and trusted. And then there was Gabriel, her lover, her solace, her companion.

There was only one fly in the ointment. Tonight Gabriel was away, so Marissa made herself a salad, then gave the rooms a quick tidy before settling down to work. A bundle of hair clips and ties had been abandoned in the bathroom; she put them in a neat pile in Isabelle's bedroom. Looking round the room, she let out a sigh. She had for some time now felt that she was failing Gabriel's daughter. Their relationship remained fragile and the teenager's attitude to her fluctuated between tolerance and hostility. Now and then, the two of them would have a good day, baking together or shopping in Selfridges, and Marissa would start to hope she had made a breakthrough. Then Isabelle would have a problem at school or spend a weekend with her mother, at her house in Cheyne Walk, and they would be back at square one, with Isabelle standing as stiff as a board when Marissa gave her a goodbye hug before leaving for work and perfecting a resentful glare for whenever Marissa addressed her.

The last few weeks had been particularly difficult. Before her most recent visit to Justine, Isabelle had been touchy and on edge, taking offence at the least thing and storming off to her bedroom, slamming the door behind her. She had kept her worst behaviour for when Gabriel wasn't within earshot. 'You can't tell me,' she had hissed when Marissa had asked her to pick up a chocolate wrapper she had dropped on the floor. 'You're not my mother!' A fortnight later, the phrase still echoed in Marissa's ears.

As the adult, Marissa knew that it was her responsibility to nurture a relationship with Isabelle, however challenging that might be. And yet she never felt her inadequacy or her childlessness more keenly than during these conflicts. She couldn't help feeling that had she been Isabelle's mother, rather than her sort-of stepmother, she would have found a better way of navigating their relationship. Worse, she felt that she was running out of ideas. Whatever she did only seemed to widen the gap between them. There was the temptation to step back and leave Gabriel to deal with his daughter. She needed to focus on her work, which was time-consuming and demanding, to concentrate on her designs for her next collection, for which she was struggling to find a theme. She mustn't let herself be distracted by difficulties at home.

Though she tried to cling to the hope that the situation would improve as Isabelle grew older, her optimism had thinned with the passing of time. Isabelle's behaviour was a consequence of her background, of insecurity and a fear of rejection, but unfortunately, knowing that didn't always stop Marissa feeling exasperated by the way in which the girl's sulks could poison a perfectly pleasant day.

Bea and Francis had split up two and a half years ago, after he had admitted to her that he had started seeing Daisy Wynyard again. He had behaved decently over the divorce and had agreed that Bea should have the Portugal Place house. A clean break, he had said. Bea knew that breaks were never clean; they were always ragged round the edges.

If she had been forced to choose a worst day from an entire pack of bad days, it might have been the one six months ago when Francis had told her that Daisy was expecting a baby. While Bea had been married to him, he had always said he didn't want a child. She had since realised that what he had actually meant was that he didn't want a child with her. The baby was due imminently. Alice and Rachel couldn't wait to meet their new sort-of brother or sister.

Bea had met her current boyfriend, Miles Brampton, towards the end of the previous year. Miles was good-looking, charming and clever. An academic and writer, he lived in a book-lined flat in Newnham. Their whirlwind affair had repaired some of the damage to her confidence that the divorce had inflicted.

Recently, though, she had sensed Miles's devotion lessening. The gregariousness that had attracted her when they had first got to know each other, in the bar of a theatre in Cambridge, had its less appealing side, she had discovered. Twice in recent weeks he had cancelled a date late in the day because something more interesting had come up.

Three months ago, he had agreed to accompany her to the wedding of an old friend of hers, which was to take place in London. That morning, meeting him at Cambridge station, he was fidgety and short with her, and his handsome features settled into sour, petulant lines as they took their seats on the King's Cross train. Bea told herself he would cheer up as the day went on. After all, who didn't love a wedding?

The ceremony took place in a register office a short distance from the Maida Vale mansion flats in which Bea had lived as a child. It was the bride's second marriage. Rather a lot of Bea's friends were divorced or embarking on second marriages. The bride looked absolutely divine in her pale grey and pink dress and coat, and the tiny bridesmaids were utterly sweet. While the couple made their vows, Bea found herself reflecting on the past. Ages ago, when she had been in her teens – before Ciaran, before Patrick – she and her friends had talked so confidently about meeting Mr Right and living happily ever after. Well, it hadn't turned out like that. Which just underlined the fact that events didn't necessarily come to pass in the way you hoped they would.

She was distracted during the signing of the register by Miles, who kept sighing and glancing at his watch. Later on, while the guests were milling round the reception room of a nearby hotel, drinking fizzy wine and chatting, she asked him whether he had somewhere else he needed to be. Their conversation quickly deteriorated into a muffled row, which culminated in Miles hissing at her, 'God, Bea, you can be so *demanding!*' Then, between the canapés and the photographs, he stormed off.

Bea made the best of the remainder of the afternoon. She told anyone who asked that Miles had felt unwell, and enjoyed herself catching up with old friends, some of whom she hadn't seen for years. But now and then his words popped back into her head. *God, Bea, you can be so demanding.* They had reopened a wound inside her.

She had left Alice and Rachel with Emma that day, so she slipped away from the celebrations shortly after five so as not to be too late picking them up. Alighting from the

Underground at King's Cross, she made her way up to the surface. Rounding a corner in a tunnel, her eye was caught by the sight of a poster advertising Marissa Flint fashions. She stopped to admire it. Unconsciously she smoothed her frock over her hips and patted her hair in place. They looked so perfect, so cool and glacially superior, those two beautifully dressed young women on the poster. Bea had worn a gorgeous Marissa Flint dress for the wedding, but she was afraid it didn't make her look like the models.

The railway station was busy, and she had half an hour to wait for her train. She thought of buying a chocolate croissant, but after another glance down at her hips decided not to. She took off her wedding hat, longing for the moment when she could sit down in the carriage and slip off her high-heeled shoes too. It wasn't that she minded awfully that she and Miles had split up. Her heart wasn't broken. She knew that she hadn't loved him as much as she thought she had in the first heady days of the affair.

The truth was that she had persisted with Miles Brampton for longer than she should have because she didn't want to be alone, and she wasn't proud of that. More than once, since Francis, she had wondered whether she was still capable of falling in love. When she pictured her heart, it looked withered and shrunken, like an old balloon.

They didn't get on too badly now, she and Francis. Bea had made sure of that, because he was, after all, the nearest thing Alice and Rachel had to a father. She had to admit that he continued to be a kind and loving step-parent to her girls and was conscientious in keeping up the relationship, and she was thankful for that. Bea couldn't stand Daisy, but she supposed she would get over that eventually.

Her mistake had been in failing to realise that Francis was the sort of man who made a better friend than husband. There had been other mistakes, she knew that, and perhaps that was why what Miles had said to her preyed on her mind. *God, Bea, you can be so demanding.* She wondered whether she was to blame for the situation in which she found herself, whether she was one of those clingy women who made unreasonable demands – though goodness knows she tried not to be. Or whether, in the past, she had fallen in love too easily and wanted too much, which was why, at the age of thirty-six, she found herself on her own again.

The platform number for the Cambridge train flashed up on the departures board. Hat in hand, Bea joined the crowd hurrying towards the ticket barrier.

The anxiety Marissa often felt before social events made her stomach churn and her heart pound. There was a certain unpredictability about these affairs. The rain might put people off. The food might turn up late, or be unappetising. The guests might not gel.

She had recently initiated a series of small receptions that took place in the design studio behind the Floral Street shop. The first two had featured the work of a goldsmith and a milliner. She invited fifty or sixty carefully chosen guests to view the exhibits and meet their creator. She kept the numbers low so that the occasions felt special and intimate. Tonight's event would feature the work of a friend of Gabriel's, a ceramicist based in Chinon.

She left the transformation of the studio into an exhibition space to David, and slipped into the cloakroom to touch up her make-up. Angie was there, peering into the mirror. They talked through the evening's arrangements while Marissa fluffed up her hair and reapplied lipstick and Angie painted a silver line on her eyelids.

When they went back into the design studio, tables had been pulled together in the centre of the room to display the bowls and vases. Beside another table to one side, the waiting staff were uncorking bottles. David was talking to Nico, the French ceramicist.

Conrad, her publicist, handed her a glass of wine. 'There. You look like you need it.'

She thanked him. Gabriel had helped her choose the wine for the event, and it was delicious, tasting of apples and vanilla. Marissa straightened a row of glasses and picked up a thread of cotton from the floor.

Smoothing the table covering, she saw Conrad giving her a wry glace. 'I hate it when I can't do everything myself,' she admitted.

'That's because you're a control freak, Marissa. It's okay, I'm the same. But we can't have the celebrated Marissa Flint doing the dusting.' He raised an eyebrow. 'I could give you something stronger, if you like. Calms the nerves, helps you go with the flow.'

'Thanks, Conrad, but this is perfect.' She tapped her enamelled fingernail on her wine glass.

The decade was approaching its end and London parties were awash with cocaine. Marissa had never tried it, because she knew she wouldn't be able to bear the loss of control. She knew also that she'd feel fine as soon as she'd had a couple of drinks, and as soon as it was clear to her that the evening was going to be a success. The first guests had begun to come through the door. She craned to see whether Gabriel was among them.

She said to Conrad, 'How's Art?'

Conrad's boyfriend, Art, a New Yorker, was HIV positive. Conrad grimaced. 'Not too good.'

'Please give him my love.'

He nodded. 'Where's the gorgeous Gabriel?'

'Flying back from Paris today. He said he might be late.' She wouldn't be able to relax completely until he had arrived. 'Right,' she said softly. 'Into the fray.' She went to greet her guests.

Soon the room was crowded and buzzing with conversation. Waiters circulated with platters of mushroom vol-au-vents and prawn cocktail canapés. Compliments were made about the exhibits and Marissa's nerves eased.

When, at a quarter to seven, she glanced out towards the shop frontage, hoping to see Gabriel arriving, she noticed that a man was standing on the pavement outside the shop. She wondered whether he was waiting for someone, for another guest perhaps, so that they could come into the party together.

She made a short speech to introduce Nico to the crowd. Everyone applauded and raised their glasses in a toast. When next Marissa looked out, the man was still there, standing in the same place. It crossed her mind that he might be the disgruntled boyfriend of one of the assistants, something like that, or a journalist from some cheap rag. Perhaps she should go out and have a word with him. Then she had to take a phone call, and when she looked out again, the stranger had vanished.

The party was on the verge of winding up when Gabriel arrived. Catching sight of him, her heart danced. He wrapped his arms round her, and she shut her eyes, secure in his embrace.

319

After the last of the guests had gone, they took a taxi to a small restaurant in Frith Street. Towards the end of the meal, when they were drinking coffee, Gabriel said, 'I was thinking, perhaps we should look for a house together.'

Startled, she looked up at him. 'Gabriel . . .'

'I know.' He made a conciliatory gesture. 'I know what we agreed, and I understand that you don't want to sell the flat, chérie, but . . .' He sighed and reached across the table for her hand. 'I've been thinking about this for some time. Perhaps Isabelle would feel more settled if we weren't moving between several homes. There's the flat and the farmhouse – and then we all go to France for summer with my family. Three different places. And she's at school in the week, of course. She must feel she's always packing a suitcase.'

'Has she said so?'

'No. But I know she's been difficult recently, Marissa, and I thought, if we were to change our arrangements, it might help. Only if you agree, of course.'

She gave a light laugh. 'Gabriel, Isabelle's sixteen. No sixteen-year-old girl is easy. I was a complete nightmare at that age.'

A line had formed between his brows, and his eyes were troubled. She drew his hand to her lips and kissed it. 'It's a big decision. Could you give me some time to think about it?'

'Of course.'

Her instinct was to hold on to the flat. It had always been her place of safety. And the practical difficulties of moving would be enormous. She struggled to find the time to buy food, let alone a house. But she thought he might be right, that Isabelle's feelings of insecurity were perhaps compounded by their unconventional lifestyle.

As they left the restaurant, she said to him, 'I'll try and find time to call some estate agents next week and get an idea of what's around. That would be a start, wouldn't it?'

Saturday morning: Alice and Rachel were due to go to their drama class. Bea was still wearing her pyjamas, and the house was in turmoil because Alice had mislaid a locket that Clive had given her when she was a baby.

All three of them were ransacking the place, trying to find it. Rachel, who at ten years old was small and dark, like Bea herself, but far more organised, came into the room and said, 'Mummy, I've been through all Alice's drawers.'

'Well done, darling. Bags and pockets next, I think.'

'Alice is crying.'

Bea went upstairs to see Alice. She was lying on her bed, sobbing. The girls still shared a bedroom. They were very close and preferred to be together. Bea sat down beside her daughter and scooped her up. Alice wailed and buried her head in Bea's shoulder. Alice had inherited Clive's good looks and striking fair colouring, as well as his wildly swooping emotions. Bea worried for both her girls, but she worried more for Alice.

'Darling, we'll find it, I promise. It'll be in the house somewhere.'

'Daddy gave it to me! I can't believe I've lost it! Why am I so useless?'

'You're not useless, sweetheart.'

'Mummy . . .'

'I wouldn't love you if you were useless.'

Alice wiped her eyes and nose with her sleeve and looked up at her. 'You have to love me. You're my mother.'

'Oh yes, so I am. I'd forgotten.'

Alice giggled. Bea embraced her and then, with promises to keep on searching for the locket while the girls were at their class, got dressed and hurried them all out of the house.

They were only ten minutes late for the class. Bea cycled back to Portugal Place. She would have a good old spring clean, she thought. The house could do with it, and with luck, Alice's locket would turn up. A cup of coffee and piece of toast to hand, she began to tidy away items into drawers and cupboards. A thought occurred to her, and she went upstairs to her room. She might have put the locket in her own jewellery box by mistake. She upended the box, then sat down on the bed, disentangling pearl bracelets and op art earrings.

Amid a knot of necklaces, she came across a silver chain. She teased it out and let it pool on her palm. Years ago, Ciaran O'Neill had given it to her. To look at it was to recall the flat in Notting Hill he had shared with his brother and father, the oily smell of the fish and chip shop, the sound of the neighbour's crying baby and the Dubliners singing 'Raglan Road'.

Perhaps all the mistakes she had made had stemmed from that very first one. It seemed to her that she had spent her adult life either searching for a man like Ciaran or trying to find his opposite. She had fallen in love with Clive because he was so sure of himself, so carefree and fun and not like Ciaran at all. And then, after poor Clive had died, she had run a mile from that sort of recklessness and impetuosity. Francis had shared something of Ciaran's sweet nature; women fell in love with him because he was understanding and gentle. All three men had been, in their different ways, a disaster.

Even now, sitting in her bedroom in Cambridge, Bea could see in her mind's eye the pond where she had stopped to feed the ducks on the way home from school. Ciaran's voice, with its soft Irish accent. *They're hungry today, don't you think?* Black curls, blue eyes, the corners of his mouth tilted up in a smile. Had his features indelibly imprinted themselves on her heart even in that first instant? She feared that they had.

She should get rid of the silver chain, she thought. What on earth was she keeping it for? Put it in the bin, give it to a jumble sale. And yet a month ago, her son, Patrick, had turned eighteen. Which meant that he was now free to try to trace her. For weeks, Bea had been imagining the ring of the doorbell or the sound of a letter falling onto the mat. It might take him a while to find out where she lived, she knew that, so she was trying to be patient. She would know him immediately, she was sure of it, because for the last eighteen years there had been a space in her heart shaped for him, waiting for him. She yearned to embrace him, to get to know him, to fill in the empty years.

Each year, she bought him a birthday card: *To My Darling Son* on the front and a picture of a teddy with a blue ribbon when he was little, dinosaurs or space rockets as he had grown older. The eighteenth birthday card she had chosen for him had an image of a car and a tall, cheerful-looking lad standing beside it, keys in hand. Inside, she had wished her son a happy birthday and told him how much she loved him. She had put his name, Patrick, on the envelope.

She never posted the cards, because she didn't know where to send them. She kept them in a drawer, in a neat pile. When – if – they were reunited, she would give him all the cards and he would know how much she had loved him and thought about him.

Patrick would want to know about his father. She had so little of Ciaran — a handful of bittersweet memories, some poems and songs they had both loved. And the silver necklace. She put it back in her jewellery box, then went downstairs.

Searching methodically through Alice's clothes and possessions, she found Clive's locket trapped in a mess of tissues and scrunchies in a crocheted bag. She put it on the mantelpiece and cycled off to meet the girls.

Monday morning: David and Marissa were returning from an appointment with the company solicitor. Marissa usually took taxis to get around London, but they had travelled on the Underground today because David had wanted her to see the advertising posters the company had recently invested in. They both admired the one at Leicester Square station. It was beautiful and striking. Marissa felt a ripple of pride at seeing her name displayed so prominently. Her hard work and talent had culminated in this success.

They left the station. As they walked down Cranbourn Street and Garrick Street, she and David discussed potential locations for a third Marissa Flint shop. She wanted Cambridge; he favoured Manchester or Edinburgh. Floral Street was a narrow thoroughfare between tall buildings. Marissa glanced at the displays in the other clothing stores, but then her eye was caught by the figure of a man standing ahead in the shadows on the far side of the street from her own shop's entrance. As they approached, he walked away, towards Covent Garden.

She took off her coat as she went into the design studio. Angie brought her a coffee and Marissa sat down at her desk. In the Underground carriage, rattling through the gloom, an idea had begun to form. Her next collection would have an urban theme. London itself, with all the varying influences that had shaped it over the centuries, would be her inspiration. She took out her coloured pencils and began to mix shades.

They often kept the doors between the design studio and the shop open, because she liked to feel in touch with what was going on in the rest of the premises. The studio was at the back of the building and the windows were high, so the light that poured through the double doors helped illuminate the space. Marissa had been working for an hour when she looked out and saw that he had come back. The man she had seen earlier was standing on the pavement again. He seemed to be looking into the shop. She found herself remembering the design studio event the previous week, when Nico had shown his ceramics. Someone had been loitering outside the shop then. Could this be the same person? It seemed an odd place to hang around, halfway down Floral Street.

His presence had begun to bother her. She squinted in an attempt to see him more clearly, but even with her contact lenses, her distance vision was poor. She was able to make out only that he was tall, broad and bulky, and wearing a fawn raincoat.

Angie came to speak to her about a problem with a garment, but Marissa was already rising from her desk. Rani, the manager, had spread out a dress on the counter; she beckoned, and Marissa went to look at it. Customers were browsing the rails; a woman was asking to try on a skirt. She looked out of the window again. The man was crossing the road, coming towards the shop entrance. Broad shoulders, reddish hair, fleshy features. The way he moved, the way he carried himself was familiar to her. Horror made her freeze, her gaze fixed on him.

Rani showed her the loose stitching round the buttonholes of the dress in question. 'We'll need to send them all back.' Marissa heard her own voice, clipped and automatic, asking whether any of the dresses had been sold yet. Rani said they hadn't, and then she and Angie went to sweep them off the rails.

But by then he had come into the shop, and she knew who he was and that he had found her at last. Rani said something, but Marissa didn't hear her, because the blood was pulsing in her ears and her heart had turned to stone.

'May I help you?' Angie asked him, but he brushed past her.

'Hello, Mary,' said Jamie Canterbury. 'Long time no see.'

Angie said again, frostily, 'May I help you, please, sir?' and Jamie said, 'I was just going to have a word with Mary here.'

'My name isn't Mary.' Marissa's voice was scratchy.

'Right.' His hands in his pockets, he looked her up and down. Then he smiled.

'You've made a mistake,' she said. 'I think you should go.'

David came to join them. 'What's going on?'

'Nothing,' said Marissa. 'This gentleman is just leaving.'

Jamie, the man she had been married to – might still be married to – looked from David to her. The years had not been kind to him, she thought; he had put on weight and his once handsome features had coarsened. His smile, though: that hadn't altered at all. She remembered that smile, the glee and the malice in it.

He shrugged, then walked out of the shop. She half expected him to leave in his wake a trail of dirty footprints.

She felt David and Angie and Rani staring at her, so she went back into the studio and sat down at her desk. Her hand was shaking too much to grasp her pencil.

Angie came into the room and said, 'Wow, that was weird,' and Marissa said sharply, 'If you would get me a coffee, please. It would be nice to have the opportunity to work without interruption.'

The coffee was a mistake, because it made her heart pound harder. She could see the pale blue cotton fabric of her blouse quivering. She pressed her hands together beneath her desk to quell their jittering. Jamie's reappearance in her life had sent shock waves crashing through her; it had the dark quality of a nightmare made real. What had he wanted? Why had he come here? And how had he found her? She kept glancing out of the shop to the road beyond, but he wasn't there any more. Perhaps he had done what he'd wanted to; he had satisfied his curiosity, and had frightened her. Perhaps that was enough for him.

She didn't believe that. She made an effort to focus on her work, but her idea of a London-themed collection had lost its appeal and seemed unattractive and overcomplicated. She scrunched up her sketches, dropped them in the bin, and left the shop. Walking down Floral Street, she seemed to feel him watching her, his gaze like twin pressure points between her shoulder blades. Emerging into Covent Garden, she looked round, wondering whether he was there among the crowds.

In Long Acre, she hailed a taxi. She told herself that he couldn't follow her if she was in a taxi, but the panicked voice in her head pointed out that he had probably been following her for weeks. It had been Jamie hanging round outside the shop on the evening of Nico's event, she knew that now. She broke out into a hot sweat, imagining him watching her, following her, finding out everything about her. He probably knew where she lived. She felt a headache starting, and when she got out of the taxi in Battersea, all the bad old habits came rushing back and she scanned up and down the street. Inside the foyer, she had a careful look round. He might be waiting for her. What if he got into the lift with her? Trapped in a small space with him, she wouldn't be able to breathe. She used the stairs instead, taking them at pace, hoping the exertion might stem the adrenalin that was flooding through her.

She let herself into the flat and bolted the door behind her. For the first time since they had met, she was relieved that she would not see Gabriel tonight, that he was away on business. It would give her time to collect herself, to work out what to do. Gabriel would have read the shock and fear in her eyes.

In the shower, she stood beneath the spray of hot water. She wished it could wash away the events of the day. She had thought she was safe, but she wasn't. Afterwards, she towelled herself dry and put on leggings and a cotton jumper. She tried to reassure herself. She had no need to worry. Jamie could have no way of knowing for sure that she, the successful and celebrated Marissa Flint, was the same person as dowdy, downtrodden Mary Canterbury.

It didn't work. Every barrier she tried to erect against her fears crumbled. Somehow, the man she had hoped she would never see again had found her. And that meant that everything had changed.

She went into the kitchen and put on the kettle. Resting her back against the counter, she went through her options. She should stand up to him. She was no longer under his thumb, as she had been when she was married to him. He had no hold over her now. If he came into the shop again, she would ask David to get rid of him. Jamie would get the message eventually.

Her gaze alighted on the copy of the *Sunday Times* colour supplement, the one with the feature about Marissa Flint that had been published a couple of weeks ago. Gabriel had asked her to keep it because he liked the photograph of her. She turned a page, and there it was, a head-and-shoulders portrait. With her hair swept back from her face, she looked naked and unprotected. Letting herself be photographed like that had been a huge mistake, she saw that now. Jamie must have seen it and recognised her. He had traced her and hung around, satisfying himself that Mary Canterbury and Marissa Flint really were the same person. She blamed herself. She had believed herself safe and had ended up getting careless.

*Marissa Flint's personal appeal and mystery are an integral part of the brand:* this was the opening sentence of the article. A quote of hers had been picked out and highlighted: *I am a very private person.* In retrospect, she had thought this remark facile. Surely even the most extrovert had their limits; surely everyone had some aspect of themselves they kept secret? Or was she the odd one out?

It had been a mistake to allow herself to be photographed for the newspaper, but three years ago, at the Verniers' house in Normandy, she had done something far worse. She turned a page and ran her gaze rapidly down the columns. Her head was throbbing as she found Gabriel's name.

*The designer's partner, Gabriel Vernier, owns Turquoise and Azure, fashionable importer of stunning ceramic tiles. The couple met three years ago, at a party in Kingston upon Thames. Until then, says Marissa with a ripple of laughter, all her efforts were focused on establishing her business. The* couple have no plans to marry. 'I don't believe in marriage,' says Marissa. 'I shall never marry. It's not for Gabriel and me. We're happy as we are.'

She shuddered. Though she ripped out the pages and tore them in pieces and pushed them down into the bin beneath slimy lettuce leaves and hardening orange peel, the enormity of the threat to her happiness made her feel nauseous. She pressed the heels of her hands against her pulsing forehead. Bitterly she wished she could turn back the clock. She should have told Gabriel about Jamie, about her marriage, years ago, on that blissful day on the beach at Arromanches. She should have told him the very first time he had said he loved her. Or before that, on their first date . . . or at the party where they had met. It was a big thing to leave out, that you had once been married, and perhaps still were, and that you had changed your name and erased such a traumatic and life-altering part of your past.

She gave up making tea and poured herself a large glass of wine. She washed down a couple of aspirins with the wine.

*Hello, Mary. Long time no see.*

Jamie's words kept coming into her head as she refilled her glass and tidied up the kitchen. They echoed as she stood on the balcony, looking out through the murky dusk to the river, raking her eyes over the street below to check that he wasn't there, waiting for her. And as she gave the oven a quick clean and vacuumed the hall carpet to get up specks of dirt.

She couldn't get it properly clean. No matter that she rubbed it over and over again with the nozzle of the hoover, it was still grubby.

*Hello, Mary. Long time no see.*

\*

Glancing at the post that had fallen through the letter box, Tamar recognised Alexander's writing on an envelope.

It was a fine, blustery day and she went to sit outside with a mug of tea and the letter in her pocket. The garden had been a wilderness of bramble and gorse that first summer they had moved to Seastone, almost four decades ago. Morgan had scythed the undergrowth but had left a gorse bush for its cheerful flowers. The bush had grown into a dense patch and was in flower now. Hedge sparrows chattered fussily as they flitted in and out of the spiky mass of gold and green.

She opened Alexander's letter and read it. He was writing to offer his condolences. News of Morgan Romilly's death must have reached the New York art world. She pictured that little pleat of a frown between his eyes as he concentrated, choosing the words he hoped might offer comfort. *I know how much you loved him. I can't imagine how greatly you must miss him and I can only hope you find solace in your family and your work.* Then a few words about his own family – he had two grandchildren now, a girl and a boy, and they were all well. At the end of the letter he had written, *I travel to London once or twice a year. If you were agreeable, Tamar, I could come and visit you in Suffolk.*

Tamar folded the letter and rose from the step on which she had been sitting. She walked across the grass. The memory of their final, painful encounter at that grim London hotel obliterated the honey scent of the gorse and the sight of the white caps on the waves. That afternoon, Alexander had said to her, *If this is truly what you want, I won't see you again. I can't stand dragged-out farewells.* But later, he had taken her in his arms and held her close.

His last letter to her she had ripped into tiny pieces and scattered on the waves. She remembered how the white fragments had danced on the surface of the North Sea. This one she folded and tucked into her writing case. She wouldn't reply to it, but she kept it nevertheless.

Francis said, 'If I could pick up the girls after lunch on Saturday rather than before – Daisy's parents have said they're coming over.'

Bea put a black coffee in front of him. Francis was sitting at the kitchen table in Portugal Place.

'Are they staying the night?'

'No, thank God,' he said, with feeling. He stared down at the coffee cup as if he couldn't remember what it was. 'Thanks, Bea.'

She poured coffee for herself. 'You can put off the girls till next weekend if you prefer.'

'I don't want to mess them about, and honestly, they're a help rather than a hindrance. They're so good with Leo. They adore him.' Leo was the name of Francis's newborn son. Francis had black shadows round his eyes and looked strung out by the broken nights. There were moments when Bea almost felt sorry for him.

Alice and Rachel came into the room. Rachel said, 'Can we give Francis the present, Mummy?'

'Yes, of course, darling, that's a good idea.'

Rachel took a package from the dresser. To Francis, she said, 'It's for Leo.'

He opened the wrapping and took out a tiny blue jacket and bootees. 'Oh!' He beamed. 'Thank you so much. They're beautiful!'

'I knitted the jacket, and Rachel and Alice did a bootee each.' Rachel's bootee was neat and exact, Alice's a flurry of dropped stitches, blotted with tears of frustration. Bea was trying to be civilised. None of what had happened was the baby's fault, and what Francis had said was true: Alice and Rachel adored Leo.

She said, 'I'll make sure they're ready straight after lunch on Saturday.'

'Thank you.' He hugged the girls. To Bea he said, 'You're such a sport. The baby clothes are divine. Daisy will love them.'

Francis left shortly afterwards to buy cotton wool and breast pads from Boots. Bea was glad he hadn't put off Alice and Rachel staying at his house on Saturday night, because she was to spend the coming weekend at Seastone, with Emma and Marissa. She could have taken the girls with her, of course, and that would have been fine, but if she was honest with herself, she knew she could do with a couple of days free from family responsibilities. She needed time to think, which didn't tend to happen when her daughters were around. She had been looking forward to the Seastone weekend for ages. She pictured herself strolling along the shingle beach, having the peace to work through some of the problems that beset her.

The prospect of having a heart-to-heart conversation with her friends felt like a lifeline. Bea was careful to maintain a pretence with Francis, because she was too proud to let him see how miserable she felt. But she never had to put on an act with Emma and Marissa, and would be able to admit to them that recently she had had a few despairing moments. Since she and Miles had finished, no other boyfriends had come into view. It seemed to her perfectly possible that she might remain single for the rest of her life. After all, as one grew older, more and more of the men one met were, frankly, hopeless. They were married, or they had been through divorces or bereavements and had never quite recovered. Or they were vain, unreliable, egotistical or plain uninterested, which was why they hadn't found a partner in the first place. She might even find the courage to tell Emma and Marissa what Miles had said to her – *God, Bea, you can be so demanding.* Her friends would tell her it wasn't true. Maybe she would be able to laugh about it then.

She needed to talk to them about Patrick, too. Though she continued to wait for him, hoping and praying that he would one day decide to try to find her so that they could be reunited, it was becoming increasingly hard to suppress her feelings of despondency. It had been unrealistic of her to hope that Patrick would try to trace her as soon as he turned eighteen. More likely he was absorbed in the usual things that eighteen-year-old boys enjoyed – sport, cars, girls – and hardly gave his birth mother a thought. There was so much she could not know, because almost all of his life was a complete blank to her.

He might be living a few streets away, or he might have moved to the other side of the world. He was no longer a child, he was a man, and that meant that whatever choices he made she must respect. In an attempt to extract a crumb of consolation from an unhappy situation, she told herself that she should be glad he hadn't tried to find her. It must mean, she reminded herself, that he was content with the life he had.

# Chapter Seventeen

## 1989

Thursday: Gabriel had stayed at the flat overnight. He and Marissa left for work together the following morning. He was to drop her off at walking distance from Floral Street before driving on to an appointment. They emerged from the block of flats into the car park. Marissa squinted at the brightness of the sun. Sunshine glittered on the puddles in the potholes that pitted the tarmac.

As Gabriel unlocked the passenger door, she saw out of the corner of her eye a movement, a shadow. Jamie was standing on the far side of the car park. Dread and horror flooded through her, and she seemed to freeze to the spot. He might call out her name. He might try to speak to her, as he had in the shop.

'*Ma chère*, are you all right?'

She realised that Gabriel was addressing her. She nodded.

'Sure?' He looked concerned

She managed a smile, then climbed into the car. As they drove out of the car park, the passenger wing mirror captured Jamie in miniature, still standing in the same place. Then sunlight flashed on the glass, and when she looked again, he had gone.

At the shop that morning, she kept looking out to the road. He would come back, she knew he would. He was playing with her. Shortly before midday, she caught sight of him on the pavement. She walked outside.

He called out, 'Hello again!' His tone was light, as if he was some pleasant acquaintance.

She crossed the road to him. 'What are you doing here?' she hissed.

'Waiting for you. You and me, Mary, we need to talk.'

'Don't call me Mary.' Though she felt frightened, her predominant emotion was fury. 'And don't ever come to my home again.'

'That's a nice block of flats. Is it yours or his?'

'Mine.'

He whistled. 'Impressive. Must be worth a bob or two. There's a café down the road, Italian place, Giulio's or some other foreign name. How about you and I go there and talk about old times.'

A vivid image sprang into her mind: Jamie grabbing her by the hair and smashing her head into the wall. The small green and white checks on his shirt and the smell of his sweat.

Her vision cleared and she cried out, 'For God's sake, just say whatever it is you want to say!'

'Temper, temper.' A satisfied look crossed his features. 'No, I'd rather we went to the café.'

He walked away from her. She thought of running in the other direction – or going back into the shop and calling the police. Then she imagined him hanging round outside her flat until Gabriel drove back into the car park. After a moment, she followed him down Floral Street, heading in the direction of Bow Street.

They went into the café. Three of the half-dozen small tables were occupied, and the air was warm and heavy with steam and cigarette smoke.

'Tea or coffee?' he asked, and she said, 'Neither.' She caught herself just in time, before she could add a 'thank you'. Politeness was too ingrained in her.

She sat down at a window table. A yellowed net curtain covered the lower half of the window, and the glass was fogged with condensation, adding to her feeling of claustrophobia. She dug her nails into her palm. At all costs she had to keep her emotions under control. Jamie enjoyed eliciting a reaction from her, because it made him think he had won, that he had the upper hand.

He bought two teas anyway and put one in front of her. 'My treat,' he said, and she stifled a shudder.

'I'm short of time. Tell me why you're here.'

'I saw that picture of you in the paper.' He shook his head in wonderment. 'You've done well for yourself, haven't you? Little Mary, running her own business and with her photo in the paper.'

She imagined Jamie ringing up the *Sunday Times* and telling the feature writer the truth about her. He would do that; he would take pleasure in informing the journalist that fourteen years ago, Marissa Flint had cut off all contact with her old life. That her name wasn't really Marissa Flint at all, but Mary Canterbury. It would make a great story.

But that wasn't what mattered to her most. She could tolerate that, the public exposure, though she would hate the violent ripping-away of the carapace she had protected herself with all these years. But all that paled beside her dread that Gabriel would find out about the marriage, and in such a way.

And Jamie, homing in unerringly on her most vulnerable point, paused, stirring his tea, and said, 'I was surprised you didn't mention in the article that you're married.'

A cold hand gripped her heart. 'That was a long time ago. And it wasn't relevant to the piece.'

A flash of anger crossed his features, and he leaned over the table towards her. So close to him, she noticed the frayed tips of his shirt collar, the sheen on the shoulders of his jacket where the fabric had worn, the nick on his jawline where he had cut himself shaving.

He said, 'You have told your chap about me, haven't you?'

She shook her head. She felt hollow with dread. Jamie sat back in the chair, his legs splayed, and laughed. 'Dear oh dear. You're priceless, you are, Mary. You haven't changed at all. You always made such a mess of things. Living with that French bloke and he doesn't even know about us.'

'There is no us.' She knew she was losing it, that her anger and fear were spilling over.

He said softly, tauntingly, 'I bet he doesn't even know your real name.'

She wanted to run away, as she had done once before. But everything was different now, and she had far too much to lose. *I was surprised you didn't mention in the article that you're married.* She had to know for certain.

She said, 'Have you divorced me?'

'No. Why would I do that? You're mine, Mary. You'll always be mine.'

How could she ever have thought herself in love with him? He was such a nasty, vicious man.

She shook her head. 'You don't own me. You never did. You thought you did, but you were wrong.'

His lip curled into that familiar malicious smile. 'You shouldn't have gone off like that. Walking out on me. It was wrong of you. You owe me.'

'I don't owe you a thing, Jamie.'

She made to stand up to leave, but he put his hand on her sleeve. 'Don't touch me!' she hissed, and a couple of students sitting at the next table turned and stared at them.

He withdrew his hand. 'Sit down,' he said, and after a moment, she did so. He took a gulp of tea. Then his eyes fixed on her. 'That nice flat. Those fancy clothes. When I saw that article, I knew you had money to spare. And the thing is, I'm rather down on my luck right now.'

Something uncurled inside her. 'What are you talking about?'

'It's up to you, Mary. If you don't want your French bloke to find out about us, that you're my wife, then you need to do something for me.'

His mouth was hard. The game-playing had stopped, and in spite of the oppressive heat of the café, she felt shivery.

She said, 'Are you blackmailing me?'

He shrugged. 'Whatever you choose to call it. You've only yourself to blame. You walked out on me. I wasted a lot of time trying to find you.'

'You shouldn't have bothered.'

But she regretted saying that: it was a mistake to engage with him, and it seemed to give him pleasure, because he cocked his head to one side, smiling.

Then he named his price, and she stared at him, aghast.

*

She must have walked for miles that afternoon, through London streets both familiar and unknown to her. In the café, Jamie had scribbled a phone number on a scrap of paper and handed it to her. 'I'll give you a week,' he had said.

Every avenue her thoughts rushed along brought her up against a dead end. She could pay him the five thousand pounds he had demanded of her. She could afford it. But he would come back for more, she knew he would – and even if by some miracle he didn't, there would be the constant fear that he would, which was just as bad. Or she could refuse to pay him; she could remind him that blackmail was a crime. Employ a private detective, even, to scare him off. But then there would be nothing to stop him approaching Gabriel. He would take pleasure in that. A letter, a phone call, a tap on the shoulder of the man she loved as he walked down the street.

Coming across a small park, she sat down on a bench and stared out at the narrow rectangular lawn edged with shrubs. She thought of Jamie in the café, naming the price of his silence, Jamie putting the cup of tea in front of her: *my treat*. She hated that he had forced on her this horrible, grubby intimacy that preoccupied her every waking hour. Sometimes she wanted to cry and sometimes she wanted to scream, but mostly she felt sick with fear and repelled by herself.

She had known in her heart for several days now, since Jamie had come into the shop, that she must tell Gabriel the truth. She had no choice, and besides, it was what she should have done a long, long time ago.

Every fibre of her being railed against it. She thought of all the different ways in which this life she loved might fall apart. The shock on his beloved face when she told him that she was married to another man would hurt beyond measure. His disappointment in her, his disillusion – how would she bear it?

But she must tell him tonight. He would read her distress in her eyes and hear it in her voice. Every minute more she waited magnified her guilt. And she felt tired beyond endurance.

She hailed a taxi to take her back to the shop. From her office she phoned Gabriel and asked him to cancel their dinner engagement that evening. She needed to talk to him, she said, about something important.

Returning to the flat in the evening, Marissa took the stairs again rather than the lift. This time it wasn't because she was afraid that Jamie might be there waiting for her. It was because she was still trying to get the words straight in her head. *Gabriel, there's something I have to tell you. Something I should have told you years ago, and I'm so, so sorry.*

As she let herself into the flat, she heard Isabelle shouting. 'Why won't you ever listen to me? It's so unfair! You treat me as if I'm a child!' Her voice was high and distressed.

Then Gabriel, his tone lower, reasoning. 'Isabelle, chérie, all I'm saying is that we need to think this through carefully.'

'You always say that! I can't stand it here any longer! I'm going out!'

Her face wet with tears, Isabelle pushed past Marissa, who was in the hall, hanging up her raincoat. The door slammed behind her.

'I should go after her.' Gabriel appeared in the entrance to the living room, looking frantic.

'Let her go for a walk. It might help her to cool down.'

Thoughts of Jamie slid just then to the back of Marissa's mind. She put down her briefcase and took Gabriel in her arms. 'Darling, she'll be fine. Give her a few moments to herself.'

'Is she right?' He stared at her wide-eyed. 'Do I treat her like a child?'

'No, you try to protect her, as any father would.' She kissed him. 'I'll get us both a drink. Then you can tell me what all that was about.'

In the kitchen, she drew the cork from a bottle of Sauvignon Blanc. She poured wine into a glass and drank it quickly. *Gabriel, I need to tell you something. The husband I forgot to mention to you is trying to blackmail me.*

Should she do it now, right this moment? Should she seize the advantage of Isabelle's absence to tell Gabriel the truth? Or would it be kinder to let him speak first, to try to help him resolve his disagreement with his daughter, which had left him deeply upset. Then, afterwards, she would embark on this nightmare conversation.

She took the glasses and bottle into the living room and set them on the coffee table. Gabriel was pacing up and down the room. He said, 'Isabelle wants to go and live with Justine.'

'Oh my God.' She stared at him, then sat on the sofa, tucking a leg beneath her. She passed him a glass. 'Gabriel, sit down, drink this. Surely not.'

'She's worked it all out.' He sat down beside her and gave a dry laugh. 'She even pointed out to me that Justine's house is near the school, so it'll be easier when she's taking her GCSEs.'

'Darling, it won't happen. For one thing, Justine won't go along with it.'

'It was Justine who suggested it.'

Marissa frowned. This was new, and it surprised her. 'Are you sure? That doesn't sound like her.'

She had met Justine Vernier on a handful of occasions. She knew what it was to live in a close relationship with a manipulative person, and she recognised some of Jamie's traits in Gabriel's ex-wife. Impulsiveness, lack of principle, the need to control, and a habit of blaming everyone but themselves. Justine was not physically abusive, as Jamie had been. Instead, she toyed with her daughter's emotions, using love and attention as a bargaining tool.

Gabriel said wearily, 'Isabelle told me that when she phoned from the school the other night, Justine spoke to her about it.'

'Then she's doing it to hurt you. She's manipulating Isabelle to get at you. You know she is, she's done it before.'

'Maybe. Or perhaps it's different this time.'

Marissa shook her head. 'It's just a whim. Justine likes to be the centre of attention. And she likes to keep you de-stabilised. Darling, you know what she's like.'

His olive-green eyes looked troubled. 'She showers Isabelle with affection and then forgets her for months. But it's possible, just possible, that she's changed. She's forty-four. Maybe she's realised that she's unlikely to have another child. Maybe she knows she needs to make the most of the daughter she has.'

'Even if you're right, it won't last. Justine isn't capable of caring for a teenage girl.'

'She'll get bored with it, yes, you may be right.' He picked a speck of dust from his trousers. 'You don't think she can change, then?'

People reinvented themselves all the time. People started from scratch with a new name and a new history.

'Anyone can change.' Her voice was hoarse. 'Perhaps you're right. Perhaps Justine has regrets and perhaps she wants to make amends. But Gabriel, even if Isabelle were to go and stay with her mother for a while, she would come back to you, because she loves you.'

He pressed two fingers to his temple, as if his head hurt. 'You do understand, don't you, that Justine tells Isabelle a different version of what happened to us, to our marriage. She says that I didn't have time for either of them, that she felt shut out by my family in France and lonely when we came back to England. She's a good liar, but there's some truth in it, Marissa. The best lies always have some truth in them.'

Restless, he stood up. He opened the patio doors and went out onto the balcony. He stood, his back to her, at the balustrade, silhouetted by the sinking sun. Her gaze rested on him. She loved him so much. She couldn't lose him; it would tear her apart.

The rain had stopped, and patches of red-gold light glowed between the clouds. She knew that Gabriel was looking down to the street below for Isabelle, that he was scouring the landscape in the hope of seeing her, just as she herself, such a short time ago, had stared down at that same patch of ground, dreading that she might catch sight of Jamie. Only a few days had passed since she had stood in Leicester Square Underground station admiring the Marissa Flint poster, and yet so much had happened. In the space of less than a week, her life had altered so drastically she was hardly able to recognise it.

She went to stand beside Gabriel. He ran a fingertip along the railing, sweeping away raindrops. He said, 'If Isabelle wants to go and live with her mother, I can hardly stop her. As she pointed out, she's sixteen now, almost an adult, old enough to make up her own mind.'

'Yes.' She leaned her head against his shoulder. For a moment, his touch and warmth erased her dread. It might be all right. Surely she would be able to make him understand that none of what she had done had been for lack of love for him.

Gabriel sighed. 'She needs to know that I trust her to use her judgement. If she chooses to go and live with Justine for a while, I think I have to accept that.' He dropped a kiss on top of Marissa's head. 'I'm so sorry you had to come home to this. You said you wanted to talk to me. What is it? Have you found a house?'

'A house?' She stared at him blankly. Seconds passed before she recalled that she had agreed to consider looking for somewhere they could all move into. 'No, Gabriel, it's not that.'

'What, then?' He was frowning now; she had his full attention. 'You're not unwell, are you, chérie?'

'Unwell? No . . . no.'

And somehow she managed to say it. There was even a fragment of relief in broaching this conversation at last. 'There's something I need to tell you,' she said. 'Something I should have told you about years ago.'

His expression altered. 'Marissa, you're frightening me.'

'Something's happened. Something difficult.' Then the words rushed out. 'A few days ago, my husband came into the shop.'

The moment she said it, she knew she had got it all wrong. She should have found a gentler way to tell him about Jamie. If such words existed.

He stepped back, gave a crooked smile. 'Husband? What are you talking about? You're not married.'

'I *was* married. It was years ago, back in the mid seventies.'

'You can't have been married.' He gave an odd laugh. 'You'd have told me.'

Marissa flinched. 'I *should* have told you, I know I should have. I regret it so deeply. But I was afraid . . .'

'*Married*.' He was staring at her, frowning. 'Tell me this isn't true, Marissa.'

'Darling, I'm so sorry . . .' The phrase tasted like ashes in her mouth. 'My marriage — it was a catastrophe. I couldn't bear even to think about it, let alone talk about it.'

'Married . . .' he said again. He shook his head, as if trying to clear it. 'I'm sorry, but I can't . . . Really?'

She couldn't speak. She nodded.

There was still disbelief in his eyes. 'You're saying to me that ever since you've known me, you've been married to another man?'

'Yes.' There were, she realised, no words that would soften the blow. There were no right words. She twisted her hands together. 'I didn't know for sure till today . . . I mean, I'd hoped he'd divorced me . . . it was such a long time ago . . . but he said he hadn't.'

She began to speak again, to try to explain, but he broke through.

'So that's why you didn't want to marry me.'

'No, Gabriel!'

'And that's why you weren't keen on living with me.'

'No, no, it wasn't like that at all!'

'What else can I believe?'

She wanted to go to him, to take him in her arms, to reassure him through the power of touch how much she loved him, but his expression stopped her. 'I love you, Gabriel,' she said. The words trembled. 'I love you with all my soul. I'm begging you to understand . . . and to forgive me.'

That he did not respond chilled her to the core. He turned away and looked over the balcony again. She saw that his gaze had alighted on Isabelle, far below them, as she made her way back to the flat.

She said softly, 'Gabriel, please . . .'

'You said that he, this man – your *husband* – came to the shop.'

'Yes, on Monday. He was there before, at Nico's event, but I didn't recognise him. And then he came to the shop. I didn't see him for a couple of days after that, and I thought maybe that was it, maybe he was just trying to scare me. But then, this morning . . .'

'Something was wrong, something upset you, when we were in the car park, I saw that.'

'Yes.' She closed her eyes. 'He was there. Just . . . standing there, waiting. And then later, he came to Floral Street again.'

'What does he want?'

'Money. He wants me to give him money.' Her head drooped and she said miserably, 'He found out who I was, where I worked, from that article in the *Sunday Times*. He recognised me from the photo. And I suppose he worked out that I was well off. He's blackmailing me, Gabriel. He said he'd tell you if . . .'

Too late she saw the trap she had fallen into. And Gabriel must have glimpsed it at the same moment, because he said, his tone bitter, 'So you've told me about him because you felt you had no choice. Because of him, because of what you were afraid he would do. Had he not approached you, I still wouldn't know.'

They both heard the sound of a key turning in the lock.

As he left the balcony, Gabriel said quietly, 'Is that what it takes, Marissa, to persuade you to be honest with me? The threat of blackmail?'

Then he went to meet his daughter.

They didn't discuss Jamie again until much later. That evening, Marissa was glad of the self-absorption of adolescence, which meant that Isabelle didn't notice the difficult atmosphere between them. They ate supper, watched a film on TV. She cleared up the kitchen. Throughout the long hours until bedtime, Gabriel did not once meet her eyes.

Later, when Isabelle was asleep and she and Gabriel were in their bedroom, he said to her, 'Tell me his name.'

'Jamie Canterbury.'

'You said the marriage was a catastrophe.'

'He used to hit me.' It was hard to say it aloud, having hidden it away for so long. She wrapped her arms round herself. 'He enjoyed hurting me, he liked to feel he had power over me.'

'I'm sorry for you, Marissa. I'm sorry you suffered.'

But his words were stiff and the shock remained in his eyes. She unbuttoned her blouse and draped it on a hanger. She wanted to implore him again to forgive her, but what if he did not?

He asked her more questions. Then he told her that she was to phone Jamie and arrange to meet him tomorrow morning. He would go with her; he would deal with him. Marissa thanked him. Again she wanted to fling her arms round him, this time in gratitude.

But he turned aside, saying, 'I've work to catch up on. I'll come to bed later.'

'Gabriel. *Please*. I love you so much.'

His gaze returned to her. He said quietly, 'I don't know what to think. I can't seem to take it in. It's too much.'

As he went to the door, something seemed to occur to him. 'Your name . . .' he said. 'What is it? Not Marissa Flint, presumably.'

'Mary Canterbury,' she murmured. 'Before my marriage, it was Mary Finch. I changed it by deed poll after I left him.'

'Dear God.' The words were a whisper. Slowly he shook his head. 'Even that . . . Even your *name* . . .' He left the room.

She hardly slept that night. Sometime in the early hours of the morning, Gabriel slipped quietly into bed. She reached out to touch him and her hand brushed against him, and there it was, the momentary consolation of the warmth of his skin, before he turned away from her.

She must have dozed off at some point, because when she woke, Gabriel, fully dressed, was opening the curtains and the summer sun was flooding into the room. He said, 'You're to phone him, Marissa. Tell him you'll meet him in the car park at nine. Isabelle will have gone to school by then.'

She made the phone call. Knowing that she was to see Jamie shortly, she couldn't face breakfast. Gabriel walked with Isabelle to her bus stop and then came back to the flat. At a few minutes before nine, they went downstairs. Gabriel said, as they walked out of the building, 'Let me talk to him. It will be all right, Marissa.' She nodded dumbly.

Jamie was already standing at the edge of the car park. His face spasmed with anger when he caught sight of Gabriel. Gabriel said, 'Is that him?'

'Yes.'

With quick strides, he crossed the car park. Marissa, hurrying after him, heard him say, 'You will not contact Marissa again. You will never again speak to her, telephone her, or approach her in any way. Do you understand?'

Jamie sneered belligerently. 'Who do you think you are, telling me what to do?'

'Someone who sees you for what you are, a coward and a blackmailer,' Gabriel said contemptuously. 'A miserable apology for a man.'

Another resident, who was unlocking his car door, turned and stared at them.

Jamie snarled. Gabriel didn't back off, and then Jamie seemed suddenly to deflate.

'I don't know what you're talking about,' he muttered. 'She must have got the wrong end of the stick.'

'Get out and don't come back.' Gabriel's voice was low and dangerous. 'If I see you again, I'll go to the police.'

Jamie's gaze moved from Gabriel to Marissa. At last he walked away.

As they went back into the block of flats, Marissa murmured, 'Thank you, thank you.' Gabriel nodded, but did not reply.

She felt light-headed, and found it hard to catch her breath. She told herself that it was over; that, thank God, she would never see Jamie Canterbury again. She need never fear him again. She remembered that she was to go to Seastone that weekend, and she tried to picture the sparkle of the sea, the cool, fresh air and the company of her friends. She would have wiped the slate clean of the past.

And yet though these thoughts should have given her joy, she seemed incapable at that moment of any emotion other than apprehension. Gabriel unlocked the front door of the flat. She was through the worst, she said to herself as they went inside. It would be all right. Though it might take a while to repair the relationship, he would in time trust her again. Yet she jangled with anxiety.

Inside the flat, Gabriel went into the bedroom. Marissa put on the kettle. She went to ask him whether he wanted tea or coffee and heard him opening and shutting drawers. There was a small suitcase open on the bed, and he was folding shirts and putting them inside it. Stupidly, she said, 'What are you doing?'

'Packing.'

Still she couldn't accept it. There had been plenty of times in her life when she had felt she was fighting to keep her head above water, but now she seemed to lack the energy to keep afloat. Her limbs thrashed uselessly. The sense of dread, that dark melody that had played so relentlessly throughout this past week, returned, and became deafening.

She whispered, 'Please, Gabriel.'

'It's over. You must know that. You lied to me.' Though his words were harsh, he did not raise his voice.

'I did, and I'm so, so sorry. I shouldn't have, but I was afraid . . .'

He put a couple of notebooks and a few toiletries into the case. When at last he looked at her, she saw that there was no anger or unkindness in his eyes, only pain, which was worse.

'And I'm sorry for that. I'm sorry for you, Marissa. I see what that brute did to you, and you have my pity.' He closed the case, snapping shut the clasps.

When she made to go to him, he stepped back. 'Please, Gabriel,' she murmured. 'Forgive me.'

'I wish I could, I truly do. I've tried to – I thought of nothing else last night. But I've been through this once before, with Justine, and I can't do it again. How can I live with someone who isn't open with me? How can I love someone who doesn't trust me?'

'Gabriel, no!' Tears spilled from her eyes. She grabbed at his sleeve as he passed her, but he pulled away.

At the front door, he turned and said, 'There have been times in the past when I've felt you were holding something back from me. Now I know what that was. The truth is, Marissa, that I've only ever known a part of you.'

Her face was wet with tears. She forced herself to say, 'Don't you love me any more?'

'I don't know.' He looked pale and weary and defeated. 'I honestly don't know. The only thing I'm sure of is that I need some space right now.'

He left the flat. She wanted to run after him, to beg him to stay, but she remained where she was. Eventually she went into the kitchen and scrubbed at her face with a handful of tissues. Then she went out to the balcony. Her gaze darted desperately over the street below, searching for him, though she knew that he had gone.

# Chapter Eighteen

## 1989

As the three of them took rugs and cushions outside to the beach – a pre-dinner drink on the shingle was a Seastone weekend tradition – Emma had a good look at Marissa, who had only just arrived. When she had been working as an air stewardess, Emma had been skilled at spotting those passengers who were afraid of flying. Her friend, she thought, had the expression of a woman who expected the plane was about to crash.

Bea must have thought much the same, because as she spread out a rug, she said to Marissa, 'Bad day?'

Marissa nodded. Then she murmured, 'Gabriel's left me,' and pressed the palm of her hand against her mouth.

'Oh my God.' Bea looked as shocked as Emma felt. 'What happened? Did you have a row?'

'Not really. But it's all my fault.'

Tamar came out with a tray of wine and glasses, which she put on the pebbles. Emma poured a glass of wine. 'Marissa. Sit down. Have a drink. And then tell us.'

Marissa sat down on a rug. Her head drooped and she

hunched her knees against her chest. Emma knelt beside her and handed her the glass.

Her own mind was whirring. She would have said to anyone that Marissa and Gabriel were rock solid. She had often thought them the perfect couple – beautiful, successful and glamorous, and the love and tenderness they shared was plain to see.

Marissa let a handful of stones trail between her fingers. Suddenly she spoke again, as if in a hurry to get the words out. 'I've been living a lie. Yesterday I had to tell Gabriel that I was married, that I got married in my early twenties.'

'Married?' This was Bea, the first to collect her thoughts.

'Yes. It didn't last long. I left him . . . I left Jamie, my husband, after less than a year.' With a hunted expression, Marissa swung her gaze between the three of them. 'I'm afraid it's true. I'm so sorry. I should have told you too, but I didn't. It was wrong of me.'

Bea said, 'But you're divorced, presumably.'

'No.' The word was a gasp. Marissa gave a violent shake of the head. 'I'd hoped that he . . . It was a disaster . . . He was . . . he . . .'

'Marissa, darling.' Tamar patted her shoulder. 'Take a breath. Have a drink. There's no rush. We've all the time in the world.'

Marissa took a mouthful of wine, then said, a little more calmly, 'So back then, fourteen years ago, after I left him, I cut off all contact with everyone I knew. I changed my name and the way I looked. Until yesterday . . . until he, Jamie, my husband, told me yesterday that I was still married to him, I didn't know for sure.' She squeezed shut her eyes, then said very quietly, 'Though of course I knew it was possible.'

'You're telling us, I think, that he was abusive.' Tamar's voice was very gentle.

Marissa nodded.

'I'm so sorry, Marissa. How dreadful for you.'

'He hit me. And he made me lose my baby. And I couldn't bear anyone to know about it because it made me feel . . . grubby. And so foolish and naïve.' Tears glittered in Marissa's eyes.

Emma felt tears sting her own eyes too. She put her arm round Marissa.

After a while, Marissa took a deep breath and started to speak again. 'For years and years I was scared that Jamie might find me. But then, eventually, I began to think I was safe. And by the time I met Gabriel, I hardly thought about him at all. I should have told Gabriel, of course I should, but I didn't because I didn't want to. But oh God, I wish I had!' Her gaze slid from Emma to Tamar before coming to rest on Bea. 'A few days ago, Jamie turned up at the shop. He'd recognised me from a photo in the newspaper and had worked out how to find me. He wanted money from me.' She sounded utterly weary.

'Oh God, Marissa,' said Bea. 'You poor, poor thing!'

'I had to tell Gabriel the truth. I had no choice. I knew it was going to be awful, telling him, and it was. I've hurt him so much. And he went away – he packed up his things from the flat and left! He told me he needed time to think. But I'm afraid . . . What will I do if he doesn't love me any more?'

Marissa put her hands over her face and began to cry. Emma found tissues. Marissa blew her nose, then rubbed her eyes on the sleeve of her linen blouse, a very un-Marissa thing to do, thought Emma.

Tamar, kneeling on the shingle in front of her, said, 'You know what I think? I think you could do with a brandy. And something to eat. I think you've been through hell this past week and I don't expect you've eaten very well at all.'

Because it was a fine, warm evening, rare on this chilly North Sea coast, they dined outside. Tamar and Emma put out baguettes and cold roast chicken and salad.

While they picnicked, Marissa told her story.

Emma found it hard at first to take in that this woman she knew so well had hidden away such a significant part of her life. And yet, now that Marissa had told them, she found that she could imagine her taking such a step. The more she thought about it, the more it added up. Marissa had always been reticent. She had never spoken much about her early life. And she had her foibles and her phobias – her dislike of crowded places, her need to shield herself from the public gaze, her intense desire for privacy.

Emma thought about Gabriel too. He had endured a destructive and deceitful relationship of his own. She found it all too easy to see why he might have reacted badly. Poor Marissa, she thought. Poor Gabriel.

'I didn't set out to deceive any of you,' said Marissa. 'All I ever wanted was to feel safe. But once you start going down that road, it's hard to go back.'

'We know, darling.' Tamar put her hand over Marissa's. 'We all understand that you made your choices in order to survive.'

Bea hugged Marissa. From the distance came the hush-hush of the waves as they lapped the shoreline. Marissa pleated her fingers together. 'I made myself into another person,' she said. 'You all befriended me, and I came to prefer that person. Mary Canterbury was so weak, so pathetic. I didn't want anyone to know about her. I didn't even want to think about her, because I was ashamed of her, you see. It would have been like going back into a nightmare. When you live with a man like Jamie, you end up blaming yourself. You think you've done something wrong, that what happened was because of you, because you were ugly and stupid and provoking.'

'That's how men like that function,' said Tamar briskly. 'They mess with your head.'

'Yes, you're right, in my heart I know that you are. But even after I got away from him, even once I'd started again from scratch and got the business going, whatever I did and however successful I was, still, sometimes, I heard this voice in my head telling me he'd been right all along, telling me that I wasn't any good. I had to put that part of me away. I couldn't have managed if I hadn't.'

Emma refilled their glasses. Then she said gently, 'Marissa, you are beautiful and clever and funny, and we all love you. I'll always remember that day I first met you, in your shop in Margaret Street. You made me feel I could become the person I wanted to be. Knowing you has made my life richer and more exciting and a whole lot more fun. Bea feels the same. And you do too, don't you, Mum?'

Marissa gave them all a shaky smile. Then she said, 'I always think of my life as splitting into three pieces. There was before Jamie, and then there was the year and a half when I knew him, and then there was after Jamie. And that's been the best bit. And a lot of the reason it's been so great has been because of you three.'

Her gaze returned to Bea. 'Do you remember, Bea, that night when I was babysitting at your house in Islington and you told me about Ciaran and your baby boy? I wanted to tell you about Jamie then. And I almost did. But in the end, I just couldn't. Earlier on this evening, when I was driving here, I thought about that. I was afraid you'd hate me for it, for keeping secrets from you when you'd been so brave and generous. I almost turned round and drove back to London.'

'We're glad you didn't.' Bea patted her hand.

'Thank you.' The words were a whisper.

Bea offered to make some tea. She and Tamar went back to the house. Shakily, Marissa stood up. Emma joined her as she wandered down the beach. Their feet crunched on the pebbles.

They stood on the water's edge, watching the waves. The shingle was finer here, the stones made so shiny with seawater they looked like fragments of amber and carnelian, like the beads in the necklaces that Emma had made for Marissa.

'Talk to me, please,' said Marissa. 'I'm so tired of talking about myself. Tell me how you are.'

'Oh, the same as ever. The usual chaos.' Emma gave Marissa a half-smile, then sighed. 'I thought that once Max had finished my studio I'd get masses of work done, but it doesn't seem to have turned out like that.'

Max had built her a studio in the attic of the Glisson Road house. A large triangular window looked down to the tops of the birches and the willow at the back of the garden. Skylights let in the sun, which reflected off a polished beechwood floor. Emma kept promising herself to get properly down to her painting now that she had a quiet space of her own, but family life got in the way – the children, her mother, a dinner that must be cooked because Max was entertaining a client or colleague – and when she next looked at whatever poor plant she was portraying, the petals had dropped off it. She sometimes felt she was letting down her forebears, that long line of artists, both male and female, who had battled through wars and penury and sickness and the demands of family and yet, in spite of everything, had succeeded in producing a lasting body of work.

They went back up the slope. Tamar and Bea had brought out strawberries and cream and mugs of tea.

Bea handed round the mugs. 'I'm thinking of making a fresh start,' she said. 'I know, I know, I've done it before, but I'm going to do it properly this time. I'm going to go back to school and take my A levels. Biology and something else, I'm not sure yet. Chemistry maybe, because I want to train to be a nurse. I wanted to become a nurse ages ago, before I got pregnant.'

'It's a brilliant idea, isn't it?' said Tamar.

There was a chorus of approval. Bea sat down on the shingle. 'I don't know how I'm going to fit in studying with everything else, with my job and the girls. But I have to try. You can end up getting so swamped with everyday life, you forget what it was you'd meant to be.'

The sun sank in a burning disc to the horizon, streaking fire across the sea as the light faded. The murmur of the sea was a backdrop to their conversation. Eventually they carried the picnic things and rugs back into the house.

Emma set off along the track, torch in hand, to phone Max so that she could check on the children. She welcomed having time on her own to absorb the revelations of the evening. After she had made sure that Max had remembered Ben's inhaler and cooked something passably healthy for the children's tea, she told him about Marissa.

'How could he?' she said. 'There's nothing to her, Max, she's skin and bone. How could her husband treat her like that?'

Anger boiled up inside her. She looked out of the phone kiosk's grubby glass windows to where a full moon cast a flat silvery light on field and marsh. 'I keep thinking I should have guessed,' she said. 'I should have known something was wrong. Marissa's always hidden a lot of herself away. How terrible it must have been for her living with this secret all these years, on her own! Maybe I should have asked, maybe I should have said something.'

'I don't think,' he said, 'that she would have wanted you to.'

She sighed. She wondered whether he was right.

Walking back to the cottage, she felt deeply worried. What if Gabriel never found it in his heart to forgive Marissa? He was a proud man, and it was all too possible that he felt humiliated at having laid bare the betrayals and mortifications of his own marriage while Marissa had remained silent about her own. Emma knew that losing him would break her friend's heart.

All that she and Bea and Tamar could do was to support her and hope that the storm blew over. Show her how much they loved and appreciated her. Phone her, write to her, visit her, make sure she knew she wasn't alone.

While Emma was out phoning Max, Bea made cocoa. Marissa perched on the table, biting her nails as she talked about Gabriel. 'I hate what I've done to him. I've hurt him so much. He thinks it means I don't trust him.'

'I expect he just needs time.'

Bea said this to console. If she was honest with herself, she couldn't be absolutely sure it was true. Gabriel Vernier was handsome, cultured and charming, and on the occasions she had met him, she had felt rather in awe of him. But she found that she could, unfortunately, imagine him being a little judgemental and given to brooding.

But Marissa latched on to her words. 'Do you think I should phone him when I go home?'

Bea was watching the milk saucepan. She chose her words carefully. 'Didn't you say that he said he needed time to think? Maybe give him a few more days. Don't rush him.' She poured hot milk into the mugs and stirred.

Though Bea had suggested she wait a while before phoning Gabriel, when Marissa returned to the flat on Sunday evening, the first thing she did was to call the farmhouse. She simply couldn't bear it any longer. She needed to hear his voice. She yearned to put things right.

The moment he answered the phone, she knew she had made a mistake. Gabriel's tone was cold and detached. When she begged him, when she pressed him to tell her how he was feeling, he told her that he was trying to come to terms with the fact that their relationship wasn't what he had believed it to be. That he'd always considered they had something special. That she wasn't the person he'd thought she was. And though he wished her well, he wasn't yet ready to see her.

Then he said goodbye and put down the phone. Courteous as always, but completely devastating. Her legs no longer seemed able to carry her. She sank down onto the sofa, and despair washed through her as she stared into the silence.

Bea and Emma were walking down the long avenue of London planes and horse chestnuts on Jesus Green. Their four girls ran hand in hand along the grass while Ben zigzagged from one side of the avenue to another, disrupting cyclists.

Bea said, 'I've called Marissa half a dozen times. She didn't pick up.'

'What do you think we should do?'

'We'll go to London. Go to the flat.'

'When?'

'Soon. I'll give you a ring. I thought maybe we could take her out somewhere. If nothing else, it'll give her something else to think about.'

They parted shortly afterwards. Bea went back to Portugal Place, where she gave the girls their supper and, once they were in bed, settled down on the sofa with a coffee and a Jilly Cooper.

She intended to keep to the resolution she had made at Seastone. She needed to move on, to transform herself, to make a fresh start yet again. Though she seemed to find it harder each time, she hoped it was not too late to find a better version of herself. She had registered to study biology and chemistry at evening classes. She wanted to make up for lost chances, for stolen time.

She had resolved also to abandon the search for love, for a while at least. Recently it had led only to disillusionment. She would socialise with interesting people and never again waste her time on hopeless men. She would have fun, but she was through for the time being with love and marriage and all the heartbreak and distraction they entailed. She would treasure what she had and give up hankering for what she had lost. And she had so much: a lovely home in one of the most beautiful cities in England. Two adorable daughters. Supportive friends in Emma and Marissa and Tamar. A civilised relationship with her ex-husband . . . and she wasn't even getting on too badly with her mother just now. As for Patrick, she would never forget the brief time they had had together, but she mustn't allow her yearning for him to knock her off course. All she could do was to go on quietly cherishing the hope that they would be reunited one day.

The following week, she and Emma went to London. Emma wanted to see an exhibition of portraits by John Singer Sargent at the Tate Gallery, and they hoped to persuade Marissa, who still wasn't answering her phone, to accompany them. They took the train to King's Cross, and then the Victoria line.

When Marissa answered the door of her flat, Bea had to disguise her shock at her friend's appearance. Marissa's eyes were puffy, and she looked pale. She didn't feel like going out, she said. She couldn't face it. When they offered to abandon the exhibition and stay with her, she said she would rather be on her own. She thought she was coming down with a migraine. She needed to lie down and would phone them when she felt better.

In the end, reluctantly, Bea and Emma left. Though they went on to the exhibition, both found it hard at first to focus on the paintings. Usually Bea enjoyed Singer Sargent – all those gorgeously glamorous women with their plumed headdresses and ball gowns, all those dangerously attractive men, darkly handsome in tailcoats and high leather boots. The allure of another age, another time.

But today the images failed to distract her. All she could think of was Marissa, and how thin and unhappy she had looked. It was hard to feel you could do nothing to help a friend in need. Bea racked her brain. Surely there was something she could do?

They paused in front of another portrait. The woman it depicted was beautiful and imperious. Bea read the caption beside the painting: *Portrait of the actress Mrs Edie Rainsford as Titania, 1908. Loaned by Mr Alexander Rainsford.* In the portrait, Edie Rainsford was wearing a swirling, diaphanous, theatrical gown and her thick red-gold hair was piled up on top of her head, in the style of her times. In her luxuriant locks there nestled a jewelled hairpin in the shape of a butterfly.

Bea squinted. For a moment, thoughts of Marissa slipped to the back of her mind. The four translucent wings of the butterfly had the fragile iridescence of mother-of-pearl. Singer Sargent had depicted the glimmers of light on the irregular oval pearl that was the insect's body and the sheen of the thread-like gold legs and blood-red rubies that formed the gleaming, bulbous eyes. But what struck Bea, and what she thought strange, was that the piece of jewellery looked just like Tamar's butterfly pin, and she said so to Emma.

The pin in the portrait hadn't *looked* like her mother's, Emma thought, after she had parted from Bea at Cambridge station and was walking home. It *was* her mother's. She was almost certain of it.

The family story was that Tamar had found the pin on a bomb site during the war. *Loaned by Mr Alexander Rainsford*, the caption by the portrait had said, and now, as she headed towards Glisson Road, Emma remembered where she had heard that name before. It had been at Tamar's private view, the occasion devoted to her mother's work at the Rochester Street Gallery. The event was seared into family memory because Morgan had walked out of it halfway through. Emma had run after him, to try to persuade him to come back, and he had refused. Later that evening, she had seen Tamar talking to a man called Alexander Rainsford.

She remembered that Nick Lauderdale had told her that Rainsford was influential in the arts world. Her mother had been wearing an elegant navy-blue Marissa Flint dress, and in her hair had nestled the butterfly pin. So that was weird, wasn't it? If it did belong to the Rainsford family, if it was the piece of jewellery depicted in the portrait of Edie Rainsford, wouldn't Alexander Rainsford have recognised it?

It occurred to Emma that she hadn't seen her mother wearing the butterfly pin for ages. And that was odd too, because it had always been Tamar's favourite piece of jewellery. She had always said that it gave her luck.

Perhaps she had got bored with it. Or perhaps, thought Emma as she let herself into the house, for some unfathomable reason she didn't like it any more.

In the mornings, waking after some nightmare-infested doze, she pulled the duvet over her head and stayed there, hidden away. After a couple of days, Angie knocked on the door of the flat again, but Marissa told her that she was unwell and sent her away. She didn't leave the flat. She subsisted on what food was left in the fridge – she didn't feel hungry anyway. When the phone rang, she had, in the first few days, answered it, hoping each time that it might be Gabriel. But it never was, and with each call her disappointment and grief became the more crushing. And in the end, she had stopped picking it up. The business would run itself for a while, and besides, she didn't care.

In the evenings, she drank several glasses of whatever

alcohol was left in the sideboard, then put on the TV to banish the silence. On her better nights, she fell asleep on the sofa. On the worst ones, the hours ticked remorselessly by, aching with his absence.

Monday morning, ten days after Gabriel had left, she was woken by the doorbell. She hoped whoever it was would go away, but they did not, and the jarring high-pitched tone reverberated, making her head hurt.

It might be Gabriel. It might be Gabriel come back, offering to talk to her, to try to make sense of what had happened. Marissa pulled on her dressing gown and hauled herself to the front door.

David Johnstone was standing on the threshold. 'I'm not well,' said Marissa.

'Then let me call a doctor for you.'

He came into the hall. She felt unable to stop him. He said, 'We're all worried about you, Marissa.'

'Don't be.'

He raised his eyebrows, then headed into the living room. Her attempt to call him back came out as a croak, so she padded after him. Naturally his gaze alighted on the wine glass and empty bottle, abandoned the previous night on the occasional table.

'Go and have a shower,' he said to her. 'I'll make us some coffee.'

Though she felt furious with him for barging in and issuing orders, she did as she was told. A glance in the bathroom mirror showed her a white-faced, hollow-eyed woman whose lank hair sprang up in tufts. She washed and shampooed and dressed. She couldn't face inserting her lenses – her head hurt too much – so put on her glasses instead. The lack of blurring made everything look worse.

She went into the living room. David was sitting on the sofa, a pot of coffee and a couple of mugs in front of him.

'Where's Gabriel?' he said.

Marissa tried to speak, couldn't, and started crying instead. David took her in his arms and patted her back. 'Hey. It'll be all right. I'm here. You know I can sort out anything. Hey, sweetie, don't cry.' Meaningless phrases that somehow leached through her despair and began to offer comfort.

At length, she recovered enough to sit down and let him pour the coffee. 'Tell me,' he said.

So she did. The entire long, sorry saga. From her marriage to Jamie to Gabriel's departure.

'I miss him *so much*.' She felt raw and chilled with crying. She cradled the mug, needing its warmth in her hands. 'I miss Isabelle too. I even miss her being sulky with me and giving me those looks. This place seems so empty, David.' She turned to him. He had a film-star attractiveness, a strong jaw, thick black curls and dark, hooded eyes. She said, 'I expect you hate me too.'

'Me?'

'I lied to you.'

He shook his head. With a wry smile, he said, 'Believe me, Marissa, there's nothing I don't know about reinventing yourself. Look at me. I come from Aberdeen and my dad was in the Gordon Highlanders. God only knows how he managed to produce a gay son who's ended up working in the fashion industry. In my dad's eyes, you were a nancy boy if you drank beer out of a glass rather than a bottle.' He took a mouthful of coffee. 'Some of us have to make ourselves into something else. We don't have an option. You've had a raw deal, Marissa. It's tough, but it's made you what you are, a strong, independent and lovable woman.'

'Oh David!' She shook her head. 'Whatever I am, I'm not *lovable.*'

'You are.' He looked serious. 'Plenty of people love you. There's no shortage of talentless poseurs and egotists in our line of work, but everyone knows you're the real thing. Now, finish your coffee and then we'll go out and I'll buy you breakfast.'

'I couldn't possibly. I couldn't eat a thing.'

'You can and you will. Here.' He handed her the pair of sunglasses that was on the arm of the sofa. 'Shoes, handbag, lipstick. Come on.'

Unexpectedly, she felt better out in the sunshine. In a café on the Victoria Embankment, David ordered bacon and eggs, coffee and orange juice. To her surprise, she found that she was ravenously hungry. She was mopping up egg yolk with a piece of toast when David said, 'I'll speak to Conrad. He can arrange a sympathetic interview with one of the newspapers. The *Guardian* might be best.'

She stared at him, horrified. 'David, I can't.'

'Darling, you need to get this out the way. Do the interview on your own terms rather than wait until someone leaks it to the press.'

By 'someone', he meant Jamie. Jamie was capable of that sort of spitefulness. Reluctantly she said, 'Do I have to?'

'I think so, yes. There'll be a bit of a fuss and then it will die down.' He made a dismissive motion with his hand. 'People will understand.'

They might, she thought. But Gabriel didn't, and he was the person who mattered.

David nodded at her glass. 'Another orange juice?'

'Please.'

'Come into the shop tomorrow,' he said gently. 'Just for

a couple of hours, if that's all you can face. I'll have a word with everyone beforehand if you like. Don't fall apart on me, Marissa. We need you. And work might help, you never know.'

David was right, it did help. It was better to be occupied and among people she loved and trusted. She was touched by her colleagues' kindness and understanding, though missing Gabriel was like a raw patch on her heart, and everything seemed to brush up against it, rubbing it, making it worse. So many places held memories of him; she still caught herself thinking, I must tell Gabriel about that. When she came home from work and unlocked the door of the flat, she couldn't help but hope that he might have come back, he might have decided to give her another chance. But then, each night, seeing that the rooms were exactly as she had left them in the morning, her spirits plummeted. She put on the lights, caught up on work, made herself something to eat and opened a bottle of wine, though she kept it to one glass – she didn't want David booking her a session at Alcoholics Anonymous – and she got by, more or less.

She phoned Emma and Bea and talked to them for hours. She went for a quick visit to Cambridge and took Alice and Rachel out to tea. Though much of the time she was able to function with an appearance of normality in spite of her anguish, the evenings that she spent on her own were difficult, and often she found herself in tears.

One Saturday, she drove to Seastone again, to stay for a night with Tamar. Tamar was a woman who knew about grief and loss, and she knew too about the struggle for creative expression, and the ups and downs that went with it.

'I can't think of a single idea for my next collection,' Marissa said to her as they walked along the path that lay between the reedbeds and the sea. 'It's as if that part of me has stopped working.'

She hadn't voiced this worry to anyone else, because to whom would she speak? To her employees, whose jobs depended on her creativity? To Emma, who, Marissa suspected, envied the time and space she herself had for work? Tamar, whom she had once consoled for her own broken heart, would understand, she knew that.

'What if,' she said, 'that's it, and I never make anything ever again?'

The wind made pennants of the reeds and whipped Tamar's hair across her face. 'Every artist hits a dry spot now and then,' she said. 'If it hasn't happened to you yet, then you've been lucky, Marissa.'

'Are you working on anything?'

She shook her head. 'I haven't painted since Morgan died. There's been so much to sort out, and besides, I can't seem to find the heart. Let's walk back along the beach, shall we?'

They headed down the slope. Tamar picked up a shell and put it in her pocket. 'I will work again, though, and so will you. When I'm going through a fallow patch, I often walk for miles along the coast. There's always something to look at, something new to spark the interest. Or I go to a gallery and have a look at what other artists are doing.' She gave Marissa a keen glance. 'Look. Observe. Think about what excites you. Take note of that first little itch of inspiration. Think about what you love. It'll come, my dear, I promise you.'

A week later, the *Guardian* article was published. Marissa forced herself to read it through. She hated to think of strangers casually glancing at the page over breakfast, or acquaintances saying, 'Well, I always thought there was something . . .'

But David had been right, and though the publication of the article prompted ripples of shock and curiosity, they soon dispersed and people moved on to the next scandal. And the odd thing was that, having got it over and done with, Marissa felt a little better. Not swimmingly, ecstatically better, because she had lost her lover, but there was a sense of relief, or revival, as if she had plunged into a clear, cold pool and in the shock of rising to the surface something inside her had begun to reset.

She reflected that she had for a long time dealt with her problems by running away. Even her marriage to Jamie had been in part a running away from the grief that had followed her mother's death. In leaving Jamie and fleeing to London, she had put an entire identity behind her. So often her instinct when she was hurt was to shut herself away, to erect barriers round herself. But this time she wasn't able to, and in time she found she didn't want to. The support of friends and colleagues helped her to keep going.

She longed to make things right with Gabriel, but as the weeks passed, she came to fear that the rift was irreparable. She could replace a zip or invisibly mend a tear in fabric, but she didn't know how to begin to fix this. David gave her the number of his therapist, but the mere thought of spilling her heart out to a stranger exhausted her. And anyway, a therapist might tell her what she knew already: that she had let down her lover in a way that was unforgivable. If she couldn't forgive herself, why should Gabriel?

One evening, returning home late after a long day at work, she took the lift to the top floor. As she stepped out onto the landing, a figure moved in the shadows. Marissa's heart fluttered.

Then, 'Marissa?' said Isabelle, and burst into tears.

'She wasn't there,' Isabelle said. Her voice quivered. She was sitting at the kitchen table while Marissa made her something to eat. 'Mum wasn't there. I'd got all my stuff. I couldn't think where to go. Fay's away this weekend with her family, and so is Jake.'

Fay was Isabelle's best friend. 'Jake?' said Marissa.

'He's my boyfriend.' Isabelle gave her a challenging glare.

'Okay,' said Marissa mildly. She wondered whether Gabriel knew about Jake. She put a plate of beans on toast in front of Isabelle. Her back to the girl as she ground coffee, she said, 'You can stay here if you like.'

There was a pause in which she held her breath. Then: 'All right,' said Isabelle. 'Just until Mum comes back.'

'I'll have to let your dad know.' Isabelle began to say something, but Marissa said firmly, 'Isabelle, I have to.'

'He's in Japan.'

'Japan? On business? Then I'll fax him from the shop tomorrow morning.'

'I don't want him to come home.' Again Isabelle looked distressed. 'Mum must have got held up or something. She'll be back soon and then I can go over to hers.'

Marissa pressed the girl's shoulder. 'Don't worry about it now. We'll sort it out, I promise. Eat your supper.'

Talking to Isabelle that evening, Marissa pieced together the story. Gabriel had agreed to let his daughter stay with Justine during the weekends while he was in Japan, as a sort of trial run before consenting to her living for a longer period with her mother. At four o'clock that afternoon, after the end of the school day, Isabelle had made her way to Justine's house. No one had answered her ring of the door-bell. Marissa hated to think of her hungry and frightened, sitting on the doorstep for hours, waiting as the evening grew colder and darker.

She phoned Justine's Cheyne Walk house first, and then her cottage in Gloucestershire, but there was no reply from either. Isabelle looked about to burst into tears again after Marissa put down the phone for the second time. She allowed Marissa to hug her, but then went into her room and shut the door behind her. Marissa unearthed from the larder cupboard a box of chocolates that someone had given her and switched on the television. After a while, Isabelle, red-eyed, came out of her room and sat down on the sofa beside her.

'I was afraid you'd have got rid of my books and things,' she said.

'I would never do that. There'll always be a home for you here, whenever you need it.' Marissa offered Isabelle the chocolates.

They were watching a TV programme, a game show, when Isabelle said suddenly, 'Don't you love Dad any more?'

'Oh, I do – yes!' said Marissa, startled. 'Isabelle, I do, so much.'

'But Dad told me you've split up.'

'It was my fault. I did something . . . But I'll always love him.' This time it was Marissa who had to staunch the tears, but she quickly got herself under control.

Isabelle said, 'Did you have an affair?'

'No! No, of course not.'

But it was hardly surprising that Isabelle would draw such a conclusion. After all, she had first-hand experience of disintegrating parental relationships. Marissa knew that she had failed Isabelle as well as Gabriel. Though she could not put that right, she must at least try to explain what had happened in terms that a sixteen-year-old could understand.

Isabelle ate more chocolates while Marissa attempted to tell her about her marriage, and its consequences.

'He sounds like a pig,' Isabelle said, after Marissa, censoring out the worst bits, had described Jamie.

'Much worse than a pig. Pigs are useful.'

Isabelle giggled.

'I should have told your dad,' Marissa said. 'I should have told him about my marriage as soon as I realised I was falling in love with him.'

'Dad makes such a fuss about that sort of thing, people not telling him stuff,' said Isabelle off-handedly.

Between them they ate all the chocolates and then went to bed early. In the morning, they took a taxi to the Floral Street shop. Marissa faxed Gabriel's hotel from her office. Fifteen minutes later, the phone rang.

'Marissa?' It was Gabriel. 'Is Isabelle all right?'

Six weeks had passed since she had heard his voice. As soon as he said her name, something seemed to flick back into place. It had an almost chemical effect on her, a bitter-sweet mixture of agony and yearning.

She cleared her throat. 'She's fine, honestly, Gabriel.'

'I should never have agreed to let her stay with Justine,' he said angrily. 'God only knows what might have happened.'

'Isabelle's well and she's safe. You don't need to worry. You should be proud of her. She did the right thing, coming to me.'

'Yes, of course, thank God she was so sensible. And thank you, Marissa. But Justine promised . . . Ah.' Gabriel seemed to hear himself, because he sighed. 'I should have known better. I'll book a seat on the next plane home.'

'There's no need. Isabelle's very welcome to stay with me. You don't need to rush back.'

'I can't impose on you.'

'It's hardly an imposition. I enjoy her company.'

Silence. Then he said, 'No, I should come back. Her school breaks up in just over a week.'

'That isn't a problem. I'll sort something out. She might like to work in the shop for a few days. I'm sure I can find her something to do.' When he made a doubtful sound, she said firmly, 'Gabriel, I've worked since I turned sixteen. It would be good for Isabelle and I think she'd enjoy it. I'm sure she'd love to try something new.'

This time the silence lengthened. Then he said, 'If you're sure . . .'

'I am. So long as it's all right with you, naturally.'

'It would help me out, it's true . . .'

He started to thank her again, but she broke in. 'That's settled, then.'

'Have you tried to phone Justine?'

'Several times. There's no answer.'

From Tokyo, a muttered French curse. 'I'll try from here. I'm sorry, so sorry about all this.'

Marissa hesitated, then said, 'Did you know that Isabelle has a boyfriend?'

'A *boyfriend*?' He said it in much the same way as one might say *a Martian*.

'Apparently he's called Jake. I can try and find out a little more about him if you like.'

'Would you? A boyfriend . . .'

'I hope your trip's going well.'

375

Gabriel said that it was going very well. She imagined him sitting in his hotel room in Tokyo, his brow creased, raking his fingers through his hair in the way he did when he was perturbed.

He said, 'Sometimes I think I don't really understand very much at all.'

'I'm not sure any of us do,' she said gently. 'We just muddle along. Would you like to talk to Isabelle?'

'Please, Marissa.'

She put the receiver on her desk and went to fetch the girl. She felt lighter. The street outside seemed a little sunnier. Though she knew that nothing was resolved between them, that nothing had changed at all, it helped to hear his voice. It helped to hear him say her name.

Marissa had a chat with Isabelle about the boyfriend, Jake, in the Ivy Brasserie in Henrietta Street. You couldn't fall into an argument, she reckoned, while eating a delicious pudding. The waiter put their desserts in front of them as Marissa asked Isabelle where she and Jake had met.

'At Fay's house.' Isabelle scooped up a spoonful of chocolate mousse. 'Jake's a friend of hers.'

'So he's your age?'

'He's three months older than me.'

This was a relief at least. 'Still at school, then?'

'He's at the same school as Fay's brother. He likes maths, like me.' Isabelle gave Marissa a suspicious look. 'You haven't told Dad, have you?'

'I mentioned it. Has he said anything to you?'

Isabelle shook her head. 'No. But he will, he'll make a fuss.'

'I thought he was surprised, but not cross. I'd say it'll be fine.'

The truth was, it was hard to tell. Gabriel phoned the flat from Tokyo every morning, his evening, to talk to Isabelle. Marissa's initial pleasure in simply hearing the sound of his voice had faded, and the stiff politeness of their exchanges was hard to bear. She ended up quickly passing the phone to Isabelle.

'He's being fine with *you*,' Isabelle said gloomily. 'He'll fuss with me, I know he will.'

'He's your dad and he worries about you. That's what dads do. Don't chew your hair, darling. Marissa Flint assistants don't chew their hair.'

Isabelle had spent the day working as a Saturday girl at the shop. Now she put on a mock-supercilious look and flicked back her dark shoulder-length hair in imitation of Floral Street's haughtiest assistant. Marissa giggled. She was discovering that caring single-handed for a teenage girl was a tightrope walk. Often she tiptoed, afraid of putting a foot wrong, but there were other times when Isabelle made her laugh like no one else could. A long time seemed to have passed since she had laughed.

Isabelle said, 'Did your dad fuss when you had a boyfriend?'

'I'm afraid he didn't get the chance. He died when I was two years old. I expect he would have, though.'

Isabelle considered this. 'How awful. Mum may be useless but at least she's *alive*.'

Neither Marissa nor Gabriel had succeeded in getting in contact with Justine. Marissa would have liked to have given Gabriel's ex-wife a good slap, but Isabelle loved her, and always would, so she chose her words carefully.

'I'm sure your mother loves you very much, Isabelle.'

'I don't think so.' She looked down at her bowl. 'I think she hates me. I think she thinks I'm a nuisance.'

'No, darling.' How to excuse the inexcusable? Marissa said, 'Some people find it hard to keep to routines. And being a mother . . . it's not easy. I haven't any children of my own, but my closest friends do, and I've seen how hard it can be.'

She put her hand over Isabelle's. 'Justine doesn't hate you. I'm sure she's doing her best.'

'It's a pretty crappy sort of best.' Isabelle scraped out her bowl. Her gaze fixed on Marissa's lemon tart. 'Do you want that?'

'Not really. You can have it if you like.' She pushed the plate across the table.

'I'm sorry I was so horrible to you when you and Dad started going out.'

Startled, Marissa said, 'You weren't horrible, darling.'

Isabelle raised her eyebrows. 'Marissa, I was. You don't have to be nice. I remember I wouldn't speak to you.'

'You were a little frosty, it's true. But I understood that. I assumed you thought of me as an interloper.'

'I was afraid you'd take Dad away and then he wouldn't have time for me.' Isabelle rolled her eyes. 'I was just a kid then, and a bit of an idiot. And you were always so *perfect*.'

'Me? Perfect?' Briefly Marissa reflected on recent disasters. 'Good Lord, I'm anything but.'

'I know that *now*.' Isabelle dug her spoon into the tart. 'But it's the way you dress and everything. Your flat, your clothes . . . they're all so *perfect*.' She scowled. 'You and Dad have got to make up. I'm fed up with him being such a misery.'

'It's not his fault.'

'He could change his mind, couldn't he? He's so stubborn. It's not as if you're anything like Mum. Dad's always been

378

lousy at admitting he's wrong. I'm sick of him being so grumpy all the time.'

In a week's time, Gabriel would return from Japan and pick up Isabelle from the flat. Marissa was counting off the days. Surely, after so long apart, his attitude might have softened a little. Surely she would find the words to make him understand how deeply she regretted the mistakes she had made and how bitterly sorry she was for hurting him. What was impossible on the phone would be more feasible in person. She longed to be with him again, to see his dear, familiar face – to recover, she hoped, at least a scrap of the old easiness between them.

# Chapter Nineteen

## 1989

It was a couple of miles from Cambridge railway station to Portugal Place, and there was a bus, but he preferred to walk. He was good at finding his way round an unfamiliar town, and he could do with the exercise. Besides, he needed time to think. The nagging voice in his head that told him this was a wild goose chase, a big mistake, intensified as he made his way through the centre of town. It was Saturday afternoon, and the streets were busy, crowded with shoppers and students. A greyish drizzle cast an uneasy shimmer. There were so many reasons why he shouldn't have come here, why he should change his mind, turn round and go back to London. After all, she had made it clear, all those years ago, that she wanted nothing more to do with him.

Portugal Place was a narrow pedestrian alleyway leading off from Bridge Street. There was a little bakery and café on the corner, and opposite, a fine medieval church. He headed down the alley, checking out house numbers. The doors were brightly painted, and scarlet geraniums flourished in pots and baskets. Bicycles were chained to metal railings. A plaque on a wall proclaimed the name of a university society.

He found he could imagine her living here, in this street. He remembered that she had always had a sense of style, a certain flair.

And there it was, the address that he had been given. He stood looking up at it, trying to decide whether to knock.

On Saturday afternoon, Emma walked to Bea's house. She took Ben with her. Ben needed to be run off each day, like a puppy. He charged across Parker's Piece, then circled the Victorian lamp post, oblivious to the cyclists and pedestrians who swerved to avoid him.

As she headed along Portugal Place, she caught sight of a man pressing Bea's doorbell.

She called out, 'May I help you?'

He swung round. He was tall, dark-haired and notably good-looking. 'Do you know the people who live here? I've rung the bell a couple of times but there's no reply.' He had an Irish accent.

'I'm afraid they're away.' As she drew closer, Emma saw that his eyes were the blue of cornflowers.

'Would you happen to know when they're coming back?'

'Tonight, quite late, I think. Can I help?'

He shook his head. 'Thank you, but it doesn't matter.'

She said curiously, 'Are you a friend of Bea's?'

'I was once, yes, a long time ago.' There was a touch of sadness in his smile. 'I'll head off then. Thank you for your time.'

He walked away. Emma noticed that he had a slight limp. As she took Bea's house key out of her pocket, an idea occurred to her, one so wild and preposterous that her immediate instinct was to dismiss it as fantasy. But then . . . black curls, Irish accent and eyes the blue of cornflowers.

He couldn't possibly be. But what if her hunch was right? She had to find out. Her gaze darted back to the alleyway, but he had gone.

She grabbed Ben's hand and they ran towards Bridge Street. She had a small bag of shopping with her – a loaf of bread and bottle of milk for Bea's fridge – which banged against her side. Because it was Saturday afternoon, the pavements were busy with shoppers and tourists milling about. Ben might be rotten at sitting still in a classroom, but he was a fast little runner, and they hurtled through the crowds. What would she say to Bea if she let this man slip through her fingers? She couldn't see the Irishman anywhere, and Ben broke from her grasp. She had a stitch in her side, but she kept on running.

She caught sight of him ahead, passing the Round Church.

She called out. 'Ciaran!' No response, so perhaps her hunch was wrong. She shouted the name again, louder.

And he paused, turned, and looked back.

Emma caught up with him. She was gasping for breath, and it was a moment before she could say, 'You're Bea's Ciaran, aren't you?'

Ciaran grabbed Ben, who was making a dash for freedom. Then he said, 'Yes. Yes, I suppose I am.'

There was a free table in the café opposite the Round Church. Ciaran bought coffees and a juice for Ben while Emma got her breath back and Ben tried to dismantle the sugar shaker.

He sat down at the table. 'So, you're a friend of Bea's.'

'Yes.'

'You said she's away?' He spoke in a low, careful manner, methodically trying to establish the facts.

'Her mother had to have an operation, so Bea's gone to Boscombe to look after her when she comes out of hospital. I'm watering her plants for her.'

'You knew my name. So she must have mentioned me to you.'

'Yes, she has. Don't do that, Ben, please. Oh good God.' Ben had unscrewed the shaker and there was sugar all over the table. Emma started sweeping it into her hand. She said, 'She told me about you and the baby and everything. For heaven's sake, Ben, what a mess you've made.'

Ciaran said, 'Baby?'

His tone of voice made Emma look up. She read his expression and pressed her sugary fingers against her mouth, horrified. 'Oh my God.'

'A *baby?*'

'Yes.' She was appalled at herself. 'You didn't know?'

'No.' His face had lost colour. 'No, I certainly did not.'

'I'm so sorry, how awful of me. I shouldn't have said . . . But Bea said . . . Ben, don't do that, please.'

Ciaran said very quietly, 'Bea had a baby?'

Emma nodded. 'Yes.'

'I think what you're telling me is that Bea had *my* baby.'

'Yes.'

He tipped back his head. His gaze was fixed on something distant, something she could not see. Abruptly he stood up and said, 'Excuse me a moment,' then went outside.

From time to time, between tidying up the sugar and cursing herself for opening her big mouth, Emma glanced out at him. He was standing beside the railings of the Round Church opposite. He wasn't pacing or wringing his hands, anything like that, but his expression was grim. She wondered whether he would walk away, but he did not. She thought of going out and talking to him, but something told her he was a man who would prefer privacy when going through emotional turmoil. Besides, hadn't she put her foot in it enough?

When he came back inside the café, he took from his pocket a small torch and offered it to Ben. 'Have a look at this, fella. See if you can make it work.' With Ben occupied, he said to Emma, 'I'd like you to tell me everything, if you would.'

'I'm so sorry. I assumed you knew.'

'Maybe I should have,' he said sombrely. 'Maybe I should have guessed. A *baby*. My God.' Softening his voice, he said, 'Perhaps you'd tell me your name.'

'Emma. Emma Hooper.'

'Ciaran O'Neill.' He offered her his hand. 'Have you known Bea long?'

'Ten years. We met through a friend, then she moved to Cambridge after her husband died, and . . .' He started to speak, but she held up a hand. 'Sorry, Ciaran. Let me start again, at the beginning.' She took a mouthful of espresso. 'Bea told us ages ago – she told me and Marissa, we're her friends – that she'd had a baby, a little boy, when she was eighteen.'

'What happened to him?'

'He was adopted.'

'Right.'

'And you didn't know about him, Ciaran?'

'No. Not a thing.'

'Bea thought you did.'

'Right,' he said again. His gaze settled on Emma. 'She must have thought I'd made a run for it.'

'Yes, she did.'

'That wasn't what happened, I swear to God. I never knew about the child.' A quick shake of the head, as if he was trying to clear it. 'I thought she'd dumped me. I was told she'd dumped me.'

Emma remembered the anguish with which Bea had spoken of that time in her life, and her aching sense of loss. She said gently, 'I'm afraid Bea thought the same thing.'

He sat back in his seat, frowning. 'My dad,' he said eventually. 'Bea's mam and dad. I bet they had something to do with it, curse them. Does Bea know where the child is now?'

'I'm afraid she has no idea. As I said, Patrick was adopted. He turned eighteen in April.'

'That's what she called him, Patrick?'

'Yes, though he probably has another name now. Bea's been hoping he'd try to get in touch.'

'But he hasn't?'

'No.'

'Right,' he said again.

Another silence. Ben had unscrewed the torch and taken out the batteries. Ciaran said, 'It lasted for a summer, Bea and me. The end was very sudden. Though I remember I'd had a bad feeling for quite a while, like, you know, when you feel a thunderstorm brewing. A heaviness.'

'I'm sorry,' she said. 'For both of you.'

He seemed to snap back to the present. 'How is she now? Her neighbour in London told me she'd been divorced. And you said there was a husband who died.'

Briefly she told him about Clive and Alice and Rachel, and then about Francis, too. When she had finished, he said, 'I'm glad she has her daughters. They must be a comfort to her.'

'They are. They're delightful. They're great friends of my two girls. The four of them are like sisters.'

'You have another two besides this fine fellow, then?'

'I do, yes. Ciaran, Bea's okay. She's had her troubles, but she's happy. She's a happy sort of person.'

For the first time, he smiled. 'I remember that. It was one of the things I loved about her.'

'And I'm so sorry,' she said again. 'For telling you like that.'

'Don't trouble yourself, Emma. However I'd have found out, it would have been a shock.'

Ben was sprinkling sugar inside the battery compartment of the torch. Following Emma's exasperated gaze, Ciaran said, 'It's fine. Let him.'

'His teacher thinks he's disruptive. She said that to me yesterday afternoon.'

Ben tipped out the sugar and put the batteries back in. 'Look at him,' said Ciaran. 'He's a great wee lad, aren't you, Ben? He'll be an engineer or a builder, perhaps.'

'His father's an architect.'

'There you are, then. There are people who like pulling things apart and putting them together again, and Ben's one of those.' Ciaran glanced at his watch. 'Train to catch. I should go.'

'You mustn't go, Ciaran!' Seeing his startled glance, she said urgently, 'You can't just leave. Bea will want to see you.'

'Are you sure?' That piercing blue gaze focused on her once more. 'I would have thought she'd never want to set eyes on me again.'

'She'll want to see you.'

Emma knew Bea. She had listened as Bea had spoken of Ciaran, and of this if nothing else she was certain: that Bea would want to see her first love again, that she would want the chance to disentangle the knots of the past. 'Please, Ciaran,' she said. 'Please stay.'

Emma offered him a bed for the night at her house, which was kind of her, seeing as she had only just met him and seeing as she'd have every reason to consider him a philandering weasel. Ciaran thanked her but told her he'd stay at a hotel. He booked a room in the Gonville, then purchased a few items – toothbrush, razor, spare socks and underwear – in town.

Though the room was spacious and the bed comfortable, he didn't sleep well. He kept going through his conversation with Emma in his mind, trying to work out what must have happened. In the middle of the night, he got up, poured himself a whisky from the minibar and stood at the window, looking out to the moonlit square of grass beyond. It was hard to take it in, that Bea had had a baby – his baby, his son. That he had a child, now eighteen years old. It appalled him to imagine what she must have endured. It appalled him to imagine her having to believe that he had deserted her when she most needed him.

Emma had left a note in the Portugal Place house telling Bea that he had turned up out of the blue and wanted to talk to her. He imagined her returning home late in the evening from her mother's house and finding the note. Surely she would tear it to bits, throw it in the bin.

His leg ached the following morning as he returned to the hotel after a run round the Backs. He'd gone out early in case Bea phoned. He'd hang round till midday or so, and if he heard nothing by then, he'd assume that Emma had been wrong and that Bea didn't want anything more to do with him. And then he would catch the train back to London and make himself forget about her and the child. He could do it. He was good at moving on.

It was a fine, bright day, yesterday's grey dullness banished by the sun. Ciaran crossed the road to the hotel. And saw the woman standing by the entrance.

He knew her instantly. He could have picked her out of a crowd. She hadn't changed at all. 'Bea?' he said, and she turned to him.


Bea and Ciaran sat side by side on a bench on Lammas Land. He had bought coffees from the café by the children's paddling pool. Neither of them had been able to face the hotel breakfast room.

They were catching up, telling their stories. The last time Bea had seen Ciaran had been getting on for nineteen years ago, at the O'Neills' flat in Notting Hill. She had to keep looking at him, as if to check he was really there. Finding Emma's note on the kitchen table yesterday evening had been a huge shock. The years had peeled away.

It was starting to sink in that he was here, that this really was Ciaran. Could she trust him? She knew that so many of her past mistakes had been in consequence of her putting her trust in people who didn't deserve it. She hadn't the knack of telling when she was being lied to and she had a fatal habit of thinking the best of people. She had never forgotten one of the last things Ciaran had said to her: *People hurt the people they love all the time. They don't mean to, but they do.* But she wasn't seventeen any more. She was thirty-six, and she didn't intend to let herself get hurt again. She was through with that.

She had told him about Clive and Francis; it was his turn now.

He said, 'There was Sarah. I met her a year or so after I returned to Ireland. She was a nice girl, but she wanted marriage, babies, all that. And I didn't. Or not with her. I was a selfish idiot and that's the truth of it. When I was twenty-one, I went back to London. I did various jobs, this and that, working in cafés and pubs mostly. I met Carolina in one of the pubs. She was American, fun to be with, a bit of a hippy. She had a couple of kids, Wren and Kyle. Nice kids. We went to the States and travelled around for six months or so, living here and there. Then one day she took off and I never saw her again. A year later, I moved up to Canada, to Ottawa. I ended up becoming a Canadian citizen. I joined the police force and I met Megan. She owned a bakery shop. I used to go in there every morning to buy something for breakfast, and she and I got talking, and then, well, you know . . .' He looked down. 'She was a fine woman, Megan, and we were good for quite a while, but in the end she got fed up being with a guy who worked a fourteen-hour day, seven days a week. The day she walked out on me, she told me she was leaving me because I was never really there. Maybe she was right about that.'

He had changed, Bea thought. The boy she had fallen so recklessly in love with had gone for ever, and in his place was a man who chose his words carefully. She had once been able to read his mood, but now there was a hardness to his mouth, and the intense blue of his eyes acted like a filter, masking his emotions. He wasn't the same person, and neither was she. They didn't know each other at all. She didn't hate him, but nor did she love him. They were strangers, and an ocean of experience divided them.

She said, 'Are you still in the police?' and Ciaran shook his head.

'I was invalided out.' He patted his thigh. 'I was shot chasing some druggy who'd stolen a car. My leg was a bit of a mess. They offered me a desk job, but I didn't want that.'

'I'm sorry, Ciaran.'

'Don't be. It's okay. The leg's fine now, it only hurts when I push it.'

'What do you do now?'

'I'm a private detective. After I left the police, I went back to Ireland. My dad was dying of asbestosis, so I came home to give Aislinn a hand. She and her husband, John, run the farm now. When Dad died, I moved to Dublin and set up the business there. I'm doing all right; there's plenty of work for me in Dublin.'

'I'm sorry to hear about your father.'

'Thank you. We didn't get on, him and me, but it was a lousy way for him to go. He didn't deserve that.' He gave her a sympathetic look. 'Emma told me your mother hasn't been well.'

'She had to have an operation. She has breast cancer, but it looks like they've caught it early.'

'I'm sorry. I hope she'll be okay. And your father . . .?'

'He died two years ago. He'd had heart problems for years. It's hard, isn't it? Tell me about your sisters. I used to be so envious of you for having sisters.'

'Nora's married. She lives in Edinburgh and has a load of kids. Clodagh lives in Dublin, same as me. She works for RTÉ. We see each other for a drink once a week or so. Emer's still nursing. She has twins, twelve years old – they're great girls. Fergal went to Australia. He's living near Canberra, and I flew out there to see him a few years back. He's happy – married, three sons, doing well.'

'I'm so glad.' She beamed at him. She was starting to see the man he had become: assured, well travelled and successful. 'A private detective,' she said. 'How exciting!'

'Right, you'd think so.' She found that she remembered the sleepy half-smile he gave her: a flash of blue beneath lowered lids. 'A lot of my time's spent on paperwork, checking columns of figures to see whether an employee's cooking the books. Or I'm keeping an eye on some poor woman's husband to find out whether he's cheating on her. I enjoy it, though. It suits me.'

One thing she noticed was that Ciaran hadn't touched his coffee as he spoke. He didn't pick up and put down the teaspoon or smooth out the paper sugar wrapper. This she remembered now: that even in his teens he had possessed focus and composure.

She said, 'Was that how you found me? Your detective skills?'

'It wasn't hard, Bea. I had some work I needed to do in London, so I came over here for a week. I got the job out of the way quicker than I'd expected and I ended up going to the block of flats where your mam and dad used to live. I spoke to your neighbour, Mrs Phillips. She gave me your address.'

During that long-ago summer when she and Ciaran had been together, Bea had helped Mrs Phillips with shopping and housework for pocket money. They still exchanged Christmas cards.

She said, 'Why? Why did you try to find me? Why now?'

His gaze shifted to the paddling pool, to the sparks of light and the laughing infants. 'I was angry for a long time after you and I split up,' he said quietly. 'I did my best not to think about you. And then, after I was shot, and after I left Canada . . . and after my dad died, I found that I didn't feel angry any more. Experiences like that, they make you reassess things.'

'Emma said you didn't know about the baby.'

'I didn't, Bea, I swear it. The first I knew was in the café yesterday.'

She found that she believed him, though it was still hard to accept that during all that time, during her pregnancy and the months of her banishment in Gloucestershire with Aunt Muriel, Ciaran had been unaware of the situation. The silence between them was broken by the shrieks of children playing on the swings and in the pool.

Ciaran said, 'I'm trying to work it out. What did they tell you, back then, your parents?'

'That you'd gone back to Ireland as soon as you'd heard I was pregnant.'

'Whatever else you think, Bea, please believe that's not true. I never knew about the baby. My dad told me your parents had found out about us. He said your dad had come to see him and I was to stop pestering you. He told me you didn't want to see me again. Obviously I assumed he was lying to me.'

'He was.'

Ciaran nodded. At last he picked up his cup of coffee. 'Maybe this is what happened. Maybe your father told my dad about the baby, and maybe they cooked up the lies between them. I don't suppose I was the sort of husband your parents had in mind for you at all. My dad would have felt the same. He wouldn't have wanted me marrying a Protestant girl, and he wouldn't have wanted me marrying the daughter of a wealthy, entitled Englishman. He always despised that type.'

Bea considered this. Was it possible? It had the ring of truth, she thought. She felt a flutter of pity for the girl she had once been, caught up in the machinations of adults.

She said quietly, 'All those prejudices. They never gave us a chance, did they?'

Ciaran hunched his shoulders. 'My dad would have believed there was no future in it for me. I should think your parents would have thought I'd ruin your life. Whatever it was, Dad had me on the boat to Dun Laoghaire three days after that last time you and I were together at the flat. I didn't have a choice. He had to beat the living daylights out of me to get me to go. He sent Fergal with me, like a bloody gaoler.'

They had been so deeply in love. She would have done anything to be with Ciaran O'Neill. Now, so many years later, memories slipped into place, and events she hadn't understood then she made sense of now. Once her father and mother had discovered her pregnancy, they hadn't let her out of the flat. A mere couple of days later, her father had driven her to Aunt Muriel's house in Gloucestershire. She had been rushed out of London with the speed of an arrow from a bow. Her parents would have told her that Ciaran had made a run for it as soon as he had found out about her pregnancy because they would have hoped it would stop her loving him.

If Alice or Rachel were to fall pregnant by some unsuitable boy at the age of seventeen, would she do the same? No, she would not. But those had been different times. A more recent memory sprang into place: herself and her mother, unpacking china after her parents had moved to Boscombe. *The only thing we've ever wanted is for you to be happy,* Vivien had said. *Everything we did, we were only ever trying to do our best for you.* Her words had contained a tinge of regret.

A toddler splashed in the pool, laughing at an orange ball bobbing on the surface of the water. Ciaran, who had risen from the bench to walk around and ease his leg, limped back to her and sat down.

'You and I, we were from such different worlds. I'm so, so sorry you had to go through such an ordeal on your own. Perhaps I should have asked more questions. Perhaps I shouldn't have listened to my dad. In the end, I believed him, and I shouldn't have done that. But I was always afraid you'd leave me. Maybe I didn't fight for you as hard as I should have.'

'Why didn't you write to me? I wrote to you every day, every single day. You never replied.'

'I never had a single letter from you. Not one. I wrote to you dozens of times, I swear it, God's honour.'

After a while, she said, 'It doesn't really matter, does it? Water under the bridge.'

'It is, I suppose.'

'We've done all right, haven't we?'

'You're right, we have.' Then, after a silence, he said, 'What was he like?'

'Patrick?' She smiled. 'He was beautiful. Such a beautiful baby. I still dream about him. I wish you could have seen him.'

They walked back to the hotel. As they reached the driveway, she said, 'You didn't go to university then, Ciaran?'

'No, that never happened. And you didn't become a nurse, I'm guessing?'

'No. But I still plan to. I'm going back to college to study for my A levels in the autumn. Biology and chemistry. I've a lot of catching-up to do, but I'm going to get there.'

'Good for you, Bea,' he said, with a grin that in an instant brought back to her the old Ciaran. 'You'll do it, I know you will.' Then he said, 'I cared, Bea. I was only a kid, a stupid, ignorant kid, but the truth is, I cared very much.'

Ciaran took the train back to London that afternoon. His Dublin flight was booked for the following morning. Sitting in the carriage, he went over the events of the last two days. So many times he had come close to changing his mind, to abandoning the attempt to trace Bea. At the mansion flat where the Meades used to live and where he had tracked down Mrs Phillips; then later, queuing to buy a railway ticket at King's Cross; and then walking through Cambridge to Bea's house in Portugal Place. On every occasion he had been tempted to turn tail and run.

It had been his sister, Clodagh, who had persuaded him to go on this mad journey. 'You can't carry on like this,' she had said to him over a drink in a pub in Grafton Street. 'You can't carry on running away.' Annoyed by this, he had protested. Clodagh's slim, pink-enamelled fingertip had tapped his chest. 'England . . . the US . . . Canada . . . And a string of women. This girl, this Bea – she meant something to you, Ciaran. You need to sort it out. You need to put it to rest once and for all.' And the bloody annoying thing, he thought, as the train pulled into King's Cross, was that he was going to have to admit to her that she had been right.

Gabriel travelled straight from Heathrow to Marissa's flat. His presence in her living room made her feel like a teenager again, bashful and on edge and aware of her own inadequacies. She was trying hard not to make a fool of herself. She knew she mustn't run and hug him, anything silly and embarrassing like that, however much she longed to.

After the long flight, he had a rumpled, dazed look. He had brought presents for both of them: a print of a reed-fringed lake and snow-capped mountains for her, and a silk kimono for Isabelle. While Isabelle was completing her packing, Marissa told Gabriel that Justine had visited the flat the previous evening.

'She'd been away with a boyfriend, I think. She didn't say that, but that's what I suspect it was. She said she'd been invited to a party in Gloucestershire and had forgotten about the arrangement with Isabelle.'

'Good God.'

'Shall I make coffee?'

'No, thank you.'

'She was very apologetic.'

His lip curled with contempt. 'She always is.'

A silence, which she filled by saying, 'Isabelle hasn't said any more about living with her mother.'

He nodded, but said nothing. His gaze raked round the room and his hand tapped his thigh. Studying him, Marissa suddenly realised that he was desperate to leave, that all he wanted after ten minutes in her company was to get out of her flat, which must hold unhappy memories for him, and drive Isabelle back to Blackthorn Farm. With bitter despair, she knew then that the phrases she had for the past weeks imagined saying to him would remain unsaid. There was no point. In a moment or two, Isabelle would come out of her room and then she and Gabriel would leave.

She made a last-ditch attempt. Surely at least they could have a civilised relationship? 'Isabelle's enjoyed working at the shop,' she said.

'Has she?' He gave her a distracted look. 'I appreciate

everything you've done for her, Marissa. I can't thank you enough.'

The rigid formality of his words appalled her. The series of staccato phrases that passed between them hardly amounted to a conversation. Unable to bear it any longer, she went into the kitchen and began to tidy up the breakfast things. She heard Isabelle come out of her room and Gabriel remind her about their journey to France, to the manoir, in a few days' time.

Isabelle embraced her, then Gabriel's lips fleetingly brushed against her cheek. Pride made Marissa put on a facade of cheerfulness and tell them to have a wonderful holiday in Normandy. The lift doors closed, and she went back into the flat.

And that was that. It was over, he was gone. She went into the kitchen and began automatically to wipe the work surfaces, but then paused, cloth in hand, and squeezed her eyes shut. She imagined Gabriel and Isabelle on the car ferry, then driving from Caen through towns and country lanes before arriving at the house. She pictured them having dinner on the lawn with Jeanne and Andrée and Michel. The warm evenings, the scents of roses and lavender.

She would not be there. She would never be there again, with the people she loved so much. There was no way back. There never had been. She had hoped that time might have softened his opinion of her, that they might at least recover a fragment of their old pleasure in each other's company, but it was not so. Too much harm had been done; too many scars still seared, red and raised, across the skin.

After her reunion with Ciaran, Bea was aware of a feeling of lightness. Picking up the girls later that day from Francis's house, she hadn't even felt annoyed with Daisy.

This emotion, which she worked out after a while was made up of contentment and comfort and relief, persisted through the ensuing days. Ciaran hadn't deserted her. He hadn't run off to Ireland once he had found out about the baby. None of that had been true. The story had been a fabrication, dreamed up by their parents to separate them.

One evening, after the girls were in bed, she made herself a gin and tonic and sat in the courtyard as the light faded. An olive tree in a pot cast a fine network of shadows. It was sobering to reflect on how sharply her attitudes and convictions had been shaped by the events of that single year in her life. After Ciaran, and after giving up her baby for adoption, she had been deeply unhappy. It had taken her a long time to haul herself up and find the spirit to start again. Clive's love and generosity had allowed her to begin the process; the births of Alice and Rachel had completed it by giving her babies to love. But she couldn't have managed without her friends. Without Marissa and Emma, she would not be the woman she was now. She would not have learned to believe in herself again.

It was funny how sometimes you could know at first glance that you were going to get on with a person. That morning more than ten years ago when Marissa had turned up at Bea and Clive's Islington house to collect the shawl she had left behind at the party: that had been one of those moments. Bea remembered how Marissa had stayed to help clear up and how the two of them had got talking. And how they had gone on talking – and laughing, and offering solace to each other and to Emma, the third of their tight-knit group – ever since.

Her friendship with Marissa had lasted longer than either of her marriages. Marissa had comforted her in the aftermath of the car crash in which Clive had died. She had listened to her for hours on end as she had talked and wept during the bleak, dreadful months that had followed. For more than two years, week after week, she had taken the train to Cambridge every Saturday evening after work to be with Bea and her daughters. Bea owed her so much.

She knew how Marissa had pinned her hopes on seeing Gabriel again when he returned from Japan. And yet the longed-for reconciliation had not taken place. Talking about it to her afterwards, she had heard despair in Marissa's voice. She longed to do something to help her.

During the time she had been sitting outside and thinking things over, night had fallen. She went back indoors. She found herself feeling cross when she thought about Gabriel. It was rather ridiculous and unfair of him to be so unforgiving and stubborn. How utterly clueless he was, like so many men, about the reality of a woman's life! Had he been at his home in Berkshire, she would have hopped into the car and driven to the farmhouse to have a word with him. She would have tried to make him see sense.

But Marissa had told her that Gabriel and Isabelle had gone to France for August, to stay with his family in Normandy. As she went upstairs to attack the ironing, an idea inched itself into Bea's mind.

Could she? Should she?

Bea and her girls were due to go away shortly, to Clive's parents in Surrey. Bea pressed T-shirts and folded dresses and considered her options.

Emma took a portfolio of her botanical paintings to an art gallery in Trinity Street. The gallery owner expressed particular interest in the watercolours of desiccated leaves and seed heads, found on the beach at Seastone, which she had completed in the aftermath of her father's death. She had, during those dreadful, dislocated days, discovered something new inside her. 'If you had another half a dozen or so like these,' the gallery owner indicated a sketch of a dried-out horned poppy, 'we could talk about representing you.'

'Okay, thank you, that's great.' Emma bundled the watercolours back into her portfolio. 'I'll get back to you.'

Her route home took her along King's Parade. A bubble of optimism rose inside her. Her only problem was that she didn't have another half-dozen paintings. She didn't have so much as another one. Here was an opportunity to further her career; all she needed to do was to knuckle down.

She would apply herself to her work and she wouldn't let anyone interrupt her. She would take the phone off the hook and wouldn't answer the doorbell. Max would take his turn looking after the children. Lucienne was twelve and Elizabeth was ten, and it was about time they learned to help more in the house. And if anyone asked her to take the minutes for the residents' association or bake a cake for a bring-and-buy sale, she would say no. She should have learned to say no years ago.

She was going to make a fresh start.

Bea said, 'I'll get that one, Mummy,' and Vivien said, 'I'm fine. I'm not an invalid,' and reached up and winced.

They were picking runner beans in the garden of the Boscombe house. Her mother didn't want to let them go to waste. It was the first week of the school holidays, and Bea had driven to Dorset to keep Vivien, who was recovering from her surgery, company after dropping Alice and Rachel for their usual summer stay with their Cornwell grandparents in Surrey. The two of them were working through a long list of household tasks.

'I'll get it,' said Bea firmly. 'Have a break, Mummy.' She stood on tiptoe and plucked the bean pod. Then she said, 'Ciaran came to see me.' She put the runner bean in the colander and looked at her mother. 'You remember Ciaran.'

'Of course I remember. I haven't lost my wits.' Vivien fumbled for her sunglasses. 'Why? What on earth did he want?'

'To talk to me, that's all. Goodness, I'm exhausted.' She wasn't, but her mother looked tired and drawn and agreed to sit in the shade while Bea made tea.

She brought out a tray and put it on a table beneath a large catalpa tree. She poured and said, 'Ciaran never knew about the baby, did he?'

Vivien opened her mouth to speak, then shut it again. After a moment, she shook her head. 'We thought it for the best, Jack and I.'

*Best for whom?* Bea wanted to cry out. But she passed her mother a cup and sat down beside her. She took a mouthful of tea. Let it go, she thought. Let it go.

Vivien spoke again. Her eyes were hidden behind the blank wall of her dark glasses. 'It was Jack's idea. He thought that if we did it cleanly, if you believed he'd run off, and then the child was adopted, you'd be able to put it behind you and make a new start.' A long pause, then she added quietly, 'Most of the time Jack let me have my own way. But the big decisions, the important ones, he was in charge. That's how it was. Sometimes I thought he was wrong. He was wrong then, and I knew it. I knew you'd never forget the baby. I knew *you*, Bea.'

'He's my son. He's a part of me.'

'Yes.' Vivien shooed a fly from the plate of biscuits. She scanned the garden, then sighed. 'It was the same with this house. It was Jack who wanted to move here.'

'You've never liked it, have you?'

'It was always far too big for us. And the garden . . . I've never been much of a gardener. Jack used to do it. What will I do with all those runner beans? I can't possibly eat them. It tires me to think of it, the topping and tailing and blanching and putting them in bags for the freezer.' Vivien picked up her cup, then put it down again. 'The boy's father felt the same as Jack and me. That surprised Jack, but I could see it. You were both so young. So Mr O'Neill said he'd get the boy out of the country.'

'Ciaran,' said Bea. 'His name is Ciaran.'

'Ciaran. Yes.' Vivien let out a puff of breath. She looked away. 'I believe Jack gave Mr O'Neill some money. He wanted to be sure the family left London.'

'Daddy bribed him?'

Vivien took off her sunglasses. 'I wouldn't put it quite like that. They went to Birmingham or Manchester, I can't remember. I hoped that in time you'd meet someone else, someone more suitable, a man you loved as much as I loved Jack.' She gave Bea an affectionate but anxious look.

There was a silence between them, then Vivien said hesitantly, 'Had he – had Ciaran changed?'

'A great deal.' Though it was a warm day, Bea felt a little chilly. She would go into the house soon and fetch her cardigan. She needed a few minutes by herself. 'It was good to see him again,' she said. 'Good to talk to him.'

Gulls shrieked, high in the sky, and cars rumbled along the road. Vivien moistened her lips. 'I'm sorry, Bea. It was hard for you. I hope you'll forgive me.'

'It's okay,' Bea said. And maybe it was. She squeezed her mother's thin hand.

'You won't . . .' Vivien flicked her a glance. 'You're not angry? You're not going to dash off, then?'

'No, Mummy, I'll stay till Wednesday.' Bea smiled. 'That should give us long enough to deal with the runner beans.'

'Wednesday? I thought you were collecting the girls on Saturday.'

'I am, yes, but I think I might go away somewhere for a couple of days.'

'Really? Where are you going?'

Bea put the cups on the tray. 'I haven't quite decided yet, but I think I might go to France.'

# Chapter Twenty

## 1989–2002

Bea had always loved France. She felt at home there, a legacy from her French grandmother. She reached Bayeux late on Thursday morning, having taken the car ferry from Portsmouth and stayed overnight in a hotel in Caen. She hadn't told anyone where she was heading, not even Emma. Emma might think this a mad venture, and that would be true. But she had to try, at least.

In the tourist office in Bayeux, she obtained directions to the Verniers' house, from where Gabriel ran the French branch of his business. Sun blistered the sky as she drove out of town. It was a baking-hot August day and the grass in the fields had browned to straw. Though she wound down the windows, the seats and dashboard were warm to the touch and the car's interior smelled of hot plastic.

Bea drove through small, sleepy villages and past half-timbered farmhouses. The closer she drew to the Verniers' place, the more her optimism and confidence faltered. She had in the past found Gabriel a little distant, a little forbidding. He might be offended by her visit. He might quite justifiably think that she was poking her nose into something that was no concern of hers and tell her to push off and mind her own business. He would be polite, but he would make his point.

Arriving at the Manoir Saint-Gilles, she parked and got out of the car. The house was breathtaking, but she was too hot and anxious to admire it. She tugged at her crumpled linen dress and tidied her hair with her hands, then rang the doorbell.

A young woman opened the door and Bea introduced herself, in French. She was a friend of Gabriel's, she said, and she would like to speak to him.

'I'm his sister, Andrée.' She gave Bea a curious look. 'He's in the garden. Come with me.'

Dust motes danced in squares of sunlight falling through high windows as Bea followed Gabriel's sister through to the back of the house. The rooms were pleasantly cool and smelled of beeswax polish and lavender. Then the heat struck her anew as she stepped out onto a terrace.

Gabriel must have caught sight of her, because he rose from a chair beneath a large copper beech and crossed the grass to her. In his navy shorts and white shirt, he looked cool in spite of the hot day.

'Bea?' he said sharply. 'It's you, isn't it? Is everything all right with Marissa?'

'Marissa's fine. But I wanted to talk to you, Gabriel.' Her voice sounded annoyingly hoarse; she tried to get it under control. 'Marissa doesn't know I'm here.'

Though his stance remained easy and elegant, Gabriel's frown returned. 'I don't understand.'

So she just went for it. Plunged in at the deep end. 'It's been so hard for Marissa. I don't mean only because of you, Gabriel, because of breaking up with you, though that's made her utterly miserable, but because of everything else as well.'

'Bea—'

'You have to listen!' She flapped her hat at him. Suddenly she knew what she wanted to say, and she was afraid that if she paused, she'd lose her thread.

'I know what I'm talking about, Gabriel. I've been married twice, and to be honest, both times were rather a disaster. But Clive and Francis were both good men. Marissa's husband – Jamie Canterbury – he wasn't a good man.'

'I'm aware of that,' Gabriel said stiffly. 'I've met him.'

She didn't know how he could stand there in this heat looking so composed and unruffled. Sweat was trailing down her spine and her brain felt fogged. She heard her voice rise again as she slipped back into English.

'You men can never really understand how it is for women. Our lives – and our bodies – they don't follow a smooth progression like a man's does. Women like me, like Marissa, we have to transform ourselves over and over again. We have to take on one different role after another. We're daughters and we're wives and mothers and we're career women and we're cooks and housekeepers . . . You have more time to get used to things. Life is more straightforward for you. It's not the same.'

'She's right.' His sister, Andrée, had come out onto the terrace, hearing the commotion, perhaps. She lit a cigarette.

'And sometimes . . .' Bea swept a hand across her damp forehead, 'sometimes we make mistakes. Terrible mistakes. And we long to erase them, but we can't.'

'Bea,' said Gabriel quietly.

'I have to sit down,' she said suddenly. She felt faint. She, who had never felt faint in her entire life, did so now. A dark green haze was clouding the edge of her vision.

'Here, take my arm.' She heard his voice as if from a long way away.

'I'll get some water.' This was Andrée.

Gabriel led her to the copper beech tree. Bea sat down in a wicker chair. She closed her eyes.

'Take a deep breath,' he said. 'I'm so sorry, keeping you standing there in the heat. It was thoughtless of me.'

'It's not your fault.' She felt both weary and mortified. She had tried, but she knew she had failed.

Andrée came out of the house carrying a tray, which she put on a rickety table. 'You must drink some water, Bea. I'll make coffee. You'll feel better once you've had a cup of coffee and something to eat.' She went back to the house, the soles of her sandals flapping on the stone terrace.

Gabriel handed Bea a glass of iced water. 'Sip it slowly.'

When she opened her eyes, the green haze had dispersed, and it was cool in the deep shadow cast by the branches of the tree. She tried not to gulp the water down. She remembered that she hadn't had anything to drink since breakfast. And she had been rushing about for days. How silly of her.

Gabriel spoke. 'Bea, everything you just said to me . . . You're right, but you didn't need to say it. I know this.'

Andrée came out of the house with the coffee. She called out as she came down the terrace steps, 'I told him, Marissa is not like that cow Justine.'

'She isn't.' Bea looked up at him imploringly. 'You know that in your heart, don't you, Gabriel?'

For the first time, he looked floored and not in complete control. He ran his fingers through his hair. 'It was such a shock when she told me about her marriage. I felt as if I had never really known her . . . To discover I did not even know her real name . . . that she had hidden so much from me . . . I thought she didn't love me as I loved her. That is what I thought.'

Andrée turned her hands palm up. 'See what I mean? Hopeless.'

'Oh Gabriel.' Bea stared at him. 'Of *course* Marissa loves you. She loves you so much. But she thinks you don't love her.'

He said softly, 'I have never stopped loving her.'

'Then for pity's sake talk to her.' Andrée swiped her brother's head with a tea towel.

'It's not so easy.'

'Isn't it?' She spread her hands. 'Talk to her, Gabriel! That's all you need to do! Tell her how you feel.'

Gabriel said to Bea, 'Everything you say is true. The thought of her at the mercy of that pathetic man . . . When I saw him, I had to stop myself from punching him. I can see how difficult it must have been for her. Marissa is a quiet person by nature, she doesn't share her troubles easily. But I'm not sure we can simply go back. I'm afraid it won't be possible. There were things I said to her that I now regret. She and I, we can't just pretend it didn't happen.'

Andrée sat down and stretched out her slim, tanned legs in front of her. She said to Bea, 'He is so *susceptible*.'

*Susceptible* meant touchy. Gabriel shrugged.

'Andrée's right,' said Bea. 'You need to talk to her.'

'I tried to, when I collected Isabelle from the flat, but she made it very clear to me that she didn't want to talk. She couldn't wait for me to leave.'

'Did she say that to you?'

'No, but it was obvious.'

Andrée gave an exasperated sigh. 'Mon Dieu . . .'

'If you had been there, you would have thought the same.' Gabriel turned to his sister. 'She was so calm . . . so soignée. As cool as . . . what's the expression? As cool as a courgette.'

'Cucumber,' said Bea. 'Gabriel, you're wrong. Marissa is in pieces.'

He rose and walked up and down the grass. Andrée went after him. Brother and sister bickered in fast French while Bea drank coffee and ate a pastry. The food and drink revived her. Perhaps it would be all right. Gabriel loved Marissa, so perhaps this journey had not been futile after all.

Her thoughts drifted back to Ciaran. Since that extraordinary moment when she had found Emma's note on her kitchen table, she had thought about him a great deal. Before he had returned to Ireland, they had exchanged phone numbers. When she went home, she would call him and tell him about the conversation she had had with her mother.

She heard Gabriel say heatedly to Andrée, 'Marissa's flat . . . it was perfect. She was managing very well without me. While we were talking about Justine, she looked at her watch! She couldn't wait for me to go. Shall I tell you what she did? She went into the kitchen to wash the dishes! I was only there for ten minutes, and there she was, going and washing the dishes!'

For an intelligent, sophisticated man he could be awfully dim, thought Bea. Feeling more steady on her feet, she crossed the lawn to them.

'Gabriel, what do you do when you're upset?'

He raised his shoulders. 'I'm not sure. I . . .'

'He gets into a temper.' Andrée gave a sly smile. 'He rages at his car or some other piece of machinery. Or sometimes he is cold and proud, like an iceberg. You are,' she added, jutting her chin at her brother.

'If I'm upset, I pour myself a large gin and tonic,' said Bea. 'Or I watch rubbish on the television. And maybe I have a little cry. But that's not what Marissa does. Don't you know that, Gabriel? When Marissa is upset, she tidies the house. She hoovers the floor and cleans the oven. It's weird, I know, but that's what she does.'

Gabriel frowned. His gaze came to rest on Bea. Then he said quietly, 'Do you think she misses me?'

'Oh Gabriel, yes!' she cried. 'All the time! She adores you!'

Marissa phoned Tamar from the flat. 'I've found my inspiration,' she said. 'I took your advice and I've been to dozens of art galleries and I've thought about what I love. My new collection will be inspired by women artists of the twentieth century, by artists whose work I admire.'

'Barbara Hepworth?' said Tamar. 'Vanessa Bell?'

'Both of them. And Dora Carrington or Gwen John, perhaps. And you too, Tamar, if you will allow me.'

From the other end of the line, a raucous peal of laughter. 'Me? Clothing inspired by me? You can't possibly, Marissa, you'd go out of business. If it wasn't for you, I'd still be putting on the first garment that came to hand. A shirt I bought when I was an art student. Morgan's old painting trousers.'

'The clothes you inspire will have a bohemian influence,' said Marissa firmly. 'And I'm going to use the colours of the Suffolk coast. Cream and terracotta and sand and the soft grey-green of those plants that grow on the beach. You'll love them, Tamar, I know you will. They're going to be wonderful.'

*

The designs flew from her pencil, hardly needing the intervention of thought. She did much of the work at the flat, sitting at the dining table, drawing and mixing colours until the light began to fade.

She missed him all the time. In the flat, there were bittersweet reminders of him everywhere. A framed photo of the two of them, a vase they had chosen together from an atelier in Paris. One warm August evening, she finished work then poured herself a glass of wine and went out to the balcony. There was always something to look at in the street below, always something going on – a couple running along the pavement, weaving hand in hand between dawdling passers-by; a smartly dressed woman walking a poodle; an open-topped car heading fast along the road, music blaring. She still found the quietness of the flat hard to get used to.

A vehicle swung into the car park. It was a Renault, of the same type and colour as Gabriel's. Leaning over the balcony, Marissa sipped her wine, idly watching the car as it circled the square, but when the driver began to reverse into one of the visitors' spaces, she squinted and put down her glass.

She let him into the flat. 'I thought you were in France. Did Isabelle forget something?'

'No,' Gabriel said. 'It was I who forgot something.'

'What was that?'

'I forgot to ask you to forgive me.'

They were in the living room. Her heart began to beat so hard it hurt. *I forgot to ask you to forgive me.*

'Gabriel, there's nothing to forgive.' Her voice scratched. 'I've been such a fool.'

'That's not true.'

'I think it is. Did you know that your friend Bea came to see me?'

'Bea?' She stared at him, confused. 'What? When?'

'Yesterday. She came to the *manoir*.'

'Bea? She went to France? To see you?'

'Yes.'

'But why? What on earth for?'

'To tell me off, I think.' His slight smile faded, and he said grimly, 'She told me that I was in the wrong. Yes, exactly that. You have good friends, Marissa.'

Nothing he was saying made sense. Bea had gone to France to see Gabriel. She had had no idea.

She said, 'Gabriel, I don't understand.'

'Bea said that you still loved me. Do you, Marissa?'

'Yes.' The word was faint, but he must have heard it, because he took her hands in his.

'Thank God,' he said softly. 'I tried to talk to you when I came here to collect Isabelle. But there didn't seem to be the right moment, and in the end I lost my nerve. It seemed to me that you were fine without me.'

'Oh Gabriel, I could never be fine without you!'

And yet she saw how it might have happened. The two of them were so easily wounded. They built up defences around themselves because they were both wary of laying themselves open to more hurt.

'Gabriel, I am *not* fine!' She looked up at him. 'I might pretend that I am, because that's what I do and because I'm very good at hiding how I feel. I've had a lot of practice at it. But the truth is that without you, nothing's much good, nothing at all. It never is.'

He wrapped her in a close embrace, and she let her head

droop against his shoulder. He murmured, 'This morning, on the ferry, I was afraid that I'd left it too late.'

His kiss brushed against the top of her head. Their lips touched, and then they kissed some more. Joy rushed through her.

She thought that she had a lot to sort out. She needed to make things right between them, and to make sure they never went wrong again. But all that could wait, because at this moment, what mattered was the heat of his skin and the taste of his lips. And the delicious sensation as he ran his thumb down the small indentations of her spine and then unzipped her skirt, which tumbled in a pale flurry of silk to the floor.

Emma said, 'All I asked you to do was to keep an eye on Ben, and you couldn't even do that.'

Max muttered something about a client phoning. The kitchen floor was scattered with volcanic heaps of custard powder, flour and sugar. Slippery trails of cooking oil had turned the tiles into a skating rink.

'He was trying to reach the matches,' Emma said. Her voice shook with anger. 'He could have killed himself. Not to mention the rest of us.'

'I know.' Max looked guilty. 'I'm sorry, Em.'

Ben began to cry. Max said, 'He said he wanted to make a pie.'

'And you let him? Then you're an even bigger idiot than I thought you were! Don't you know by now not to let him out of your sight? I mean, hasn't it struck you, after all these years of living with him, that the last thing you should do is let him out of your sight?'

Lucienne and Elizabeth peered through the doorway. 'As

for you two . . .' Emma glared at her daughters, 'I asked you to play with your brother.'

'Mum, that's not fair!'

'It's not my fault, you can't blame me!'

'It's not much to ask, is it, that I can do a few hours' work?'

Max said, 'I'll get him some clean clothes.'

'If you can find any,' she flung scornfully after him. 'I told you, the washing machine's playing up.'

Emma went upstairs. She was on the verge of saying something awful, and though Max thoroughly deserved it, there was a limit to the language she should employ in front of the children. She heard bawling from downstairs, presumably as Ben was stripped of his grubby clothing.

She was sick of the lot of them. In her studio at the top of the house, she stood biting her lip as she studied the painting on the easel. It was of a teasel head, and she was halfway through it. This, half a teasel head, was all that she, who tried to think of herself as a botanical artist, had managed to paint during the time that had passed since she had shown her work to the gallery in Trinity Street. Half a flipping teasel head. Frustration boiled up inside her.

Suddenly she gathered up her sketches and shoved them into her portfolio. She swept up her watercolours, brushes, inks, pens and pencils, and took them down to the bedroom. Grabbing an overnight bag out of the wardrobe, she put inside it a spare pair of jeans, some T-shirts, underwear and a warm cardigan.

Max came into the room. 'What are you doing?'

'What does it look like? Packing.' Emma zipped up the bag.

'Emma, I'm so sorry.'

'Good, you should be. I'm going away for a few days,

Max, to stay with my mother. I'll be able to work there. You can look after the kids.'

'Yes, fair enough.' He took a step towards her, to offer a conciliatory hug, perhaps, but she waved him away.

'Fine, you're sorry. But it's a bit late and I don't really care. I need to work. And actually, I need time to myself, to think. Clear up the kitchen, Max,' she added coldly, as she checked her purse was in her handbag. 'Sort out the kids. Have a go at finding out what it's like to be me. And then maybe, just maybe, I'll give you another chance.'

When, towards the end of that afternoon, she arrived at Seastone, the house on the shingle was in chaos. Her mother appeared to have upended the contents of every drawer and cupboard onto the floor.

'Mum?' she said.

Tamar looked up. A smile flashed across her face. 'Emma, darling! How lovely to see you. Did you tell me you were coming?'

Emma shook her head. 'I had to get away.'

'School holidays.' Tamar was sympathetic. 'They used to drive me mad. I found the best thing was to make you all a jam sandwich and send you outside and tell you not to come back till teatime.'

'I remember, Mum.' Emma stepped cautiously between heaps of books, clothing and artists' materials to hug her mother. 'We're not allowed to do that these days.' Tamar's embrace comforted her. 'I needed to get some work done.'

Tamar put the kettle on. Emma surveyed the mess. 'What are you doing, Mum?'

'I can't find the butterfly pin. It must be here somewhere.' Tamar looked distracted. 'I know I put it in a safe place. And then I thought, why not take the chance to sort out Morgan's belongings at the same time? I haven't touched anything since he died. I haven't been able to face it. You know he never threw anything away. I thought that if I made a start, the butterfly pin would turn up.' She gave a fond smile as she picked up a navy-blue fisherman's jersey and ran the palm of her hand over it. 'I'll keep this. I wear it when it's cold. I might be able to find a good home for some of his other nice pieces of clothing.'

Her father hadn't possessed any nice pieces of clothing. Whenever Emma pictured him, he was wearing a thread-bare tweed jacket and corduroy trousers so old the pile had worn off.

She said, 'I'll help you.'

Tamar was stirring the tea. 'No, you should get on with your work.'

It was such a relief to be with someone who understood, without question, how she felt. 'I'll give you a hand,' Emma said firmly. 'Then I'll work.'

An hour and a half later, Emma, teetering on a chair, found the small blue leather-covered jewellery box at the back of the top shelf in the wardrobe. Now Tamar remembered putting it there, safe but out of sight, after her final parting with Alexander.

Morgan's clothing was in neatly folded piles on the bed: some to keep, some for the Oxfam shop in Woodbridge, and the most down-at-heel items for the bin.

Tamar thanked Emma and opened the box. 'I couldn't bear to have lost it.'

'Tell me about it, Mum.'

Emma had always been sharp-witted. She had the knack,

416

which Tamar shared and sometimes thought double-edged, of understanding what other people thought and felt. Reading her daughter's expression and catching her tone of voice, she knew that Emma was asking for more than the bomb-site story.

Then Emma said, 'I saw the butterfly pin in a portrait. And I remembered seeing you with a man called Alexander Rainsford at the gallery.'

'Singer Sargent,' said Tamar steadily. 'Edie Rainsford as Titania. The pin was made for her, for Edie Rainsford. She was Alexander's grandmother.'

Tamar had worked out that Emma had quarrelled with Max. Emma hadn't told her in so many words, but Tamar guessed that was what had happened. Emma loved Max and Max loved Emma, but now and then they clashed.

Tamar put the butterfly pin back in its box. 'That day when I first met Alexander Rainsford, in the war, I learned that lives can change in a very short space of time. I hadn't believed in love at first sight until then. I thought it was an invention of movie-makers and novelists. I was wrong.' She put the jewellery box in her bedside cabinet, a more sensible place for it, then looked her daughter in the eye.

'I don't regret anything at all. If I hadn't lost sight of Alexander back then, I would have had a different life. I wouldn't have had you and Gale and Rob and I wouldn't have had all those wonderful years with your father. You – Morgan and my family – you have meant everything to me.'

'Where is Alexander Rainsford now? Are you still in touch?'

Tamar shook her head. 'He moved to New York quite a few years ago. He has family there. It's a long time since I've seen him. I hope he's happy. He deserves to be.'

*

Since Morgan had died, Tamar's sleep had been fitful, a series of naps punctuated by wakefulness. Wistfully she recalled the deep, refreshing sleep of adolescence; at other times she found herself remembering occasions when she had stayed up all night and still had the energy to work in the mornings. An impromptu party in someone's studio. A painting that a surge of inspiration had driven her to continue working on into the small hours. A quarrel with her lover, with Morgan: she had stormed out of the flat and walked the streets of the ruined city until dawn. Their fallings-out had been heart-wrenching, their reconciliations magnificent.

During the war, the air raids had kept her awake at night. A memory rose to the surface of her mind. She was crouching beneath the table in one of the flats in the house in which Evelyn Carrow had lived as debris hammered and bombs exploded and sirens wailed. The smell of plaster and ash and brick dust; the next day, travelling to work, she had kept looking up at the sky, because that was where terror and threat came from.

Her life had often been patched and dislocated. Only here on this remote coast had she found stability. The last time they had met, at the hotel, she had tried to give Alexander back the butterfly pin. He had refused. *I always knew it would suit you*, he had said.

But now she needed to return it to its owner. Alexander's granddaughter, little Edie Rainsford, should have it. The butterfly pin was not hers to keep.

One more time, she thought. She needed to see Alexander Rainsford one more time.

The phone rang. Bea answered it. 'You must let me thank you,' Marissa said, in a rush. 'Honestly, Bea, I can't believe that you would travel all the way to France to speak to Gabriel. But thank you, thank you so much.'

'Oh, no need for that,' said Bea. 'What did he say?'

'That he loved me.'

Bea felt gleeful hearing the happiness in her friend's voice. Marissa said, 'What are you doing?'

Once, years ago, this was how their nightly phone calls had begun, back in those days after Clive had died and Bea had moved to Cambridge. *What are you doing? I'm sewing a button on Alice's dungarees. I'm clearing up the kitchen. I'm sitting on my own feeling sad.* They had talked about everything, she and Marissa.

Bea said, 'I'm trying to make sense of chemical equations. I thought I should make a start, before my course begins. Ciaran's been helping me.'

'Are you two all right now?'

'I think so. And you and Gabriel?'

'I think so.' A pause, in which Bea swallowed a gulp of coffee, then Marissa said, 'When I look back, I can see why I did what I did. I wouldn't do the same now, but I understand the choices I made then. Colouring my hair, my new name, those were superficial changes. I'm trying to make more lasting ones now. I'll make other mistakes, but at least they won't be the same ones. Gabriel and I, we've started to look for a house together. I'm going to sell the flat and he's hoping to rent out the farmhouse. He'll keep the barn for the business. We're going to look at houses in Richmond and Twickenham. Oh, and he's asked me to marry him.'

'*Marissa!* What did you say?'

'I said yes.'

Bea whooped. Alice looked up from the book she was reading.

'It won't be for a while,' said Marissa. 'I've a divorce to

sort out first. But I've seen a solicitor and we're setting the process in motion. Oh, and I've decided to see a therapist too. I thought it was about time I faced up to the past and talked it through with someone.'

'Good idea,' said Bea.

'Once Gabriel and I are able to marry, whenever that is, I would very much like it if you would agree to Alice and Rachel being my bridesmaids. Will you?'

'Oh Marissa. They'll love it.' Bea didn't even have to think about it. She could hardly wait. She had always adored a good wedding. She had always loved a party.

Emma was kneeling on the shingle drawing the mullein flowers that flared their yellow flags along the beach. It was her last morning at Seastone. She stood up, stretched, then walked down the shingle bank. She had been staying with her mother for the last three days. They hadn't talked about Alexander Rainsford or the butterfly pin again, and Emma suspected they never would. The two of them had fallen into a pleasant routine of working in the mornings and then going for a walk after lunch. Morgan's clothing had been sorted out and Emma had driven bags of his belongings to the Oxfam shop in Woodbridge. Tamar had begun to catalogue Morgan's paintings and prints.

Emma had called Max a couple of evenings ago.

'I think my mother has just told me that she had a love affair,' she had said to him.

'Are you thinking of doing the same?'

She pictured him. He would have jammed the phone between shoulder and chin, and he would be taking off his glasses and polishing the lenses on a grubby tea towel or handkerchief, as was his habit.

'No, Max. I'm not like my mother.'

'I think you are. You are so like your mother.' Then he said, 'I miss you, Emma.'

'I miss you too.'

'Honestly?'

'A little bit, yes.'

'I've cleaned the kitchen. I've fixed the washing machine. I think I've found someone who'll vacuum for us a couple of mornings a week, though she may run a mile as soon as she sees the place. Still, fingers crossed. Oh, and the children are still alive. Even Ben. I will do better, Emma.'

She remembered the first time Max had come to Seastone. She had showed him a piece of blue glass in the shape of a teardrop that she had found on the beach, and he had told her he loved her. She had kept that piece of blue sea glass. Max might be hopeless at some everyday things, but he had a rare ability: to make a vision real. Back when they had first met, when she had been in her early twenties, she had wanted adventure. Falling in love with Max, that had been her adventure. Marrying Max, that was an adventure too, and it was still going on.

She planned to drive back to Cambridge in the afternoon. Standing where the waves licked the smallest stones, she turned the pages of her sketchbook. It was almost full. It was hard to put your head over the parapet and it took courage to reveal the innermost workings of the heart. Maybe in the past she had found excuses not to do so. She had seen the pressures that ambition and a creative vocation had placed on her parents. Maybe she had filled up her time with other duties, even with her three children, whom she loved more than life itself, because the prospect of taking on a new role daunted her. Well, there was nothing wrong in that, she thought. Sloughing off an old skin, transforming yourself into something else and flying off into the unknown: none of that was easy.

Ciaran visited Cambridge for the second time in September. Bea introduced him to the girls. She had told Alice and Rachel that Ciaran was the father of their half-brother who had been adopted, and she showed the three of them her mementos of her son: the pencil sketch she had done in the nursing home, the scrap of blue wool from the matinee coat she had knitted him, the birthday cards she had bought for him each year. They all had lunch together, and in the afternoon they went for a walk at Wandlebury. Later, Ciaran drove them back to the house and then returned to his hotel.

He came to Cambridge again in November, for Emma's private view. Bea wore the silver chain he had given her years ago, when she was seventeen. Meeting him at the gallery in Trinity Street, she saw him look at it. She wondered whether he remembered giving it to her. When the evening was over, he walked her back to Portugal Place. They sat side by side on the living-room sofa, and she flicked on the television and together they watched the footage of the fall of the Berlin Wall. It was late, and he stretched out his arm along the back of the sofa, and she let her head relax against his shoulder as, piece by piece and brick by brick, the world changed.

In the December of 1989, Alexander came to the house at Seastone. Standing at the kitchen window, Tamar caught sight of him heading down the track to the house. She went outside to meet him.

'What an extraordinary place,' he said. Still lithe and energetic, he climbed easily up the ridge to her.

'A change from New York.'

His smile melted her heart. He kissed her cheek. 'How are you, Tamar?'

'I'm very well. And you? You look just the same.'

'I'm as fit as a fiddle. And you look beautiful.'

They went inside the house. After coffee, after they had asked after each other's families and compared photos of grandchildren, they went for a walk. It was a typical Seastone day, fine and blowy, with great puffy clouds scudding shadows now and then along the shingle. She showed him all her favourite places: the Martello towers, the marshland behind the ridge, the decaying Second World War fortifications on the headland. History was deeply incised into this scrap of coast.

He said, 'I can see why you choose to stay here.'

'It's a place that holds on to its memories. I like that.'

'I've missed you, Tamar.'

His voice was tender. They were standing on the breeziest part of the walk, looking out to sea. 'And I you,' she said softly.

They started back to the house. The skies darkened early in December, and they were heading into the wind, but she didn't mind that. She and Alexander, they had always had to walk into the wind.

In the back room, he admired the early stages of her new painting on the easel. Tamar made tea. When she came back into the room with a cake she had baked, she saw him studying a small portrait on the wall.

'It's you, isn't it?' he said.

She put the plate on the table and went to stand beside

him. 'My father painted it, during the war. I was fifteen, I think.'

In the portrait, she was wearing a plum-coloured blouse and she had borrowed her mother's necklace of blood-red garnets. The following year, she had left Cornwall for London. The girl in the portrait looked directly at the viewer; her gaze challenged.

'I was such an intense little thing,' Tamar said.

'You were lovely,' Alexander said. 'You still are.'

They had their tea and cake and then she went to fetch the butterfly pin. She took it out of her bedside cabinet and opened the box. Cradling it in her palms, she looked down at it. So many memories, so much joy and heartbreak. She touched it with her lips and whispered, 'Fly free.' Then she put it back in the box.

'Thank you,' he said, when she gave it to him, 'for looking after it so well for me.'

He took her in his arms. Tamar closed her eyes tightly, breathing in the scent of him, treasuring the warmth of his embrace.

'Every now and then,' he said, 'I'll see a stranger who reminds me of you. A woman who walks like you, so straight and so proud, or who has that habit of brushing her hair back from her forehead. I know that I'll go on seeing you for the rest of my days. It won't matter where I am. I'll see you in the street, Tamar, or I'll glance out of a subway carriage and there you'll be, standing on the platform. On the beach, I'll catch sight of a woman who smiles like you, and when I walk in Central Park on a hot summer's day, I'll hear a peal of laughter and I'll turn, thinking it might be you. And it will give me such delight. You will always have a piece of my heart.'

*

Bea was never afterwards able to pinpoint the moment when she fell in love with Ciaran for the second time. Perhaps it was when he came over to England for Marissa and Gabriel's wedding in the March of 1991. There was a moment that evening when she and Marissa and Emma were holding hands and dancing to Bruce Springsteen, bawling out the chorus to 'Dancing in the Dark', and she looked over to where Ciaran stood at the side of the room and he smiled. Just that. Perhaps that was all it took: a smile.

Or maybe it was a few months later, during that frantic summer when Bea was taking her A levels. She had just completed her first chemistry exam when Alice fell off her bicycle and broke her arm. It had to be reset, which necessitated an overnight hospital stay. Then, a week later, her mother phoned and broke the news to her that her cancer had come back.

That night, she phoned Ciaran in Dublin. 'I don't know what to do,' she said. Tears poured down her face. 'I need to go and see Mum. But Alice needs me here, Ciaran. And Emma has an exhibition coming up and I'm for ever asking her to help out. Francis is no use at the moment, what with Daisy expecting twins.'

'I'll come over,' he said. 'I can give you a hand with the girls.'

'But Ciaran . . .'

'It's no problem. And I'd do anything for you, Bea, you know that, don't you?'

He flew into Gatwick the following afternoon. The day after that, Bea drove to Boscombe to stay with her mother while Ciaran cooked meals for Rachel and Alice and made sure they got to school on time. His business partner, Gareth, took care of the Dublin agency. Ciaran set up a desk and phone in the spare bedroom so that he could keep an eye on things.

He ended up staying on. There was just so much to do, and besides, she liked him being there. Once she had recovered from her treatment, Vivien put her Boscombe house on the market. She planned to move to Cambridge, so that she could be closer to her family. When Bea received the letter telling her that she had passed her A levels with flying colours, she and Ciaran and Rachel and Alice celebrated together. He was still staying at Portugal Place when Bea embarked upon her nursing course. And he picked up Vivien from Boscombe and drove her to Cambridge on the day she moved into the new flat.

One evening he cooked dinner for the four of them. He was a good cook. As he lifted chicken pieces out of the pan, he said, 'I've been thinking of setting up another branch of the agency, here in Cambridge. I've found the right premises. Gareth will continue to take care of Dublin. I'll have to do a bit of toing and froing, Bea, but I can make it work.' He spooned mushroom and tomato sauce on top of the chicken. Then he said, 'I've lost you once before, love. We've spent so much of our lives apart and I don't want to be apart from you ever again.'

'Oh Ciaran . . .' And without thought, she was in his arms and kissing and kissing him, until Rachel came into the room and asked whether dinner was ready.

The years passed. Bea attained her nursing qualification and worked four days a week at Addenbrooke's Hospital. The girls grew up and did well at school. In 1995, Alice left home to read psychology at Edinburgh University.

Being with Ciaran made the joys of life – a summer

travelling round France, a trip to Australia to see Fergal — more intense. It made the sorrows — losing her mother and her daughters leaving home — more bearable. Though she still sometimes had the dream about Patrick, and though she still now and then wandered alone through the dark tunnels looking for her lost baby, the fact that he held her in his arms on those nights consoled her, and she felt comforted.

The letter arrived in the spring of 2002. Bea guessed what it was even before she opened it. She had been waiting for a letter like this since her son had turned eighteen, thirteen years before. She sat down on the stairs. Moments passed before her hands stopped shaking long enough to open the envelope.

She read the single page through once, then again, though by the time she got to the foot of the letter, she was weeping too much to make out the words. They were tears of joy. Her son was well and happy, and he wanted to make contact with her. He was called Richard Turner now, and he was thirty-one years old and lived in Bath with his wife and two sons. He taught history at a local school. *I've always wondered what you were like*, he wrote. *I've wondered where you lived, I've wondered what you looked like and what you did for a living. My mother preferred not to talk to me about you. Sadly, she died last year, and I made the decision to try to trace you. It's taken me a while and I don't know what your situation is now. You might be married, you might have a family and you may not have told them about me. But if you were happy to do so, I would very much like to meet you.*

Bea wrote back to him. *I was afraid you would never want to know me. I was afraid you would hate me or that something dreadful might*

427

have happened to you and I would never see you again. I can't tell you how happy your letter has made me, Richard. There are no words.

Six weeks after that, her son travelled to Cambridge. It was arranged that Bea would wait for him on Jesus Green. After they had got to know each other a little, they would come back to the house so that he could meet the rest of the family. They had exchanged photographs. In the snapshot, Richard looked out with calm dark eyes. His black curly hair was like Ciaran's, and he had a firm jaw and an upward tilt to the corners of his mouth, as though a lot of things amused him. They had exchanged the photos so that they would recognise each other, but Bea saw in his image the baby he had once been, the baby that had been taken from her when she was a girl. She would have known him anywhere.

PART FOUR

# THE LIGHT IN THE HOUSE

# Chapter Twenty-One

## 2005

They are all to go to Seastone today.

Rising early, at half past five, Emma gives thanks for blue skies and fair weather. May can be such an unpredictable month, especially on the east coast. Max is still asleep, the duvet kicked off him, so she slides out of bed, careful not to wake him. Downstairs, in the back room, watery squares of sunshine filter through the windows and shimmer on the floorboards. She opens the door, letting into the house the scent of roses and the sound of birdsong. Outside, dew dampens her feet as she crosses the grass to fetch a basket and secateurs from the greenhouse and then searches out those perfect blooms on the verge of opening. Rose after rose, pink and cream and white and apricot and buff, tumble into the basket. She's taking them to Seastone, to decorate the house and the village hall.

Tamar, who lived through the Great Depression and the Munich Agreement, a world war and the Cold War, has gone. She died six weeks ago, at the age of seventy-eight, following a long illness. Emma wonders how she will get through this day. She puts down the basket and screws shut her eyes. She would rather go up to her studio to paint the roses; she would rather close the door behind her and lose herself in the task of representing their impermanence and soft summer colours on paper. She would rather do anything than this.

But hearing a cry from an upstairs window – the youngest member of the family, Lucienne's son and Emma's grandson, Oscar, is stirring – she picks up the basket and goes indoors to put the kettle on.

Bea steps round Alice's belongings, dumped in the hall when she arrived at the house in the middle of the night, her arms full of coats, bags and a pot plant she's trying to nurture into life, talking loudly of a breakdown on the motorway and an emergency phone call to the AA.

There is another scene at breakfast, after Alice discovers that the zip has broken in the skirt she planned to wear for Tamar Romilly's memorial service. 'God, Al, why do there always have to be *dramas* with you?' Rachel moans at her through a mouthful of toast. But she accompanies Alice on her dash into town, where Alice buys a plum-coloured skirt from Noa Noa, Tamar having stipulated in an addendum to her will that no one is to wear black. Then Ciaran herds them all out of the house and they set off for Suffolk only half an hour later than Bea had intended.

Tamar Romilly's memorial service is to be held in the village hall. Marissa and Gabriel have stayed overnight at a hotel in Woodbridge, and so, arriving comfortably early, they secure both a parking space and seats near the front of the hall. The funeral took place six weeks ago, a small private affair for close family only; today's occasion, Emma has said, is to be a celebration of Tamar's life. Marissa greets old friends: Rob and his partner Ursula, Gale and Douglas,

Nick Lauderdale. She keeps four places for Bea and her family, who are on their way.

Several of Tamar's late paintings are propped on easels at the front of the hall. During her last years, her work became more abstract, and these oils are vibrant slabs and smudges of colour. Emma is standing near an easel, talking to Nick, who is to be responsible for the order of service. Marissa darts forward to give her a quick hug and kiss, then sits down again. Music ebbs and flows as guests file into the room. Bea and Ciaran and the girls come through the door and Marissa turns and waves at them. Rachel takes the seat next to her and she squeezes her hand. When she looks back, she sees that every seat is taken. People are standing against the walls and flooding into the central aisle. Someone props open the double doors so that those who can't fit inside can hear from the vestibule.

The memorial service begins. Pieces of music are interspersed with readings and recollections and eulogies. Nick Lauderdale gives a tribute to Tamar, listing her achievements as an artist. When Ben Hooper plays a work he wrote especially for his grandmother, Marissa threads her fingers through Gabriel's and tries not to cry. In her other hand she holds the scrap of paper on which she's written notes for her own short speech. She doesn't need it, she knows it by heart, because what she felt for Tamar is forever in her heart, so she tucks the paper back into her handbag, and when the music comes to an end and it's her turn, she takes a deep breath then stands up.

Ben and his grandmother were always close. Once, not so long ago, Emma came across the two of them sitting in the little paved area to the side of the Cambridge house, chatting and sharing a joint. Tamar was a rule-breaker, as Ben is. Aged sixteen, Tamar fled from the safety of rural Cornwall towards the dangers of war-torn London. She strode through life doing what she wanted, falling in love with whomever she wanted.

Emma is dreading giving her eulogy. Each time she has practised reading it through, whether alone in her studio or to Max, she has always ended up in tears. She is afraid she will go to pieces now, that she will weep and blubber in front of friends and neighbours and Tamar's fellow artists. She's typed out the speech in case she has to hand it over to Max.

The music, an orchestral section from Britten's *Peter Grimes*, comes to an end. Emma's mouth is dry. Max, who is sitting beside her, gives her an encouraging smile. Emma stands, then turns to face the congregation. And in the end, she gets through it without stumbling at all, and the words she wants to say about her mother, whom she misses so much, flow like a river.

The service is over. There's a sort of collective sigh of relief and then an outburst of chatter. They all tramp down the track through the fields to the house, where Gale has prepared a buffet lunch.

The house is now jointly owned by Emma, Gale and Rob. With her siblings' agreement, Max is going to do some work on it so that it doesn't blow down in the next storm. He's planning to bring the modest building kicking and screaming into the twenty-first century. A second bathroom, a new kitchen, a studio attached to the house rather than teetering on the edge of the shingle dune like Morgan's. Nothing will be out of proportion or grandiose, because

Max doesn't do grandiose. What alterations he makes will complement the extraordinary nature of the setting. Emma and her brother and sister have decided that they will lend the house to those who have need of it, to family and friends and starving artists who have nowhere else to go. Tamar and Morgan were starving artists once, so that seems appropriate.

Gale and Douglas have been staying at Seastone for the past week. Efficient as always, Gale has cleaned and tidied the rooms and is sorting through Tamar's work. When Emma dropped in that morning to give her the roses she had picked, her sister showed her a drawing she had discovered inside a portfolio.

It is of Emma and her friends, on the beach. Emma looks at it and remembers. Tamar has captured a perfect day. Max had taken the children for a week with his parents while Emma went to Seastone to spend the weekend with her mother and her friends. It was summer, and warm, so they lazed on the beach, reading and chatting. In Tamar's pencil sketch, Emma is lying on a sunlounger while Bea kneels in the shingle, her cupped hands full of shells, her dark hair curtaining her face. Marissa stands beside them, slim and bare-legged, her loose linen kaftan flaring in the breeze. The three of them were born in 1953, the year of the Coronation, and those images of a beautiful young queen in a golden coach have accompanied them throughout their lives. Privately Emma has always believed that the fortuitous year of their birth has cast its magic, has scattered fairy dust.

A long line of white pebbles weaves from the house. It circles round a patch of sea holly and winds across the shingle bank to the place where Tamar liked to sit and sketch the sea. It dips and curls over the rises and falls, then loops round a crescent-shaped pond. It pauses at the place where Morgan passed away before heading on, further down the beach, until eventually it hurtles, almost straight now, over shining wet shells and stones. And then, at last, the sinuous white trail disappears into the waves of the North Sea.

Late that afternoon, Emma sketched out the line. Her family and friends gathered up white pebbles. Small children collected them in buckets; old men with walking sticks stooped creaking in the shingle. This is her memorial to her mother.

It's late now, and growing chilly, and the family have gone back indoors. There are children to feed, journeys to embark on. Only Emma, Bea and Marissa remain, standing by the shore. Bea places the last few pebbles. The sun is sinking, and in the dusk, the winding line seems to glow, pale and luminous, delineating the warp and weft of a life. Emma looks up and sees the light in the house. Then the three women walk back across the shingle, arm in arm.